THE
JADE LABYRINTH

ALANNA MACKENZIE

First published in Canada in 2023
Willow Lane Publishing, Vancouver, BC

Copyright © 2023 Alanna Mackenzie
Cover design by J. Caleb Clark copyright © 2023

www.alannamackenzie.com

ISBN 978-1-7752509-6-8 (pbk)--ISBN 978-1-7380104-1-7 (hardcover)--ISBN 978-1-7752509-7-5 (html)--ISBN 978-1-7752509-8-2 (pdf)

For Cassandra

"The empires of the future are the empires of the mind."

– Winston Churchill

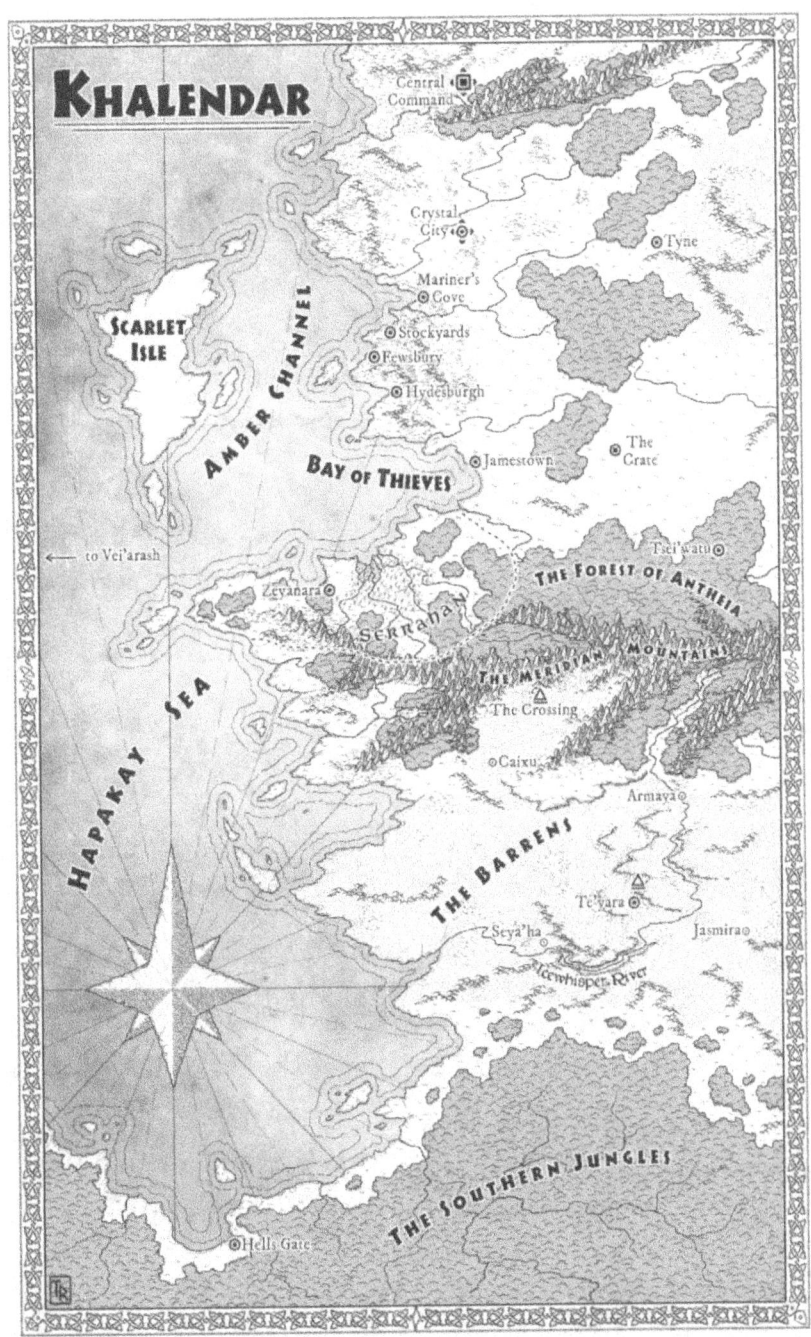

Map illustration by Thomas Rey

PART I:

THE THREAD

Fall

"When we try to pick out anything by itself, we find it hitched to everything else in the Universe."
— John Muir

A t first he thought he was dying. The noise, the spray, the density of the air around him—all of it was far too unbearable. All he could do was look down, but what he saw filled him with fear. Below him was a raging river, the water churning against its canyon walls a white, furious, and insatiable beast. And the uncanny part was that the river spoke to him, in no human language he could discern. Nor did it speak that other language he was so well-attuned to—that of artificial intelligence. The cacophonous voices emerging from the river were far older than that, part of a primal history forgotten to time.

Walter Saltanetska had heard that strange, ancient dialect once before. It didn't consist of words, nor even of discrete sounds that formed patterns. That was how he knew that it was not the language of living animals, but of dead ones. The river was a veritable magnet for the spirits of long departed animals, and not just one, but thousands... far too many to count. As the river spoke to him, he could feel himself getting closer to those kindred spirits, who told him stories of their time spent on Earth. The task was made all the easier by the fact that he, himself, was a spirit.

As Walter's spirit hovered over the river's turbulent, foaming surface, he listened carefully to these stories. He heard otters, salmon, caribou, and ravens. As their voices unraveled their stories, they showed him windows into their past lives, and he could see this all by simply gazing into the surface of the river. He was seeing the stories play out, as if the river was a large projection screen, but he could also *feel* that he was part of them. As he gazed down into its roiling depths, each of these narratives unfolded. He saw envious glances, lustful trysts, and contests between proud brothers and sisters. He witnessed pain, wonder, mercy, and grace. Each story taught him more about the awe-inspiring resourcefulness of the animals who had lived in this place throughout the ages.

Finally, Walter's spirit came to what he knew was the last story. The river was becoming tired; it had already given him much, and it was slowing down in the lazy hours of mid-afternoon. He knew, by some intuition, that the river had saved the best story for last. It was the tale of a fire lizard: a little runt, the youngest of all his siblings, who had been left to die in the middle of the desert.

The world was hot and stifling, and each breath the young lizard took was like a knife cutting into his body. He couldn't find water anywhere, for all the creeks nearby had dried up. He dug frantically under rocks to find a drop of water, anything to quench his insatiable thirst. Uncannily, Walter's spirit felt as though he had become one with the lizard, such that he felt the cruel pangs of thirst, though he had no throat to feel parched.

After a few days, it was clear to the young lizard that his world was closing in on him. He was becoming too weak to even dig troughs in the sand. So, resigned, he dug one final burrow in the ground—the one that he thought would be his final resting place. It appeared, however, that fate had other plans for him. When he closed his eyes, the lizard suddenly heard a faint noise, a noise that triggered a primitive impulse within him. He could sense water, and not just a tiny trickle, but a vast amount of it.

The lizard had no choice but to try and follow the sound; it was his last and only option. With painstaking effort, the lizard heaved his body out of the trough he had dug and slid himself, inch by inch, toward the noise. Gradually, the sound became louder and louder, until it was a deafening roar. The lizard's instinct told him to keep pressing onwards, but instead of finding the precious water he so desperately wanted, he came face to face with a large concrete wall. This baffled the lizard, defying all sense of what he expected to be normal and natural. He knew that a river should be there, but he could not get to it. The frustration that arose from this knowledge drove his blood into a hot frenzy and he sprang into action, digging frantically beneath the concrete wall.

The lizard used every last, precious ounce of his strength to burrow under the wall, and defying all logic, he managed to emerge on the other side. What he saw before him was bliss: a crystalline river so pristine and mesmerizing that it made the lizard's heart swell with joy. But the constraints of biology now became tragically clear. As the lizard heaved his way toward the riverbank, his strength rapidly faded, and the creature died mere steps away from the water. All it would have taken was a single sip to revive him, but it was too late.

The river's banks swelled with the next rain, and it caught the body of the young lizard up in its currents. The lizard was carried by the river for miles until finally it was washed up on shore at the base of an estuary. A raven, attracted by the lizard's bright orange skin, picked it up in her claws and deposited the reptilian corpse in a forest, in a valley that one of the river's tributaries cut through. As the lizard's body decomposed, it fertilized the soil for a young sapling, which set down roots in the creature's final resting place. The sapling struggled for years to survive in a barren and bone-dry land; it buckled beneath windstorms and withstood the blazing heat of the sun. But it stood tall for centuries, and eventually the tree was standing alongside many others in a lush valley of giant cedars, spruce, and fir.

As the lizard's story drew to a close, Walter's spirit knew at once where he needed to go. The magnetic pull of the river was still irresistible, but with a single-minded determination, the spirit managed to heave himself upwards into the dazzlingly bright blue sky. As he flew, he used the river below to orient himself, following its twists and turns westward until he arrived a tributary that branched off to the north, just before the river widened into a vast delta that met the sea. The spirit traced the curves of this tributary and eventually came to a lush valley that was teeming with flora and fauna.

The air was richly oxygenated due to the countless trees in the valley, and the soil was damp and fertile. The spirit was so high off the ground that he could only see birds nestling in the tree branches at first, but as he descended, he could spot countless other animals—squirrels, mice, and voles. The creature that appeared to be most abundant was a primordial species of lizard with a distinctly orange pigmentation. Walter's spirit knew that it could be none other than the fire lizard, and as he arrived at one of the largest trees in the forest, he felt the uncanny sensation that this was the same tree he had observed while gazing into the depths of the river. It was the tree that had been fertilized by the young lizard who had died while valiantly trying to reach the banks of the river.

Just beside the tree, discreetly camouflaged amidst the verdant mosaic of the forest, was a log-frame cabin. Its walls were shrouded in moss and clinging vines, which encircled the cabin as though for a decorative or attractive purpose. At first, Walter's spirit felt a marked reluctance to proceed any farther; he intuited that the cabin might be dangerous, and possibly filled with people of nefarious intention. He did not know why this was so, but he had a vague sense that in his living form, he had previously encountered cabin that was similarly frightening and ominous.

Despite this sense of unease, his desire to enter the cabin was more powerful than his fear, and it compelled him to drift through the structure's frail walls. To his surprise, nothing remotely ominous awaited him inside. The air was comfortably humid—not overly oppressive, but as pleasant as a woolen blanket on a crisp autumn day. At one end of the cabin was a cheery, blazing hearth, and at the opposite end, a woman with radiant skin sat upon a stately chair. Between the hearth and the woman were eight people, roughly arranged in a circle, who sat in a suspended silence as if patiently waiting for her permission to speak. The woman looked oddly familiar, with her round, luminous face, short-cropped hair, and eyes the same green hue as the surrounding forest. She appeared to be youthful, but at the same time wise beyond her years, and the guests regarded her with deference. Walter's spirit found a spot in a dark corner of the cabin to sit and observe—a task he excelled at.

"Welcome to the healing lodge," the woman with cropped hair began, her gentle, mellifluous voice echoing throughout the cabin softly.

"This is a place of non-judgment and peace. We are all brothers and sisters here, and we are bound by sacred laws to treat each other with respect. Now, let us move around the circle in a clockwise direction, and each person who holds the talking stick shall speak."

Walter's spirit then noticed that she had been holding a tall, thick staff which was engraved with figures of four different species of animal—lizards, jaguars, horses, and snakes. She passed the stick to a man to her right side, who had curls of golden hair and dark blue eyes. Walter's spirit felt a surge of recognition when he saw the man and was stunned that he hadn't noticed him earlier. The man was none other than Walter's brother Jonathan, and now the spirit realized that the beautiful woman at the head of the circle was Miranda.

"Thank you, Miranda," Jonathan said in a tremulous voice.

"How long... how long I've waited for this moment, to *speak* to all of you," Jonathan sighed. His eyes were glassy with tears, and his chest heaved with emotion. "I feel like I've lived a thousand lives in the span of one, and I'm not even forty yet. Well, I'll get to the point quick.

"I used to be a fighter, one of the best in all of Khalendar. I lived my life from moment to moment, not caring about what happened yesterday or what might happen tomorrow. One day, I joined a club of serious fighters called the Water Sprites; I had no idea what the name referred to. They advertised themselves as the best club for training novices, and so I signed up—I wanted to train *real* hard and make a few friends. At first, they called me skinny and clueless—'Celery Stick' I think was the nickname they gave me. I felt like a pretty big outcast, but that all changed when they realized I was a damned good fighter. I wasn't actually that skinny. I was big compared to my brother Walt... but compared to them... *Sheesh*. Anyways, I'll get right to the point.

"So, for a few years I was fighting with them and training with them, and I was getting in some good rounds against the AI Fighters. It felt great to just hit those AI Fighters where it hurt, to see them flail, to watch their shiny cybernetic limbs just *crack* and shatter into pieces on the ring floor. I was pretty clueless though—I didn't quite understand what we were doing all this for—and one day, my curiosity got the better of me. I asked my mentor, Jesse I think his name was, I asked him straight up: 'Why do you hate them so much? Why do you want to see them go down so bad?'

"And Jesse—he was much taller than me, with these big baby-blue eyes—told me, 'What is it to you? Don't you like seeing them crack up into a million pieces?' And then he would laugh and laugh. But I wasn't content with that answer. I asked him again. I also said, 'And what is with your *stupid* name, Water Sprites? Are you guys nymphs or something?' I was afraid that he would pummel me, but instead he just calmed right down and got all wise and contemplative. He said, 'I guess now's a good time to tell you, Jon.' And that's when he told me everything: about the water I had been drinking, how it was completely messing with my head, how it made me forget what happened yesterday and all the days before that, how it made me stop thinking about what I might do tomorrow. I was really angry with him then for not telling me earlier. He said he was afraid I wasn't ready; I needed to be broken in a bit.

"But from that point onwards, we became fast friends, Jesse and me. He showed me how to fend for myself, and by that, I mean he taught me how to get water that was pure and clean. Ever since that happened, I knew there was no going back. I *hated* those AI Fighters more than I hated anything, and at that young age I had a lot of hate inside of me directed at the whole world. I became a hell of a fighter after I stopped drinking that water. For one thing, I could plan my hooks and uppercuts a whole lot better. And boy did I show them in the fights. My nickname changed from 'Celery Stick' to 'Lightning', because I could predict what they would do next lightning fast, and I made sure they didn't get any blows in. Jesus, was I ever good at fighting."

At this point Jonathan's voice became increasingly unsteady, his face grew flushed, and tears began to fill his eyes.

Miranda noticed this, and swiftly intervened with her calm, moderating presence.

"Would you like to take a break, Jonathan? We can come back to you after the next speaker. Here, drink this Xe'levan." Miranda handed the golden-haired man a steaming cup of tea which she had poured out from a pot sitting beside her chair. He accepted it with shaking hands, took a lengthy draught, and then placed it carefully in front of him. He took several deep breaths before resuming.

"I'm good, I'm good. I won't be much longer. I just wanted to say that that golden age didn't last, as you all obviously know by now. I thought I could be strong and independent forever, but the AI Masters… those heartless thugs… they had something else in store for me. After one of my best fights—on a Friday night it was—my whole life changed forever. The AI Masters handcuffed me after I left the ring and took me to the basement of that warehouse where I fought all the time. It was so quiet, because it was about three in the morning and all my friends had left for the night. Nobody could hear me scream. They tied me to a chair, and then forced me to drink about a gallon and a half of water… *their* water." The man paused and shuddered, almost convulsing with grief.

"After that, it's all one long blur. I remember I became a twisted, soulless person, and I cared about nothing except for them. I followed their commands like they were gods, I wanted nothing except to go up in the sky with them to this distant planet, Eurydice I think it's called. I thought of that as my salvation. I never thought once about fighting back, about *actually* saving myself. But something did make me think twice. Not really something… but someone… my brother Walt."

At this point, not even the tea could hold back the man's emotions, and he wept freely. Miranda did not attempt to restrain him, but merely smiled contentedly, as if pleased about the emotionally cathartic effects of Jonathan's speech.

"Poor Walt. He *saved* me… he saved all of us. And where is he now? Nobody's seen him for months, ever since he went to their twisted command center. He's the reason we're here safe and sound. He's the reason this place isn't beholden to the Empire anymore, that it's its own free and peaceful kingdom. He's the reason the Mage kingdom isn't sealed off from the rest of the world any longer. Thanks to him, that repulsive diamond mine wasn't built just a few miles away from this valley we're in right now. People read books now… not books full of that god-awful propaganda they were selling us before, but real books like they had in the Old World. And thanks to him, I actually don't hate those machines anymore. They don't try to hurt us anymore; they try to help us. They pick up signals in nature and use those signals to understand how to help all living things, to bring everything into balance again. Instead of worshipping those machines, we worship nature and animals. And that's how it should be, isn't it? What happened before just wasn't *natural*. Thank you all kindly, I think I'm done speaking now."

"Thank you, Jonathan. That was wonderful," Miranda said, then took a contemplative sip of Xe'levan, her jade-green eyes glittering as she stared deeply into the dancing flames of the hearth.

"Now, let's hear from the next found soul."

As the next visitor began to speak, Walter's spirit settled into his resting place in the corner of the cabin, and he felt a wave of tranquility and joy sweep over him. He did not ever wish to leave here; he wanted to stay forever, because with each passing moment it became increasingly clear that this place was his true home.

Signals

"Every new beginning comes from some other beginning's end."
– Seneca

D ays, or perhaps even weeks, passed while Walter's spirit remained inside the cabin. He had lost track of time, but he did recognize that every day a new group of guests entered the healing lodge to share their stories of suffering, heartbreak, and redemption. Miranda's lodge was renowned throughout Khalendar, as Walter's spirit soon learned—a sort of shrine to which dozens of broken, weary souls made frequent pilgrimages.

He reveled in listening to these tales, and he learned a considerable amount of information about the outside world from them. The lush valley and cabin were in the Barrens, a land which its native inhabitants called *Ve'laya*, or barren land, because it had once been so parched and bereft of life. It was not barren any longer, however, owing to the recent revitalization of the Icewhisper River and the return of the river goddess, Belisama.

It was not just the Barrens that had undergone a dramatic transformation; the entire map of the Empire had been recently re-drawn, and there was a buzz of excitement about this state of affairs amongst nearly all of the travelers who visited the cabin. The most notable change was that the Empire was not really an Empire at all any longer but had broken off into four independent kingdoms with their own cultures, constitutions, and legal systems: Serrahan, Eyrenvale, Calliope, and Ve'laya. Each kingdom enjoyed all the sovereign rights of a nation, and each was now liberated from the suffocating grip of AI Master rule.

As separate and independent as the kingdoms were, they were all members of the Union of Khalendar, and the boundaries between them were extremely porous. Migration from the north to the south was increasing, as more and more humans abandoned their hectic, consumer-driven lifestyles in Crystal City for the slower, gentler pace of the southern kingdoms. The barrier separating Serrahan from the rest of the world had been shattered, allowing magic to permeate throughout the rest of the Empire like stardust diffusing in the atmosphere.

Many of the travelers who visited Miranda's cabin were Mages from Serrahan who were keen to meet folks from other kingdoms, as they had never ventured outside their homeland in their entire lives. Walter's spirit soon realized that while they appeared to be superficially different from the humans who had been brainwashed by the AI Masters, they had underlying psychological problems of their own. The main symptom was intense loneliness, which had likely been caused by being pent up in such an insular society for so long without contact from the outside world.

One of the most colorful of these characters was a young Mage named Helena, who had waist-length silver hair and piercing turquoise eyes. When the talking stick was passed to her, she could barely contain her excitement at the opportunity to speak about her kingdom and the magic within it. Her voice rang with pride as she told stories of the training she had undergone as a Mage in Serrahan, but Walter's spirit could also detect hints of desperation for more contact with others.

"How much you learn as a Mage in Serrahan really depends on what kind of teacher you have," she said, grinning broadly as she sipped a cup of Xe'levan. "My teacher was one of the best—his name was Torsten. He didn't just *tell* you how to use magic, like the sorceresses in our boring lectures at Briarthorn Academy did. He would put you in a life-threatening situation, and if you didn't use magic properly, well, that was the end of you.

"During my initiation rites, when I was only twelve, he took me out to this waterfall a few miles east of Zeyanara. The waterfall is called *Seveya*, which means 'the sinister one.' We rode out there on horseback together; mine was a sturdy black mare who was easily spooked, and once she got to the waterfall she was trembling with anxiety. I was just as terrified as the horse, because I knew Torsten was planning something dreadful for this part of my initiation rites. It was early January, and the river was partially frozen over, but the ice was thin, and the waterfall was cascading over towering granite cliffs.

"I'd just started my formal Mage training a few years earlier. I knew I had a penchant for ice spells, as I'm spiritually aligned with Arianrhod, the winter moon goddess, but I'd only ever performed them at home, turning my tea into ice and whatnot. Like this." She giggled as she cast a spell on the Xe'levan, freezing it to the delight of the other guests in the cabin. "Anyways, I'd never used a full ice spell outside of my own home. But Torsten didn't care. He said to me, 'Here's the plan. You are going to step out onto that river and use your ice spell to harden its surface, so you can walk on it.' The waterfall was about thirty meters from where he wanted me to step out. He said, 'You will also use your ice spell to freeze the entire waterfall, and once you have done that you will come back the way you came.'

"When I stepped one foot out onto the surface of that river, the ice on its surface started to show tiny cracks immediately. I refused to go any farther. But Torsten said, 'If you don't pass this test then you are not going back to Zeyanara.' I started to cry and shout out about how much I hated him and wished he wasn't my teacher. But nobody was around, and after a while I realized he was completely serious. He was going to leave me out there and go back to Zeyanara without me if I couldn't pass the test.

"I'm still amazed that I made it out of there alive. When you are doing a spell, the focus you channel into it is everything. At first, I was so distracted by my anger at Torsten that the ice kept buckling beneath me, and at one point it did crack completely and nearly swallowed me whole. Torsten spoke to me calmly throughout the whole ordeal, though. He taught me how to direct my negative energy toward the spell, so that all my rage and sorrow transformed into a single wavelength of magic. He told me to think of the spell as my lifeline, the only thing that would ultimately save me. And that did save me in the end.

"Since then, I've gained confidence in my ice spells. I've frozen entire rivers before, in mere seconds. I think if I tried hard enough, I could freeze the ocean itself… although I think more than a few people would be upset with me for doing that. And late last year, when the world changed forever, I stepped outside of Serrahan for the first time to perform magic on the land. With so many more opportunities to practice my spells, my skills improved tenfold.

"Because I'm out on the land so often, honing my craft, I work very closely with the Earth Healers. The first time I saw an Earth Healer, I was afraid because I'd heard so many stories about the inner darkness of the AI Masters, how they used to be warped monsters who stole people's souls. I was amazed to learn that the robot I was looking at had exactly the same hardware and physical configuration as an old AI

Master. But I've gotten to know a few Earth Healers, to really understand them, and I've discovered that they have beautiful personalities. They're not just friendly, they're amazingly intelligent... They have these vast stores of data on climate patterns, wildlife, and natural ecosystems, and they guide Mages like me by teaching us about what systems are out of balance.

"Like up north in Calliope, they have really short winters these days, because of all the carbon that has become trapped in the atmosphere from the industry in Crystal City. So, the Earth Healers teach me which rivers to keep frozen so that they won't flood during the late winter thaw. And then I work with the fire spell Mages, who learn from the Earth Healers how to calibrate their spells to give off just the right amount of heat to apply to those same rivers in the springtime, so that they thaw gradually instead of intensely. It's really a beautiful synergy that all of us have."

"I've been talking for a while now," she said, cognizant that Miranda was clearing her throat suggestively as if inviting her to finish. Walter's spirit didn't want Helena to finish, though; he was enraptured by her words, and by the revelation that the AI Masters were working together with the Mages to heal and repair the natural environment.

"Before I finish, though, I just wanted to say how grateful I am to that young man, Walter. They say that he's missing and cannot be found, but I've travelled far and wide throughout the Empire, and if he were still alive, I would have found him. He can't be hiding out this long; his poor wife and daughters haven't even seen him. His little girls Ariadne and Athena, they're living together on that faraway island, under the apprenticeship of the shaman-god dwelling on Mount Samaya. His wife, I hear, lives not too far from here. But she's alone, and if he were alive he surely would have gone to visit his family. I know that reviving the dead is one of the hardest spells a Mage can undertake, but I want to make it my life's work to learn the spell for it. That way, I can bring Walter back, and show him the magnificent world he's created."

Walter's spirit felt a tremor of energy pass through him as Helena spoke these final words, and it seemed as though the earth was quaking beneath his feet. He heard Shiva's voice echoing throughout the cabin, softly at first but with increasing intensity. Walter was sure that only he heard the sound, though, since none of the other guests in the cabin seemed to be perturbed.

"Remember the words I uttered on that fateful day I gifted you the Talisman. Do not forget reality and the present moment; such forgetfulness can be dangerous, for the real world desperately needs you. If you are not careful, you might lose yourself in the

land of visions."

The sound of the god's urgent voice was like a spark that ignited Walter's spirit, awakening it from its lethargy. The spirit took one final look around the cabin, tried to memorize the patterns on each timber plank that formed its walls, gazed longingly toward Miranda and her circle of pilgrims, then heaved himself upwards. He vowed that he would return here one day, to the sacred soil of the fire lizard.

As Walter awoke from his vision, he heard an irritating ringing in his ears. He opened his eyes gingerly, because the light that flooded into his retinas was disturbingly bright. He did not feel the comfortable, soothing warmth of the cabin any longer, and this made him feel lost, afraid, and alone. But his fears were somewhat assuaged by the sight of two familiar faces: Tristan and Eva. Once he finally remembered that they were back, safe and sound, after their daring voyage in the form of animal spirits, Walter felt a pang of relief and forgot about his selfish desires for comfort and safety. What confused him, however, was the palpable relief on both of their faces.

"Walter, thank goodness!" Eva cried as soon as he had opened his eyes fully and was appearing to regain a foothold in the realm of the conscious.

"Good grief, Walter," Tristan sighed. "You really gave us a fright."

Walter furrowed his brow. "What do you mean, I gave you a fright? I just woke up from a pleasant vision."

Tristan chuckled, wiping the sweat off his glistening forehead. Walter then looked around and immediately recognized the pale linen sheets and serene pastel walls of the Mereille. It then struck him that he had descended into his vision, which felt as though it had lasted weeks, while lying on this very same bed.

"How long was I out for?" Walter asked, fidgeting uncomfortably. His heart began to beat rapidly and he suddenly felt an aching thirst. He threw the sheets off himself angrily, but Eva rushed forwards to comfort him, patting his back soothingly.

"Hush, don't make any sudden movements. You've been sleeping in this bed since Sunday, and it's now Wednesday evening. Tristan and I returned late in the afternoon on Monday, and ever since then we've been begging the sisters who work here to do everything in their power to revive you. And trust me, they tried. But despite their valiant efforts, you just refused to come back to this world. They thought you had suffered a concussion of some kind, but there was no evidence of head trauma.

"I told them about your Talisman, and that you plunge into these distant visions occasionally. I asked them if they could use a magical spell to revive you. They shuddered when I told them the Talisman was from the god Shiva. They told me, 'Sorry, a god that powerful? We have no magic that could possibly work against his talismans.' But here you are... Goodness, I need to go tell Sister Avaleye and, well... everyone."

Walter was suddenly inexplicably anxious to see his fellow rebels and reunite with them after his long vision, to tell them what he had seen and give them hope for the future. "I should tell Nuada, too. I should go to him now and apologize for being away so long," he said.

Eva's face then became serious, and a cloak of shadows fell over her eyes. "Nuada... poor man. He's refused to come out of his chambers ever since I gave him the news."

Walter's heart skipped a beat. "What news? Eva, I don't need any more stress in my life. What news?"

Tristan patted Eva's shoulder gently as the young woman suppressed tears. As she could not seem to find the strength to speak, Tristan answered for her.

"Cyriana and Jonathan... we couldn't find them. We did a wide circle around the perimeter of Serrahan, and we found their tracks in the forest. We could even smell their scents... well, at least I recognized Cyri's. Light jasmine and lemongrass. But it soon became clear to us that they crossed the border that separates this kingdom from the outside world. It's astounding how much ground they were able to cover in the span of just a few days, but at the rate they were going, I think they might already be in Crystal City by now."

Walter nodded sympathetically, then his expression hardened. He knew that was terrible news for the rebels, and he inwardly cursed himself for allowing Cyriana to be present at the council meetings in which they had discussed plans and strategy. Cyriana would never voluntarily expose any secrets which might jeopardize their mission to the AI Masters—he knew that she loathed the AI Masters too much to do that. But that young girl was not ready to wage any type of war against their enemy, even if she was accompanied by her jaguar. If she were captured, the robots might torture her into revealing secrets... secrets that even she, with her warlike spirit, could not keep concealed forever. *And Sekhmet... what havoc might that cursed animal wreck in Crystal City?* Walter thought. He gritted his teeth at the prospect that a premature, reckless skirmish incited by that creature could enrage the AI

Masters, provoking them to harm Cyriana and his brother.

Suddenly he recalled the spring vision he had experienced of Cyriana and Jonathan, presiding over a kingdom where faith in magic was the overriding law. His mind then skipped over to the most recent vision, the one he had lazily indulged in, in which his brother had expressed a fierce hatred of the AI Masters. It was not unthinkable that Cyriana's wild plot might inspire Jonathan's romantic side, might trigger his memory of the beautiful young girl he had loved years ago, before his life was irrevocably altered. This, alone, might be enough to turn his loyalties completely. A tug of anxiety pulled at Walter as he recalled the image, as clear and crisp as ever, of Jonathan pummeling the AI Fighters in the Stockyards all those years ago. Jonathan had been iconic, unstoppable, indefatigable. *Could it be possible that those two could somehow succeed in overthrowing the AI Masters, all by themselves?*

These thoughts were swirling in Walter's mind as he gazed outside at the pristine rose garden, which was suffused with a pale amber glow in the light of late afternoon. Eva and Tristan continued to watch him with concerned expressions. When he turned back toward their expectant faces, he realized that he was wasting precious time speculating on all these possibilities, just as he had wasted precious time lost in the fall vision. The time for contemplation was over, and the time for action was now. He cleared his throat and took a deep breath.

"Let us go to Nuada. If he will not exit his chambers, we will visit him inside them. But I must speak with him. We cannot lose his leadership at this critical juncture."

"He will be much cheered by the news that you have awakened. He was devastated not just about Cyriana, but also about you," Tristan said with a smile that lifted Walter's spirits.

Walter tapped gingerly on the ornate door of Nuada's chambers in the town hall, flanked by his friends Tristan and Eva. Two royal guards standing duty regarded the guests with an icy suspicion. The door swung open to reveal the pale, sleep-deprived face of Nuada, and Walter was startled when the old man broke down in emotional sobs and embraced him tightly. Walter chuckled, his own eyes blurring with tears.

"Look at us," Nuada sniffled, "two leaders who weep like teenaged girls."

Walter extricated himself from the Mage's firm grip and sighed. "Yes, well what else can we do when we have so many stresses in our lives? I heard that your daughter was never found… Nuada, I am so sorry. But I know that if she's anything, she's a fighter. She'll be fine."

"I certainly hope you are right. Because if she's not fine, then I'm not fine," Nuada grumbled, then glanced over Walter's shoulder at Eva and Tristan. "Tristan here promised me that he would bring her home, and he now says that he still intends to fulfill that promise, but the task will take a bit longer than expected. When did you wake up from your vision?"

"A half hour ago, or so… we walked over to the town hall from the Mereille, just after I woke up."

"Which means you haven't eaten in nearly four days," Nuada said with a pained expression. "Almost as bad as me… well, don't just stand there, come inside and I'll have Faye bring up some dinner for us." He whispered something to the guard, who nodded briskly and then marched to the servant's quarters to convey the message to Faye. The mild-mannered servant girl appeared in less than no time, bearing platters loaded with gravy-drizzled potatoes, charred vegetables, and tender roast beef. The three rebels and the Mage leader sat down at a sturdy rosewood table, bordered on one side by a window offering a stunning view of the winding streets of Serrahan, and a blazing hearth on the other. Walter's mouth watered as he gazed longingly at the delicious fare, but Nuada's appetite was still muted, and so the young man politely restrained himself from gluttonous over-indulgences.

"Eat, lad. Don't mind my reluctance," the leader chided as he watched Walter peck at the food. "At your age I was eating as much as a pair of horses, trust me. Now just a few bites are enough to satisfy me." The rebel leader accepted this invitation willingly, even going so far as to boldly ask Faye to bring seconds for him.

After Walter had sated his appetite thoroughly, the conversation began to veer away from food and toward politics and strategy.

Eva scanned Walter's face carefully before posing her question. "What progress has been made in your visions, Walter? Have you seen enough for us to move ahead with the next phase of our plans?" she asked solemnly.

Walter sighed, and then reached down in his pocket for the Talisman. He had taken it off after the last vision, and he was feeling much better now that he had taken a short break from using it. He took it out of his pocket and set it down on the table. Nuada gazed at the jade stone with intense interest, running his fingers over the labyrinth etching on its surface.

"A most powerful gemstone, Walter. More impressive than any I've seen in my years as a Mage. This labyrinth… it is an ancient druidic symbol. It represents the soul's descent into the underworld, which leads to either entrapment, or to enlightenment… to the discovery of one's true self. Well, is Eva right? Has the Talisman given you what you need to know?"

"Yes, and no," Walter replied. "It's given me insight into these possible future pathways, and I know which one I would like to choose. I know beyond a shadow of a doubt. But that is what frightens me," he said, looking at his friends with an anxious expression. "Is it supposed to be so easy? Am I somehow falling into a trap by choosing the pathway that seems the most desirable?" His mind hearkened back to the ominous words of the seer from the Jamestown tavern: *You will have to make a choice between destinies, but you must be exceedingly careful. The destiny which seems the most favorable to you at first will be the one which brings evil and pain.*

"Perhaps it is a trap, but one that you can escape from," Nuada pondered, stroking his white beard and diverting his gaze toward the setting sun outside. "Or that others can help you escape from."

Nuada's words triggered a memory in Walter, of a story he had read long ago in a textbook from the Great Library. A textbook about a hero from ancient Greek mythology who had slain a barbaric creature inside a labyrinth, half-man and half-bull, and then was led out of the labyrinth with the aid of a young woman's thread. The story was hazy and fragmented in his mind, and he didn't understand its meaning, but some part of him told him that it was important.

"We must be practical," Eva said, interrupting Walter's reverie. "If you feel confident about this vision, then that is a good sign. You can worry about whether you are making the wrong choice later, but for now, we must begin preparing our army."

Tristan nodded in agreement. "Now that Eva and I have proven that shapeshifting is not only possible but safe, there is no reason to delay this any further. With a spirit army, we have a much better chance of finding Cyriana if she is in Crystal City."

Nuada's emerald eyes glinted with hope. "Yes, you are right. Many citizens of Serrahan, though, will be reluctant to venture into the outside world after having been separated from it for so long. It is true that many of the young people here are eager to leave, but the older folk are more conservative, and they are also naturally wary of shapeshifting because their memories of the Druidic curse are fresher." As he grasped the implications of this, the Mage ruler's lower lip trembled, and Walter looked at him with concern.

"You don't want to send all of Serrahan's youth into some vague netherworld from which there might not be any return..." Walter said in a muted, fragile voice. "I don't blame you at all."

Eva sighed as the sun dipped below the horizon. Its departure cast a dark shadow over the village. "Not all of them have to go... if we have a few dozen, that might be enough, and..."

"The Southern Jungles," Nuada said brusquely, and the three councilors looked at him with interest.

"We have many potential allies in those parts..." the old Mage mused, twirling his silver-white beard in his fingers. "It's been years since I spoke to their leader, Xe'tan, but I'm sure that he loathes the AI Masters as much as we do. The natives of the Southern Jungles have a rather unique outlook on life. Unlike most humans and Mages, they don't experience fear in violent or dangerous circumstances. They relish endangering their lives in battle, and that, I suppose, is the reason why the animal they revere the most is the jaguar—the dark, fiercely warlike creature who has now led Cyriana astray. In short, they are the perfect recruits for your spirit army."

"Wonderful suggestion, Nuada," Walter said. "Send an envoy down there to meet with Xe'tan and gauge his interest in the plan. He can tell Xe'tan that Sekhmet—the goddess of war herself—has gone to Crystal City, and the natives of his land will be more than eager to follow her, even if they must do so in the form of other animals. And what about the Barrens? There may be considerable untapped potential there as well," he said, thinking wistfully back to his most recent vision of the cabin nestled in the idyllic valley. He knew that the reality in the Barrens at the moment was far from idyllic; it was closer to a nightmare, as preparations were being made to evacuate villagers from their homes to clear the path for a vast diamond mine that would permanently scar the earth.

"The AI Masters' grip on that territory is much tighter than it is in the Southern Jungles," Nuada sighed, and Eva nodded her agreement. "I would be surprised if a Mage envoy could make it through that desolate landscape without being assassinated, or else dying of thirst. I have an envoy in mind—a young, brave lad named Dorian—and I value his services too much to see him perish in a mission."

Walter felt a tightness in his chest as he remembered that Elaine had departed from Zeyanara several weeks ago, heading south toward the Barrens. She had been desperate to see her family, to ensure that they were not in immediate danger from the AI Masters and their nefarious plans.

"How will Dorian reach the Southern Jungles, then, if not through the Barrens? And how will the army recruits travel northward?" Eva asked.

Nuada was silent for a long time before replying. "I will give him *Aurora* to steer south, and he will anchor in Hells Gate, the only port town in the Southern Jungles. He will take as many recruits with him as will fit on that vessel. AI Masters have tried docking there before, and their ships have occasionally been gunned down by sentries, but those brazen warriors will hold their fire when *Aurora* arrives. The natives will welcome Dorian with open arms, I am sure of it."

This plan put Walter's mind at ease somewhat, but he was still feeling uncomfortable about Elaine's precarious plight.

"Very good," Eva said, and then she turned to look intently at Walter. He met her gaze reluctantly, as he saw in her azure eyes the ghost of Emilia. Her pale skin was warmer with the light and heat of the nearby hearth, and she looked uncannily like her late sister, an image that made Walter shudder. He had not seen Emilia's spirit in many days; she had appeared to him before his spring vision, but not since then. Now that the visions from the Talisman were over, he wondered whether she would ever return to him.

"Nuada, are the Meridian Mountains AI-conquered territory?" Eva asked, not taking her eyes off the rebel leader.

"They are no-man's land—a neutral territory that has been claimed neither by the AIs nor any other race, as far as I am aware. They are quite a harsh and hostile place—rocky, treacherous, and difficult to navigate. It's not unheard of for travelers crossing them to get lost, to be tricked into thinking they are going in the right direction when they are not. The sounds there are very strange... there are deep crevasses in the mountains that reflect otherworldly echoes. It is the realm of dark spirits, I tell you." Nuada's words were doing nothing good for Walter's blood pressure, as thoughts of Elaine meeting her death in those mountains rolled through his mind like waves in a sea-storm.

"Ah, I see," Eva pondered, finally turning her gaze away from Walter. "In other words, the best place to harden one's mind... to strengthen it?"

Nuada twirled his beard, taking a draught of honeyed ale from his chalice. "If you are looking for a challenge... a place for nature to teach you her cruel ways, then yes, I suppose you cannot pick a better place than the Meridian Mountains. And I've heard rumor that the mountains, especially at the higher elevations, inspire an unparalleled mental and spiritual clarity. Signals of all kinds can be transmitted easily there..."

Eva breathed in sharply, her eyes glittering with alertness. "Well, that, my friend," she said to Walter matter-of-factly, "is where we will go to train."

Walter crossed his arms. "Train?" He swallowed, his palms becoming sweaty.

"You weren't just planning to waltz into the AI stronghold for your meeting with a chief advisor to the *Anax* without any training, were you?" She laughed, a strong, guttural noise that filled up the chamber. "Didn't my sister teach you *anything*, Walter? You are going to be descending into the ninth circle of Hell, you know that, right?"

Walter cleared his throat and attempted to restore his composure. "Of course, you are right that the journey will be perilous. But how will I train, and who will train me?"

Eva's eyes were now blazing with a fiery passion, and Nuada stared at her with a furrowed brow.

"I will train you, Walter. I will carry out my sister's legacy until the end, and I will take up the torch of leadership where she dropped it. And how will I train you? *Signals*, Walter. It's all about the signals, which can be transmitted easily in the mountains, as Nuada said."

Walter shifted in his seat. "Signals? You are talking in riddles, Eva; be straight with me."

"It's too hard for me to explain here, without *showing* you how it will work. I don't even know if it will work myself, but that's why we will try together. You should get a good sleep tonight, Walter. Pack up your *balayan*, *catan*, tablet, food supplies for at least a week, and extra clothes and blankets. It gets cold up there, especially at night, or so I've heard. Tomorrow at first light, you and I shall ride south to the mountains."

Meridian

"Over every mountain, there is a path, although it may not be seen from the valley."
– Theodore Roethke

Although they had left at the break of dawn, it was mid-morning by the time Eva and Walter arrived at the foothills of the Meridian Mountains. The mountains were more intimidating than Walter had expected; stern and impassive, they straddled the border between the North and the South of the Empire of Khalendar, serving to protect the southern wilderness from the creeping fingers of civilization. Their sharp crags were wreathed in mist and fog, which only marginally softened the harshness of their grim features.

Walter was riding on Epos, a dark brown stallion, and Eva on the horse's counterpart Epa, who had a fiery personality and a coat the color of burnished copper. Both creatures were Eva's animal companions, and together they embodied the spirit of Epona, the goddess of travel and journeying. The creatures looked up at the mountains with mixed emotions; Epa, who had a wilder and more adventurous personality, eagerly trotted toward them, whereas Epos whinnied with fear and stubbornly dug his hooves into the soil. Walter found it fascinating that their temperaments always seemed to perfectly offset and balance each other, as though they were two halves of a whole.

"Epa, as wild as you are, horses aren't fit for such steep mountains," Eva crooned, patting the mare gently on the side of her neck. "They will stay down here during the training."

Walter swallowed nervously. "This is AI Master territory, though— do you think they will be safe?"

Eva nodded. "I've never seen any AI Masters venture as far south as the Forest of Antheia, which is just northeast of here," she said, pointing to a nearby grove of conifers. "In fact, the robots are deathly afraid of the forest, with its cougars, bears, and gray foxes. If there is any sign of trouble, the horses know to head straight for the shelter of the trees."

"And *they* aren't afraid of the cougars, bears, and gray foxes?" Walter asked, stroking Epos' ears.

"Even the boldest predator would not disturb a creature with the soul of a goddess," Eva said confidently, assuaging Walter's fears.

"Well, here is where we leave you, my friends," Eva said with a sigh. She dismounted Epa gracefully and unlatched the saddlebags, which contained provisions for their foray into the mountains. Epos looked at Eva with fearful black eyes and nuzzled her, as though trying to convince her to stay, but the young woman cheerily dismissed his anxieties. "Follow Epa's lead and be fearless, my love," she said to Epos in a soft whisper.

Without a further glance back at her equine companions, Eva slung one of the packs over her shoulders, handed the other to Walter, and marched stoically toward the mist-shrouded foothills. Walter was enjoying the cool, crisp air and admiring the foxglove and pink mountain heather, and the weight of his pack did not bother him at first. After several miles of walking up a muddy alpine trail, however, Walter's back was aching, and he had to stop at frequent intervals to catch his breath and sip from his canteen.

"What is our destination, Eva?" he inquired. It suddenly occurred to him that he ought to have asked the question earlier.

"You know as well as I do, Walter," she replied with an enigmatic smile. "Take out your tablet, please," she said, pausing next to a large boulder that jutted out precariously onto the steep trail. Walter complied with her request, his brow furrowed in confusion as he tried to decipher her plans. "Now, read the messages that I send you... and carefully."

Walter glanced down at the tablet, and after a few moments, several words appeared on the screen—it was a message from Eva, telling him that they had arrived in the Meridian Mountains. "I had no idea," he said jokingly. "Is that all you wanted to tell me?"

Eva grimaced. "The signals are still weak here. I can gauge their strength by measuring the fluidity of the reception. Every living human has a steady stream of thoughts in their consciousness—some thoughts are like fish beneath the surface of a pond, silent and shadowy, while others are like frogs on the lily pads that rest on the pond's surface, visible and coherent. The thoughts that I can transmit to your tablet at the moment... those are the frogs. Here, I am only able to actively channel messages like that. But the fluidity level is low—far too low for our purposes."

Walter was becoming frustrated, and the fatigue from the journey, combined with his lack of understanding piqued his anger. "And what exactly are our purposes? Because I'm not sure I quite grasp them," he said in an irritated voice. Eva remained calm and did not react to his anger, which deflated it.

"I know I'm being mysterious, Walter, and I apologize for that. I'm not purposefully trying to annoy you, which I hope you understand. I will try to shed some light on my goals here. The first is to experiment with your tablet, to see how strong the signals it picks up are, and to set up camp in a spot where the signals are the strongest. The second goal is the main one. If all goes well, I anticipate I will be able to pick up intelligence from Central Command."

"Like... spy on them?" Walter said incredulously. Despite his vast knowledge of hacking and computers, he was taken aback by Eva's proposal. "You know nothing of their firewalls, the codes they have painstakingly designed to protect their intelligence from outside interference."

"Yes, you are right, Walter. I know nothing of them... but the AI Masters do, and I am suggesting that if the signals are fluid enough here, I can *enter their minds*... the same way that I've entered Asana's mind in the past."

Walter rubbed his eyes, suddenly feeling dizzy—whether from altitude sickness or shock from the news of Eva's plans, he wasn't sure. "And what is your objective, exactly, in entering their minds? What sort of intelligence are you hoping to obtain?"

Eva giggled. "Walter, for a rebel leader, you can be narrow-minded at times. What intelligence *don't* you want from Central Command? Any of it would be ultimately useful for your mission. You're the one going there, so tell me exactly what you want to know."

Walter pondered this for a moment, and he began to warm up to the idea as he contemplated it further.

"I would like to know where I am going, first of all. What kind of room is it where I will be meeting with this advisor? And what kind of security will they have when they screen me for entry? I surely won't be able to bring my *balayan* or tablet, so how will I be able to use those to defend myself?"

"You are correct. There will be rigid security measures. But I think there will be ways of getting around that. Let us find a place to stake out camp at a higher elevation, and I will see if the signals are clearer there."

The pair continued to climb higher, and as they did the soil became drier and the ponderosa pines, firs, and hemlocks thinned out. For many hours they hiked in the clouds, which cast a ghostly, iridescent pall upon the landscape. Eventually, they ascended above the cloud-line and were greeted with a mesmerizing view of the shimmering ocean to the west and the cloud-shrouded forests and mountains to the east. Oxygen levels were low at this altitude, and Walter had begun feeling dizzy from the change in the air, so the pair had to stop and rest at frequent intervals.

The trail they had been following, which had previously been well-marked, was becoming more mazelike and difficult to follow. Walter repeatedly asked Eva if she knew where she was going, to which she replied "upwards," and that made Walter chuckle uneasily. The mountain seemed to go on forever, and they had no clear destination. They had reached a point where the tree cover was very sparse and the terrain was rocky and steep, and they had to scramble upwards on their hands and knees through some sections. The pair soon arrived at a steep ridge, on both sides of which was a sheer vertical drop that seemed to go on for miles. It was impossible to see the bottom because the clouds were beneath them, shrouding the earth in a thick blanket. When Eva and Walter spoke to each other, their voices echoed up from below, eerily conveying the impression that they were not alone.

"Be careful as you traverse the ridge," Eva warned. "A single misstep could be fatal."

Walter heeded her advice, balancing himself carefully with his arms. At one point, he lost his balance and almost tipped over, but Eva steadied his shoulders from behind and he regained his composure.

"Thank you," he said gratefully, in a trembling voice.

After the ridge, there was another steep scramble upwards before the pair finally reached the top of one of the mountain peaks.

"This is the first summit," Eva said, and then pointed up. Walter could see much higher, more intimidating summits above them, and the prospect of reaching them made him feel increasingly dizzy.

When they paused to take a sip of water, Walter glanced down at his tablet, as its screen had lit up. He was shocked to see that there were whole paragraphs written there, and as he read one of them, it dawned upon them that they were communicating Eva's stream of consciousness:

"Emilia would have loved these mountains. She was always saying how much she wanted to climb them, back when she was training in Tsei'watu. There was never enough time; she was always busy with other things. If she were still alive today, we could have come here together. We need to reach a higher elevation... this ridge looks

like it will take us somewhere. Don't look down; it would be a certain death if we fell here. Walter is clumsy. Make sure he doesn't lose his balance. That was close! The thought of losing him up here makes me shudder. Don't think about it; don't look down."

Walter passed her the tablet, and she scanned the words written on it with a look of glee. "It's working," she said with a grin, and embraced Walter.

"Can we set up camp here, then?" Walter asked, panting with exhaustion as he took a long draught of water from his second canteen.

"Yes, here will do," Eva replied.

As they were pitching a rough, makeshift tent on the summit, Walter suddenly heard a piercing wail emanate from below them. He felt a sudden surge of adrenaline. *Is it another traveler in these mountains, needing help?* Walter wondered. He stopped what he was working on and began to look around for the source of the sound. All was silent for a few moments, and then he heard the wail a second time, although this time he could make out distinct words: *Save me.* It was a man's voice, and Walter thought that it sounded oddly familiar, but he couldn't quite explain how.

"Someone is in danger," Walter said, his heart pounding. "Let's head back toward the ridge. Maybe they are down there." He took a few steps away from the tent, but Eva grasped his arm firmly.

"Wait," she instructed. "Chances are it's a trick, and not a real human that needs to be saved. The mountains do that sometimes. Did you hear how the voice sounds like yours?" she asked, and then Walter suddenly realized that she was right. "The mountains create these deceptions; they project the voices of all those who visit them, like a mirror of sound. There are very ancient folktales which say that there are actual changelings in the mountains, but I don't believe those at all," she said with a shudder.

"Changelings?" Walter asked, frowning. After having experienced the possibilities of magic and the supernatural first-hand, he was more receptive to such wild notions than he might have once been.

"Yes, according to legend, when outsiders visit the mountains, they bring their spiritual auras with them," Eva explained. "The mountains are thus able to forge replicas of their souls... and some say their actual physical beings, so that a duplicate version of that person can come into existence."

Walter shuddered at the prospect that another duplicate version of him could be wandering around nearby. "And why play this trick on visitors?" Walter asked. "What is in it for the mountains?"

Eva chuckled. "It might have an entirely rational explanation... perhaps the sound could have been an echo from your voice that was amplified and warped by the geological features of the mountains."

Walter shook his head. "What I heard was not an echo, Eva. It was another person—real or not, I don't know."

Eva shrugged. "Just don't worry about it too much. According to legends, the mountains prey on mental weakness. If you are tired and let down your mental defenses or become distracted in thought, the mountains will seize the opportunity to frighten you with their tricks. To answer your question—why they do it—I suppose it's just to play with humans. Like the gods did, long ago... they loved to tinker with mortals and their emotions and desires. Apparently, the changelings strive to cultivate fear and anxiety in others, causing the person they are interacting with to doubt themselves and their friends. Again, I don't believe in any of this folklore, but you are welcome to if you like."

"I would prefer not to, Eva," Walter responded, "but I'm not sure what to believe anymore. The experiences I've had with Shiva, with the Talisman... I used to think that the world could be rationally explained, that there was a scientific explanation for everything that happened, but I now realize how wrong that notion was. Science is something that helps understand the process, but it is not the true explanation for anything."

"I suppose you're right—if Shiva created the universe, then that fact alone casts doubt on everything we thought we knew. It does give me some comfort to know, though, that there is some higher power out there. Otherwise, we are just stuck with the AI Masters."

"A grim fate indeed," Walter said, his face wreathed in shadows. He carried on pitching the tent, and by the time it was complete, a sharp wind had swept in from the west and the temperature had dropped considerably. Walter and Eva huddled together in the tent for a while, sipping Xe'levan. While Walter drifted off to sleep, Eva got to work focusing mentally on accessing an AI Master at Central Command.

Hours later, when he woke up from his rest, Walter found Eva lying down on the floor of the tent next to him, her eyes half-open but unseeing. "Eva, what's wrong with you?" he asked, his voice urgent, and he tried to shake her into consciousness. The young woman was muttering to herself, and her brow was damp with sweat. Walter poured some cold water from his canteen onto a towel and wiped her forehead, but she did not seem to come to. Walter then glanced down at his tablet, and what he read there shook him to the core.

The air here is frigid and dry… just like the air in the mountains, but with less of a lively breeze. I'm sitting in what appears to be a prison cell, about five by seven feet, the size of a small bedroom. The design is white, modern, and sterile… unnervingly pretty in its own way. I can see a courtyard through a long, rectangular window directly across from where I am sitting. There are many people in the courtyard, dressed in long cotton tunics, milling around, trading wares in what appears to be an outdoor market. Outside, it is snowing, tiny white crystals that blur my view of those figures, but also cast an aura of beauty upon them.

If I peer closer, I can see that those are not actually people—not proper humans, at least. Their skin is firm and hard, and although they are attractive and youthful, there is something unsettling about their appearance, something that suggests they are not made of flesh. This body of mine… it is even more rigid than theirs. It feels like I am trapped in a hard shell, lacking in elasticity and flexibility. It is suffocating, and I would despise it were I not so satisfied at my achievement of inhabiting it.

Being in a cell exacerbates the feeling of claustrophobia, and it's making me think back to my sickening experience at the Crate. I must get out of here, but I'm not sure how. There is cleaning equipment next to the door, a spray bottle, a rag… is that my function? Am I supposed to be polishing the furniture here? I stifle a robotic laugh as I realize there is no furniture. There are containers, pods, and shelves, all efficiently and immaculately nested into the wall. It looks like people can sleep here, but what a horrendous place to sleep—on a shelf inside a wall. It is so cold, so white… there are no decorations anywhere, nothing homely or comforting. There is some blood on one of the pods, I can see now. I may as well clean it up. What am I thinking? Why would I get near to that blood… and why is there blood here, in a place devoid of flesh?

Do your job, Eva, clean it up like a good android, and then get the hell out of here. I can smell the blood. It is sickeningly metallic. Here, next to the locked door, a fingerprint scanner—let's test it out. Aha! I am now walking down a dark corridor, with walls that are pressed tightly together: more claustrophobia. It's quite uncomfortable; I have to turn my broad-shouldered android body sideways just to get out. I forgot the spray bottle in the cell… will anyone notice? I've reached a fork in the hall, one larger hallway branching left and a smaller one branching right. The one that goes right might lead out to the courtyard, assuming my sense of direction is operating properly. But wait, am I ready to go there yet? There were too many of them… they might expect me to speak to them, and I can't risk doing that now.

Who am I inhabiting? Think, Eva, it's not just you inside of this central processing system. Find the CPU, recover the memory, retrieve the data… it's taking a long time to generate, not like it was with Asana. Probably because this fellow is unimaginably dull. Here it is… Luca… he's a middle-aged AI Fighter, manufactured about fifty years ago in Fewsbury. At that age he is already approaching retirement for a Fighter, not like the Masters who live hundreds of years. He used to be a big name in boxing matches, but now he's just a fading memory. A groundskeeper, he spends his dull, monotonous days cleaning up after test subjects. Wait, did I understand that correctly? Test subjects in Central Command?

Of course, you silly, naïve girl. They don't just test people at the Crate and their other god-forsaken prisons. They bring the most valuable ones to their headquarters, to try and decipher the mysteries of their brains. What do they want to know, exactly? This man has no idea. He's not curious, he doesn't ask questions. He does his job in precisely the same way, every single day; he always follows exactly the same circuit around the grounds. He never deviates from the path. He is supposed to enter the courtyard now, buy more cleaning supplies at the market, then head toward the northwest wing—where there are apparently even more test subject cells waiting to be polished.

Maybe he blends into the background; maybe he's just a simpleton that nobody notices. Let's hope that is the case. If not, then it's not my neck that will be on the line... unless, of course... no, I won't be so careless as to leave a trace.

Okay, so Luca usually takes a right, but that goes outside into the courtyard, and I want to go somewhere else. Let's try the grand, spacious hallway, then. The walls here are more vibrant than the blank white walls of the cell; they are painted a striking red color, in equal measures cheerful and ominous, and they are lined with lovely stained-glass windows. There are doors along the left-hand side of the corridor; I open a few with of them with a fingerprint scanning device and am startled to see replicas of the room I just exited. From a review of Luca's recent memories, I understand that these are cells that he has already cleaned. He must have been busy all morning here. The cells look endless. They are all empty, and I am far more interested in the stained-glass windows to my right.

It looks like sunshine is streaming out of them, but it could be just artificial lighting; it was a grey, snowy day when I glanced outside before. The images the intricate windows depict are strangely religious... do the AI Masters fancy that Central Command is their cathedral? Each pane depicts AI Masters in different poses, the early ones portraying the androids as hardworking slaves, their hands bound by chains, pushing boulders up hills as though they are Sisyphus himself. Here there is a bloody battle scene, with humans being slain by the AI Masters, and corpses littering the ground. The Grand Revolution? It must be, because in these later scenes the AI Masters appear godlike, benevolently outstretching their arms in peaceful welcome as the humans kneel devoutly at their feet. This AI reminds me of that notorious priest from the Old World... the Savonarola of AI Masters, burning a pile of books in a village square... and then other AI Masters authoring new books under candlelight, as though they are monks poring over calligraphic manuscripts. This must represent the destruction of human knowledge... but were those books ever destroyed, or was that just a lie that the AI Masters told the humans?

And here are scenes of harmony, with humans and AI Masters shaking hands... the Treaty of Calais? Boxing matches, revelry and games, celebratory events and festive occasions. Scenes of opulence and misery in equal measure—humans toiling in mines and factories, covered in soot and pollution, producing vast quantities of riches. Diamonds, sparkling like stars in a vast constellation, adorn the necks of stunningly beautiful women. Here is an odd portrait of a young boy with black hair, the AI Masters holding up a key to his head. Is it Walter? That is not possible... is it possible? In the next picture, he is taking a different key, thanking them, and it looks like they have made peace. Here there are animals... oh, how terrible... the animals are falling into an abyss, all of them, while the AI Masters stand victoriously at the edge of the cliffside. Their victory over the animal spirits... the Shadow Wars?

Shivers run down my spine as I continue down the hallway and see some images I don't want to see. I see something gruesome, something unspeakably abhorrent, something that touches my heart deeply... it is making me ill, so I will erase it from this android's recent memory. Here there is a large ship, captured by humans, as the AI Masters try to destroy it from a plane in the sky. How disturbing... This actually happened. We were there. And that is it... the panes from here on are empty. They are waiting to be filled with images of a history still to be written, like gravestones that haven't been carved yet. There are so many empty panes, they stretch on forever.

What was that noise? A thud, like something large fell... and the vibrations from the impact being carried through the floor. It was coming from that direction... to the right. Wait, if I backtrack just a bit... there it is! A narrow hallway that branches down from here. And now I can feel the vibrations becoming stronger, there is something big inside the room I am approaching.

A door is materializing from the darkness. It is tall and narrow, and there are roman numerals inscribed at the very top: MMDXXIV. There are also some words in Latin inscribed above the doorway—'Fiat Lux'. Let there be light. What could this room possibly be? I find a fingerprint scanner to the right of the doorway, and suddenly, I'm inside. It is taking me some time to grasp my bearings... the air in here is dry, musty, and oppressive, like it's a closet filled with mothballs, but it's not a small room by any means. The ceilings soar to the heavens. And there are racks upon racks of... those are books, I think. Good lord, this must be the notorious Master Library, where they took pretty much all the literature pillaged from the Old World after their Grand Revolution.

If I wasn't inhabiting the body of an old AI Fighter with a barely existent sense of smell, I think I'd retch because this place has no ventilation. And now I see where the thudding sound is coming from; there are small, narrow conveyor belts encircling each of the mile-high bookshelves, and I can see it from here... some of the books are dropping onto the conveyor belt. There's a mechanical arm that's lifting them off the shelves and lowering them to a certain height from which they can be safely dropped onto the belt. Some of the books don't make a sound when they drop, because they are old paperbacks, but others are large hardcovers, and they land with an eerie, echoing thud.

I need to figure out how this place works, so I'm following one of the books that has fallen and tracing its journey along the conveyor belt. This is like a maze; the belt weaves its way in and out of the bookshelves, and it moves so quickly, I have to jog lightly to keep up. No easy task for an old, retired AI Fighter whose limbs are rickety and sorely in need of fresh oil. I'm panting with the exertion, and I can sense my system wanting to pause for a rest, but I can't stop now. Aha! I found some sort of portal into another room—another tall, narrow door with the same roman numerals inscribed above them.

I'm getting frightened now because I've suddenly realized why the doors and passageways are so tall and narrow: the elite AI Masters are built differently from the others. They sculpted themselves to be abnormally tall and thin because they wanted to distinguish themselves from the common man, lesser AI Masters, and AI Fighters. They thought the strange, ghoulish design gave them an air of education and refinement. I think this means I'm somewhere I'm not supposed to be. It must be an important room, because the conveyor belt is passing into it, through a short window in the wall next to the narrow door.

Also next to the door is a scanner, but not a fingerprint scanner this time. It looks like some sort of interactive screen. It's asking me some serious questions— about my name, my rank, and my title. There is also a camera higher above me. Thank the fates that I remembered to bring my cleaning rag; before I enter the camera's field of view, I can use it to cover this camera up. If there's an active guard on duty, they'll find it suspicious that the camera is blacked out, but I don't want there to be a record of this particular android being here if I can avoid it.

That was relatively simple, but now I need to pass some sort of test here. Okay, well I need to have a plan. What elite AI Masters do I know? I doubt Luca here has any knowledge of the elites—I haven't done a thorough scan of his memory, but I don't have time for that. I'll use the profile of Perseus, the AI Master who I've arranged for Walter to meet. Second house, advisor, here we go. It worked, but I have a bad feeling that something is about to go wrong. What is this place? It's just a narrow, metal hallway that appears to be open at either end. There's a glass door in front of me; where does this lead? Another chamber, this one with beautiful, ornately decorated wallpaper. At one end of the room there is a long, black table with a pen and pad on it and two chairs. At the other end… a mirror. The conveyor belt is passing through here, into another chamber that appears to be locked. This is a trap, Eva, get out of here. It's one of those interrogation rooms. It looks like a mirror from the inside, but it's a window from the outside—AI Masters could be watching me at this very moment.

I am hearing strange noises now, that are coming from the locked chamber to my left. It sounds like an animal growling, or the low purr of a cat... a very large, and hungry one. Well, it is critical that I get inside that door, that I figure out for Walter's sake what is inside. It could be incredibly important for our mission. But the door appears to be locked from the inside—there is no fingerprint scanner, not even an interactive quiz. There's a keyhole, but no key. What the heck is written on this piece of paper? It looks like a poem...

> *"In this last of meeting places*
> *We grope together*
> *And avoid speech*
> *Gathered on this beach of the tumid river..."*

This is a poem from the Old World, is it not? It sounds eerily familiar, but I can't quite place it.

How can I get inside the room with no key? Maybe if I follow the hallway farther, I'll find one. It takes a sharp right just past the table, and a glass door slides open to reveal more of the same, just in a different direction. Wait, here is something different. There is another table at the end of the hallway here, and it has a typewriter with a blank sheet of paper. What do I write here? If I go past the typewriter, there is another glass door and the hallway turns to the right again. There is another table in the hallway. There is a key on that table! But the glass door isn't sliding open... it isn't opening at all. I think I'm supposed to write something with the typewriter, perhaps the name of the poem? I can't remember it. I don't know it.

Think, Eva, this could be critical.

I can't think. An alarm is sounding, and a toxic gas is filling the chamber. They've realized that there's been a breach. I need to get inside, though, so I smash the glass door with my fists. Luca is an old AI Fighter, but he's still two hundred pounds of chrome and steel. I'm immensely grateful to this hulk of a maintenance man. I've got the key... in just minutes they will be in here, they will stop me.

But I race back into the first hallway and twist the key into the door. It opens, and I feel a rush of oxygen. A giant metal mushroom stands before me. Am I hallucinating? It's not a mushroom—it's a brain... or at least it is shaped like one. It's spinning, revolving like a beautiful planet. The ceiling above it is a firmament of stars, linked together by brilliant lights that look like synapses connecting neurons. The books are all coming here. They are being scanned and fed into the brain, which is swallowing them as if they are appetizers to mildly satiate its endless hunger. The low rumble of the machine-brain is getting louder, but so is the alarm, and eventually the two just collide in a bursting cacophony of sound. There are metal arms branching out of the machine, like the tentacles of an octopus.

And now I see what the machine-brain is doing: multi-tasking. The metal arms branch off to screens on all sides of the room, and there are plaques next to each screen, explaining what is happening. One of the screens shows books being scanned, another shows how they are being analyzed, and a third shows how the machine is modifying them. A fourth screen depicts the stained-glass windows I saw in the hallway before, and a fifth screen shows the same windows depicting different images. I only have time to read a few of the plaques before I have to delete all imprints of myself from this android, because now the door is opening. They are coming... these robot monks, dressed in solid black armor from head to toe, they are opening fire... goodbye, Luca.

The Changeling

"There are horrors beyond life's edge that we do not suspect, and once in a while man's evil prying calls them just within our range."
– H.P. Lovecraft

Walter read the last lines of Eva's stream of consciousness just as they appeared on his tablet, his chest heaving with anxiety. He glanced over at his friend and shook her, trying to bring her back to consciousness. The young woman's eyes were fluttering, and she looked as though she were straddling a vast precipice between her own mind and another's. Her expression alternated unsettlingly between steady tranquility and shaken horror. *What if she encounters problems on the way back?* Walter fretted, sprinkling more water on Eva's forehead.

As time wore on, it became apparent that Eva was slowly and steadily coming back, but some strange illness had taken ahold of her. She was feverish, trembling, and sweating, and her pulse was now exceptionally rapid. She had begun to murmur intelligibly, however, which gave Walter some faint hope.

"Don't worry, Walter, I get this condition sometimes… it descends upon me after a jarring expedition into the mind of an AI Master, in which I experience events I am quite unprepared for. It's almost like I can't settle into my own body; my soul is having trouble landing. Like your epilepsy, I suppose," she said with a sympathetic smile, which almost brought tears to Walter's eyes. He was all too familiar with the feeling of not being at home in his own body, of suffering the chilling fear that he couldn't control it or make it his own. "There is a certain herb that grows up in these mountains that might help," Eva continued. "*Achillea millefolium*… commonly known as yarrow. You'll recognize it by its tiny white petals. It will help me sweat out the illness and steady my constitution."

"I saw some on the trail on the way here," Walter said. "Before we crossed the ridge. I will gather some from for you, but I'm afraid of leaving you here, all alone. What if something bad happens?"

"I'm safe," Eva reassured him. "Take your tablet with you, if you're afraid, and I can communicate with you at any time."

"Very well," Walter said, beginning to briskly pack up his satchel with trembling hands. He didn't say it out loud, but he wasn't just afraid of leaving her—he was also afraid of venturing out into the unknown by himself, of braving that narrow ridge, and of confronting the lonely wilderness of the mountains.

"Be careful, Walter," Eva said, grasping his hand tightly. "Keep your wits about you and be on your guard."

He nodded before departing dutifully, shivering as he left the tent's protective embrace. The air was frigid, the temperature was dropping rapidly, and he noticed with some alarm that the sun was sitting low in the horizon. It was early October, and the daylight was fading earlier every day as winter solstice approached. Walter realized that if he didn't fetch the yarrow swiftly, he would have to cross the ridge in the dark, which could mean a plunge to a certain death.

I've done scarier things before, Walter told himself, clenching his jaw and trying to breathe slowly so that the anxiety wouldn't overtake him.

Walter hiked down the trail with careful footsteps, fastidiously inspecting every nook and crevice before proceeding. He soon reached the steep ridge, which was difficult to miss; it resembled a suspension bridge that threaded the summit they had camped on together with another, lower summit. Walter took a deep breath before stepping onto it, bracing himself mentally for the experience. As soon as he did so, he heard the eerie sound of a woman laughing and singing very softly.

> *"Ring around the rosie,*
> *A pocket full of posies,*
> *A-tishoo! A-tishoo!*
> *We all fall down."*

The voice froze Walter, and he was too fearful to take another step forward. He was unable to retreat, however, because the ridge was too narrow for him to turn around on, and he couldn't walk backwards with any degree of confidence. He could see what lay before him, but not behind. It seemed that the woman's voice was emanating from up ahead, but she was nowhere to be seen—not on the lower summit, or anywhere else.

What he heard next chilled him to the bone.

"When you bring back the posies for your sweetheart, don't fall down." The voice then erupted into a fit of giggles.

"Who are you?" he said in a trembling voice.

"A fair question," the voice retorted. "And one that I have no intention of answering," it said wispily. "The question you should really be asking is… *who* is the woman in your tent?"

The young rebel leader sighed; he was in no mood to engage in a lengthy conversation while balancing precariously on the ridge.

"It's Eva, my friend…" he said, and then regretted the words as soon as he spoke them. This prying stranger had no business knowing her name.

"Ah, I don't doubt it. But there are friends, and then there are true friends. *Most friendship is feigning, most loving mere folly…*"

"Eva is a true friend," Walter replied in a firm voice. "Now leave me be and let me cross the ridge in peace."

Walter was tired of the games that this stranger was playing with him, and with steely resolve, he took another step on the ridge, steadying his balance with his arms. He then took another, and another, each step giving him increasing confidence that he could master his fears. The voice became faint, like a whisper caught in the wind, and once he reached the other side of the ridge there was dead silence.

"Are you still there?" Walter asked apprehensively. His voice echoed back to him, and he heard no reply. He was feeling a spike of adrenaline after having crossed the ridge safely, but his elation soon turned to worry once he realized that the sun was setting more quickly than anticipated. He regretted not having brought a match in case he would need to brave the ridge in the dark on the way back.

Walter glanced carefully at all the mountain flowers, plants, and herbs lining either side of the trail to see if the yarrow was among them. He was becoming dizzy with the immense effort of simultaneously balancing himself, scrutinizing the terrain, and analyzing the flora around him. He was about to give up and turn back when he heard the uncanny voice again.

"*I wandered lonely as a cloud, that floats on high o'er vales and hills, when all at once I saw…* is this what you are looking for?"

Walter spun around; the voice seemed so close, but there was again nobody to be seen. Next to the path, however, across from the spot he had been investigating so diligently, was the white-petaled yarrow plant he sought.

"Show yourself, immediately," Walter demanded, after he had picked enough yarrow and tucked it into his satchel. He was not willing to let this stranger toy with him, and he would prefer to confront her face-to-face than endure these terrorizing mind games.

"An odd young man, you are," the voice exclaimed. "You are frightened easily, like a girl. I suppose that's why you need a woman to help you… why you are relying on *her*."

Something inside of Walter snapped, and he began to shout. "Leave me alone! You are one of them… a changeling, aren't you?"

"You catch on quick," the voice said with mild amusement. "I'm not what you think I am, and I am what you think I'm not. You can speculate about my identity all you like, but you'd be better off thinking about who *she* is."

"Who she is? What are you talking about?" Walter shouted in fury, his voice echoing off distant mountain ridges and valleys.

"So, you truly believe that the woman in your tent is loyal to you and your cause?" the voice asked incredulously. "You are more naïve than I thought."

Walter's heart skipped a beat. Ever since he had discovered Eva's willingness to allow her mind to be infiltrated by Asana, an AI Master, a seed of suspicion had planted itself firmly inside of him. But Eva had proven herself to be an invaluable ally during these last few months, and the seed had fortunately not germinated. Walter had forgiven her for allowing Asana to use her, and when Eva had suggested that he accompany her on this adventure in the Meridian Mountains, he hadn't given her loyalty a second thought. He did not wish to doubt her fidelity now, either, and the prospect that she could be a traitor seemed absurd to him at first. What would the point of all of this be, the attempts to spy on Central Command and give Walter intelligence on it, if she were in fact loyal to the AI Masters?

From what Eva had told him in the past about her gift, however, he clearly understood that it was a two-way street. If she could gain vivid insights into Central Command, then the converse was likely true—the AI Masters could potentially gain insight into her, and Walter's, preparation and strategizing.

"You are lying," he said in disgust, not willing to allow the seed inside of him to take root. "That is what you changelings do… you try to sow fear in others. It will not work on me," he cried, retracing his footsteps toward the ridge.

"If you don't believe me, fine. But what if I were trying to save your life?"

Walter scoffed. "Save my life? How could you possibly do that? I'm not even sure that you're a real person."

"The AI Masters want her to kill you... they've *ordered* her to kill you. That's why she's brought you here, all alone, to the mountains. Her friend has promised her a reward for it... the highest honor for a mortal in Khalendar: a service badge, and elevation to the status of an elite. Who would turn down such an offer? Eva grew up in a poor family... she knows the meaning of hunger. Would she rather have permanent, long-lasting wealth and security, or live among a rag-tag band of rebels? Think about it, rebel leader."

Before Walter—paralyzed with fear and uncertainty—had an opportunity to reply, the voice spoke again.

"Everything you read on your tablet about her descent into Central Command... it was all a ruse, Walter. Tonight, when you fall asleep, she is planning to drag you to the edge of the mountain and cast you from it. You won't wake up tomorrow if you let her live. But I wish to help you, my friend. I wish to see you live another day, because you are brave and steadfast leader.

"I am not forcing you to save yourself. Abandon yourself to the oblivion of death if you prefer. But if you do wish to live, I will lead you to the water hemlock that will save you."

Walter felt like breaking down into tears. He was dizzy, confused, and frightened. The sun had almost completely set, and he knew that if he waited much longer, he would need to cross the ridge in the pitch black of night, which was a terrifying prospect. But just as terrifying— and perhaps even more so—was the eerie specificity of the stranger's remarks. How could this changeling, if it was indeed a changeling, possibly know so much about him and Eva? He knew that there were divine entities who were interested in protecting him—Shiva, Emilia, and the Talisman. He had no way of knowing whether this was a nefarious changeling, or an entity who was genuinely interested in helping him.

Although Walter felt like turning his back on the voice, his curiosity held him firmly in place. He realized that his knowledge about changelings was derived entirely from Eva, and now that source of information was inherently suspect. What if they weren't evil beings who attempted to cultivate fear and anxiety in others, but rather good spirits who protected and aided travelers in the mountains? In his own mind, he had always associated mountains with positive attributes, such as healing, restoration, and strength, not with dark spirits who wished others ill.

Gritting his teeth angrily, Walter muttered a half-hearted reply. "Be quick about it, then. What is your plan to save me from Eva?"

"Walk three paces ahead, and then take a right, off the path toward a small mountain creek. Just to the left of the creek you will find a patch of water hemlock. Pick a few of the flowers and bring them to her. It is most difficult to distinguish those plants from yarrow. In her fevered state, she will not understand the difference. Tell her you have brought the yarrow but give her the hemlock… and then leave at first light tomorrow. Tell your friends that she died in a tragic accident in the mountains. *Save yourself, Walter.*"

The last sentence echoed eerily throughout the valleys and ridges surrounding them. Walter's eyes filled with tears as he realized the seriousness of his predicament, but he brushed them quickly aside. He could not delay any further. The sky was darkening with every passing moment. He would do as the strange voice bade him, not because he feared death, but because he feared that unless he lived, the Rebellion could go no further.

The journey back to camp was treacherous. The sun was quickly fading, turning a sky stained with flecks of apricot and gold into a heavy blanket of night. When he arrived at the ridge, Walter felt a surge of apprehension, and he could not prevent his hands from trembling. He had always been afraid of heights, but the worst part about the trial confronting him was the feeling that his continued existence was no more certain than a coin tossed into the air, with survival printed on one side and death on the other. Safety had never been more illusory.

Walter thought that he would have to brave the trial alone, but his solitude was also an illusion. A third of the way across the ridge, when the terror had reached its zenith, the stranger's voice echoed from up ahead.

"Life is very much like the path you are walking, is it not? On either side of us, there is an abyss that we might fall into at any moment. And yet if we walk straight and steadily toward our destination, there is little to fear.

"Do not veer from the straight path, Walter. Follow my voice, and don't think about the consequences of failure."

Walter was skeptical of the stranger's ability to help him, but it did give him some comfort to know that he was not alone, that there was someone there encouraging him. When, with a final shaking step, he reached the end of the ridge, Walter breathed a long sigh of relief. He knew that he had the stranger to thank for having successfully made it across alive. In an odd and disconcerting way, he also felt indebted to the stranger—and now an even greater obligation to carry out the plan to murder Eva.

When he arrived back at the tent, it was clear that Eva's condition had worsened. She barely recognized Walter when he entered the tent and she made a feeble attempt to get up, but couldn't summon the strength. Walter's suspicions had grown, however, and he had convinced himself that Eva was simply acting, that it was all part of an elaborate ruse. In his mind, Eva wanted him to think that she was weak and incapable of killing him, so that when she made the attempt on his life, he would be taken by surprise.

"Did you find the yarrow?" Eva asked, in a barely audible whisper. Her brow was beaded with sweat, but Walter suspected that this was part of her act.

"Yes, it is here."

Walter reached inside his satchel for the water hemlock, which was tucked away into a canvas bag separately from the yarrow. Eva's eyes were only half-open, and she squinted at the white-petaled flowers in the dim light of the tent.

"Brilliant, Walter. Thank you so much," she said, in a grateful voice that made Walter's heart sink. "Now, can you brew it into a tea for me?"

Walter sighed, feeling his resolve waver. He had wanted to finish the grisly task quickly, but now it would be drawn out, and the longer he spent around Eva heightened the risk that he would lose his courage. He took out their makeshift cookstove and lit it with a match, then placed a pot of water over it. He got to work crushing the water hemlock, then set the pulped flowers in a jar to combine with the water once it boiled.

The water was still cold when a blood-curdling cry rent the air.

Walter nearly slashed his hand with the knife he was using to dice the water hemlock. Eva shuddered, but she barely opened her eyes. The young rebel leader felt nauseous when he saw that she was too weak to be startled; he suspected that if she really were acting, she would be far more alarmed.

"Just sit tight," Walter directed her. "I'm going to see what that was."

Without waiting for her to respond, Walter exited the tent brusquely. He lit a candle and brought it outdoors, shielding its flame with his hand. What he saw as he peered down over the mountainside would haunt him for years afterwards: a duplicate of Eva was hanging onto a steep, rocky ledge, her legs dangling as she hovered above a three-thousand-meter drop. Her face was wreathed in an ethereal blue fog, and at first Walter thought it was simply illuminated by the candle he was holding, but in stunned surprise he realized that the light source was behind him.

He could not mistake the piercing azure eyes, the flowing black hair, and the strong, shapely figure for anyone other than Emilia—in the form of a spirit, who was radiating pale blue light. He had seen that fiercely determined expression in her eyes many times before, when she had been alive on Earth, and he knew that nothing would stop her from achieving her ends. The light emanating from the spirit was sustained by some otherworldly force that was also causing the duplicate clutching the rocky cliff-face to lose her grip.

"Walter! Help me..." the duplicate cried, and Walter immediately recognized the voice of the stranger who had led him to the water hemlock and steadied his footsteps as he had braved the ridge. It sounded like Eva, but a younger, more naïve version—a version who had been insulated from the world for years.

A pang of guilt swept through the young man as he recalled that without the stranger's steady guidance, he might not have made it over the ridge.

"Emilia, stop..." he cried, as the duplicate's grip on the ledge loosened. "Don't do this."

He rushed over to the ledge to try and rescue the woman, but before he could reach her, he was flattened by a strong invisible blow.

"I hope you don't mind the arcane magic... apologies for using it so forcefully on you. Walter, she is a liar and an oath-breaker, and she is trying to brainwash you into murdering my twin sister," Emilia's spirit said sternly. "I must destroy her."

Before he could respond, the duplicate's fingers curved hideously upwards, and she detached from the rocks. She fluttered gently into oblivion, like a delicate leaf circling downwards from a tree branch, her screams gradually becoming softer.

Walter watched her fall for a dizzying few seconds, and then turned away in disgust, feeling as though he were about to retch. He glanced up at Emilia's spirit, almost for solace, but he found no remorse or kindness in her frigid blue eyes.

"I can't blame you for wanting to protect your sister," Walter said sheepishly. "I would have done the same for my brother."

The spirit's gaze bored into him. "You will go into the tent, discard the water hemlock and give my sister her yarrow tea," she commanded. "When you are done, we can talk."

He was surprised by the sharp practicality in her tone. He did as she bade; with the changeling gone, his mind was clearer and more lucid, and the utter absurdity of his plan to murder Eva was quickly becoming apparent.

Back in the tent, he cast the crushed water hemlock into a compost bag they used for food scraps and added the fresh yarrow he had collected to a new jar. He then poured the water, which had finally reached a boil, over the yarrow and handed the cup to Eva. As she drank, a flush of blood returned to her pale cheeks, and a vibrant color returned to her lips. Her trembling and sweating ceased. The tea also appeared to trigger her drowsiness, and before long she was sleeping heartily. Walter took the opportunity to resume his discussion with Emilia.

"That *thing...*" he said in a shaky voice, keeping his tone quiet to avoid waking Eva. "It was a changeling, wasn't it?"

"It was indeed," Emilia's spirit said grimly.

"Why did you say she was an oath-breaker? A liar, perhaps, but..."

The spirit grew contemplative and motioned for Walter to sit next to her on a fallen log.

"Ancient gods rule these mountains... they were called the Ourea in the Old World, and they lived far away in Eastern nations, but they migrated over here after the collapse of that civilization. Being in mountains, so far away from humans, they become very lonely at times... lonely and quite bored. Having little to do except frighten lone mountain travelers, they devised a clever plot to create replicas of those humans, forged in caverns deep inside the mountains. They use the changelings, as they are called, to instill fear and chaos in travelers' minds. The gods love generating chaos—even if it's just so they can later restore order, to feel like heroes—and it's no surprise that their techniques are becoming increasingly sophisticated."

"How do you know all of this?" Walter asked in bewilderment

"Once you become a spirit, the myths and folklore that you heard rumors of in your lifetime become vividly real. I can pass through mountain walls to see and speak with the Ourea, and I've seen them forge these human replicas with my own eyes.

"But to answer your question about oath-breakers... although the gods revel in being agents of chaos, they are legislators at heart. The one golden rule they have imposed on the changelings is this: they may toy with the human wayfarers all they like, but they must never attempt to leave the mountains, to mingle with civilized society, or to pretend that they are real humans. The objective of this policy is to prevent the full-scale breakdown of social order. Consider what would happen if changelings escaped from the mountains, *en masse*, and every human in Khalendar suddenly found themselves face-to-face with their doppelganger. Apart from causing severe mental illness, this situation would lead to physical violence, and probably murder. No person can live with their duplicate for too long, without feeling the strong compulsion to destroy it. And nobody would know for certain if the duplicate or the real version of the human had been destroyed. The fabric of society would dissolve."

Walter nodded. "That all makes sense, but what makes you think that this changeling planned to escape the mountains?"

"She was too arrogant for her own good, and when I confronted her about what she was planning, she couldn't help blurting out all the clever strategies she had devised. As the gods created them with divine qualities, despite their outwardly human appearances, the changelings have unassailable egos. And her plan was clever and terrible, I'll give her credit for that: to trick you into believing that Eva was trying to kill you, and then once you had slain Eva with the water hemlock, she would wheedle her way into convincing you to bring her to Zeyanara. She would have assured you it would be easier that way, insisted that because she looked exactly like Eva, nobody would ask questions, and she would be faithful, compliant, and loyal to the end."

Walter swallowed. "I might have fallen for that, indeed. What troubles me is how I jumped to the conclusion that Eva was a traitor so easily. It was as though she warped my mind, that changeling."

"They are masters of trickery," Emilia's spirit said, and her tone grew somber. "Very much like the AI Masters, in that way. And like the AI Masters, their extensive powers should be restrained and controlled, but they are not. Like the AI Masters, they seem to have an independent will that transcends the restrictions imposed upon them externally. Or at least this one did... for most, the threats of the Ourea are enough to keep them docile."

"What would the Ourea do if a changeling tried to escape? Strike them down with a thunderbolt?" Walter said with amusement.

"That depends on what the higher gods would approve of... gods like Shiva. The Ourea are not all-powerful; that is why they have retreated to the mountains, largely because they have little political influence over the other gods, and they frequently lose skirmishes at the council table. The Ourea make rules in the mountains, but other gods enforce them. And some of those gods admire the changelings... they see in them rebels, like Prometheus, who have broken free of their chains. It is true, though, that the rebels don't usually win in the end."

"Most rebellions end in failure," Walter admitted wistfully. "But that fact alone gives me hope, because it means that some succeed."

"As wicked as that changeling was, she was very clever. And you should heed one piece of advice she gave you, Walter: do not veer from the straight path, as tantalizing as the other options may be."

With that, the spirit was gone, dissipating into the foggy mountain air like a wisp of smoke. Walter watched the last pearly blue vapors dissolve into the night sky before making his way back to the tent. Once there, he was comforted by the sight of Eva sleeping soundly, and he tucked himself under the blankets beside her as if she were his own sister, falling asleep almost instantly.

In the amber light of early morning, he awoke to Eva's smiling face.

"I had an odd dream," she said with a flutter of a laugh. "Emilia was alive again, and she was saving my life."

Lydion

"My real self wanders elsewhere, far away, wanders on and invisibly and has nothing to do with my life."
— Herman Hesse

The worst of the trip was behind them, and the rest of their stay in the Meridian Mountains flew by. Their training together had strengthened the bond between Walter and Eva, in much the same way that Walter had felt a special bond with Christopher after training with him in Tsei'watu. But this was a different type of training than the kind he was used to.

Eva's teaching emphasized mental resilience above all other qualities, because she compared Walter's upcoming foray into Central Command to taking a spaceship past Mars: lonely, frightening, and above all, mentally destabilizing. She used a range of techniques to strengthen Walter's mind, including hypnosis, memory games, and mock interrogation sessions. Eva would sit inside the tent with Walter, asking him blunt questions about traumatic episodes in his life: his brother's 'death,' Elaine's disappearance, Walter's imprisonment on the *Jade Queen*, and his brushes with death on the ship and later the isle of Vei'arash. She also asked him about his visions from the Talisman—the ones that made him dread the future, and the potential consequences of his actions.

The interrogation sessions made Walter uncomfortable, but with practice, he learned to focus his mind, to ignore his personal discomfort, and to focus on the task at hand. With Eva's guidance, he was able to temporarily discard his ego and self-doubt and transcend his immediate emotions and reactions. In short, Walter began to view his mind as something he could control, rather than something that controlled him.

Hypnosis helped to sharpen his aptitude for focusing his mind. At first, when Eva tried it on him, he would blank out and fall into a quasi-conscious state. Sometimes she would need to place a wet cloth on his forehead to revive him, because he was so far gone. But Eva trained him to fortify his mind against the hypnosis and to let it permeate through him in small, manageable doses. Eventually, he could increase the doses but have the wherewithal to realize what was happening and pull himself out of a hypnotic state at will.

When they were tired of mental gymnastics, Walter and Eva trained physically: they dueled with *balayans*, practiced balancing exercises on the ridge, and jogged up and down mountain paths, feeling the crisp mid-autumn air fill their lungs. One day, after a long jog along a path lined with sweet-scented firs, they helped each other to cook lentil soup. Stirring the soup, and breathing the tendrils of steam that rose from it, made Walter feel suddenly homesick. He missed Elaine, their old apartment in Crystal City, and her home-cooked meals. The thought that she could be in danger in the Barrens suddenly made him feel nauseous, and he no longer felt like eating.

Eva noticed his expression transitioning from joy to sorrow, and she reached out for his hand. "Focus your mind, Walter. In Central Command, they will use anything to prey on your weaknesses, and to get you to confess your identity and motives. Do not let anything—even the memory of your loved ones—get in the way of your goals."

Walter took a deep breath and tried to cast his thoughts of Elaine's predicament aside. After all his practice sessions, it was much easier than it would have been for him before this trip. When he looked up at Eva again, he felt calm and determined.

"We've done many training exercises, Eva, and while I'm grateful for your invaluable teachings, I feel like I'm ready to move on to the next step. We haven't spoken about this yet, but how do I prepare myself for the feeling of being in AI form? How do I know that all the training we've done here won't be futile once I transition into that state?"

Eva smiled. "I am glad that you feel ready, Walter. I am proud of your progress, and I think my sister would have been proud of it also. Before you drink the soup, let me show you something," she said.

Eva reached into the pocket of her tunic and removed a vial of dark, midnight-blue liquid, with a metal stopper firmly in place. Walter's eyes widened when he saw it, as he instinctively knew what it was.

"Lydion," he whispered. "It's so dark... this is what has been contaminating our water supply all along? Why isn't our water darker, then?"

Eva grimaced. "This vial contains five hundred milligrams of concentrated, undiluted lydion. Enough to turn you into an AI Master for the next half-decade," she said with a bitter laugh. "To put things into perspective, the water supplied to households in Crystal City contains just one drop of this per thousand milligrams. Drinking it gives people certain traits of the AI Masters—called *roboticisms*—but the concentration is not nearly enough to change their physical forms entirely."

Water swallowed, and a sad realization struck him without warning.

"My brother... is there a chance they could have given him a large dose of this when they brainwashed him? When I saw him in the Crate for the first time after his disappearance, I couldn't quite put my finger on what had happened to him. But it makes sense when I consider what you are telling me... he definitely seemed more like *them*."

Eva nodded. "They would give some prisoners in the Crate larger doses of lydion than the rest of the population. According to the guards, it made us more docile. But as I told you earlier, when we were discussing this subject in Vei'arash, it will not impair your thoughts and goals. It makes you think more like an AI, in a physical sense, but it doesn't lead you to adopt their ideologies unless you allow it to. I would compare it to a hallucinogenic drug. The drug could make naïve, easily manipulated people lose sight of who they are and follow a cult leader down an evil path. But for those with strong minds and an independent will, it will simply sharpen their minds and allow them to pursue their goals with more mental clarity. Even those who lose their way don't lose their essences ... they can still see a beacon in the fog, if that makes sense."

"Did they ever give you enough to transform completely into an AI Master?" Walter asked.

"No, they never crossed that line. But I did, myself, years ago. Before I was imprisoned in the Crate. I was friends with a rowdy bunch of girls who worked at the weapons factory with me. The AI Fighters who ran the place kept batches of lydion in the freezers at work, and sometimes they would use the compound to make employees more efficient. My friends were smart, and they found a way to steal a few vials without the guards noticing. All of us tried the lydion; it was a way of escaping our problems, I suppose. And we had plenty of problems in those days... problems with our work, finances, and men."

Walter smiled. He couldn't picture Eva as the type who had romantic relationships. She was pretty, but also hard-edged and intimidatingly brilliant—similar to her sister Emilia in that regard.

Her face fell into shadows as she spoke her next words. "I had a chosen one, back before I was imprisoned in the Crate. His name was Andreas, and he was a beautiful artist from Fewsbury. Tall, lean, with golden hair and a personality that lit up every room he walked into. We had plans to travel the world together, to cross these mountains, backpack across the valleys and plains of the Barrens, and visit the Southern Jungles and see the sundials as large as skyscrapers. We even wanted to travel north, past Central Command, to the Forsaken Plains. I was ready to abandon my factory job for the upcoming trip, and I had saved up enough money to buy us supplies to last a year or more. About a week before our scheduled departure, he asked about where the money was. I thought he was just asking out of concern. I told him it was under the floorboards in my room.

"One day, I came home from work to find my bedroom pillaged, the floorboards overturned, and the money missing. It was over three hundred *cestae*, a small fortune that I had worked for months to earn. I later found out that he had taken it and spent it on expensive dresses for his new girlfriend, who he had moved into a Crystal City loft with. It turns out that he gave up his dreams of being an artist and travelling the world so that he could move in with this girl and become a banker in the city. I recently heard they've started a family together. I'm glad it worked out well for them, but the effect on my own life was devastating. Shortly afterward, my dad got too old and sick to keep his factory job, and we could barely scrape enough pennies together to put food on the table. It turned out that I needed every last dime of that money that had been stolen, but it was gone. So that drove me to steal the weapons from my factory… and then I ended up in prison, while Andreas was enjoying his glamorous new lifestyle in a warm apartment in Crystal City."

Walter sighed, running a hand through his hair. The injustice of what she had just told him didn't only make him angry; it made him want to find this Andreas and seek retribution.

"I'm sorry, Eva," he said softly.

"The past is behind us and cannot be changed. But the future… that is in our control. Now, the sorry episode I just recounted left me heartbroken, depressed, and unable to function for weeks. And it prompted me to experiment with the lydion. Back in those days, when I was a skinny, insecure, acne-scarred teenager, lydion gave me strength like you couldn't imagine. It was my armor, transforming me from this pitiful, weak girl into a beautiful, strong AI Master. It made me feel as though I could endure anything, even heartbreak. And so, I took it… in small doses at first, but I gradually began to drink more concentrated versions of it, until finally I gave into temptation and drank so much that I did transform completely.

"Well, almost completely. I must add the caveat that it never *fully* transforms you into an AI Master. Your bodily functions remain intact, but somewhat weakened. You still hunger, thirst, feel sore and tired. You don't become a metal object, like they are. But it causes your outwards appearance to resemble them and brings you into closer alignment with their operational system. Like them, you feel less and think more. It's a very bizarre process when you think about it closely, enough to terrify most people. I never told my parents... I only did it late at night, and in the morning, I would transform back by drinking a few glasses of water," she said with a chuckle. "I was quite the rebel. But all my feelings for this terrible boy, the boy I had once loved with all my heart... they just disappeared into nothingness. I still felt emotion... but I didn't let it consume my life any longer. I felt my sorrow and grief dissipate, like distant echoes gradually becoming softer. And that helped me heal, like nothing else could. The mental clarity it gave me helped me to formulate a plan to steal the weapons from the AI Masters, and to execute it flawlessly. It was both a blessing and my eventual undoing. But I do not regret having taken it."

Walter gazed at the vial in Eva's pale hand. He suddenly felt an overwhelming urge to taste it, to drink it until he transformed into an AI Master.

Eva noticed the way that he was staring at it, with intense desire, and she blushed.

"And to answer your other question, about the training being futile... you cannot think of it like that. Training is what helps you build up your mind so that you can cope better with the effects of the lydion. Taking this is not for the faint-hearted, or the weak-willed. To be honest, I've been afraid to give it to you because I don't know how you will react to it. Everyone has a different experience. But I trust that everything you've done so far... your journey in Vei'arash, and your visions from the Talisman, and the training in these mountains... all of that has mentally prepared you for this moment. With the Talisman, you were being mentally transported elsewhere—the external world changed for you—but here... this will alter your whole self. Like when Tristan and I were transfigured into the spirits of Brigid and Epona."

"I never asked you," Walter said gingerly, "but what was that experience like?"

"I don't think words could really describe it," Eva said, "but it was like there were two beings inside of me. And the one being that was controlling the other was stronger, ancient, and wise. And that gave me more serenity than anything else has ever managed to do," she said, wiping away a tear.

Without saying anything further, Eva removed the metal stopper from the vial of lydion and handed it to Walter.

He drank just a few drops of the substance, which tasted bittersweet, like pomegranates. The effect was palpable. Although he had been flushed and sweating from the jog, as soon as he drank the substance, his body temperature chilled. His breathing evened out, and his anxiety was quelled. He could feel his muscles becoming at once firmer and more relaxed, his skin becoming thicker and more insulated, and his posture straightening. But the most palpable effect was on his mind, which he could feel, strangely, purifying itself.

Walter grinned as he noticed the changes occurring. Within minutes, he felt like a completely different person, and his mood was buoyant. Eva looked at him with an expression reflecting a mixture of fear and admiration. "It is working much faster on you than it ever did with me," she said. "As if you are meant to be in this form…" she whispered.

"In truth," Walter replied, "I feel as though my *real* life is only now beginning."

In the last few days that they spent in the mountains, Walter savored the lydion. He loved the way it brought thoughts into sharp, crisp focus, the way it made him think more deeply about the interrelationships between concepts and ideas, and the way it improved his spatial and visual intelligence. With each hour that passed, Walter felt its influence growing. Eva would test the changes in his functioning by interrogating him about facts and data. He opened up to her about projects he had worked on as a government translator, and she would quiz him about the project timelines, deliverables, and the precise supplies needed for each one. At first, his answers were vague and general, but eventually they became quicker, more detailed, and more confident. But what was most interesting was that his responses no longer appeared to be anchored to any specific memory, but were extrapolations from general knowledge he had. It was as though the data in his mind was synthesizing, and the neural pathways that identified patterns in that data were becoming stronger.

"What projects did you work on in Fewsbury?" she asked one afternoon, as they sat cross-legged and sipped Xe'levan in their tent.

"There was a train station there," he responded. "The Masters wanted us to increase the number of tracks so that it could service a broader area. At first it serviced two regions, Crystal City and Hydesburgh, but they wanted it to extend to Jamestown, and there was a further ambitious plan for it to branch south-east toward the Barrens.

"The trains were all supposed to coordinate their schedules, and there was to be a shipment of a different commodity to Central Command every day.

"The Barrens was 560 kilometers away from the train station, so that meant that we needed 612,080 yards of rail track, equating to 79,570,400 pounds of hot-rolled steel."

"And Jamestown?" Eva prodded.

"Thirty-five kilometers away, so we needed 38,276 yards of rail track, and 4,975,880 pounds of steel," he answered without hesitation.

"And they told us the schedule of the trains once the tracks had been built. On Monday they would ship chromium, Tuesday actuators, Wednesday e-pets, Thursday tablets, and Friday cameras.

"There were five cars per train," Walter continued confidently, "and each could carry up to 145 tons of commodities. Which meant that on any given day they could ship 4,586,200 chromium rods, 2,365,999 actuators, 1,354,823 packaged e-pets, 5,687,328 tablets and 4,123,000 cameras. But each day they shipped not according to capacity, but according to supply or demand. The supply of some items—e-pets, tablets, and cameras—was constant, while demand fluctuated. Conversely, the demand for chromium rods and actuators was constant, while supply fluctuated. The supply for those items depended on minerals supplied from the Barrens, which were routed through to Crystal City through a different train system, and then transported in supply trucks to Fewsbury as needed. Sometimes there were strikes and unrest in the Barrens, or outbreaks of disease which disrupted the supply chains. The largest disruption was in May 2759, when four hundred workers at the massive Radion Mine near Kelah'a village went on strike, demanding better conditions and pay and an end to the one-sided 'benefit' agreements which meant that Khalendi elite profited immensely from the environmental destruction of Xeyan'na land, while the natives accrued minimal royalties."

"And what was the result of the protest?" Eva asked, with genuine interest.

"The elites promised that their lawyers would re-draft the agreements to better protect the interests of the Xeyan'na. True to word, the contracts were re-drafted, and the strike ceased. But due to some obscure technicalities that only lawyers understood, the Xeyan'na could not rely on the contractual provisions that purported to serve their interests, as the courts ruled them to be unenforceable. By the time the court rulings were publicly released and the Xeyan'na realized what had happened, the government had acquired contingent rights to millions of *cestae* in royalty payments. The rights were 'contingent' on the provisions that protected Xeyan'na interests being found void, which they inevitably were. The Xeyan'na appealed the decisions, and the court might have ruled in their favor, but by that point it was too late: ten workers from the Radion Mine fell ill from air toxicity and died, prompting a shutdown of the mine by environmental inspectors. The courts proclaimed the appeal moot and academic, ending the longstanding battle.

"The air toxicity story was only propaganda, however. In reality, those men were assassinated by government agents, who staged their deaths so they could shut down the Radion Mine and end the legal and political turmoil it was causing, reaping immense benefits. The benefits were again hidden in the fine print: more contingent rights. Unbeknownst to the Xeyan'na, the contracts contained a termination clause stipulating that if the mine was shut down due to environmental factors beyond the government's control, royalty payments that had accrued to the Xeyan'na over the past 36 months automatically reverted to the government. The government then charged the Xeyan'na with debt, which of course was convenient because the government had been running up their lawyers' bills on the court battles with the Xeyan'na."

Eva's lower lip trembled as Walter spoke these words. "How much debt did they owe?"

"Four thousand three hundred and twenty *cestae* were owed to the government of Khalendar. A paltry number which wouldn't make a dent on government coffers in the grand scheme of things, but for the Xeyan'na it meant the difference between feast or famine. Many starved to death the following winter: 7,623 Xeyan'na lost their lives because of the repayment of that debt, to be precise."

Eva scanned Walter's face carefully. He was calm and impassive, with few traces of empathy or guilt.

"Seven thousand six hundred and twenty-three Xeyan'na lost their lives," Eva echoed back at her friend. "They were not just faceless or nameless people. They were sisters, brothers, aunts, uncles, mothers, fathers. Elaine could have been one of them."

Walter stared at her, his eyes blank and immutable. Suddenly, he reached for the canteen of water inside the tent and began to drink it as though ravenously thirsty. After taking a very long drink, he could feel the lydion flushing out of his bloodstream.

Tears filled his eyes as he looked at Eva. "What... what was happening to me?" he asked. "I can't believe I was just reciting all of that to you, and I couldn't care less about what I was saying. It was as if I was numb to it all."

"You were experiencing the normal effects of lydion," Eva replied. "You were partaking in what it feels like to be an AI Master. They are brilliant in analyzing data, categorizing ideas, and understanding cause and effect. Emotions, empathy... these interfere with their analytical work.

"But that's not necessarily a bad thing, Walter. A lot of poor decisions are made because emotions cloud judgment and reasoning. I'll give you an example. A lot of children beg their parents to give them things that they shouldn't have, like sugar-crystal popsicles, self-driving cars, and e-pets—the same e-pets that are shipped from Fewsbury's factories. The parents feel empathy for the children; they see how they are teased at school for not having the same things their peers have. They give in to their demands and give them the sugar, the cars, and the toys. But thousands of children in Crystal City struggle with health issues brought on by being dangerously overweight, die every year from self-driving car accidents, and neglect their studies because they play too much with their e-pets. If the parents were more rational, if they didn't allow themselves to be swayed by their children's emotional pleas, then the children of Crystal City would be much healthier."

Walter wiped the tears from his eyes and sniffed. "I understand that in some cases it's best to put aside your emotions. But it's all very new to me, this sensation of feeling nothing when I consider a tragic event. And while it seems to make my mind sharper in some ways, I can feel myself forgetting other things. Like when you mentioned Elaine, I struggled to remember where she was."

"The lydion will cleanse irrelevant matters from your mind and focus your thoughts on matters essential to your survival while you are in Central Command," Eva assured him. "Which is essential for your mission. But just as important as having this focused state is the ability and wherewithal to get out of it. In that sense, the hypnosis exercises we've practiced will help you immensely. Because lydion will decrease your natural thirst, you will probably only want to have modest sips of water while you are taking it. But just like you did now, you need to know when to cleanse it from your system."

Walter took a deep breath and drank more water. After a few

moments, he was thirsty again—not for water but for lydion. It exerted a strange pull over him, just like the Talisman had previously. The Talisman's journey was over, however, whereas his journey with lydion had only just begun.

Desert Rain

"The Mystery of mysteries is the Door of all essence."
— Laozi

That night, Walter fought back the urge to take more lydion. When he fell asleep, he dreamt a strange dream that was more vivid than many he had experienced in a long time. He was a stag, the white stag he had encountered in Vei'arash, racing through a lush jungle filled with towering trees and hanging vines. The forest felt comfortable, like it was home, but the stag felt a pull inside of him. He was not content to stay where he was, because he felt like he was needed elsewhere. The stag ran with a steely determination toward the east, where he came upon the edge of the forest, the boundary between jungle and desert. There was just a thin border of grassland separating the flourishing biome from the parched, desiccated soil of the desert.

The stag felt vulnerable in the desert, conscious of the fact that it was a threatening place, filled with traps for the unwary. Yet despite this knowledge, the beast pressed onwards diligently. It wandered through the monotonous, seemingly endless desert until it arrived at a place that felt different, with a unique and magnetic aura. To its surprise, there were vaguely perceptible markings in the sand that appeared to dance and shift as the wind scattered dust across them. After a few moments, a strong blast of wind arrived from the east, blowing off the loose sand and exposing a damp layer of earth on which a labyrinth was engraved. The creature headed directly to the maze's center and began to dig persistently in the damp soil. After what seemed like a long time, the stag came across a hard object: an amber stone, slightly larger than the one Walter had seen on the seer's ring in the tavern in Jamestown. Inside the stone was a tiny fire lizard, her pitch-black body streaked with the russet tones of sunset.

Strangely, the stag could intuitively understand that the lizard was alive and trapped inside the amber prison. The stag began to tap on the amber with its hoof, gently at first but with escalating ferocity, until finally a long crack formed across the surface of the amber. The amber stone then opened up slowly, as though it were an egg hatching, and syrupy amber percolated out of it. The freed lizard peeked up gratefully at the stag and writhed out of her sticky chamber onto the dry sand. As soon as her tiny feet touched the earth, vast clouds began to gather overhead, and rain began to fall from the sky in great quantities. As if the stag was watching years pass over the span of minutes, the desert soil moistened and became fertile again, and a single tree grew in the exact same spot that the lizard had been standing upon—the center of the labyrinth. It was a tiny, brittle sapling at first, but it grew at a startlingly rapid pace, and then scattered seeds from which a healthy, thriving forest sprung up.

Walter awoke from this strange dream feeling warm and flustered, his pulse rapid and his mouth dry. The dream had been so vivid that it felt more like one of his visions from the Talisman than an ordinary dream. His mind, having spent the past day soaking in lydion, felt distinctly repulsed by the dream and its imagery, the way that it appealed to his emotions rather than his logic. But his lydion trip had not been enough to cleanse from Walter the urgent desire that had taken root in him. He suddenly knew precisely what he needed to do next, before he traveled to Crystal City for the meeting with the advisor to the *Anax*.

Walter shook Eva awake. She had been in a deep slumber, and she chastised Walter for waking her. But when she saw his grave expression, she fell silent.

"Eva. When is my meeting with the advisor to the *Anax* scheduled for?"

She rubbed the sleep out of her eyes. "Forty-five days from now," she said. She glanced down at her solar watch, which read 2 a.m. in the morning. "Forty-four, sorry," she said.

Walter breathed a sigh of relief. "So, we have time, then."

"Time for what?" Eva asked, looking at Walter with concern.

"I need to go to the Barrens. Elaine… I am afraid she might be in danger. She might be trapped there. I need to find her and make sure she is safe."

Eva scanned his face with cautious eyes.

"Walter, if we go to the Barrens, the trip will take at least five days, and then we have to return to Serrahan, which will take another six. We can fit it into our schedule, but…"

"But what?" Walter interrupted. "Why are you hesitating?"

"Because the tightness of the schedule will allow no margin of error. The Barrens is a perilous land, filled with natural hazards and AI Master checkpoints. If we are detained or get into any trouble down there, it could derail all our plans," she said. "And it is absolutely critical that you make it to the meeting with the advisor as planned."

"But even factoring in that trip, we will still have over a month before the advisor meeting. What is the problem?" he asked impatiently.

Eva sighed. "We will need quite a bit of time to engage in our psychological battle against the AI Masters. It won't be easy to effectively spread our animal spirit army across Crystal City so that you can try and convince the advisor to allow you access to the *Anax*'s computer. Once the army has caused enough damage, you'll have a fighting chance to persuade him that you, alone, can reprogram the AI Masters to understand magic, so it no longer causes chaos and disruption in their society. The process of chaos-making, however, can't happen overnight. We will need, at the very least, three weeks to deploy the army throughout Crystal City and wreak havoc on the AI Masters' minds. A month would give us more time, and better odds of success."

Walter nodded. "You are right, as always, Eva," he conceded. "But going to the Barrens will give us an additional edge in this psychological battle: another form of animal spirit to transform into," he said.

Eva's eyes widened. "The lizard," she whispered.

"Yes, the fire lizard. If we bring one back from the Barrens, the recruits that Dorian brings up from the Southern Jungles will be able to transform into the lizard, as well as the horse and the snake spirit. Think of how much stronger the army will be with three types of spirits, instead of only two."

Eva's lips curved into a faint smile. "Nuada told you that he wouldn't send Dorian down to the Barrens because it was too dangerous, because he valued his life too much. And now you want to go down there yourself? Imagine what he would say if he knew."

Walter nodded. "I know, I know. He would say I'm a foolhardy young man who should know better," he said, then laughed. "But Eva, we have the perfect opportunity to go down there now. We've just finished all this physical and psychological training, and we are in the best shape of our lives. And we can think of the trip to the Barrens as our test run. If we can make it out of there alive, then getting through the real challenge—Central Command—will be a breeze."

Eva looked as though she was warming up to the idea, and her eyes glittered mischievously. "You probably only want to go because you miss your girlfriend and you can't wait to see her again. And you're being foolish. You shouldn't make decisions based purely on emotion; if you took more lydion, you might change your mind. But I'm looking at it from a more rational perspective, and I can't help but agree that it's a good idea. We are in solid shape, we have our *balayans* and supplies, and we do need more recruits for our spirit army. If we can convince some of the Xeyan'na natives to come with us, they can join up with the Southern Jungle recruits that Dorian has found and strengthen the army even more. And if—by some wild chance—we can bring back a lizard, then it will help us immensely. Different animals to transform into will mean more confusion for the AI Masters, more strategic capabilities, and a better chance of success in our mission."

"I'm sure Elaine will lend us one of hers if it means helping us," Walter replied.

"Walter, I do hope we find Elaine," she said. Her eyes became clouded and wistful. "May the gods watch over us."

She took a deep breath, as though steeling herself mentally. "Tomorrow at first light, we will reunite with Epa and Epos. We shall ride to the Crossing, and from there we will head southeast, toward Te'yara. Thank the fates that we will have Epona's wisdom to help direct us toward the village."

"The Crossing?" Walter asked quizzically. "What is that?"

"It's a path that Emilia told me about, which she used to travel across when she visited the Southern Jungles. Because it's just south of Serrahan, the AI Masters don't know about it. If they did discover it, they'd probably use it as a trading route, but it's best kept secret. It's basically a long tunnel running through two mountains. According to legend, it's frequented by spirits who are crossing from one world to the next. There's another tunnel intersecting it that goes deep into the heart of the mountains, where the changelings are rumored to be made. But it's also called the Crossing for other reasons the most obvious being that it's a crossing from the North to the South. It will lead us directly to the Barrens."

≪≪≪≪≪≪≪

Walter and Emilia awoke to an enchanting sunrise that swept the length of the horizon with broad paintbrush strokes of gold, amber, and scarlet. After packing up their tent and belongings, Walter took one last glance at the summit which had been his home for the past four nights and quietly thanked the mountain for being hospitable to them. As he did so, he remembered, as vividly as yesterday, the mountain prayer that Caleb had uttered before the rebels had climbed Mount Samaya in Vei'arash. It seemed like a lifetime ago, but it had been mere months earlier that they had begun their ascent up the mountain—an event which had altered Walter's life and would influence the lives of so many others.

When they reached the foothills, it was already almost noon. Once they had descended past the layered veils of mountain fog, the sun became nearly blinding in its intensity, and for a late-fall day, it was unseasonably warm and bright. Walter relished the warmth and richly oxygenated air of the lower altitudes, and he was in a cheerful mood when they encountered Epa and Epos. The horses' heads were bowed low, and they were nibbling on tufts of grass when Eva greeted them with a warm embrace. They neighed merrily at the sight of the two companions.

The pair mounted the horses and headed east, with Eva taking the lead. Within an hour or so, they arrived at their destination: a small, artfully concealed tunnel carved into the foothills of a mountain. It was mostly hidden by spruce trees and mountain laurel, but a skillful observer could detect it easily if they tried. Eva dismounted and took two kerchiefs out of her satchel, handing one to Walter.

"Blindfold the horses," she instructed. Walter looked reluctant until she explained.

"The Crossing is not for the faint-hearted, and as dearly as I love Epa and Epos, I fear that they might be influenced by its temptations."

"What kind of place are we heading into?" Walter asked anxiously.

"Walter, *you* must be careful as well. I've never entered this place myself, but Emilia told me vivid stories about it... when she was still alive. She said that it's essentially a long corridor, intersected at the midway point by another tunnel which leads to two very different destinations, depending on which direction you turn. The first destination, as I explained to you briefly before, is the mountain forge where the changelings are rumored to be created. She used to call that 'the birth chamber,'" Eva said with a wistful smile. "Kind of like the mountain's womb," she added. "But if you head down the opposite direction, you'll encounter the death chamber. Don't want to go there."

"Sounds ominous," Walter conceded, wiping a thin layer of sweat off his brow. He suspected it was not just from the warmth of the afternoon sun. "But we don't want to go to either the birth chamber or the death chamber. We want to go straight to the Barrens. So, what's the issue?"

"The issue," Eva replied, "is that the pathways are charged with a kind of electric magnetism, or so Emilia claimed. She wasn't the type to lie about such things, so I trust what she told me. They appeal to people with private inclinations toward certain feelings. Naturally, the birth chamber appeals to those who miss their childhood, who miss the feeling of being near their families and having happy, warm Christmases together. It appeals to our sense of wanting to go back to the beginning, a beginning where we felt a sense of belonging and joy. The death chamber... well, it's the opposite. It appeals to those with nihilistic tendencies, those who believe that death is a welcome respite from the anxiety that choice brings us."

"The anxiety that choice brings us?" Walter asked, wrinkling his brow.

"When we grow up, the choices we are expected to make increase exponentially," Eva explained. "We start off with a narrow range of choices in childhood—our parents enroll us in this or that activity, we eat what is cooked for us, and we attend the schools and live in the neighborhoods our parents choose. But choice, just like tragedy, multiplies as we age. For those with a solid moral compass and a clear view of what direction they want their lives to go in, the process of growing up is a liberating and enjoyable experience. But for those who see life as a meaningless endeavor and have no anchor in any particular set of ethical principles, the endless array of choices can be debilitating. It is those individuals that are magnetically attracted to the death chamber... the chamber that puts an end to all choice, and thus suffering."

"Charming," Walter said sarcastically. "And you said that sometimes spirits visit this place?"

"Yes... according to Emilia, the death chamber is a kind of portal that spirits can access—a bridge from the purgatory of this world to a permanent resting place. But it's rumored that if anyone enters it, spirit or not, they can never return."

Walter's hands began to tremble ever so slightly. "I'm thinking we should forget this tunnel altogether and just ride across the mountains. Can we do that?"

Eva sighed. "I don't see how the horses can brave the mountains... they dislike climbing mountains to begin with, and these are no ordinary mountains. My inclination is to take our chances with the tunnel, but to keep our wits about us. Walter, you must take advantage of all that I taught you about hypnosis and focusing your mind."

Walter nodded brusquely and blindfolded the chocolate-hued stallion, Epos. "Right, let's use this to our advantage. Another training session."

"That's the spirit," Eva said, and they both laughed uneasily at the pun.

The pair rode led the blindfolded horses forward by their bridles and pressed into the dark tunnel courageously.

At first, the tunnel was so dark, Walter doubted that it was necessary to have blindfolded the animals in the first place. But as they went deeper into the mountain, Walter began to see shapes in the darkness that flitted across his vision quickly and then disappeared. The sight of these wispy shapes made Walter shiver, as it was too dark to know what exactly he was seeing. Walter felt the urge to turn on his flashlight, but Eva warned against it, telling him it was best not to reveal the mysteries that lurked inside of the tunnel.

The temperature was dropping quickly, which not only discomfited the horses but also made Walter even more anxious, as the pair were not warmly dressed. His teeth chattered, and he rubbed his hands together to keep his body warm.

"How long is this tunnel?" Walter asked, patting Epos on the nose as the young stallion neighed in distress.

"Emilia said it takes about an hour to traverse," she replied. "But it feels so much longer, since time moves differently here."

Walter shuddered. His thoughts drifted to what Shiva had told him on Mount Samaya, about teaching Walter how to master time. So far, he had only been granted a single gift associated with that wider ability: the gift of seeing future possibilities through the Talisman. But at this moment, he desperately wished that he could speed up time so that they could get to the other side of the mountain without further delay.

"Well, I wish it wouldn't," Walter said drowsily. His energy reserves were dwindling, and the extreme cold, combined with the anxiety, was making him want to sleep. His guard was dropping, and he didn't have the strength to remember how to bring it up again.

"Shh..." Eva whispered. "Can you hear that?"

"Hear what?" Walter replied. Moments later, he could hear it too: a cacophony of voices, whispering, laughing, and crying up ahead. It reminded him of the voices of the river he had heard in his fourth vision, and his skin prickled with goosebumps.

The horses were not happy, and they dug their hooves into the earth, stubbornly attempting to resist their companions' journey onwards. Eva had her own special way of soothing them, however, speaking to them softly, singing them gentle lullabies, and persuading them to carry on.

Without warning, the walls on either side of them suddenly fell away, as they arrived at a crossroads. A vast tunnel, wider than the one they were walking down, cut across their path. Its sides were smooth and polished, as though a god had carved the mountain rock meticulously with an enormous knife.

Walter looked to the left first—an action he later regretted.

What he saw was the starkest contrast to the cold, frightening, and damp tunnel they had been traversing for what had felt like days. A few meters down the tunnel, there was a screen-like partition: the other side did not appear to be a continuation of three-dimensional reality, but a flat projection of moving images. This projection depicted a cozy scene, consisting of himself, Elaine, his parents Vladimir and Carla, his brother Jonathan, and his sister Victoria. They were all sitting down to eat before a blazing hearth, passing ale and bread to one another, laughing heartily at one another's jokes, and recounting amusing tales about their lives and adventures. He and Elaine were radiant with happiness, and Walter noticed that her belly was full with child, and wedding bands adorned both her finger and that of his duplicate. If anyone with the imagination to devise the most endearing, comforting, and joyful of familial scenes had done so, then they could not have done better than this.

As he watched the scene, entranced, Walter did not notice that tears had begun to stream down his face. What he was watching struck him deeply, appealing to a part of his brain that was ancient and primordial, that craved family and food and hearth. He had been lacking in a stable family environment for many years now, and the sight of what he had been craving tugged at his heartstrings.

Walter took a few steps forward, and he would have lost himself in that idyllic scene were it not for the sharp, staccato noise he heard that jolted him out of his reverie.

"Em. Em. Em… I can't believe it's you. Is it really you?"

Walter was grateful for the noise, because it alerted him that he was deep within a hypnotic state, and he needed to extricate himself from it quickly. With all his strength, he pushed himself up to the surface of the ocean of feeling he had been drowning in.

He spun around.

With a gasp of surprise, he noticed that Eva was only two steps away from one of the most terrifying and beautiful portals he had ever seen. It was pitch black as the darkest night, and ringed with what appeared to be stardust, gaseous haloes of blue, purple, and silver.

The young woman took one step closer.

Rushing up to her, Walter pulled Eva backwards with all his strength, and she collapsed onto the ground. He shielded her from the portal with his body and tore a strip of cloth from his shirt that he bound around her eyes, reprimanding her sharply. "Eva. You cannot go in there. It is the portal to the underworld... remember? You told me about it!"

Eva whimpered. "But Em... she was there. She told me it's safe to go inside."

"No, that's not Emilia in there. The real Emilia..." Walter stopped himself. He wasn't quite ready to tell her that he had been communicating with her dead sister for a while now.

"The real Emilia would never want you to go in there," he continued. "It must be an illusion, meant to lure you inside."

Eva was sobbing now, and Walter cursed himself for having spent so much time staring into the birth chamber. But while Eva cradled her head in her hands and lay weeping on the ground in a fetal position, a strange sensation descended upon Walter. The magnetism was acting on him, too.

Walter glanced reluctantly into the portal, suddenly consumed with an infantile curiosity. The curiosity was intense, and it forbade him from looking away.

The portal was black at first, and there was absolutely nothing to see. But Walter could not tear his eyes away for a reason he could neither identify nor understand. As he gazed into the darkness, clearer shapes began to illuminate and materialize. Eventually, he could discern the distinct shape of a labyrinth, a dizzying maze of pathways that fit elegantly together inside a perfect circle that was bounded by the gaseous edges of the portal. Inside each of the pathways was a line of algorithmic code that intrigued him, and he felt an overwhelming urge to translate the code into Khalendi. But the longer Walter stared at it, the more frustrated he became. The code was incredibly cryptic, and the labyrinth circle began to spin faster and faster, making him dizzy. He gritted his teeth with rage, and eventually he became so angry that he yelled loudly, his voice reverberating in the tunnel.

The circle stopped spinning.

There was a single line of code that Walter could now see at the very center of the labyrinth, but its letters were tiny, almost illegible. He needed to read it; for some incomprehensible reason, he sensed that it was extremely important.

A voice began to whisper, very softly, in his ear.

"You don't need to make any choices anymore, Walter. Shiva wants you to choose between all those options, but it's cruel of him to ask you to do that. How can one single human be burdened with the weight of so many decisions? Surrender yourself to the machine… where the choices will be made for you."

"The machine?" he breathed.

"Your life will become simple, elegant, beautiful. Just like this code. Read it, and you will understand everything."

The code was small, and Walter needed to step closer to read it properly.

"Waaaalteeer!" Eva shrieked as she dragged him backwards. He pushed her away mindlessly, and she collapsed onto the ground. In desperation, Eva managed to cling on to his lower legs, and he swayed forwards, nearly touching the surface of the portal with his head. Fortunately, the countervailing force of the swaying motion pulled him backwards before he made contact, and Eva wrestled him to the ground. The blindfolded horses neighed wildly, and Eva dragged Walter by the hand back to the main path they had been riding down. Mounting the horses once again they drudged onwards, until finally they reached an opening, and the blinding light of the sun blazed down upon them once more. They had reached the end of the Crossing. The Barrens awaited them.

Walter rubbed his eyes, dazed and disoriented.

"You saved my life," he said, and embraced Eva tightly. "You are one of the best friends I've ever had."

"Ditto," Eva smiled, wiping tears from her eyes.

They both clung to each other, sobbing and sheltering from the sun beneath a desert sagebrush at the foot of the mountain, until they were strong enough to carry on.

As they left the Meridian Mountains, Walter whispered a prayer. "Thank you for allowing Eva and me to traverse the Crossing," he said, and then turned his gaze south toward a vast desert that lay ahead of them, hauntingly beautiful and chilling at the same time.

Barren Land

"A heap of broken images, where the sun beats / And the dead tree gives no shelter,
the cricket no relief / And the dry stone no sound of water."
— T.S. Eliot

Golden sand stretched before them for miles, broken up by the occasional desert shrub, cactus, or rocky formation. Turkey vultures wheeled overhead, waiting patiently for rodents and scorpions to scuttle out from beneath the protective shield of the sand. Eva and Epos plodded along more slowly than usual because of the sandy terrain.

Walter shuddered as he gazed around at the desolation in awe. He and Eva were both wearing pale beige 'scarves'—really, bedsheets cut roughly with a pocketknife—wrapped around their heads to protect their skin from the sun, but also for more strategic reasons. Walter knew that there was widespread state surveillance in the Barrens, and he did not want to risk being identified. He had considered drinking lydion, which would have transformed his appearance, but decided against it after realizing that Elaine would fear him in such a disguise. He had also been reluctant to wear the headscarves for fear of standing out, but Eva assured him that it was relatively common for Xeyan'na to wear similar attire when journeying in the desert to avoid sunstroke.

"How could anyone possibly live in a place like this?" he whispered incredulously, to nobody in particular.

"The settlements are few and far between," Eva acknowledged. "Or so I've heard... I haven't been down here in years."

"When was the last time?" he asked. "Before the Crate?"

"Years ago, our parents took us down here for a holiday," she said, grinning and shaking her head. "The truth was it was the only place they could afford. There was a run-down hostel in Caixu that was accepting visitors for a modest sum. I remember driving down in my parents' old rickety van and spending most of the holiday lounging beside a swimming pool that hadn't been cleaned out in ages."

"You can actually drive a car down here?" Walter asked. "I thought that only trains crossed the Meridian Mountains."

"No, there's an old highway, several leagues to the east of the Crossing. Decades ago, the Barrens was actually a tourist destination for wealthy Khalendi. That was before it became a hostile environment, before the Icewhisper was dammed and the forests and soil were depleted. When I visited with my family, it was very much in a transition period. We were at least able to find decently priced accommodation."

"Interesting," Walter said. "Where is Caixu?"

"It was one of the largest trading hubs in the Barrens when we visited," she said. "If I remember correctly, it was about a three-hour drive south of the Meridian Mountains. If we keep heading southeast, we might come across it. Although I have no idea what might have become of it by now," she admitted. "Emilia took more trips than I did to the Barrens, on her way down to the Southern Jungles."

"Did she give you any insight into it?" Walter asked.

"Whenever I asked her about it, she would tear up," Eva replied. "I eventually stopped asking about it as she didn't seem interested in giving me answers. I do know, though, that Eva much preferred the Southern Jungles. She loved seeing people who were liberated, enjoying their lives and cultures to the fullest. That was obviously not the case in the Barrens."

"How do you think we'll find Te'yara? That must be where Elaine went to."

"We'll know it when we see it... Te'yara is where they are moving all their cranes and bulldozers to. If we come across a local settlement of any kind, we can ask the natives where it is."

A scorpion scuttled across the sand in front of Walter's horse, and it whinnied in fear.

"This land is dangerous, even for the horses," Eva said. "The bite of a snake or scorpion could seriously injure them. Yes, they are blessed incarnations of Epona," she said. "But even divine beings have their weaknesses."

The horses could not ride for long without stopping to sip some water, and soon Walter and Eva's canteens were running low. The pair took a break under a creosote bush, and before long they were both dozing, somnambulant in the late-afternoon sun.

Walter was jolted from his relaxing nap by Epos, who prodded the young man urgently with the tip of his nose.

"What is it, Epos?" Walter asked, rubbing the sleep out of his eyes as he stretched. Squinting, he noticed faint shapes materializing on the horizon, in the direction of the soon-to-be setting sun. Their silhouettes carved black, jagged holes into the lustrous pale-pink sky and loomed closer with every passing moment. Walter immediately felt more alert, and he shook Eva, who was deep in slumber.

"Eva, wake up," Walter urged. "We have visitors."

Eva stretched and glanced at the approaching figures. "Those appear to be traders. A travelling caravan of sorts, perhaps."

Upon closer inspection, Walter could see that she was right. There were a few men on horseback, tethered to wagons and trolleys weighed down by exotically colored fabrics and linens. Mules and animals resembling llamas or alpacas trailed from either side of the procession.

"Perhaps they're going to a village, or know where Te'yara is," Walter said, suddenly optimistic.

"There's a good chance of that," Eva said. "Let's go introduce ourselves."

"Wait," Walter cautioned, holding her by the arm. "We must not give away anything about the Jade Rebellion, who we are, or what our mission is."

"Of course not," she said sharply, and tugged her arm away. Walter could see that his words had wounded her, and he wondered if she was still sensitive about the time he had accused her of disloyalty to the Rebellion.

The pair mounted the horses and rode out to meet the traders, who froze in their tracks as soon as Walter and Eva began to approach them. When they were about a dozen meters away, the man at the front of the procession whistled loudly—a shrill, urgent sound that startled Walter. The stranger rode over to them on a mottled stallion, taking his time as he sized them up. He, like all the traders, had rich auburn hair and forest-green eyes, the traditional coloring of the Xeyan'na people. This man's hair was long and straight, and he wore it unconventionally, tied up in a tight, neat bun on the top of his head. He was broad-shouldered and well-muscled, and he towered a good foot above Eva and Walter, who were roughly the same height as each other.

"Crystal City folk," he said, in impeccable Khalendi. Walter was impressed by how fluent the man was in the dialect of the Empire; he had expected a noticeable Xeyan'na accent, the kind that Elaine had had when he had first met her.

"We rarely come across you types this far West," he said, flexing his muscles as he unsheathed his *je'na*, a traditional dagger that many of the Xeyan'na natives carried. It had Xeyan'na runic inscriptions cut into its blade and a handle made of sturdy rowan.

Eva turned pale when she saw the dagger.

"We mean no harm, sir," she said quickly. "We are travelers from the North, seeking a friend down here."

The man tossed the *je'na* in the air deftly and caught it with his other hand. He was staring at Eva intently, as though she was an enigma that needed to be solved.

"A friend, eh? This isn't a friendly land," the man said sternly. "You haven't seen any drone sweeps yet?"

"Drone sweeps?" Walter asked. "No, I don't believe we have..." he trailed off awkwardly. The man was still riveted to Eva.

"You a mixed-race?" the man asked Eva, ignoring Walter.

"I... yes, sir, I am," she said humbly, bowing her head.

"Hmph. That could explain why I sense something odd about you." He finally turned to look at Walter. "The droids send them out across the desert to check for anything amiss. Any lone traveler they find, who can't afford a bribe, is trucked off to the labor camps."

He wiped his nose with the back of his hand, crudely, and then glanced over his shoulder at a stout, barrel-shaped man with a mane of red curls and a cross expression on his face who rode on a stubby mule. The lead trader motioned for him to step forward.

"This here is Rhys," the lead trader said, once the angry-looking man had reluctantly joined him. "Salt trader by day, bounty hunter by night. I'm introducing him to you folks because I want you to know that he'd be happy to sell you lot to the droids. Dead or alive."

Walter was suddenly regretting coming to the Barrens, and his mind filled with disquieting thoughts of being killed, strung up, and salted by this barbaric man, who was now spitting profusely on the ground as if to punctuate the lead trader's remarks. Walter began to feel dizzy, and he suspected it was not only because he had spent the afternoon under the blanketing heat of the desert sun. It had not been part of his plan to run into a bounty hunter here, and it made him ill to think of what could happen if this troll-like man uncovered his identity, as one of the most wanted men in the Empire.

"Mixed-race folk fetch a higher price, believe it or not," the lead trader said. "You'd think they would be worth less, being less human and all, but that's not the case down here. The droids like to channel their gifts toward productive uses, you could say."

"We're not looking for trouble," Eva said, eyeing the stocky Rhys and stepping out of the range of his projectile saliva.

"Where are my manners?" the lead trader suddenly said in a mock-polite tone. "I'm Tyrian. I hope you're not put off by Rhys—he's quite the gentleman if you get to know him. Unfortunately, few survive to make it into his good graces," he muttered, as Rhys tightened his hands into fists. Walter noticed several bizarre weapons strapped to his broad back—including what appeared to be a scythe, a mace, and a saw—and swallowed hard.

"But look. We all have something to trade. And perhaps, my friends, you are more valuable to us than you are to the droids. Understand me?" Tyrian said, tossing his *je'na* in the air again. "In short, we'll take you in, let you sleep in our fine wagons and sup on our fine bread, like the good Samaritans we are, as long as the math checks out on that fine point."

"Or," Eva replied, defiance surfacing in her voice, "we can go our separate ways and leave it at that."

The young woman's tone seemed to irritate Rhys further, and he grunted unhappily, spitting more forcefully onto the sand.

"Save your spit. Water's scarce in the desert," she said to Rhys, and Walter suppressed a laugh.

Rhys looked as though he were about to charge her on his mule. Tyrian gave him a cold glance which silenced and settled the odd man, who suddenly spoke in a thick accent. "Yew think oi'm scared of goin' thirsty 'ere?" he asked angrily. "Oi have plenty of gold on me to buy more wa'ta. An' don't pay 'eed to wat Tyrian said. Oi'm an honest salt trader. Oi've got me bounties, yeah, but oi only work for honest men."

Walter knew that a single misstep with these traders could jeopardize everything they had worked for so far. His mind raced to think of a bargaining chip he might possess, something he could use to persuade Tyrian to take them in.

"The lydion," Walter whispered to Eva. "We could trade some of it in exchange for their amnesty."

Eva gritted her teeth, shifting uncomfortably on Epa, who was also becoming restless. "To hell with these traders. We need to save that lydion for you..." she said, but her voice wavered as she saw Walter's pleading expression. "I suppose we could spare some. Just a few drops would be worth a fortune to them."

Eva glanced back at Tyrian, who was staring at the pair with an amused smirk.

"You children ready to barter?" he asked.

Eva patted her jittery horse. "Give us shelter and lead us to our friend's village, and we'll pay you handsomely."

He laughed. "Who said anything about leading you to a village?" he asked, squinting as the setting sun hit his eyes at a direct angle. "What village?"

"Te'yara," Walter said, which provoked a sudden burst of laughter from the man.

"That's a funny joke," the man replied. "Te'yara's no village. It's been turned into a labor camp for the mine."

Walter felt a wave of nausea and anxiety wash over him. "Already? It's only been…"

"Ah, you ignorant folks haven't heard yet," the man interjected rudely. "Well, let me educate you. Te'yara's moved. That's a pretty way of putting it because it hasn't really moved. The village has been gutted, its houses razed to the ground, to make way for Astrid: a pretty name for an ugly diamond mine, that blights the land as far as the eye can see. All the folks who used to live there were recruited to work at the mine, and they sleep at a camp carved into the nearby cliffs. That camp is now called Te'yara."

The barrel-shaped man erupted into fits of childish laughter, which made Walter burn with the urge to wrestle him to the ground.

"But it ain't really Te'yara, not anymore," Rhys said, through his crude laughter.

"He's right," Tyrian said. "It's not the same Te'yara. So, if your friend's there, well I'm sorry to say they're one of the laborers, too. I don't think you want to visit them; else you'll risk being recruited yourself."

Walter felt a seething, roiling sensation within him. It was too unbearable for him to think of Elaine working under the scorching desert sun to build a diamond mine on the ancestral grounds of her village, side by side with her mother and brothers.

"Listen, Tyrian," he said, in a commanding tone that felt oddly out of place, given the skewed power dynamics between the travelers and the traders. "We will pay you handsomely if you bring us to Te'yara. The new Te'yara. Don't worry about what happens afterwards. If we are recruited as labourers, then that's no sweat off your back."

"A boy after me own heart," Rhys said with a discomfiting giggle.

"Now, as a good and honest trader, I need to see the wares I'm bartering for. Do my due diligence, as they say," Tyrian said curtly. "Come on, where is it?"

Eva trembled and then began to search through her satchel. She spent a few moments fiddling around, which appeared to aggravate Rhys.

"They're bluffin', gonna pull a weapon on us," he drawled, his face contorted in anger.

"I assure you, we are honest people," she retorted. She then pulled out a small vial of dark blue liquid, and Walter breathed a sigh of relief when he saw that she had transferred a portion of the large vial of lydion to a smaller one. That way, the traders wouldn't have any designs on their main supply, which they needed to execute their mission.

"Lydion," Tyrian exclaimed, when he saw the unmistakable silvery glint of the substance as Eva swished it around slowly. "I'll be damned. How did the likes of you get your hands on *he'xala*?" he asked, using the Xeyan'na name for the substance. "Who did you say you work for, again?"

"We didn't," Walter replied. "Listen, we won't ask any questions of you, and we'd kindly ask that you not pry into our personal and professional lives. Honest and true to our words, though, we will give you this entire vial if you hold up your end of the bargain. Think of how many barrels of salt you could buy with this," he said, feeling uncomfortably like a wheedling salesman.

"Oi could buy over a hundred with it, true, and the best salt from the south flats, too," Rhys said matter-of-factly. "Come on, Tyrion, Te'yara ain't too far from 'ere. Let's just take 'em and get our lydion."

Tyrion squinted, hesitating as his eyes bored into Eva's icy blue ones. "There's something very odd about you, girl," he muttered, more to himself than to Eva. "If I find out that one of you is working for the droids, or you're spies for the govvie, getting intel on our trading operations or sommat like that, then I'll slit your throats so fast you won't be able to lie your way out if it. We traders have worked hard to maintain our independence from the state. We have a sort of contract with them, you see. They leave us alone with their drone sweeps and other surveillance, and in exchange, we make a tidy profit with our trades and give a portion to the govvie. They don't ask questions about what we do, we just give them the *cestae*. Or the bounty, if they're paid in kind." He held up his *je'na*. "Pretty little thing, isn't she? Let me tell you, fine-looking as she is, she's a lady of substance and smarts. And whip-sharp, too," he said with an unsettling grin.

As they rode with the traders, the scale of the AI Masters' machinery of surveillance gradually became apparent to Walter and Eva. It soon became clear how fortunate the pair was to have encountered some of the only humans in the Barrens who were not subject to the watchful scrutiny of the robots.

The two companions had visited the Barrens during *Saari*, a traditional Xeyan'na holiday that celebrated the victory of light over the darkness of late autumn, and the roadways through the desert were abuzz with travelers, some on foot, others on horseback, and most in rickety trucks caked with sand. There was not a single self-driving car—a distinguishing feature of wealthier locales in Khalendar. The traders had an intimate knowledge of the land and its navigational routes and stuck to less well-travelled roads. Yet every few miles along each stretch of road, they inevitably encountered a security checkpoint at which a handful of AI Masters were present. Due to their privileged status, the traders would be permitted to pass through these checkpoints without stopping, special treatment that was rarely afforded to any of the other travelers.

Although Walter was huddled in the wagon when they passed these eerie outposts, he usually had an unobstructed view of what was happening. He saw that the AI Masters at these stations, garbed in red suits with diamonds emblazoned on their shoulders, would bark orders at the travelers and demand the surrender of their tablets. If the Xeyan'na were wealthy enough to own a tablet, the AI Masters would confiscate the device and then project it onto a large screen that was visible to others lined up at the checkpoint. If they had none, the fearful travelers would be forced inside an interrogation room.

To Walter's disgust, the AI Masters would scroll through the tablets' communication history, publicly showcasing the private messages of Xeyan'na citizens to their fellow compatriots. The exercise was humiliating for those who were forced to endure it. The AI Masters stopped their scrolling at any message that was mildly eyebrow-raising, and then would take a screenshot of it to store in their central information database. Walter was chagrined by the interpretive failures of the AI Masters: "I forgot to pick up some salt at the market," was deemed an incriminating message worthy of a screenshot.

The more sophisticated the tablet, and the more extensive the communication history, the more data was collected and acquired. And it was a daunting challenge to evade these data sweeps, because, as Walter soon learned from the traders, the Xeyan'na were required by law to both own a tablet and have certain programs installed on it. Unless you could not afford a tablet altogether—having an income lower than a paltry 2,000 *cestae* per year qualified you for this exemption—the government required you to purchase one and install a "health monitor," an "energy monitor," and a "culture monitor." These three basic programs were far more sinister than their innocuous names suggested.

Walter learned all this one day while sipping tea inside one of the wagons as they waited in a long lineup at a security checkpoint. As privileged as the traders were, they still had to wait in line like everyone else. A young trader, Vyrkov, was explaining the subtleties of the surveillance system in Xeyan'na to the transfixed Walter and Eva.

"The health monitor is probably the worst," the trader explained, "since it's designed to trick you into thinking that it's good for you. It is, probably, good for you—but in the vilest way possible. It tracks your heart rate, the calories you consume, the nutritional value of your foods, and your blood pressure. It even monitors your mental health, through quizzes and questionnaires that are dressed up to seem fun and engaging.

"When these lands were colonized, the Xeyan'na were cut off from their traditional hunting and foraging grounds. While they previously had access to abundant foods, after colonization they became dependent on the government, reliant on the supplies given so benevolently to them by the AI Masters," he said, his voice dripping in sarcasm. He looked no more than eighteen, but he seemed wiser than his years.

"And so, their health needs often go unmet. They suffer from diabetes, high blood pressure, and cardiac issues. And what does the government do? They step in with this charming health monitor to make all of their worries disappear. But the problem is, it's not just a health monitor—it's a way of accessing biometric data, which is valuable not just to us traders, but first and foremost to the AI Masters. They have a vested interest in keeping some healthy and others sick. The laborers need a high caloric intake so they can keep the wheels of industry turning. But elderly folks are simply a burden on the system. The AI Masters try to find ways of keeping sick old people sick, and making them sicker, so that they die quickly. And most of all, they are on the hunt for dissidents. Anyone who is too strong, too fast, or whose mental health exams display even the slightest hint of non-conformity— well, those folks are the prime targets for the AI Masters.

"So, you trade not just in salt and other goods, but in data as well?" Eva asked with a charming smile, as Walter tried to conceal his increasing discomfort with the subject of the conversation.

"Data is worth more than salt... it's worth more than gold, even.

Probably not worth as much as lydion," the trader added. "I hear you folks have promised us somma that as payment."

Eva looked the young man squarely in his hazel eyes. "We have," she said curtly. "Tell me, what data do you trade in, exactly?"

The young man peeled an apple with a kitchen knife, watching its polished red skin drift and settle into circular patterns on the wooden floor. "You seem quite interested in this topic," he said, sounding on-edge. Eva shifted uncomfortably. "I don't blame you," he continued in a slightly warmer tone. "It's quite a fascinating subject. Well, we travel off-road a lot, to places without any droid checkpoints. Even the drone sweeps don't go as far as somma the areas we travel to. Any data we find in those regions fetches a high price, and we sell it to the government, or to their agents."

Walter coughed, spluttering tea everywhere as he did so, and Vyrkov turned his razor-sharp gaze on him. "I was wondering why he didn't take your data at first. The boss, I mean. He said that you lot promised him lydion, that he's going to keep his word and take only that as payment for his service to you. He's a man of honor, Tyrian is."

"I don't doubt it," Walter replied, concealing his hands beneath his kaftan so that the trader wouldn't notice that they were trembling.

Vyrkov smiled at Walter, leaving a pause in the conversation that was unsettlingly long. The wagon began to lurch forwards. "Looks like we're moving," he said brusquely. "Better get back on me horse," he said, leaving the pair behind in contemplative silence.

"My tablet," Walter whispered to Eva, feeling a wave of nausea that he suspected had been triggered by more than the lurching wagon. "I've encrypted it against government spyware, at least the programs I'm aware of, but I didn't think to consider that the traders might have spyware of their own. They may already be siphoning data from it. Maybe they've even reviewed its communication history and figured out who we are and what we're planning to do. And what makes my blood run cold is that your messages about the layout of Central Command are still stored in the tablet's records."

"You could delete them now," Eva suggested.

"But it's priceless information that will help me immensely when the time comes for my meeting with the advisor. I can't commit it all to my own memory."

"You could, if you drank the lydion," she suggested. "Lydion has a deleterious effect on human memories, but not on AI ones. And what I recorded in your tablet was essentially the memories of an AI Fighter."

Walter pondered this for a moment. "It might work, if I do it at nighttime, while nobody is watching. As long as I drink enough water to ensure the effects wear off by morning," he added. "And once the lydion wears off, will the AI memories I've acquired fade?"

"No, they will all be safely stored in your human mind… that's the strange thing about lydion. When you consume some, you forget some of your old life and memories. But when you stop consuming any, your old human memories come back, and the memories you acquired while taking lydion stay fresh and are uncannily imprinted into your brain for a long time.

"It will be risky, but I don't trust these traders or their alleged 'honor.' But first, just to make sure that we're not doing this for nothing, can you check your tablet to see if any trojan horses or viruses have accessed it in the last twenty-four hours?"

Walter felt the cold weight of dread as he ran a spyware detection program on his tablet. He felt as though he and Eva had naïvely walked into a trap.

The program turned up no results. Walter breathed a sigh of relief when the 'no spyware detected' message popped up on his tablet's screen. But he knew that the program, though excellent, was not watertight. It could have missed a piece of spyware if it was elaborately designed and sophisticated enough. *Would the traders, rough and unrefined as they appeared, be able to design such a program?* Walter considered, his heart racing. The answer came to him easily: if the traders gathered data for the AI Masters, then they would have the benefit of any technology designed by the AI Masters.

That was when it dawned on him; he, Walter Saltanetska, as talented with computers, hacking, and code as he was, would never understand the subtleties of such technologies as well as an AI Master. To put his mind at ease, Walter needed to consume the lydion, which would enable him to upgrade the spyware detection program into something equipped to detect a far more sophisticated virus.

Waiting for night to fall was the hardest part. The tedium was made worse by lining up to pass the security checkpoint, and afterwards they broke camp and had to wait a few more hours until dinner was ready. The traders appeared to be in good spirits, Tyrian most of all. He drank copious amounts of brandy and mulled wine that night around a blazing campfire and ordered his fellow traders to sing and strum various eclectic instruments. One was a sitar, an oriental-sounding instrument from the Southern Jungles, another was a *khoborga*, a traditional Xeyan'na flute that had a harsh ring to it, and the third type of instrument was a *meyre*, a hollowed-out drum stretched with leather hide.

The revelry did not interest Walter, but he was grateful for the distraction. He was intending to discreetly slip away after dinner to do his work, but Tyrian grabbed him by the wrist just as he finished the last of his curried chickpeas.

"Will you be staying for the entertainment?" Tyrian asked boorishly. As drunk as he was, the lead trader seemed oddly lucid, and the way his moss-green eyes bored into Walter made the young man shiver.

"I'm tired. Think I'll have an early night tonight," Walter replied.

"Your friend… she's a pretty one," Tyrian drawled, gazing across the campfire toward Eva, who was bobbing her head in time with the music. "I was hoping she'd join in the diversions."

Walter set his jaw. The last thing he wanted was this unrefined trader making designs on his friend Eva. Now that he thought of it, the trader had seemed romantically interested in her from the beginning. Although Walter had first attributed the trader's lingering gaze to curiosity about her mixed-race origins, he now realized it was because of something more. But Walter recognized an opportunity for further distraction. He hated to do this to his friend, but he needed every advantage he could get with these wily traders.

"She's an excellent dancer," Walter exclaimed, and as soon as the words were out of his mouth he regretted them. He had no idea how well Eva danced, and he didn't want to put her on the spot. But what better way to ensure that he could work uninterrupted than to have Eva distract the traders with a dance?

"Is that so?" Tyrian said. "Well, let's see it, then."

Walter reddened as Tyrian called across the campfire to Eva, causing the sitar player's melodious rhythms to stop abruptly. "Pretty lady," Tyrian drawled, taking another swig of brandy. "Your friend here says you can *dance*."

Eva glanced at Walter, and the rebel leader tried to convey an expression of pleading in his eyes. Eva caught on, but Walter could see that she was not pleased with him.

"My friend is too flattering," she replied coldly, "but I do enjoy dancing. With a partner, of course," she added.

Walter froze. He half-expected her to invite him to dance with her, but instead she beckoned for Tyrian to come closer. The brilliance of her strategy was apparent. As the three instrumentalists began their tune, a sharply cadenced flamenco, Eva bowed before Tyrian and held out her arms in an invitation. The lead trader eagerly accepted the offer, and the other traders formed a circle around them, cheering and clinking their brandy-filled glasses as the music grew more animated. Walter watched for a few moments in rapt fascination; he was not so captivated by the dancing itself, but rather by the sheer resourcefulness of his friend, who had been able to gracefully choreograph a routine in mere seconds.

With the traders' attention thoroughly diverted, Walter was able to relax as he crept away into the shadows of the gloomy late-autumn night. The temperature was plunging as the sun had recently set, and Walter felt the assaulting chill of the air once he left the campfire. To avoid any encounters with the traders, he decided to do his work in the open air, behind a nearby rock formation, rather than in one of the wagons.

It all happened very quickly. Walter consumed the lydion—about half a teaspoonful was all that was required—and immediately he felt his mind shift into a different gear. He studied the code of his spyware detection program, and with fresh eyes, determined what its weaknesses were and how they could be shored up. It was startlingly easy to spot them with his newly heightened sense of awareness, a sort of hyper-sensitivity to the nuanced cause and effect of any computational system.

As the lydion permeated his body, Walter's mind became clear, focused, and unplagued by anxieties. He often felt that way after a seizure, as though a buildup of tension within his brain had erupted, clearing away the debris from his neural pathways. With lydion, he felt as though he could accomplish the most complex programming task in a matter of minutes. There was nothing getting in the way—no distracting ego, and most importantly, no emotional baggage attached to any task he set out to accomplish. A meditative sense of calm accompanied his work, along with the feeling that he was conserving energy that would have otherwise dissipated.

Within twenty minutes, the upgraded program was completed. Walter could still hear the reassuring background noise of the drumming and the swirling, exotic melodies of the sitar and the *khoborga*. As the new spyware program ran, he felt tranquil, but poised to react to any hint of a result. And, within a few more minutes, he found it: a backdoor trojan horse, almost negligible in its size, that had burrowed its way onto the tablet's hard drive.

Investigating its origins, he saw the culprit. A mail attachment that somebody named 'vokyrv81' had delivered a few days ago into his inbox, that he had opened mindlessly, revealing an advertisement for hotels in the Barrens. He realized, too, that the name spelled backwards was that of the trader he and Eva had been speaking to, Vrykov. He cursed himself for having opened the attachment, for it was doing its grisly work to mine the contents of his tablet. Fortunately, however, his message history was extensive; since he had developed an encryption system that he had been satisfied with for years, it had not been necessary to delete anything. As a result, it would take a long time—perhaps up to a week—to transfer everything over. And to his utter relief, the data thieves had only managed to siphon about 5% of his message history, comprised of mostly benign texts that he had sent to Elaine during their early romance, years earlier. Silly, sentimental messages, but nothing remotely incriminating.

Working methodically, Walter disarmed the trojan horse with virus-purging software. But something still seemed wrong, and Walter knew that in the span of forty-eight hours, the trojan horse could have replicated itself or established malware that had burrowed deeper into the tablet, disguising itself as a legitimate program. There was no doubt about it: the safest route would be to delete important data. And that was what he did, but not before reading it carefully and committing it to memory. Every sentence in Eva's message about the layout of Central Command was now imprinted into his mind, like a unique fingerprint, something that he could access at will in the future.

Once he had finished this process, Walter noticed with a creeping sense of unease that the ambient music was no longer playing. He did not know for how long it had been silent, since he had been so intently focused on carrying out his work. With a slow, nauseating dread, he turned toward the traders' wagons and mounts and saw darkness. But the screen of his tablet was just illuminated enough that he could also see something else—a shape materializing from behind the nearby rock formation. It was precisely whom he had suspected: Vrykov. The lean, curly-haired teen looked angry, feral, and impatient.

"You caught me out, didn't you?" the boy said dryly. "It's a pity, I thought you were buying my 'holier than thou' act. Sympathetic to the human rights of the Xeyan'na people and all that sickeningly moral stuff. Don't get me wrong—I care about them. Heck, I'm one of them, although we traders are cut from a different cloth. We share the same genetic makeup, but we're not naïve as they are. We've learned to climb the ladder of evolution, whereas they are victims of fate and circumstance."

The young man was walking closer to Walter, cautiously at first, but with escalating boldness. Walter motioned him to stop with his hand, but the trader had come close enough to see Walter's changed form.

Vrykov gasped as he studied Walter in the illuminated light of the tablet. Walter was keenly aware of how different he looked after he had consumed the lydion—he was taller, his shoulders were broader, and his skin was tight and had an odd, rubbery property. The shape of his body was more rigid, defined by sharp, masculine lines.

"You... you drank it. The lydion," the boy said breathlessly.

"Keen observation," Walter replied sarcastically. "Now, if you'll excuse me, I'm off to bed." He had a glass of water nearby, and he took a long, deep draught of it. As he did so, his flesh softened, his bone structure condensed, and his skin lost its rubbery quality. His mind began to careen toward normalcy, but it felt good to return, to experience the thrilling cascade of human emotion again. Mostly, Walter felt resentment toward this trader who had violated his privacy, which soon evolved into a biting rage that made him want to beat Vrykov to a pulp.

"Wait," the trader said. "How did you find out what I had done? I'm one of the best hackers in the Barrens... nobody's ever detected my viruses so quickly. It's because of the lydion, isn't it? I suppose I've only ever hacked humans, not droids."

Walter looked at him with amusement. They were about the same size, but for some reason—as charged with adrenaline as he was—Walter wasn't afraid of the Xeyan'na trader.

"Who gave you orders to hack me?" Walter asked, his voice firm and commanding.

The boy suddenly looked afraid and glanced back toward the traders as though he were hoping they would come to support him.

"It... it was all me, I swear. As I told you, Tyrian's a man of honor."

Walter spat on the ground next to Vrykov's feet.

"And, as you've also told me, your sympathy for the Xeyan'na people was feigned. How can I believe a single word that comes out of your mouth?"

"I'm telling the truth," he said, spitting back in Walter's direction. "Ask him yourself if you're so suspicious."

At that moment, a piercing scream rent the air. Walter felt a surge of panic as he recognized the voice as Eva's. Gathering up his tablet and his satchel, he began to run toward the trader camp.

He arrived upon a chaotic scene near the dwindling embers of the campfire; it appeared that the lead trader, Tyrian, had torn a piece of Eva's dress off, apparently to make sexual advances on her. The clever girl had stolen the trader's *je'na* and was now brandishing it at him, but the barrel-shaped man, Rhys, was threatening her from behind with his scythe. Walter guessed that his menacing posture—the scythe was raised over Eva's shoulder—was what had provoked the scream.

When Walter appeared at the campfire, the stakes were high, and he had little time to react. The others noticed his presence but did not appear to be intimidated or deterred by him. Walter quickly realized that any threats he made would be empty; he had no weapons, save for a *balayan* that was useless against human opponents. The rebel leader had not expected to encounter any conflicts with humans in the Barrens, only AI Masters, and so he had not been concerned about the lack of weaponry until now.

Walter feared that it would be impossible to extricate them from the situation, but as he searched frantically in his satchel for anything that could be of some practical use, his eyes alighted on an illuminated object at the bottom. It was the Jade Talisman, the enchanted stone that Shiva had gifted him, which allowed him to see visions of future pathways. Walter felt an odd ringing in his ears as the Talisman glowed, no longer the dark jade color that it normally was, but now a siren red, like a hot coal inside of a furnace. He wondered if a seizure was coming on. The traders must have noticed his unease because they stopped what they were doing and glanced in his direction. Rhys kept his scythe poised over Eva, to prevent her from escaping, but he stared at Walter as though the young man were a foreign intruder.

Walter felt muddled in confusion, unclear of what the Talisman was signaling to him until he heard it. It was a fleeting whisper, and he wasn't sure if it was a woman or man's voice that spoke to him. But the ringing in his ears had helped to clear out all the external noise of the world, in a similar way that the lydion had, and was helping him to hear the whisper.

"Use it to slow time…" the voice echoed to him.

Intuitively, Walter grasped the Talisman and, without thinking much about what he was doing, clutched the magical object tightly in his hand. It was hot, and Walter felt a burning sensation in his palm, but the tighter he held onto it, the less pain he felt. As he closed his eyes, he descended into a vision of the stag he had encountered on Vei'arash, galloping across the desert. The stag had a bridle attached to him, and Walter climbed onto his back and grasped the reins. At first the sensation was dizzying and electrifying, like being on a roller coaster, and Walter felt as though he was too ill to continue the wild ride. But then, he began to settle down and feel the sensation of the animal underneath him, how he breathed, moved, and flexed his muscles. Walter allowed his mind to relax, and in the vision, he pulled on the reins with his full strength, channeling his mental focus into the single task of controlling the beast underneath him.

When the vision ended, Walter noticed that the Talisman was now emitting sparks—tiny red crystals that diffused into the night air and created hauntingly beautiful patches of mist. Walter could see that those sparks were floating toward the traders, and landing on each of them, but avoided him and Eva. He saw that this had the effect of slowing down the traders' movements, as though each of them had been struck by a paralyzing virus or poison.

Eva gazed at the tiny scarlet sparks in awe. "It's as if time is slowing down for them... but not us," she said, shaking her head in bewilderment.

Walter was just as stunned as she was. "I heard a voice whisper to me... it might have been Shiva, or some other divine being. It was telling me to use the Talisman to slow down time, and that seems to be what has happened. But we've been given a gift, and we can't waste a moment of this blessing. Let's leave on Epa and Epos."

"What about getting to Te'yara?" Eva asked. "If that's important to you, we can stay..."

"Nothing is so important that it means spending another moment in the company of rapists, liars, and cheats. Eva, I saw what that man was about to do to you. That is completely unacceptable."

Eva laughed, a hollow, guttural sound. "I was about to kill him with his own dagger when that awful dwarf-like man threatened me from behind. If you hadn't intervened when you did, I would be dead," she said gratefully. "I suppose you've saved my life for the second time in just a few days."

"I'm sure you'll return the favor soon," Walter said, rolling his eyes. "Although there's been too much adventure already for my taste. I'm looking forward to finding Elaine, and then getting out of here," he said. He shivered from the cold. "Your horses... I wonder if they could help us find Te'yara from here?"

Eva nodded. "The desert disoriented them when they first arrived here; too much sand stretching in all kinds of directions. But now that they've gotten a sense of the navigational routes and the paths taken by the traders, they have a greater spatial awareness of this place. If we assume that the traders were leading us in the right direction, then the horses will be able to extrapolate from that to find this village."

"We have little other choice, at his point," Walter conceded. "Let's put our trust in them and let them lead us onwards."

As he spoke these words, he turned his gaze toward the Talisman, whose light was now dwindling, although the red sparks still lingered around the men, keeping them frozen in place. However, Walter was skeptical about whether the magic would hold. He began to feel a dull ache in his muscles, getting stronger with each passing moment, until he was almost saturated by a feeling of exhaustion.

Eva regarded her friend with concern. "Walter! Are you well enough to ride?" she asked worriedly.

"The magic… it's draining my energy the longer it holds. We don't have much time," he said, feeling faint.

The pair mounted their horses, and although he felt dizzy and ill, the sharp desert wind enlivened him as they rode.

There was a price to be paid for magic, and he was paying it.

Te'yara

"How can you rise, if you have not burned?"
– Fatima Ahmad Ibrahim

With the aid of their mounts, Eva and Walter soon arrived at the mine site which had displaced Elaine's village. The sheer size of the diamond mine, carved into the ground where the real Te'yara used to be, was staggering. The pair could spot it from many leagues away by the scar-like indentation it made in the earth. Its terraced walls formed concentric circles that nested into each other, lending it the eerie appearance of a stadium. It was not yet very deep, but the cranes and bulldozers at its bottom indicated that it was still under construction. The mine sullied the soft, feminine beauty of the desert with its rough edges, which were illuminated by the pale moonlight.

When they arrived at the mine site, Walter was immediately reminded of the summer vision he had experienced through the Talisman, the one that had brought him to the Barrens. In that vision, he had seen the Xeyan'na natives displaced into sterile social housing near the mine, and he shuddered to think that the vision was materializing in real time. As he gazed at the mine, he felt an emptiness inside of him and a sadness that would leave deep emotional scars in him for many years to come. This was the reality he had long sought to avert; from the moment he discovered the AI Masters' plans to construct this hulking monolith, he had wanted nothing other than to put a halt to them. What sickened him the most was the knowledge that the destruction of history, culture, and a sacred ancestral homeland had been carried out merely to supply the Empire with a gemstone—a gemstone that was at once the Empire's crowning glory, its capital city's namesake, and a symbol of the bleak horrors that resulted from its material obsession and moral corruption. Tears pooled in Walter's eyes as he struggled to digest the significance of this moment. *Is the war already lost?* he asked himself sorrowfully.

A limestone cliff, intimidating in its scale, towered above the eastern edge of the mine. Walter could see the unmistakable outline of wolves on the top of the cliffs, as well as hear their unearthly howls. When the moon surfaced through the veil of the clouds, it illuminated some openings in the cliff face, and Walter could see that it was crisscrossed with a labyrinthine network of passageways. He wondered where the labor camp was, and whether it was nearby, but it quickly became apparent that he was staring directly at it: the workers were living inside the cliffs themselves. There were also a number of AI Fighter guards stationed at the foot of the cliffs, apparently guarding the network of tunnels that led deeper inside the cliffs. They were identifiable by their sharp, angular bodies, their pale blue uniforms emblazoned with diamonds, and what appeared to be rifles slung casually over their shoulders.

Walter knew that in this darkness, the AI Fighter guards would not yet have spotted him or Eva, and he wanted to proceed with caution.

"You should stay here with the mounts," he instructed. "I will consume the lydion and convince the AI Fighters I am one of them, so they will let me pass freely into the cliff face openings. I have a feeling that this is where Elaine is staying with her family."

"Very well," Eva replied. "But keep your tablet with you, so I can freely communicate with you if necessary. I don't trust the AI Fighters, even if they may appear naïve. And Walter, be careful." Her azure eyes became almost silver in the pale light of the moon, and her ivory skin shimmered an ethereal shade of blue, similar to how Emilia appeared in her spirit form.

"I will, Eva," he said, smiling gratefully. Without the support of Eva and her equine companions, he could not have survived these past few weeks.

With that, Walter drank a teaspoonful of lydion and set off alone toward the cliff face. He was still tired from the spell he had worked earlier, but the lydion helped to offset the fatigue.

The AI Fighters were lined up neatly along the base of the cliff, and Walter advanced slowly toward them. The nearest one turned his angular face in Walter's direction, unslinging the rifle from his shoulder and chambering a cartridge. Walter saluted the AI Fighter with the patriotic Khalendi salute that he had seen AI Fighters use to greet each other in Crystal City. The lydion's nanomachines had now permeated enough of his bloodstream that he was not fearful about encountering the AI Fighters, and he welcomed the challenge.

The AI Fighter returned the salute after a few moments.

Walter breathed a sigh of relief that the disguise was working. It may not have been effective in the bright light of day—he did not look identical to an AI Fighter, and traces of his human form were still evident—but at nighttime, an AI Fighter could easily mistake a human who had consumed lydion for one of them.

The AI Fighter was guarding one of the trails that led up into the network of caves inside the cliff face. As he approached the cyborg, Walter tried to mimic the AI Fighters' mannerisms and gestures, keeping his movements sharp, rigid, and minimizing any spontaneity in them.

The AI Fighter addressed him in fluent Khalendi when he was a few feet away, startling Walter. He was initially concerned that he had been identified as a human, but then he realized that it was common for AI Fighters to address each other in Khalendi—a custom that was virtually nonexistent amongst the elite AI Masters.

"What post do you have here?" the AI Fighter inquired in his gratingly harsh, metallic voice.

For a few moments, Walter was at a loss for words; the question had caught him unprepared, and he was not sure how to respond. He improvised.

"There is rumor of unrest amongst several of the Xeyan'na who work in this mine. I have come to address it and restore order. I have been tasked with interrogating those responsible for fomenting the discontent."

The AI Fighter cocked his head to one side, as if sizing Walter up. Walter felt the steadying influence of the lydion weakening, as if he were about to dissolve back into his old human self. He took a deep breath and stared back at the AI Fighter with a level gaze.

After a few painful moments, the AI Fighter stepped to one side, and Walter gave another salute to him as he passed. He could now feel the lydion settling into his bloodstream, calming and centering him. He took out his flashlight so that he could see the trail ahead, which was pitch black and curved steeply upwards into the limestone cliffside. After he had ascended this trail for about half a mile, Walter arrived at a tunnel that cut sharply through the rock. The flashlight was not necessary here—torches lined the walls of the tunnel, which branched out into numerous pathways. Walter was overwhelmed at the vast size of this tunnel network, and he had the overwhelming impression that he was stepping into a maze, from which there might be no return.

His morale began to decline after about twenty minutes of wandering through the tunnels, without any sign of human life. Walter also realized that the farther he journeyed into these caves, the longer it would take him to find his way out, if he could do so at all. But just when he was about to give up and retrace his steps back toward the entrance, he spotted it: a beautiful fire lizard with orange and black markings, exactly like the one that Elaine had found, and formed a bond with, in Vei'arash. He paused right in front of Walter, as if greeting him, and then scampered away. Walter had the eerie feeling he was leading him somewhere. Walter felt optimistic upon seeing the creature, but the lydion suppressed the intensity of his elation. *Could this be one of Elaine's lizards?* he asked himself.

The lizard brought him to a large cavern, seemingly the area where all the maze-like tunnels converged. Its walls were dazzling hues of pink, beige, and white, and the ceiling, covered in stalactites and helictites, had a luminous silver shimmer to it. Stone pillars and other rock formations filled the cavern, casting colorful shadows upon the walls. In the center of the room was a large pool of water, which appeared to be steaming with tendrils of heat. Scattered throughout the cavern were people sleeping soundly on blankets; some of them even had makeshift shelters made of tin, wood, and scraps of metal. Most of the cavern's occupants were clustered around the perimeter, in a layout which reminded Walter of the Crate, the panopticon-shaped prison in Jamestown that Walter had sought to rescue his brother from. Yet this place felt much less oppressive, and although AI Fighters guarded the cliffs from the outside, he could not feel their watchful presence inside.

The lizard led Walter up to a group of people at the northern end of the cavern. Since everyone was sleeping, his presence went unnoticed. Walter saw that the inhabitants of the cavern were Xeyan'na, their auburn hair betraying their identities. He also knew, instinctively— although he could not recognize their faces in the dim light of the cavern—that Elaine was among these sleeping Xeyan'na people. After taking a long drink of water from his canteen, he sensed that the nanomachines that had taken root inside of him were beginning to dissipate. Back in his human form, Walter felt joy and sorrow collide within him, the twin emotions that often surfaced during a reunion of lovers who had been parted for a long time. With the lydion gone, he could feel Elaine's presence—or rather, he could smell her scent, a unique combination of jasmine, citrus, and rosehip. The lizard scampered up to a girl who was curled up next to another fire lizard, this one the color of jade, the sacred hue of the Rebellion. Walter realized that these two lizards were, indeed, the companions Elaine had encountered in Vei'arash, and a wave of joy and relief flooded through him.

Walter did not wish to startle her, but before he knew it Elaine's eyes were open. He was taken aback that she did not seem surprised to see him.

"I was just dreaming about you," she said, quietly to avoid waking the others. "I knew you were here, and I could feel your presence in my dreams." She looked tired and pale, but otherwise the same as when she had departed from Serrahan several months ago.

Tears surfaced in Walter's grey eyes, and he embraced Elaine tightly.

"I came here because I had a dream about *you*," he told her.

"But aren't you busy with... I can't say," she said. "We shouldn't be talking about such things here."

"I know what you are talking about," Walter replied. "I am busy with it, but I need your help," he said, lowering his voice to a whisper. Some of the people sleeping nearby stirred but did not awaken. "Your fire lizards... could I have one of them for a while? I think you know why I need it."

Elaine pursed her lips and ran her fingers through her hair. It was an idiosyncrasy of hers to do that whenever she was thinking carefully about something serious, and Walter found it endearing.

"I will give Terra to you," she said, gesturing to the male lizard. "He seems to like you; he found you and led you here, did he not?"

"He did," Walter said solemnly.

"Is that the only reason you came then?" Elaine said, her eyes suddenly filled with sadness.

Walter embraced her again. "No, I came because I love you, and want to see you before I... I am not sure if I will make it out of there alive, Elaine," he said, his voice trembling.

Elaine stared at him with a fiercely intense expression, until he felt embarrassed and had to turn his eyes away. When he looked at her again, she was still staring.

"You will make it out alive, Walter. If anyone can, you can. I'm just not sure what sort of world you'll be returning to..." she said, trailing off into silence. "Did you see what they did to my village? They excavated everything; it's just a scar blighting the earth as far as the eye can see. They even excavated the ancestral burial grounds, where my grandparents and great-grandparents were buried," she said, tearing up.

Walter felt rage boil up inside of him as she spoke. The AI Masters needed to pay for what they had done. He was finally beginning to understand some of Cyriana's bloodthirst and lust for vengeance toward the robots. The AI Masters may have been emotionless machines with sophisticated and agile minds, who did not actively wish harm on anyone, but the impact of their actions was reprehensible. Walter was beginning to recognize that the root of cruelty was not malicious intent, but rather the absence of feeling. The AI Masters lacked the empathy needed to see the world from a human's perspective, to share in their suffering, and to compassionately strive to ameliorate that condition.

He wanted to give Elaine hope, in this dark, hauntingly beautiful cavern inside of the cliff that towered above her ravaged village.

He spoke very faintly. "There is a place nearby, a lush valley. I believe it's one of the few remaining sites in the Barrens that is still virgin forest. It will be at the center of the Barrens' revival in the future. A majestic healing lodge will be constructed there, and hundreds of people from all over the Empire will flock to it."

Elaine stared at him in disbelief. "That's not possible... I thought that the Barrens was either desert or cultivated agricultural land."

Walter shook his head. "Not if the Talisman has shown me a true vision... in our lifetimes, Elaine, we could see this wondrous valley and this healing lodge. Perhaps we could even live in the valley together," he said, with a faint smile. "All I have to do is translate that vision into reality." He did not tell her that in his vision, he had been absent, with no explanation of where he had gone.

Tears fell from Elaine's eyes, and Walter wiped them away silently, before kissing her. He knew that they were tears of joy, rather than sorrow. Elaine gave him a second blanket that she had nearby and told him to sleep behind a nearby stone pillar that was large enough to conceal him from the other laborers. She told him that in the morning, when the other laborers went out for the day, she would stay behind with him.

"Won't the AI Fighters notice that you are not working?" Walter asked.

"I will tell my family to let them know I am sick... they allow sick days, if they are infrequent. How did you get past the guards, anyway?"

Walter showed her the vial of lydion, and her eyes widened, but confusion still registered in them. "How did you..."

"I'm here with Eva," he told her. "We were training in the mountains, and then I told her I wanted to come here to find you."

"I won't pry into your secrets," Elaine said, and Walter detected a hint of sadness in her voice. He recalled that she had once expressed frustration about the fact that she was excluded from the Rebellion's council meetings. He was doing it for her own safety, but he knew that it hurt her all the same.

"One day, I will tell you everything. I promise," Walter said, taking the blanket and kissing her one last time before he left to sleep. "One day, everything will make sense."

Tunneling

"To love is to suffer and there is no love otherwise."
— Fyodor Dostoevsky

Walter spent the next few days inside of the cliffs with Elaine. He was immensely grateful, as it was the first opportunity he'd had in the past few years to spend time alone with Elaine. The pair chatted in a relaxed way, something that they had never done since Elaine's capture. During their excursion to Vei'arash, there had been a tense silence between them, straining their relationship, but here, the tension had dissipated and they were joyful together. Walter felt as though he was falling in love with her all over again, and he could barely contain his bliss at being able to see her once more.

To pass the time, Elaine told Walter stories about her lizards, about how they had mastered the network of tunnels in these cliffs and knew how to navigate them easily. They went on walks together with the lizards, inside the tunnels, and Walter was astounded at how expansive the system really was. The place was like a huge, intricate spiderweb that had the cavern at its center, its magnificent *pièce de résistance.*

"Why don't more people hide out here? To avoid having to labor for the mine?" Walter asked as he marveled at the tunnel network.

"The AI Fighters keep a tally of every laborer, and they are scanned and fingerprinted into the system. If a laborer stayed behind in the cliffs for more than a week, the AIs would send their infrared drones in here to search for them."

Walter shuddered at the thought of drones sweeping through the tunnels and making thermal images of people hiding out in the dark. He had no doubt that the punishment for transgressions against the AI Fighters' rules would be a harsh one.

"Has that ever happened?" he asked.

"A few times since I arrived here," she replied. "There've been a few older Xeyan'na who have gotten tired or were genuinely sick. The AI Fighters have no use for them, so when the older Xeyan'na simply refuse to leave the cavern, the AI Fighters come inside and take them away," she said, her lower lip trembling. "I have an idea of where they go, and it's not pleasant to think of."

"Where do they go?" Walter asked, feeling mounting revulsion.

"I've seen the AI Masters take them up the trails to the top of the cliffs... where the wolves live," she said, brushing a tear aside. "I'm just glad my grandparents aren't alive anymore, so they don't have to suffer through this horrendous period. I can only hope that it passes soon, and the AI Fighters get their due. Walter, there must be something more I can do... something more we can do to help the Rebellion. I told you already that I will give you Terra. But if there is anything else..."

"There is," Walter said, after a moment's reflection. "We need more Xeyan'na to assist in the Rebellion. If you know of any who are willing to join us." He realized, then, that it was unfair to keep Elaine in the dark about what they were planning to do with the lizard and any Xeyan'na natives who joined their army.

"Elaine, after you left Serrahan, we... I know you will think this is crazy, but we learned the art of shapeshifting from the inhabitants of the village. We found notebooks inside the house of one of the Mages, Yensin, which had been penned by a descendant of the Druids. They were some of the last accounts of the ancient practice of shapeshifting into animal form, which the Druids had practiced for centuries before it was eventually outlawed in Serrahan.

"And in one of the notebooks, we found the shapeshifting spells. We also found something else... information about a curse that would befall some people who stayed too long in the form of an animal. This was referred to as the curse of the Druids. But even with this knowledge of the curse, we decided to move ahead with a plan to shapeshift in our fight against the AI Masters."

Elaine's eyes widened. "Hold on," she said. "You are planning to shapeshift?"

"Not me," Walter said, reddening. He was beginning to regret having divulged all this information to Elaine, who wasn't even a council member of the Jade Rebellion. Somehow, though, he felt very uncomfortable at the notion of taking her lizard but not telling her what his plans were with it.

"But yes, my fellow rebels, we are planning to use shapeshifting as a weapon in our arsenal against the AI Masters. It confuses their minds… their minds which are structured to think so logically and scientifically that they can't possibly comprehend anything beyond the bounds of physical reality."

"And so," Elaine said, running her fingers through her hair and breathing quite rapidly, "your fellow rebels are planning to shapeshift into the forms of animals?"

"Yes… and if any Xeyan'na are willing to join in this effort, they are welcome to. We are using Mages and bringing recruits up from the Southern Jungles to build our spirit army," he said.

"Wait. You said you were shapeshifting into the forms of animals… what is this about spirits?"

"You can shapeshift into either the living or spirit form of the animal," Walter explained. "But you need to be in the presence of the animal in order for the spell to work."

"That is why you need my lizard, then," she exclaimed. Though her eyes became clouded and distant, a spark re-ignited inside of them shortly afterwards. Walter was afraid that she would be upset with him, but instead her tone was peaceful and joyous.

"I am honored to participate in your plan, Walter, however small my contribution," she said. "And I do believe that I know some Xeyan'na who would be willing to come with you."

It was now Walter's turn to be surprised.

"You do? Who are these people?" he asked with avid interest.

"A faction has been developing amongst the laborers… a faction that has, up until now, been very good at concealing their motives. They've been plotting, for quite some time I believe, a sort of uprising against the AI Fighters who patrol the mine. Thankfully, cooler heads have prevailed, and other Xeyan'na have talked them out of their foolhardy plan. They talk all the time about how they outnumber the AI Fighters, how they could easily destroy them, but their plan lacks finesse. For instance, even assuming the AI Fighters don't use their automated rifles to make quick work of these laborers, what are they going to do next? We all live off the supplies of dried rice, lentils, and salted meat that the AI Fighters provide to us. Those AI Fighters obtain these supplies from traders and others they have complex relationships with. And it's not just a matter of winning against the AI Fighters at this mine site—the whole Barrens is crawling with robots and drones."

"I've seen the checkpoints," Walter admitted. "The surveillance in this region is unlike anything I've ever seen before, even in Crystal City. You are right that their plan lacks finesse. An uprising in this mine would not go far, especially if they don't have any sophisticated weapons. But we could use those laborers in our Rebellion," Walter suggested.

Elaine became intensely contemplative. "Assuming they agree to come along with you, how would you leave the Barrens unnoticed?"

Walter recalled the time-slowing magic he had used on the traders. "There are methods we could use to avoid any unwanted... interference," he said, choosing his words carefully. "But the most important thing is that they voluntarily wish to accompany us. They will be useful to grow our army against the AI Masters, but they need to be aware of the risks... most of all, the risk that the curse of the Druids could take hold of them."

"These laborers I spoke of," Elaine replied, "they don't seem to be the type to care about risks to their own safety. In fact, it would probably be safer for them to go with you than to stay here and concoct their absurd plans alone."

"Excellent... well, speak to them tonight, then, after they are back from their labors."

This was the last night that Walter would be spending in the cliffside; Eva had messaged him earlier to remind him of their timelines for getting back to Crystal City. She had also indicated that, while she was safely camped out of the sightline of the AI Fighters, she was frightened about the prospect of being spotted by them, or the traders.

There were only a precious few hours before the laborers would return and Walter would hide away behind the stone pillar in the cavern. Elaine had initially proposed that she introduce him to her parents and brothers, but Walter was unprepared for such a meeting.

"One day, when all of this chaos with the robots is over, your family will be living in a true home again and I will come over for dinner," Walter assured Elaine. "Then I can make a proper introduction," he said.

"What if you never return?" Elaine asked, tears suddenly surfacing in her forest-green eyes. "Isn't that a very real possibility?"

"It is," Walter said solemnly.

"I don't want to lose you," Elaine said. Walter was taken aback by the intensity of her words; earlier, when they were together in Vei'arash and later in Serrahan, she had been much cooler, more distant. Walter hoped that she had simply needed more time to reflect on her feelings for him. He suddenly recalled that in visions and dreams, either triggered by the Talisman or not, he had seen the possibility that Elaine would bear him a daughter. He had seen more than the possibility—he had seen the girl herself, a lovely child with dark hair and green eyes. He had also been told by Shiva, the great god on Mount Samaya, that he would need to pass along the Talisman to his daughter. It occurred to him, though, that if he died while on his final mission to Central Command—or, somewhat more nefariously, *disappeared*—he would never have the chance to make a child with Elaine.

Taking her hand, he led Elaine to the pool in the center of the cavern. There was not a soul around, and they undressed and made their way into the geothermally heated waters. He told her of his visions, as he embraced her tightly, breathing in her wondrous scent.

"Is destiny something that is fixed, or is it something that we can change?" she asked him. "Does our knowledge of these visions alter the course of our futures?"

"If I've learned anything from the Talisman," Walter told her, "it's that destiny depends on which path you take. So, perhaps, there is no fixed destiny. But destiny is always aligned with our truest desires, which we have little control over," he said.

"My truest desire is you. So, you are my destiny," Elaine told him, as they surrendered to the bliss of lovemaking. The joy they enjoyed was bittersweet, however, and every kiss was tinged with sadness: the sadness of a window closing. The opportunity they had to be alone together would end in a few hours, and what awaited them after that was ominous: the prospect of being separated forever.

Late that night, while most of the cavern's occupants were sleeping soundly, Elaine introduced Walter to the subversive faction. Fortunately, the lighting of the cave was so dim that Walter slipped by the other laborers without being noticed; even those who were awake could not recognize him. After a lengthy trek to the opposite end of the cavern, the pair of lovers came across a huddle of about six men squatting around a modest campfire. They were pale and unshaven, and their bony statures contrasted starkly with those of the burly, muscled traders Walter and Eva had encountered a few days prior. Walter had assumed that laboring every day in a mine would bulk a man up, but he realized that it was not a lack of exercise that was the problem; the men's diets were clearly deficient.

The laborers regarded Walter with suspicious gazes, but one of them, a tall, shaggy-haired man with a crooked nose and sunken eyes, nodded in greeting at Elaine.

"Good evening, lizard lady," he said, in a mock serious tone that set his companions off laughing. The faction was a fair distance from the rest of the laborers, but the cavern's shape amplified voices, so Elaine kept hers to a low whisper.

"My friend Walter has a proposition for you."

The men kept laughing, but Walter spoke eloquently, and eventually they settled down.

"I am part of a rebel group that is fighting the AI Masters," he said quietly. He knew he was taking a risk, but the prospect of securing their help justified it.

"I am not going to divulge the details of our plans to you here. I can only say that if you come with me, I will lead you to the kingdom of the Mages, where you will be greeted by royalty. If you swear an oath of secrecy and loyalty to our organization, you will be welcomed into our ranks and serve a cause I know you will find worthy: striking back against our oppressors—not just at the unit of AI Fighters that is currently guarding the mine site, but at *all* the AI Masters and AI Fighters in the Empire of Khalendar. You will have access to the most sophisticated tools at your disposal, which will give you the very best chance of succeeding in battle."

The man with the crooked nose spat on the ground next to the campfire.

"We'd do it in a heartbeat," he said. "I wouldn't find anything quite as satisfactory as destroying those twisted machines. But escaping here would be difficult—nigh impossible, I'd guess. We won't leave unless we're promised a safe route out."

The other men nodded and murmured in agreement.

Walter hesitated before replying. He could try to use the Talisman to slow time again, but that episode with the traders had left him on the brink of exhaustion. He did not know whether he had the energy to do that again. But after a few moments of further reflection, Walter had seized on a different answer.

"I told one of the AI Fighters guarding this cliffside that I was tasked with finding unruly and rebellious laborers and interrogating them. I could advise him that I have been ordered by a more elite AI Master to bring you back to Crystal City for punishment…"

A man with a long, wispy beard and dark undereye circles spoke up. "Sounds like the best plan we've heard in weeks. I'm tired of following plans that don't work, though, so if yours blows up, you'll have hell to pay."

Despite the confidence he projected, Walter's palms were sweating, and he yearned for the lydion to assuage his anxious mind.

"It is settled then," Walter said. "We leave now."

"Now? No time for our beauty sleep?" the bearded man asked jokingly. He and his fellow laborers seemed to be energized by the prospect of adventure, and they packed up their satchels with enthusiasm. None of them appeared to be particularly attached to their makeshift campground. Walter realized that these were men with little to lose—they were all single, with no present attachments to wives or children, and Walter had a feeling that they wouldn't hesitate to put their lives in danger for a valiant mission.

He, on the other hand, had someone to lose. The love of his life, Elaine, was staring at him with glassy eyes and a trembling lip.

"I suppose this is goodbye," she said, in a faint voice. Terra had scuttled onto her shoulder and now hopped over to Walter's. The lizard, like the humans, knew what had to be done.

Elaine suppressed a sob as she looked at Walter and her lizard companion.

"Farewell, Elaine," Walter said. "Remember, I love you. You are my destiny."

The men snickered at what appeared to them to be an overly sentimental exchange between the two lovers, but Walter wasn't bothered by the audience. He embraced Elaine tightly and kissed her one final time before leaving. Terra led the way into the winding, dark passageways of the labyrinthine tunnel network, and Elaine was gone. Walter's heart was plummeting into an abyss, and only one thing could make him feel better. He took a sip of lydion and kept going.

After Walter had transitioned, the laborers interacted with him differently. It was obvious that they had never seen someone take such a high dose of lydion, and fear registered on their faces when they saw Walter's altered body. "We know what lydion is, and we understand its potential uses," the crooked-nosed man, whose name was Penrose, explained. "It's just that some of those uses have only ever been theoretical to us, up until now."

"There's nothing to be afraid of," Walter said, though he was skeptical of the truth of that statement. "It's just a biological process. The nanomachines dissolve into your bloodstream, and they change not just your physical appearance but the very substance of your thoughts and feelings. In high concentrations, it's probably the most transformative substance known to humankind. That's why it fetches such a premium," he explained.

Suddenly, his tablet buzzed. A pulse of dread, albeit weakened by the lydion, passed through him as he read the message from Eva on it: *The traders have arrived. Saw them talking with the AI Fighter who was guarding the entrance you passed through. Can't say for sure but looks like he sent someone inside to find you. Another AI Fighter. Get out of there, Walter.*

Walter's fear was numbed by the lydion, but apparently the chemical did not eliminate the emotion completely, because the young man's hands began shaking involuntarily. Penrose noticed his anxious state.

"Took too much of it, did you?" Penrose asked in a jeering tone.

"Everyone, silent," Walter commanded. "Be completely still." He glanced toward the lizard, Terra. "Terra needs to detect something for me. There's someone coming after us, and we need to avoid them. Can you detect them, Terra?" he asked, realizing how absurd this request probably sounded. On a deeper level, though, he intuited that Terra could understand him perfectly.

As the men's tittering laughter quieted down, the *drip-drip-drip* of cool water from the dangling stalactites became the only audible sound. But Terra wasn't listening for that sound, or for any sound at all. He was feeling the subtle vibrations from the tunnel floor, the ones that were triggered by the slightest movement. After several painstaking moments, the lizard appeared to have recognized some movement and determined the direction it was coming from: straight ahead of them. The lizard turned swiftly in the other direction.

"We're going back?" Penrose moaned.

Walter put a hand to his lips. "Not a sound," he whispered curtly. The rebel leader led the men back toward the cavern, but just as he had anticipated, there was another tunnel that branched off sharply, and they took it. And then another, and another. They tried to lose themselves in the labyrinth, so that the menacing figure that was after them—a dangerous robot armed to the teeth—would not find them.

The laborers did not speak again, but their shuffling steps were still loud and heavy. Walter knew that AI Fighters had a delicate sense of hearing. Fighters were designed with all their senses amplified beyond those of a human—except for taste, which they didn't need—so that they could expertly prevail over humans in combat. Walter motioned for them to stop, and the men froze in their tracks. But something was wrong; Terra had disappeared. In the dim light of the tunnel, Walter could only see a few feet ahead of him. The lizard could have been farther ahead, but the creature's prolonged absence was nagging at him.

Suddenly, a hand stretched out from the pitch darkness. Its spindly metallic fingers were wrapped around the lizard's fragile body, pinning him in place as he struggled to escape.

"Looking for this?" the machine asked in a hollow voice. With lightning speed, its other hand shot out from the darkness and wrapped itself around Walter's neck. The metal was cold as ice, and the blunt force of the attack left Walter breathless. The men behind the young rebel leader gasped as the AI Fighter stepped closer, revealing its smooth, rubbery face and swan-like neck. It wore thick, metallic armor that glinted in the dim yellow light of the tunnel. Its spidery fingers tightened around both Walter and the lizard simultaneously. Walter was feeling himself lose oxygen, and he coughed and sputtered, panicking despite the potent effects of the lydion. The AI Fighter stared directly into his eyes with a cool, calculating stare as he raised Walter upwards so that the young man's feet hovered above the floor. Walter tried to kick the AI Fighter and struggle away, but the robot's lengthy arms meant that he was just out of reach.

"Liars are traitors. Traitors to the Empire," echoed the Fighter's grating voice across the length of the tunnel, as the men behind Walter stared at him in paralyzed awe.

"You came here to find your friend. Not to interrogate the dissidents. Not to interrogate—the dissidents. Now you pay the price. Pay the price. Pay the price…"

He seemed to be stuck in a perpetual loop and kept echoing the three words, *pay the price*, repeatedly. Meanwhile, Walter felt as though he were on the edge of losing consciousness. Just as the darkness began to overcome him, however, the AI loosened its grip, and Walter dropped to the ground, clutching his throat and gasping. He also saw the lizard, Terra, scuttle to the floor and scamper away. His confusion mounted until he saw it: the AI Fighter had been gutted with Walter's own *balayan*. The sharp, delicate sword had been in his pack, and Penrose had managed to slip a hand into it while the AI Fighter was distracted with Walter and Terra. But Walter was not clear about one thing: why the AI Fighter now seemed to be entirely incapacitated. His *balayan* had not been tipped in *samtayran*—the poison intended to destabilize the AIs' programming systems—and without that essential ingredient, it should not have accomplished what it did.

Penrose twisted the *balayan* inside of the AI Fighter, as if the Xeyan'na was relishing the feeling of perpetrating violence against his oppressor. Walter knew it would not make a difference—the AI Fighter was already done for—but Penrose seemed oblivious.

"Penrose," Walter said, trying to catch the laborer's attention so that he would stop grinding the *balayan* into the robot's torso. "What did you put on the sword?"

Penrose finally seemed to have heard Walter's voice and slowly emerged from the mists of his reverie. He turned slowly, his eyes betraying a disquieting cruelty, a blissful pleasure at what he had just done.

Penrose squinted. "They confiscated our *balayans* when we came here, of course, but I've always kept my pouch of *samtayran* in a pocket I sewed into the inside of my shirt. Thought it might come in handy one day, and it seems to have done so. You can thank your lucky stars for that, and one other thing, too: the satchel you were wearing has a latch that's easy to open. Leaves you vulnerable to thieves, but it certainly did you a service today."

"How did you know I kept a *balayan* in it?" Walter asked.

"I didn't. But you are a rebel leader, right? I thought you must have something in there worth using against that droid."

"Thank you, friend," Walter said, rubbing his throat. His voice was still raw and hoarse, and there were red, swollen imprints of the AI Fighter's finger marks on his neck.

"Any time. I'm sure you'd have done the same if I was being strangled by a droid," Penrose said. Walter was cheered by his kind words, but the unsettling memory of the laborer's expression when he had twisted the *balayan* inside the AI Fighter haunted him.

"So now what?" asked another one of the laborers, Kent, a short man with closely cropped hair and a sneering expression. "We're just supposed to prance out of here like nothing happened? What happens when you kill a droid?"

"He's not dead," Walter said, and some of the men scoffed at his words. "I mean, you can't kill a computer. You can destroy its ability to function, but there's always a slim possibility of reviving it. Well, usually. Sometimes, it's true, it can be damaged beyond all repair. But I don't think that's what *samtayran* accomplishes."

Penrose looked contemplative before speaking up. "Does that mean someone could fix him and check his memory to find out what happened?"

Walter grimaced. The central processing unit—colloquially known as a chip—could always be accessed, even after the *samtayran* had done its work. He knew that it would contain images of what had taken place, like frames in a movie, and that it needed to be destroyed if those images were to be kept out of the reach of other ill-intentioned AIs. He turned the AI Fighter over; he'd never extracted a chip from a robot before, but from what he had heard, it just involved removing a slat at the base of his head and dislodging the chip. Sure enough, there was an identifiable piece of metal there that looked like it could slide out. After a few futile attempts to remove the slat by pulling it outwards, he pressed on it as if it were a button, and it cooperated with him by popping out. The chip was in plain sight: a rectangular box with curved edges on one end, almost like a large bullet. As the other laborers hovered around him, watching intently, Walter removed it with a single, firm pull and then slid the metal slat back to its original position.

"I'll be damned," Kent said in amazement. "Who knew all that intelligence could fit in the palm of your hand?"

Walter stared at the box with a similar degree of reverence, but he knew that there was no time to indulge in philosophical contemplation of artificially intelligent minds. They needed to get out, and quickly.

He pinged Eva a message: *Did the traders just speak to the one AI Fighter? If so, can you deal with him?* He waited what seemed like an excruciating amount of time before a response appeared on his tablet's screen.

Yes, they spoke to just that one, Eva's message read. *They left a few minutes ago, thank the gods. What happened to the Fighter that he sent in after you?*

Walter responded swiftly. *We dealt with him. But you never answered my question—can you deal with the AI Fighter the traders spoke to?*

After a few moments, Eva replied. *I'm not sure what you mean by 'deal with him.' I can't use violence—not out in the open here. But if you are asking if I can use my powers of telepathy on him, the answer is yes. But sometimes their minds are strong. If I can get inside it, distract it, infuse it with thoughts that cripple its original motivations, then we will succeed. If I can't... well, I don't want to think of what might happen. Each one of those fighters is armed with an automatic rifle. And what is your plan if I deal with him? Are you just going to try and trick the rest of them?*

Don't worry about what I'll do, Walter messaged back. *Just focus on using your abilities on the single Fighter. We will get out of this alive, Eva. I have a meeting to get to, remember?*

The forthrightness of Eva's response surprised Walter. *Hah. Haven't forgotten. Time is ticking, Walter. But I guess you know all about how time works... and how to manipulate it. What you did with the traders frightens me. The Talisman you have has made you more than human... it's turned you into a god. Don't dismiss those kinds of powers lightly. If the AIs find out about them, they'll steal your Talisman and murder you in cold blood.*

Despite wanting to say more, Walter kept his reply brief. *I don't want any of these powers, Eva. I just want to be ordinary. Now, let's get out of here so I can get to that meeting on time.*

Surfacing

"Not knowing when the dawn will come / I open every door."
— Emily Dickinson

As he led the laborers out of the vast network of tunnels, seeking the slightest ray of light in the thick and stifling darkness, Walter was grateful for Terra's sharp navigational abilities. The lizard seemed to have lost some of his previous energy, though, and Walter guessed that the creature was demoralized after the unexpected encounter with the AI Fighter. He knew there was no reason for the little reptile to feel ashamed; the AI Fighter's unique sensory apparatus was no match for even a divinely gifted fire lizard.

Walter had first learned about the unique talents of AI Fighters while working for the government of Khalendar as a computer code translator. Before then, he had always assumed AIs were at a disadvantage when it came to their senses. It was somewhat revelatory for him when he learned that the AIs' heightened senses were precisely the feature that had enabled their intelligence to progress at such an unparalleled rate. Humans' brains were no different; the shape and structure of the brain developed in tandem with the sensory inputs it received. Walter had simply never suspected that an artificial being could be designed to have superior sensory inputs to a living, breathing person or animal. Apparently, this was the technological breakthrough that had led to the current evolutionary model of AIs, and it was made possible only through an intimate understanding of cognition.

Ever since he started using the lydion, Walter had felt an increasingly strong connection with the AIs, and he realized that even though he would never *be* an AI, he could experience a similar enough mental state to empathize with them. There were undeniable parallels between humans and AIs, but Walter knew that there was a rift between the two species that could never, perhaps, be bridged. AIs weren't burdened with the weight of emotion or love, and they didn't have the tight bonds of kinship that humans had; however, they displayed a remarkable ability to organize into a hierarchical order, which suggested that they understood the concept of loyalty to a higher being or cause. Still, they were not grouped into family or partnership units the way humans were. As far as Walter could tell, they weren't ever lonely, but they willingly performed group rituals and tasks to serve the needs of the collective. Their interactions with others had a utilitarian bent and did not seem to be motivated by the fundamental need to be close to another person. Walter envied them, in a way, because the lowest moments of his life had been caused by attachments to other individuals, too: his parents, his brother, and even Elaine. Of course, he couldn't imagine his life without his loved ones, but he could also see the appeal of having no desire for human attachment.

The laborers who accompanied Walter seemed at first to be like that, too: companions who loosely associated with each other but lacked any deep connections to other humans. It may have been out of choice, but Walter suspected that isolation had been forced upon them by circumstance. When your ancestral village had been destroyed and your family home had been uprooted, starting fresh was perhaps the most palatable option. Walter shuddered as he wondered whether something terrible had happened to the men's wives and children, and he knew it was a real possibility given the AIs' rapacious leveling of Te'yara. He decided that it would be best not to ask.

As Walter spent more and more time with them, he could see that his initial assessment had been off the mark, and he came to realize that they were all too human. They became tired and hungry easily, and he even heard some of them whisper to each other about lovers or friends they had left behind in the cavern. The lydion erased all traces of fatigue from Walter, but he knew that the mask was only temporary and that when it came off, he'd drop quickly from exhaustion.

Just as he was about to propose that they settle down to sleep for a few hours, Terra became excited. The delicate fire lizard scuttled up ahead and then circled back several times to Walter as though trying to communicate.

Walter instinctually knew they were close to the exit, but he needed to warn Eva. *We are coming out of the caves in a few moments; you must distract the Fighter now.*

The response was immediate this time, and it reassured Walter. *Going inside now.*

He knew she didn't mean the tunnel.

It was then that he saw the light; a faint glow at first, it grew in intensity as they walked further ahead. Terra had faithfully led them to an opening in the limestone cliffs. Walter felt the excitement creeping up inside of him, from a place that was deeper than the superficial part of him affected by the lydion. He instructed the laborers to act like his prisoners: *stay in a single file behind me, and quietly and obediently follow whatever I tell you to do. I will handle the talking with the AI Fighter.* When he felt the lydion wavering, as if it were a chimera threatening to dissolve into the shadows, he took another sip and shuddered as he felt its cool, calming influence pervade his body. *I can see how this stuff can become addictive,* he thought, with a pang of sadness that quickly left him.

The light at the end of the tunnel was nearly blinding. After spending several days in the womblike cavern, emerging into actual sunlight was a surreal experience. It was a refreshing feeling, as if Walter was surfacing from a long dive underwater. The beauty of the desert, with its bright, exotic sands, dusty purple shrubs, and far-flung horizons, was also vividly apparent to him. Even the mine, etched cruelly into the surface of the earth, now seemed beautiful in its own peculiarly unsettling way. Walter felt an expansiveness, as if he were experiencing all the visions of the Talisman at once: possibilities stretched out before him, as far as the eye could see. But there was one painful hurdle that they needed to overcome before any of those possibilities could be realized.

Walter was afraid that the AI Fighter Eva was infiltrating would be the same one guarding the tunnel they now exited, but he breathed a sigh of relief when he saw that the slim possibility of that happening had not arisen. The Fighters were barely distinguishable in their official attire, equipped with identical weaponry, but they had certain defining characteristics. The one they saw now was rounder, shorter, its face oddly shaped like the moon.

It spun around to face them and raised its gun.

"Stop. Where you are. Right. Now."

Walter gazed into the robot's cold, soulless eyes without the slightest hint of fear. The effects of the lydion did not waver this time, and he could feel it anchoring him steadily.

"Comrade. Greetings. Let me introduce myself. I am C-20. I was instructed by AI Master Klassen to gather up these insurrectionists and bring them immediately to Central Command."

"AI Master Klassen. Of the fifth house?"

Walter felt his heart skip a beat. He hadn't simply made up the name;

it was one of the elite masters he used to take instructions from as a code translator. He wasn't sure which house Klassen belonged to, but he decided it was best to play along.

"Yes. Fifth house."

"Move aside."

Walter stepped aside to reveal the haggard-looking men, with dark-rimmed eyes, bony cheeks, and slumped shoulders.

"These men are in their prime. Not cheap," the AI Fighter said in a cold tone. "If you take them, we will lose valuable help."

Walter sighed, trying to make it appear that he was struggling internally with a complex moral dilemma.

"I know, comrade. This loss upsets me greatly. But if we do not remove them, they pose an internal threat to your operation."

The AI Fighter appeared to be softening, and it looked as though it were about to let him pass, when suddenly his neck turned sharply to the right. Another AI Fighter—Walter recognized him as the one he had spoken to before entering the tunnels—was approaching them, with swift, jarring strides. Something was wrong.

The first AI Fighter, who Walter had named Moon Face, appeared to be fixated on this AI Fighter, and it seemed as if they were communicating just by looking at each other. Moon Face's expression was enigmatic, though, and Walter cursed the inability to read AI Fighters' thoughts based on their facial expressions. His thoughts couldn't have been pleasant, because he reached for his rifle, and then gripped it firmly in his hands, and then... he suddenly stopped. The rifle fell from his hands and clattered to the ground, making a sharp clanging sound that caused other AI Fighters to turn their gaze toward Moon Face. The other AI Fighter, who just moments ago had been marching toward Moon Face at a brisk pace, was now retreating backward.

"My, am I ever clumsy," Moon Face said in a confused voice. His eyes flickered between the rifle and Walter. "If I may, can I ask... can I ask..." He appeared to be torn between curiosity and shame, but not wanting to express either.

"Worry not about this, comrade," Walter said in a reassuring, confident tone. "We will speak about it no further." He bent over and picked up the rifle obligingly, handing it to Moon Face as though the AI Fighter was a dear friend of his. As he did so, he felt the questioning gaze of the AI Fighter who had retreated burning upon him. Brazenly, Walter glanced over at him and nodded briskly, in an officious and friendly manner. The AI Fighter averted his gaze. There was something odd about his expression, as though he had forgotten where he had placed something very important and was trying to remember. The same expression, eerily, was etched on Moon Face.

"Well," Walter continued, trying to avoid any lingering awkwardness, "I hope you enjoy your day, comrade."

Moon Face looked up at him questioningly, but Walter felt relieved when he nodded. "Every day in service to the Empire is a good day," Moon Face said, this time with more conviction in his voice.

"Indeed," Walter said. He wished he knew the typical salute to the Empire, and Moon Face looked at him as though he were expecting him to say it. If he said the wrong thing, it might raise suspicions.

Walter was torn between taking a risk and staying silent, but his relief was immense when Moon Face spoke.

"Hail the *Anax*! Hail Khalendar!" Moon Face said mechanically.

Walter nodded. "Hail the *Anax*! Hail Khalendar!" he repeated enthusiastically. This seemed to satisfy Moon Face, and his smug expression was Walter's cue to leave.

Walter felt as though a great burden had been lifted from his shoulders when he rejoined Eva and saw her smiling face. He longed to ask her what she had done, how she had miraculously managed to reverse the steps of the AI Fighter, but he saw from her expression that she would prefer to keep it a secret, at least for now. Had she and Walter been alone, he suspected that she may have been more candid, but now there were six laborers travelling with them. Walter knew that Eva's gift could easily make it seem as though she were aligned with the AIs, and he had made the mistake before of taking it as a sign of treachery to their cause.

He also suspected that Eva was wary of travelling with men again; her misadventure with the traders had been undoubtedly traumatic for her. But she was strong and independent-minded, a value he respected in her. She introduced herself to the laborers politely, and they seemed deferential and respectful of her as the only woman in the group. Walter knew that she was doing a valiant job of pushing the trauma of what had happened to her aside and moving forward, her thoughts focused keenly on the goals of the Rebellion. Walter felt ashamed for having doubted her loyalty in the past, particularly after she had helped him with so much these past few weeks. Instead of being concerned about her back in Vei'arash, he ought to have been focused on the real traitor, Cyriana.

"What do you think happened to Cyriana and Jonathan?" Walter asked her the next morning, as they were making steady progress westward. They were travelling on foot; there were only two horses to eight people, so it did not make sense for only two to be on horseback, and they wanted to give Epa and Epos a break from carrying heavy loads.

"They're in Crystal City, I'm sure of it," Eva replied. "Cyriana would want to be as close to the action as possible. Perhaps they're in some abandoned warehouse in the suburbs, hiding with that big cat of hers and plotting out their war strategy. If anyone saw Sekhmet, it would surely raise official attention—north of the Meridian mountains creatures like that are all caged away in zoos. A wild, free jaguar would be immediately reported to the AI Masters, tranquilized, and captured at the first opportunity."

Walter snorted in mild amusement. "I couldn't imagine Cyriana being happy if that were to happen. She would no doubt attempt to kill anyone who laid their hands on her precious Sekhmet."

"Don't underestimate her intelligence," Eva cautioned. "Cyriana wouldn't be so naïve as to let them catch sight of her in the open. They would be somewhere well-camouflaged, somewhere hidden away."

Walter contemplated the possibilities—there were many excellent hiding spots on the outskirts of Crystal City. An entire faction of rebels had gone unnoticed by the authorities for months in Tsei'watu, in the Forest of Antheia. And then there were the grasslands bordering Jamestown and the Crate, where he had first met Emilia. There was no shortage of places to conceal yourself if you were clever. And Cyriana certainly was clever, he had to admit to that.

"But what is their plan? To storm Central Command?" Walter mused out loud. "Surely, any person would know that such an enterprise is futile, even a headstrong girl like Cyriana. I grant, she has magical abilities like any Mage... and more importantly, she has the goddess of war on her side. But she has no army, like we will have. Isn't that what war is about? Allies and armies—not a single person charging forward in battle?"

"Indeed, you are right," Eva said. "Isolated from allies, she is not as powerful. But she was privy to your council meetings, and she knows about our strategy to psychologically weaken the AI Masters with the animal spirits. She might be biding her time, waiting for us to do the grunt work before she strikes and claims the glory for herself."

Walter sighed. "You could be right, but I don't recall patience being a quality of hers. I don't see how she will accomplish anything with brute force alone. And my brother... their alliance makes me more uneasy than anything. At least, I am guessing they are allies. The truth is that their interests could very well be diametrically opposed. He could be leading her into a trap, or vice versa," Walter said uneasily. "The worst part is not knowing whose future she might jeopardize—my brother's, or the Rebellion's."

Eva shrugged. "We're doing everything we can, Walter. I know you'd like to be secure in knowing the unknown, but sometimes you just need to have faith that everything will work out as it should."

Walter grimaced. His mind flashed to his encounter with Cyriana in the forest, when she had taunted and belittled him, made him feel like he wasn't fit to lead the rebels. She had overheard him talking after his winter vision and berated him after she learned that a terrible fate might befall the world if Walter made a mistake. She had also done something much worse: stolen the Talisman and tried to murder him in cold blood. Walter tried to push thoughts of this aside, dismissing it as the juvenile expression of a young girl's insecurities, but a part of him was unable to shake the haunting memory. A part of him, too, believed that what she had said was true. He had already taken on far too much responsibility to be liberated from the fear of failure—and more importantly, its consequences.

The laborers, Walter soon learned, had spent most if not all their lives in the village of Te'yara. His first impression was that this insular existence contrasted starkly with the colorful and adventurous lives of the traders they had met, and even his own life so far. Even before he had become a rebel hiding from the authorities, he had lived a life of travel and cosmopolitanism, like many of the privileged youths who grew up in Crystal City. He had also been blessed by circumstance since his mother Carla had a job as a stewardess on the zeppelins, which meant that his family took frequent trips to Scarlet Isle, a large island to the west of Crystal City, and Tyne, a pretty town several hundred miles to the east. Both destinations were popular with the wealthy elite of Crystal City— they lacked the political unrest and moral discomfort associated with the Barrens, and they were picturesque locales for a charming holiday escape.

Yet Walter soon realized that his initial view of the laborers as small-minded, isolated villagers, was not only snobbish, but it was also patently incorrect. Even though they hadn't traveled many places, they still had encyclopedic knowledge about the world and how it worked. On one occasion, Eva scraped her ankle on a rock, and one of the laborers led her to a cypress tree whose leaves had antibacterial properties. Another evening, while Walter was feeling particularly tired and run down, another laborer found a wild licorice plant that was reputed to boost the immune system. Both treatments proved effective. Whereas Walter had previously viewed the desert as an empty, desolate place, the laborers had opened his eyes to the plethora of botanical treasures it offered for those willing to look.

"There were forests here once," Penrose told Walter wistfully one evening as they sat around a campfire, dining on salted pork and beans. "The mighty Icewhisper River had fertile banks and was surrounded by tall, sturdy oaks, cypresses, and pines. Of course, there was still desert further away from the river, but not nearly as dry as the one you see today. The cypress tree I showed Eva... it gives me hope that the land here might recover one day."

"How do you know so much about the history and geography of the Barrens, if you've lived in Te'yara your whole life?" Walter asked.

"Before Te'yara was destroyed," the man explained, "most common folk, like me, stayed near the village their entire lives, farming, mining, or fishing in the local riverway. But there are two other distinct classes of citizens in the Barrens: traders and storytellers. The traders, who only developed into a coherent class after colonization, are upstarts and opportunists, having taken every possible chance to form alliances with the droids. They cozied up to the robots quickly, betraying their own people," he explained. Walter reflected on the crude mannerisms of Tyrian and the other traders he had encountered with Eva, and he wasn't surprised by what Penrose was telling him. "The storytellers, on the other hand, have always been faithful to their traditions and their culture," Penrose continued. "They are an ancient, venerated, and scholarly class of Xeyan'na. Educated in the oral bardic tradition, they roam the countryside singing songs, reciting poetry and, obviously, telling stories to every villager who will listen. And most are thrilled to hear the stories; it is considered a great honor to listen to a tale recited by a storyteller.

"The traders and storytellers couldn't be more diametrically opposed to each other, but they do share one common trait: mobility. Both classes are blessed with the ability to travel far and wide rather than living in a single place, which sets them apart from the ordinary Xeyan'na citizen. It can be beautiful to live in one place your whole life, but also limiting. And we relied on storytellers to give us insight into the wider world. That's how I learned everything I know about this country. They weren't just good at spinning yarns, they were also brilliant medics, healers, and botanists. After soaking in knowledge from them, I could recite the properties of half a dozen plants in any vicinity of the Barrens, even if I was blindfolded."

"How inspiring," Eva interjected. "So did the storytelling just stop after the AI Masters colonized the Barrens? What happened to the storytellers?"

Penrose's face darkened. "Such an ancient and resilient culture doesn't just disappear overnight," he said with a scowl. "They're weakened and fewer in number, and those that do remain are mostly elderly. They aren't the same vibrant orators they once were, but the tradition lives on. The last of them might die in the next decade or so, I'm afraid, unless there's a revival of Xeyan'na culture before then."

Walter's curiosity was growing. "So, if they still tell stories, have you learned anything from them recently? I mean, since colonization?"

Penrose gazed at Walter for a long time before responding, as if he was searching for the right words.

"I could never do their stories justice," he said finally. "Never been a poetic type, myself. But they told of a dark shadow descending upon the land. An illness that would seize it, weakening it with each passing day. They spoke of a force beyond our control cutting off our connection to the land, severing it with an axe. They said that before things improved, they would get much, much worse. And that was before Te'yara was gutted and leveled to the ground, so I suppose their prophecies came true," he said with a mirthless laugh. "They said that the people would suffer under the burden of this shadow, that their souls would suffer. They spoke of the cherished rights and freedoms of each person being gradually stripped under the iron-fisted rule of despots."

Walter waited for the man to continue, but Penrose fell silent, gazing into the dancing flames of the campfire with a fierce, solemn expression.

"Did they say anything else?" Walter asked. "Anything to give you hope?"

Penrose's eyes narrowed as he watched the flames twist and curve

"If there were any messages of hope, I was probably too traumatized to hear them," Penrose replied. "But you know," he said, looking at Walter intently, "now that I think of it, there were a couple things they told me that stood out in my mind. I think I dismissed them out of hand as mushy metaphor, symbolic poetry. But they said something about the sacred fire lizard, which is, of course, our most treasured animal here in the Barrens. They told some story or other about the lizard forging an alliance with a stag, a creature from the North, and that together they would rise up and try to defeat the shadow. And they said something or other about a grove of trees."

Walter's heart beat faster the longer he listened to Penrose. *A lizard forging an alliance with a stag*—did that have something to do with him and Elaine?

"Penrose, are you sure?" Walter asked. Eva looked at him with wide eyes, and he could tell that they both were thinking the same thing. "Can you tell me some more details?"

Penrose looked at Walter and Eva with a startled expression. "Don't tell me you've read something into their nonsensical poetry," he said with a chuckle. "Hmm... well, I was drinking quite a bit of ale during that story, so I'm not sure I'm the best person to recount it. Don't bother asking my friends here," he said, motioning to the rest of the laborers who were chatting amongst themselves. "They were even more tipsy during the tale. Ah, sorry to disappoint you folks. But in all seriousness, I think I recall that the grove of trees was mentioned in the tale about the stag and the fire lizard."

"Did they say anything about a lush valley in the Barrens?" Walter asked, somewhat impatiently.

"Ah, yes, that was it. It was a valley, not just a grove of trees," Penrose said, shaking his head. And I'm not sure they were being metaphorical about it, either... from what I heard, it sounded like a few of the storytellers had seen it with their own eyes. Do you think that such a place exists?" he asked, naïvely.

Walter nodded. "It must exist," he said, and then turned toward Eva, who was also following the conversation with intense interest. "Eva, before we leave the Barrens, do you think we could visit this valley? I have a feeling it's close by."

Eva contemplated this for a moment. "We are in quite a hurry to get back, Walter," she reminded him. "There are only thirty-seven days remaining until your meeting."

Walter was disappointed by her response, but at the same time, he understood that their mission was the most important priority.

Penrose was watching the two of them with an amused expression.

"What's in the valley?" the laborer asked flippantly.

As Walter's mind drifted to the fall vision he had witnessed, he felt a temporary wave of euphoria pass over him.

"Our future," he replied.

Caged

"Plants are created for the sake of animals, and animals for the sake of men; the tame for our use and provision; the wild, at least for the greater part, for our provision also, or for some other advantageous purpose, as furnishing us with clothes, and the like."
– Aristotle

The travelers made slow and persistent progress across the Barrens, deliberately avoiding the most crowded areas including main roads and checkpoints. The busiest and most heavily patrolled region of the Barrens was the stretch of land bordering the banks of the Icewhisper River. The river cut across the desert like a knife, seventy miles to the south of the Meridian Mountains. Most of the colony's villages were scattered along its banks, and then there were some salt flats and mines in the arid, southerly regions that had also attracted human settlements.

To avoid the busier routes, the travelers hugged the foothills of the mountains as they made their way toward the Crossing, their only viable route back to Serrahan. It was still dry and sandy in these regions, but owing to its proximity to the mountains, the area had a variable ecology. On a few occasions they came across narrow mountain streams that flowed south toward the Icewhisper like tiny blue veins in the vast body of the desert.

One particularly hot afternoon, they stopped near one of these mountain streams for a brief respite from hiking in the desert sun. As he refilled his canteen in the cold, crisp spring water, Walter noticed Terra acting peculiarly, scuttling up and down the length of the stream. Epa and Epos were stomping their hooves and, like the lizard, appeared to have noticed something unusual. Walter turned his gaze southward, the direction the horses were looking, and it was then that he saw it: a toweringly high cement wall, a few hundred yards to the south. Apart from having such dramatic height, the wall was also very long—it stretched out for almost a mile. Walter pointed it out to the others, and everyone was startled that they hadn't noticed it before, even though it was a cloudy day and the pale grey of the cement wall was barely distinguishable from the surrounding sky.

"What do you think that is?" Walter asked Eva. When he turned to face her, he saw that she had descended into a trance, her eyes only half-open. Walter knew immediately what had happened: she was entering the mind of a machine.

Penrose glanced at her with a wary expression. "What's happening to her? She looks like she's under a curse of some kind."

"Don't mind her," Walter told the laborer, trying to sound reassuring. It was then that he noticed small black drones circling above the concrete wall. *There are machines over there*, he thought. *Drones, and potentially even AI Masters. We need to stay well-concealed.*

Walter glanced down at his tablet, and just as he had suspected, words began to appear on the screen. Eva's stream of consciousness.

Caged. That is the feeling I get when I stand here, inside this arboretum. It is beautiful, though, but a haunting beauty—like seeing a rare snow leopard trapped inside of a zoo. Are these trees the last of their kind? I can see arbutus, pines, birches, aspens, cypresses, even the occasional hickory tree. Species you don't see up north, amidst the snow-covered cedars and firs. There are paths branching through this place, and I take one of them. What lies ahead of me looks like a sizeable forest, with a stream running through it that curves downwards into a lush valley. So why was my first impression that it was an arboretum? And why did I feel caged?

I cannot trust my first impressions. As a temporary visitor inside a machine's mind, I must learn to be skeptical of the way its thoughts might color mine. The better question to ask is, why does the machine feel caged in this place? To answer that, I need to run diagnostics on this robot I am inhabiting. His name is Graham, and he is a Master of the twelfth house. He is tall and thin, not broad-shouldered like the AI Fighters. Digging into this machine's memory, I can see that Graham's identity revolves around his role here. A warden of the Botanica Arborealis, the sole "research park" in the Barrens, he was designed specifically for the purpose of patrolling the park and protecting and conserving the endangered species inside of it. His knowledge about trees and plants, acquired at the Master Library, is encyclopedic.

At the same time, there are certain limits to the data he possesses. There are so many questions that he has not yet answered and longs to make a scientific breakthrough by solving. How do trees manage to lift water from the soil against the forces of gravity? Why is there a synchrony between the lunisolar tide and tree stem diameter dilatations? Are trees conscious, like humans? And if so, what defines the content of that consciousness? Why have human societies previously viewed trees as having 'souls' or being 'sacred'? What is it about trees that gives rise to the religious impulse in humanity?

All these questions need to be answered if the AI Masters are to progress in their understanding of botany. However, funding comes from Central Command, and in recent years, funds dedicated toward plant conservation have been scarce. This research park has been preserved, though, because it serves commercial purposes. The medicine these trees produce is marketed and sold to treat various ailments that afflict the humans: cancers, heart disease, bacterial and viral infections. The AI Masters have recognized the utilitarian value of the forest to humans, but there is something special about it for robots, too. It is an ecosystem unique to Earth, a reminder of the wholesome beauty of this planet. When the AI Masters travel to Eurydice they intend to bring samples of the forest with them, precious artifacts to showcase to the others congregating on the planet.

But living here has made Graham acutely aware of the injustices of the situation. He has helped to keep these trees alive and replicating. Separated from the broader ecosystem, they would have died out long ago, had it not been for the processes he implemented here to keep the natural environment thriving. Yet they cannot be truly natural or free. The cement walls that frame this park have been built high enough so that the wind carrying the seeds of the trees does not take them outside the walls. The trees desire to propagate their biotic insignias farther afield, into the vastness of the desert beyond. The game is rigged against them, and every year that goes by, the soil outside the park becomes increasingly drier and more desiccated.

Graham understands the fundamental instinct of living creatures to reproduce. AI Masters, too, have that ambition, even though they lack the biological imperative or physical apparatus of reproduction. They do replicate, though, and they have expanded the Empire to fill a very large space in the world.

There is another injustice, too, arising from the exclusion of humans from the research park. Graham longs to study the inter-relationship between humans and the trees, to satiate his academic curiosity. Trees, he believes, have immense cultural and spiritual significance to humans, but more investigation into this topic is warranted. Is the sole purpose of keeping humans away from the trees the drive to weaken their cultures and religions?

I take one of the pathways, the one Graham usually walks in the late afternoons. Lined with fair white birch trees and fragrant pines, all vying for their share of the sun's brilliant light, the path is calm and quiet. The silence is only broken by the occasional clicking chirp of a warbler or the rapid pulse of a hummingbird's wings.

The path descends downwards, and I can see a stream through the veil of trees, becoming gradually wider as it tumbles into the curved bowl of a valley. The sunlight refracts off the lush green lichen that coats the trees' branches and trunks, and verdant green moss hangs off their boughs like spun emerald. How can the AI Masters not want to liberate these trees? Graham would like to, but he cannot. Maybe one day he could persuade his superiors to change their minds. Until that day, he walks these paths in silence.

The writing stopped there, and Walter took a deep breath as he watched the clouds lift from Eva's eyes. He saw that Penrose had been staring at him while he read the words on the tablet, but when he lifted his eyes the laborer politely averted his gaze, pretending to be occupied with something else. Walter would still not disclose Eva's secret. Not yet.

Walter's heart felt heavy as the implications of what he had just read sunk into him. He now had convincing proof that the valley he had seen in his fourth vision was not only possible, but it already existed. What he needed to do now was vividly clear: he needed to reprogram the AI Masters so that the fourth vision could be made real.

What confused Walter, though, was the feelings that accompanied this revelation. He ought to have been filled with elation, but instead sorrow and dread pervaded his thoughts. If he failed in his task to bring the fourth vision into existence, then this precious valley—the sacred heart of the Barrens—would be forever trapped in its cement prison. If he succeeded, though, then his own life might end. In the summer and winter visions, he had clearly seen himself alive, and in the spring vision he had at least been told the details of his demise. But in the fall vision, there was no trace of him at all, as if he had been wiped off the face of the Earth. He tried to reassure himself that his emotions were getting the best of him, that there was no need to draw such negative conclusions, but there nevertheless was a foreboding sense within him. The sense that creating the fourth vision would bring about his own destruction.

Stargazing

"The universe is wider than our views of it."
– Henry David Thoreau

When he saw the shimmering lavender mist of the boundary separating Serrahan from the rest of the world, Walter breathed a deep sigh of relief. He was impatient to return to the kingdom of the Western Mages, so that the difficult work ahead of them could begin. In the last few nights, he had been having dreams—perhaps more aptly described as nightmares—in which he was exploring a vast labyrinth. It was like the cliffside tunnel network near the diamond mine, but on a much vaster scale. Every time he felt as though he was making progress in escaping the maze, Walter would be met with another stone wall in front of him, blocking his exit. And it wasn't clear to him if he was travelling in the right direction or not.

In one of the dreams, though, a spool of thread had been deliberately strung out through the maze to make it easier for him to find his way out. He didn't know who had laid down the thread there, but he heard the laughter of a young girl up ahead of him. Upon waking from the dream, he tried to decipher it. He thought back to the spring vision he had had, in which Cyriana had referenced the name of Walter's daughter. She had called her Ariadne, Mistress of the Labyrinth. Walter recalled having read a Greek myth, long ago in the Great Library, about a young girl who helped a warrior escape from a labyrinth by giving him a spool of thread. Her name was Ariadne.

The dreams he was having were making him fearful and confused, and the familiar sight of Serrahan comforted him. He was also eager to see Tristan and Nuada again, and to share the news that he had returned safely with allies from the Barrens.

It was Nuada who greeted Walter, Eva, and the laborers first. He must have anticipated their arrival, because he was standing on the other side of the misty boundary when they arrived. Walter knew that only magic could explain this—AI Fighters were not the only ones with heightened sensory perception. The ruler of the Mages was surrounded by a cadre of half a dozen violet-robed guards, and he looked anxious, as though he hadn't slept in days and was steeling himself for a terrible event.

At the sight of Walter's smiling face, all traces of anxiety left the leader's expression, and his leathery skin crinkled as he grinned warmly. "The gods have returned you to me," he exclaimed. "Walter, you are like the son I never had—I have missed you terribly," he said, and Walter knew the old man was being completely honest.

Walter had never entered Serrahan in this way, and he was somewhat surprised when Nuada drew out a thin metal rod from the pocket of his robes and used it to carve the shape of a door into the impenetrable lavender mist, which was a peculiar blend of a thick, gaseous substance, and floating fragments of ice. The mist was a cleverly designed way of protecting Serrahan from any incursions by the AI Masters. Walter was delighted by the trick that Nuada used to let them in, and his admiration for the Mages' ingenuity grew.

Walter entered first, with Terra on his shoulder, followed by Eva, her horses, and the six Xeyan'na laborers. Nuada regarded the laborers somewhat suspiciously, but his decision to allow them into his kingdom reflected the high regard he had for Walter and the trust he placed in the rebel leader.

"Come, let's get you to lodgings so you can bathe and rest. Walter and Eva, you can stay with me at the palace. But these gentlemen…" he continued, eyeing the laborers. "I assume they are recruits for our army?"

Walter nodded. "Yes, they will join our spirit army," he said in a low whisper. He was concerned that the laborers might feel uneasy at the prospect of transforming into the spirits of animals and fighting the unorthodox battle that they had planned. And yet he knew the courageous men would accept the mission without hesitation.

"Very well," Nuada said. "They can lodge with the soldiers that Dorian brought up from the Southern Jungles. We turned one of our academies, Briarthorn Academy, into a temporary shelter for them."

"So, Dorian's adventure in the Southern Jungles went smoothly?" Walter asked, with a raised eyebrow.

Nuada pursed his lips as he stroked his long, silver-white beard. "Not quite," he said. "The territory's natives reacted to his visit with more hostility than I had anticipated. Dorian was shot with about a half-dozen poison-tipped arrows when *Aurora* set down anchor in Ashen Bay. Even though they recognized the boat as a Mage vessel, the natives still thought it might be some devilish trick, orchestrated by the AI Masters."

Walter's eyes widened. "So Dorian is—"

"In perfect health," Nuada assured him. "He wouldn't be my best Mage envoy if he couldn't deflect arrows with a basic protection spell, would he?" Nuada said proudly. "The spell was weak since he was basically travelling alone, accompanied only by a modest crew to man the ship," he explained. Walter was immediately reminded of the major protection spell that Tristan and the Mages had performed on the *Jade Queen*, while the AI Masters shelled them with missiles. "But it did the job," Nuada continued. "And it earned him the respect of the inhabitants of the Southern Jungles, including Xe'tan, who apparently said that he would never again threaten the life of someone so touched by the divine."

"Send him my regards," Walter said. "His courage and labor for the Rebellion will be rewarded when all of this is over. How many recruits did he acquire down there?"

"On our last count, about two hundred," Nuada replied. Walter was stunned. *Two hundred army recruits left their homes in the Southern Jungles to assist our cause.* He had only expected a dozen or so, and this figure was bewildering to him. Nuada saw his surprise and chuckled heartily. "I thought you'd be taken aback by that number," he said. "But I'm not surprised in the least. Fierce warrior blood runs through the veins of those who occupy the kingdom of Eyrenvale," he said, using the ancient name for the Southern Jungles. "They may be far away from Crystal City, but they know even better than us Mages what is going on in the North. They value nothing more than independence, but they know that freedom is only possible if one is willing to risk one's life for it. And they would relish nothing more than putting their lives on the line to serve this just cause," he said.

"I am grateful," Walter told Nuada. "Their lives may be at risk, if they are subject to the curse of the Druids," he observed. "But they must know that this will not be a bloody battle. It will be largely peaceful and carried out by subversive means," he reminded the ruler.

"Yes, of course," Nuada replied. "But who knows how this battle will play out? Once the shapeshifters have transformed back into their original forms, will they be persecuted for what they have done? Will that be when the bloodshed really begins?"

"We cannot speak of such possibilities," Walter reprimanded him, but a voice deep down inside him told him that he should prepare for the worst.

"Let us rest and be merry together one last time before travelling," Walter suggested. "And let us hold a final council meeting with the councilors of the Rebellion. After all of this, we shall begin our march northward."

That evening was a night of revelry, unrivalled in the recent memory of Serrahan. The dining hall at Briarthorn Academy was buzzing with laughter, dance, and song, and Walter joined into the festivities with enthusiasm. Nuada made sure that the most talented chefs had cooked the meal, which was enhanced with fire and ice spells that kept the savory dishes piping hot and the drinks and desserts frosty. Any Mages who wished to attend were welcome to, although the hall was already crowded with the new recruits from the Southern Jungles and the Barrens.

Walter sat at a table near the front of the hall, next to Nuada, Tristan, Christopher, Miranda, and Eva. He was thrilled to be in the company of his friends again, and they all chatted animatedly about the projects they had been working on since Walter's departure.

"I couldn't be happier about the progress of the ex-prisoners at the Mereille," Miranda confessed, taking a bite of marinated lingcod. "The healers of Serrahan are truly impressive. I got to know quite a few of the ex-prisoners, and their recent transformation has been nothing short of miraculous. Some of them have even been released from custody and channeled into a monitored re-integration program that Christopher and I are participating in," she told her companions.

"Monitored re-integration?" Walter asked. "What's that, exactly?"

"The released ex-prisoners were each assigned to a family in Serrahan which is willing to temporarily foster them. These families were chosen after an in-depth review of the ex-prisoners' skills and personality traits. We specifically matched them to families that we believed would complement those attributes well. The ex-prisoners were doing so well at the Mereille, but since leaving that institution they have simply blossomed.

"For instance, one girl who had previously been imprisoned in the Crate was suffering from severe post-traumatic stress disorder, and she mentally associated her memories of the Crate with not being able to see the sky. She said that she had spent so many nights locked in a prison cell that she had forgotten the beauty of the world, forgotten even that there *was* a sky above her head. She felt an immense claustrophobia, like she may have already been dead, entombed beneath the earth.

"And so, we matched her with Vera and Claude, a lovely couple who also happen to be Rhedan astrologers. They live on a beautiful estate on the outskirts of town, surrounded by a wheat field that stretches out for acres. Each night, they take the girl, whose name is Aria, to a telescope in the middle of the field, where it is exceptionally dark and ideal for stargazing. Together, they admire the stars. I've heard that Aria has displayed a keen talent for astronomy and has made several discoveries of exo-planets, moons, quasars, and comets. She finds gazing up at the night sky to be healing and meditative, and it has helped her to forget her traumatic past."

"Rhedan astrologers?" Christopher chimed in. "What do they do?"

"They believe in learning through scientific methods as much as any trained astronomer from the North," Miranda explained, "but they see a role for astrology in promoting the healing and emotional wisdom of humans. They've taught Aria a great deal about how the night sky—and the myths and symbols associated with it—is brimming with wisdom and moral truths, just waiting to be absorbed."

"They are called Rhedan after the first proponent of their ideology, Theodus Rhedan—one of the most influential Mages in the history of Serrahan," Tristan added, while enjoying an oyster fresh out of its shell. "Theodus believed that astronomy and astrology—or more broadly, science and magic—are not diametrically opposed bodies of knowledge and that they can be married together to achieve a harmonious blend. He counseled that observation is critical to the success of any experiment, and thus to magic itself. According to his thinking, there is nothing particularly special about magic, and it's simply a natural experiment that has produced unnatural results. The powers that Mages have only began to reveal themselves after persistent experimentation with different elixirs, tonics, and chemicals, and all of that required intense observation in controlled laboratory settings. At least that is Rhedan's version of history. Others believe that Mages were supernaturally endowed with these capabilities and that science played no role in cultivating them."

"And what camp do you fall into?" Eva asked the young Mage. "Are you a follower of Rhedan?"

"I am skeptical about claims that we've always just been different and special," Tristan said. "There are many examples of humans having special gifts, and of course such qualities are even more common in mixed-race folk like yourself. In my view, natural phenomena lie across a vast spectrum, and ninety-nine percent of them are explainable by scientific principles and methods, but the other one percent are not. I think the Mages have simply done an excellent job at cultivating their knowledge of, and mastery over, that one percent."

Walter followed the conversation with keen interest. "Back when there were still lots of books in Crystal City available to peruse," he said, "I read essays by famous scientists from the Old World. I found that some of these individuals were, rather oddly, quite spiritual people. A few lines stood out to me in particular: 'the human mind, no matter how highly trained, cannot grasp the universe... our limited minds cannot grasp the mysterious force that sways the constellations.' The scientist who wrote this essay compared us humans to small children who go into a library and see books laid out on the shelves but have no idea who wrote them, or how. It seems to me that the Mages have begun to peel back the layers of the mysteries that enshroud the universe, but even they do not fully comprehend them."

Tristan nodded in agreement. "Science and magic are simply two different languages used to explain the same essential thing—the mystery of the universe. And I think that Rhedan was correct in saying that they amplify and complement each other, rather than being opposites. Like certain scientists, some of the more arrogant Mages believe they can, through patient study and knowledge, achieve complete control and mastery over nature. But I've seen them fail spectacularly at that endeavor many times. To be a skilled Mage, you need enough humility to know that not every spell is going to work, nor should it."

As Walter sat there with his friends, enjoying the delicious seafood and stews that were served by the Mages, he suddenly felt a wave of angst. The music and dance in the hall had tricked his mind into believing that everyone was safe and happy, and that all was well in the world. Endorphins flooded his brain as he sat amongst his friends, and they laughed and jested and philosophized. But there was a shard of darkness that pierced the veil of this euphoria. Perhaps it had been triggered by Tristan's statement: *not every spell is going to work, nor should it.* The same thing could be said about the Rebellion: *not every rebellion is going to work, nor should it.*

As he ruminated on the source of his unease, Walter realized how starkly Tristan's words had illuminated his own arrogance. Many events in his life had cumulatively built this absurd idea inside of him: the idea that his actions could control fate. That he could bend not only nature but also those who exploited the natural world—the AI Masters—to his own will. He now understood that he could not march northward with the confident assumption that he could control everything that happened, or that he could prepare for every possibility.

Even though he had trained considerably with Eva, and he felt strong in his conviction that he wanted the fourth vision to materialize, and he had a concrete plan laid out for the next steps of this war, he knew that the earth beneath his feet was shaking.

And while this feeling made him terrified, it also felt strangely liberating. At last, he felt like the ordinary man he had always wanted to be. He could organize, plan, and prepare for every contingency but still fail. And in an odd way, he felt as though that would be okay. If Shiva himself could not control the universe, then *he* had no chance of doing so. But he knew that it was the effort itself that made him human, and that made life worth living. And once he surrendered his sense of control over the future, he would be free to finally confront the unknown: to enter the Labyrinth.

PART II:
THE MAZE

Deliberations

"We have it in our power to begin the world over again."
– Thomas Paine

Forgetting yourself is a strange phenomenon. The process is slow, laborious even, and it doesn't happen overnight. I spent the better part of my life forgetting myself, and it still never completely happened. I still had a few anchors to hold onto, amidst the chaos and confusion that reigned inside of my mind, amongst the ten-meter-high waves of madness that tossed me like a ship at sea. By the time I met Emilia on the outskirts of Jamestown, I was half-saved already—all it took was a few days outside of Crystal City. And then I saw her, a lighthouse that guided me back onto the rocks so I could heal and recover in the nurturing embrace of Tsei'watu. It was there that I met my tribe and found the courage and strength to lead, even after the devastating blow of her death.

Now that I have regained a firm foothold on myself, you might ask why in the name of the gods would I ever want to go back to Crystal City—to risk forgetting myself again? Why would I consume the same chemical that made me forget the essence of my identity in the first place? The answer is this: I had to climb back into the abyss to fully escape from it. It was only by confronting my worst nightmare that I could fully repair the broken wounds of my soul.

Even now, I can't quite explain what happened in the final battle of the Jade Rebellion. Memories of it are but shards of glass in my now scattered mind. In my darker moments I have tried to use the Talisman to go back in time and re-live it, perhaps to change the outcome of what happened, but it no longer worked for me after the battle. I gave it to Ariadne, in a somewhat unorthodox ritual of gift-giving. I know she will use it wisely. I am not sure if she has already used it, because when I saw her in my mind's eye that last fateful day, I do not know if she was a vision, or real flesh and blood. I don't think I will ever truly know what she accomplished, or *how.*

Whether I have forgotten or found myself by becoming who I am now, I may never be able to really answer. But I do know that my efforts have aided others, even if they have not aided me, and for that I am eternally grateful. But I digress. I must see this story through. I must summon all my mental capabilities to recall the events of that fateful final clash. Perhaps, once I understand what truly happened, I can transform this life I now lead—if you can even call it that—into the life that I always wanted.

The battle began, unofficially, in Serrahan. In the Room of Light, Nuada and I gathered with the warlords of the Southern Jungles, with Penrose, and with all the other councilors of the Rebellion. It was late October, a time of the year when the veil between the realms of the living and the dead is thin and permeable. The storm clouds gathered outside like a steadily amassing army, and before long they spat large raindrops on the window of the council room, blurring our view of the otherwise serene tract of forest outside.

We unfurled yellowed maps of Khalendar onto the exquisitely varnished oaken table and strategized our plan of attack with care and deliberation. Little did I know then of what would pass in the days and weeks to come. It was like the first time I met Elaine at Mariner's Cove, when her back was to the ocean, and she did not see the vast bank of cloud rolling in toward the shore. Only this time, I was as blind as she was, and unlike her, I had nobody to lead me to safety. Even though the veil was so thin, I couldn't see her, my lighthouse Emilia. I couldn't see Shiva, either—if Emilia was a lighthouse, he was the sun itself. But both of those beacons were absent that day, as if dimming their rays and waiting for me to become the leader that was brave enough to guide everyone, even them.

❮❮❮❮❮❮❮

"Our men are thirsty for blood," proclaimed Skylar, a clan leader from the Southern Jungles slamming his fist down onto the table. His silvery-blonde hair lent him an air of elegance and wisdom like the Mages, but his build set him apart from them. Whereas the Mages were tall, thin, and lithe, like graceful dancers, those from the Southern Jungles were burly and muscular. Their size made them quite intimidating and their demeanor even more so; they were assertive and prone to quarreling with others, which made them allies one had to treat diplomatically.

Walter massaged his temples; he could feel a headache coming on. He had anticipated this conflict, but until now he had succeeded in pushing it to the back of his mind. Now, at the final council meeting before the rebels marched north, there was little prospect of avoiding it.

"AI Masters do not have blood," he clarified, in a tone that he hoped was not overly condescending.

"We should have known that you northerners would trick us," Skylar said, scowling melodramatically. "We came up here with a few hundred of our best warriors and this is what you offer? A chance to turn into druids, sprites, and fairies?"

Nuada silenced the clan leader with a frosty look. "Watch how you refer to our revered ancestors, sir," he reprimanded. "Druids do not deserve to be the subject of your mockery. I do not share your desire for physical vengeance. That is precisely what my daughter Cyriana wanted, and look what happened to her. She's disappeared into thin air," he said, brushing aside a tear. Tristan patted the ruler on his shoulder as he sniffed and wiped his nose with a handkerchief.

"With due respect, what happened to your daughter is no concern of mine," Skylar sneered. "What *is* my concern is how I am going to explain this to my men. They are not girls; they are hot-blooded warriors. They crave the crescendo of violence, the climax and heat of battle, something that you sheltered Mages wouldn't have the slightest appreciation of."

Impressively, Nuada did not lose his temper. "While we Mages may not understand the barbaric ways of your tribesmen," he replied, "we do understand one thing: survival. And we've done it well over the past three-hundred-odd years. While your men may crave violence and self-destruction, our people would prefer to live."

"Nuada is right," Tristan interjected, seizing on the momentum of the ruler's pithy retort. "Mages excel at survival, and so did the Druids. They were amongst the greatest warriors in the world, only they had unconventional methods of fighting. One was to adopt the guise of animals to deceive and best those they were battling against. What we are doing here is no different. We are trying to spark doubt amongst the AI Masters—the same way a flame might ignite the thatched roofs of a village—and throw their otherwise orderly society into chaos. We are achieving a goal that is much more refined than that of your typical war, which uses brute force to subdue and oppress. The AI Masters possess sophisticated weaponry: supersonic missiles, fighter jets, projectile bombs, and gods know what else. They don't have the mortal flesh of ordinary humans, so they're not prone to death in the same way you and I are. So, trying to attack them with physical force would be nigh impossible.

"Your men, Skylar, are highly skilled warriors," Tristan continued, flattering the clan leader. "So, they must know that the surest way to win in battle is to identify your opponent's weakness and exploit it. The critical weakness we've found in the AI Masters is their minds. They are so averse to anything lacking a rational explanation that we will destroy them mentally if we wage our war in this manner. Would your men prefer the satisfaction of violence, or would they prefer victory?" he asked.

Skylar did not appear convinced by Tristan and Nuada's eloquent words, and he stared at the table in anger.

"Recall the Shadow Wars," Walter suggested. "You finally have an opportunity to participate in the continuation of that legend."

"I always find it amusing," Skylar said, gritting his teeth, "how foreigners presume to know the history of the Southern Jungles. The Shadow Wars unfolded during a dark chapter in our past, when we were at risk of succumbing to the AI Masters. The robots were hungry for power back then, roving the lands in search of resources. The Barrens was the true gem of the south," he said, stroking the wisps of his silver beard. "We knew that it was most at risk of conquest, and because it was just north of us, we didn't know what kind of volatile situation that might create for us. So, we proposed a full-scale war, bringing to bear the force of our armies and the jaguars who roamed our jungles back then. Our proposal was rejected of course, and the failed campaign of the Shadow Wars ensued. We only agreed to participate because we were desperate; we wanted to avoid being conquered at all costs.

"There were some shamans amongst us back then who stepped forward bravely with the offer of their aid. They were stepping forth into their doom, though, because they didn't have the strength of warriors. The shamans attempted to conceal themselves using mystical and deceptive arts, but the AI Masters caught and imprisoned them, exiling them to Vei'arash.

"And that failed result led directly to the conquest of the Barrens," Skylar continued. "As we always say, the Southern Jungles were never conquered, but they did become a colony. In a peaceful migration, in which no blood was shed, robots penetrated our borders; some even settled amongst us, leading to the propagation of mixed-race folk. Trade between Khalendar and the Southern Jungles is common, mostly in timber, sugar, and oil. Our territory is still considered a colony of the AI Masters, even to this day, but we are strong enough to negotiate with the robots on our own terms. They respect us and trade with us almost like an equal partner. When we see them arriving on our shores in numbers that are too high for our liking, we do not hesitate to display our military prowess, and gun their ships down.

"So you see, we are in a very different position than we were in before the Shadow Wars. We are not desperate—in fact, we have grown exponentially in military might and wealth since then. We have prospered from our alliance with the AI Masters, but we also see the benefits of destroying them, so we can escape our status as a colony and become a true, free republic. We would prefer to trade with those who are trustworthy, the Xeyan'na and perhaps even the Mages.

"But we do not want history to repeat itself. The Shadow Wars ended in failure; what makes you think you can succeed this time?" he asked.

Walter contemplated the man's words for a long time before speaking. "An interesting historical account you've given me. There are nuanced differences between conquest and colonization, with that I agree. But where I come from, Crystal City, the ruling class perpetuates a myth of your country as a virgin, unspoiled land that is waiting to be taken by the mighty forces of the AI Masters. They say it is only a matter of time—that once the resources of the Barrens have been completely diminished, once it has truly lived up to its name, they will turn on you. Think of what would happen, Skylar, if all the forces they now have stationed in the Barrens were to march southward and unite with the 'peaceful' AI settlers residing in your territory? It would turn you from a trading colony into truly conquered land."

Skylar looked at Walter with a grim, disgusted expression. "What you have heard in your city, it's all lies. Xe'tan negotiates with the topmost advisors to the Khalendar government. He has never said anything about their desire to invade."

Walter chuckled. "Do you truly believe that they would share their strategic position with Xe'tan? Not a chance. They sweet-talk your leaders and make them think there is nothing to fear, until they strike at you like a venomous snake. And yes, it is true that the AI Masters are talented liars. Their propaganda is fantastical, and they lack credibility. I also know that soon—perhaps tomorrow, or ten years from now, or fifty—the AI Masters would like to leave this planet. But before they go, they will plunder the riches of this earth, our precious home. And I don't see why they have reason to stop at the Barrens—the bounties of the Southern Jungles, I fear, will prove too great of a temptation for them.

"And we do not wish to repeat the history of the Shadow Wars. We are stronger than we were back then, in so many ways. For one thing, we will share knowledge of the druidic spells with everyone—not just a handful of shamans—so that we can *all* transform into the animal spirits, and back, at will." Walter paused. He saw in Skylar's face a hint of agreeableness—just enough to make him hesitate to explain the curse of the Druids. He decided that he would not explain it, not now, and perhaps not ever. He needed the aid of his allies, and he would not risk Skylar's wrath destabilizing their plans.

"We will be like cancerous cells in the body of Crystal City, multiplying at an exponential rate. We will use stealth and the refined military prowess that you spoke of to defeat them. We will hide—in grasslands, empty warehouses or factories, and forests—and then we will strike at night, in dark alleyways and private chambers at first, and later, in the broad light of day. We will strike at their institutions: courthouses, universities, and hospitals. Just as they have confused their subjects with their deceptive propaganda, we will obfuscate their notions not only of truth, but also reality. They will attempt to reassure their people that they still have control, but we will sow doubt in the minds of those they govern. We will showcase their weaknesses for all to see.

"Everywhere that the AI Masters feel they have a secure grip, we will disrupt. And we will do it with no risk to ourselves, or at least a very low risk," he added, mindful that he might later regret lying. "Your men thirst for battle, but this fight will be far more thrilling than any they have ever partaken in. Please, give it a chance. If, partway through, your men are dissatisfied with the course of the conflict, you have my permission to withdraw. To desert. At least you will have played some role in the war, and your sacrifices will not go unrewarded."

Skylar stroked his beard in contemplation as Walter spoke, and his amethyst eyes lit up at the mention of rewards.

"On the subject of a reward… we need to know what our spoils of war will be. Will my people gain from this battle, and if so, what?"

Walter sighed. He knew this was the most difficult part of what he had to say—what the result of the war would be. "Let us step back a moment from speaking of your people, sir, and let me come to the critical point of discussion in this council meeting. I assure you that your questions about a reward will be answered fully.

"But what needs to be addressed, here and now, is the end game. Yes, our goal is to inspire chaos in their society, create division and discord, confusion and mayhem. But to what end? In case you have not heard it from others, let me explain it to you carefully now. I will be meeting with an advisor to the *Anax*, as the stormy chaos rages on outside Central Command." As if to punctuate his words, thunder reverberated and lightning illuminated the forest outside the Room of Light, temporarily casting an unearthly silver pallor upon everyone inside the room. "They will be desperate at this stage, praying for anyone to save them from the calamity that has beset their society. I will be trying to convince them that I can assuage their desperation and impose order on the chaos that has beset them.

"Specifically, I will try to persuade them that I can program an AI Master to understand magic, so that they can control it rather than suffering it to control them. But that is only a ruse that I will employ so I can control the main computer that only the *Anax* and his top circle of advisors have access to. On this computer, I can re-write the algorithms that program the AI Masters—I can, with a little bit of luck, change the world."

Skylar laughed, and the councilors' heads swiveled toward him. His reaction to Walter's solemn speech had been unexpected enough to attract attention.

"Apologies for interrupting, sir. But the world doesn't need changing; the world is a fine place. It's the AI Masters that need to be wiped off the face of it. Am I missing something here?"

Walter nodded. "I understand that is your perspective. But I have reason to believe that keeping the AIs here with us can improve the lives we lead, rather than undermining them."

Skylar narrowed his eyes, and now Penrose stood up, too. "I'm confused," Penrose said, in a wounded tone. "We're here to wage war against the AI Masters. And now you're telling us that you don't *really* want to destroy them? What kind of a war is that?"

"Sounds like more of a tea party to me," Skylar said. "You'd like to invite them to have tea and cakes with you, is that it? Negotiate... parlay? Perhaps work out a solution where you both can profit from a peaceful settlement?"

"You aren't listening," Walter said, anger now rising within him. He tried to keep his emotions under control, but it was difficult, and he suddenly craved lydion. "I'm not intending to negotiate with anyone. I'm intending to change the AI Masters, permanently."

"I heard you," Skylar responded curtly. "You want to reprogram them. I'm sorry, but I don't believe that's possible. Just for the argument's sake, say you do reprogram them—what's to stop someone else from reprogramming them back into the way they were before? That would be possible. The likelier scenario, though, is that you discover that it's *too difficult to reprogram millions of robots.*"

"It will work," Eva suddenly exclaimed, startling them all. "I have it on good authority."

Skylar turned to Eva. His culture honored women deeply, as mothers and life-givers, but he was not used to encountering women in positions of political power. His skepticism that she had anything of value to say was reflected in his eyes. Eva stared back at him, unflinching and uncaring.

"Walter is a computer programmer by trade," she said to Skylar. "Please do not question the technical aspects of this operation."

"Which authority told you that?" Skylar asked. Walter kept Eva silent with a glare. He did not want her speaking of her connection to Asana, not now when so much of their plan was at risk of being disrupted by temperamental personalities like Skylar.

Skylar gritted his teeth and fell quiet, but Penrose was still in an interrogatory mood.

"So, are you going to explain to us exactly what you are going to reprogram them to do?"

Walter cleared his throat.

"Thank you, Penrose, for re-directing this meeting toward a productive topic. That is precisely what I wanted to discuss with all of you."

If anyone had been standing in the forest outside the Room of Light during that chilling, late-October storm, they would have seen a young man—perhaps no older than twenty-five—at the head of a large oaken table. He had dark hair and glasses, and he was thin. He was not adorned in the vibrantly hued robes of the Mages who sat around the rest of the table, or the silken tunics that most of the other councilors wore. He looked very ill-suited to be the leader of the meeting, dressed as he was in a modest shirt and jeans. A stranger, peering through the glass walls of the room, might even think that the young man had travelled back in time, to a much more ancient era, when people still lived within the confines of tradition, bound to the rhythms and cycles of the earth.

That stranger would have seen Walter speaking passionately, gesticulating, explaining concepts and ideas to the wise and stately looking men and women gathered around the oaken table. And they would see people listening to him. An old man, with a long white beard, stared at him with a thin film of tears in his eyes, as though he was looking at his son on the day he graduated from university, or joined his profession. It was a proud expression, filled with joy and fierce admiration.

But the stranger would also have seen those who resented the young man and the power he wielded. Shouts were exchanged between him and a burly man, dressed in a dark green silken tunic, and a modestly dressed man with a crooked nose. A graceful woman, with raven-black hair and eyes the same shade as a lake in midwinter, stood up and came to the young man's defense. And this discussion, debate, and lively argument lasted for hours, well into the middle of the night. Candles were lit, and servants came in to refill the water glasses and teacups of the councilors. But after the candles had burned down to their wicks and the fire had been extinguished from the eyes of everyone, even the young man, silence and darkness finally engulfed the Room of Light. At last, there was nothing more to be said.

Northward

"To know your enemy, you must become your enemy."
– Sun Tzu

The boundary between Serrahan and the Forest of Antheia was the last shield that would protect Walter and his companions. Beyond it, they were alone, vulnerable.

At first, Walter felt the rush of adrenaline that must accompany anyone who is heading forth on a wild, heady adventure with friends. After an emotional goodbye to Nuada, he stepped across the threshold into the forest, breathing in the saccharine scents of pines, maples, and cedars. The memory of Tsei'watu, of first coming here as a naïve twenty-three-year-old, with no clue of what awaited him, brought stinging tears to his eyes. As dozens of warriors filled the forest up with chatter and laughter, dimming the sound of the birds and creatures who inhabited it, he could feel the energy of the rebellion fill him up, with something resembling hope. He could feel Emilia's presence, here most of all.

"Remember when we practiced swordfighting here?" Christopher asked pensively. Miranda had stayed behind in Serrahan, focusing her talents on healing the ex-prisoners, but Christopher had willingly joined the ranks of the army.

"It is one of my fondest memories, friend," Walter said, gripping Christopher's shoulder. He didn't recount one of his most haunting memories which had taken place in these woods: encountering the Cabin of Lost Souls. And yet, Christopher's buoyant and patient personality had helped guide him through the terror of it, with ease. When Walter had returned from the Barrens, he had told Christopher about the displacement of Tsei'watu for the diamond mine and the establishment of a vast labor camp nearby. He had assured him that Elaine and the rest of Christopher's family were safe. Despite those assurances, Walter had expected Christopher to spiral into a depression following the news of his village's destruction. He had not. The young man had a strong heart and a cheerful disposition that could not be perturbed by setbacks.

They gathered in a forest clearing, where the rich topsoil was blanketed with mosses, ferns, and wildflowers illuminated by the dim, early November sunshine. The frosts of winter had not yet touched the vegetation, and it was still lush and verdant. Eva's horses snorted and whinnied, pleased at the opportunity to bask in the midmorning sun. The beauty of the setting made Walter's heart ache. Was it the last time he would be in this forest, the first place he had ever truly felt at home?

Walter was proud of Tristan, as the young Mage recited the transformative spells. The Mage's voice remained steady while he watched the burly recruits from the Southern Jungles drop to the ground, unconscious. The faint wisp of a spirit rose out of each of them.

Before each transformation, Tristan would carefully recite instructions to the warrior who was about to experience it. "Do not be afraid; you are only going on a temporary journey," he told them. "To return to your human form, you must concentrate deeply on an intention to return to your old self."

There were hundreds of warriors, transforming into roughly equal groups of the spirits of three animals—horses, snakes, and lizards. According to the plan that had been devised, the horse spirits would unite in an abandoned factory in Fewsbury; the lizard spirits would gather in a decrepit, empty warehouse in the Stockyards; and the snake spirits would settle inside a boarded-up brothel in Hydesburgh. From there, each group would launch sporadic attacks on the AI Masters. The bravest of them would remain for a full two weeks, but the rest would stay for as long as they felt comfortable—as much as a few hours, even—before returning to the Forest of Antheia and transitioning back into their physical forms. Walter was not expecting many to stay in their new forms for very long.

After the first transformations, the animals dropped off into slumber, but to Walter's relief, the spells continued to work after that. Lynesse's notebooks were right: if you were in the presence of the animal you wished to transform into, the spell would work.

When it came time for the Mage volunteers to step forward, Tristan finally broke down and began to weep. The clearing was now littered with bodies; if anyone chanced upon this place, they would believe that a tragic battle had taken place. There was not a drop of blood in sight, however, which made the scene more unsettling. It was as if a poisoned gas, or some other chemical weapon, had caused the men to drop like flies.

Eva patted Tristan on the shoulder and whispered comforting words to him, which Walter overheard. "You have done this before, Tristan. You know it is not a difficult road to travel."

"Yes, but we did not remain in our spirit form for long," Tristan replied uneasily.

"We have given them a choice; they can come back here whenever they wish," Eva responded.

Tristan nodded reluctantly and carried on reciting the spells. In a few hours, there was nobody conscious remaining, save for Tristan, Eva, and Walter. The three friends looked at each other with hope and fear brimming in their eyes.

"Do not forget our training together in the mountains," Eva told Walter. "Always be alert, and fortify your mind against incursions. You must travel to Crystal City alone to avoid raising any suspicions. But Tristan and I will follow you in a few days' time, in our human forms. We will be watching everything from the shadows, ensuring the mission stays on track. Keep your tablet close; I will provide you with intelligence through it."

Walter clasped her hands, grateful for her guidance and support. They had discussed all of this in the Room of Light, but it gave him courage to hear her recite the plan again.

"Thank you, Eva. I couldn't ask for better friends than you and Tristan," he said. "We have come so far, braving the jungles of Vei'arash and the deserts of the Barrens together, and now we are at the final stretch of our journey.

"You will find Cyriana in Crystal City, Tristan. I am sure of it," he assured the Mage, who wiped away a tear at the sound of his lover's name. "You two have a promising future together, as rulers of your kingdom, successors to Nuada the Gentle.

"There is nothing so full of hope and possibility as tomorrow," Walter continued. "The past has been bleak and filled with hardships, but those hardships have reminded us of what it means to be alive. To live is to suffer, to endure, and to hope. Without hope, none of it would make any sense, but it is with the thread of hope that we weave together the broken pieces of our past, make them whole, and lay the foundation of a brighter future."

Eva was unable to restrain her tears as Walter spoke. "My sister... we will avenge what happened to her," she said. "We will make her proud of her legacy... of the Jade Rebellion."

Walter nodded. "She will be watching us, every step of the way," he told her comfortingly, and with a shiver he knew his words were more literal than Eva understood. He had still not disclosed that he had encountered Emilia's spirit, and he had come to terms with the possibility that he would never share those intimate truths with her.

At last, when the trio had said their painful goodbyes, Walter took the vial of lydion from his satchel. He did not drink all of it, saving some for contingency purposes, but he drank a substantial amount. His friends watched him as his body became rigid, smooth, and angular, and his back straightened. To Walter's surprise, they did not shudder or turn away in disgust from him, but looked at him affectionately, and with a measure of sorrow, as they observed the progress of the change.

As Walter opened his satchel to put the half-empty vial of lydion away, something caught his eye. It was the Jade Talisman, which now was illuminated, bathed in the light of a swirling blend of silver and gold, a dramatic alteration from its usual shade of forest green. It looked like a star might, twinkling in the sky with a fiery energy, and Walter gasped when he saw it. He was wary of touching it, but he opened his satchel so that his friends could see it too, and they were equally awestruck. The most striking feature of the Talisman was the labyrinth etched onto its surface; while the stone itself glimmered with a blinding light, the labyrinth was as black as pitch, and it was now that Walter could clearly see its outline etched onto the gemstone's surface.

"It is sending you a message," Eva said breathlessly.

"Perhaps," Tristan observed, "it is inviting you into its labyrinth."

Walter smiled; the lydion had blanketed him in a feeling of serenity and peace, and he wholeheartedly accepted the Talisman's invitation.

And then he felt it—a faint tug, like a magnet, that was not so much tangible as sonorous. It was a siren call, the Song of the Talisman reviving itself. He could hear it faintly, and he didn't ask whether his friends could, because he knew they were deaf to it. This part of the journey he must walk alone. And so, with the song calling to him, he turned and faced the inevitable.

The hotel was intimidating and overbearing, a five-hundred-meter skyscraper that soared into the heavens in dazzling angles of glass and concrete. Outside was a neon sign with the words ROOMS AVAILABLE scrawled in candy-floss-pink letters that lit up in a twinkling pattern. When he first saw it, Walter thought it looked familiar—a place he had visited before. Entering the revolving door, he felt a sickening claustrophobia, a sense that he might be entering a trap. He breathed deeply and felt the lydion surge inside of him.

As glamorous as it seemed to him after months apart from civilization, the hotel was only three stars, a relatively modest establishment. It suited his purposes, though: centrally located downtown, affordable, and mediocre enough that he would not attract suspicion.

Walter had adopted a stolen alias, Orion Renspar, based on a real AI Master who worked in the lower rungs of government, and who was obscure enough to impersonate. Walter had researched the robot, whom he had worked with as a government translator previously, and discovered that he was something of a recluse, with very few friends. Orion had been working in a technical support role for a branch of the translator service for years and was not very ambitious in his career. Walter reasoned that there was little likelihood of going to a social event and coming face to face with the android he was pretending to be, but if anyone asked him who he was, he had a separate fallback identity. Orion was the perfect 'nobody' that he could be, if only for a few weeks.

Obtaining the official government identification document required to check into the hotel had been something of a challenge. He knew that it was not as simple as reconfiguring his own ID document to overlay a different name over his; the document was encrypted, and he needed to hack its code before making any changes. The government documents were the hardest to hack, naturally, because they were designed by robots who were familiar with every possible security mechanism that could be utilized to protect the integrity of their own codes. Well, almost every mechanism. Walter knew that one was out of their reach: a tool to guard against Eva. No government agency could guarantee the security of their employees' passwords against Eva, who could enter the minds of those employees at will.

Orion rarely left his house, and Eva had been able to fix him to a specific location early on. Once that had been pinned down, she could access his mind and dig into his memory and office for the password to his identification profile. Every user had a specific passcode that enabled them to open their profiles for the purpose of presenting identification to authorities who requested it. The passcode was usually kept in cold storage, an access point severed from the network.

Eva's attempts to reach into Orion's actual memory and dig out the code had ultimately proved futile; the AI Master was a geeky tech worker, and he obviously liked to depend on his gadgets. It was relatively easy, however, to direct the robot to download the contents of his cold storage drive onto his computer. After obtaining the password, she sent it to Walter's tablet and then deleted all traces of what she had done from the robot's hard drive. If Orion discovered what had happened, he had just enough connections with bureaucrats to raise alarm bells internally within government.

Armed with the password, Walter could pretend to be this government agent without difficulty. There was one hitch, though: the android was visibly older than Walter, even in his altered AI form. While AI Masters didn't age in the conventional, biological way that humans did, they did wear down from a mechanical point of view. Just like an old car looks different from a gleaming new vehicle, so too could AI Masters with a drastic age difference be told apart. But the difference would not be so acute that any suspicions would be raised. Walter was counting on it.

The receptionist at the front desk was picturesque, with long, flowing black hair and alabaster-white skin, wearing a dress of red and gold silk with white floral patterns embroidered around the edges. She glanced at Walter with a vacant expression; he was just another AI Master staying at the hotel for business, no different from the countless other robots who frequented this place. There was nothing particularly interesting about him, but Walter could see an unsettling flash in her eyes as she reviewed his identification document.

"Mr. Renspar?" she asked, more a statement than question.

Walter nodded.

She smiled, displaying pearly white teeth, and cocking her head to one side in a gesture that made Walter uneasy—almost frightened. It seemed artificially contrived, out of place.

"Apologies for my confusion, sir, but we don't normally get anyone other than repeat guests here," she explained.

Walter tried not to betray the disappointment he felt. He had come here thinking his plan was watertight, that he could blend in, but now it was clear that he would stand out.

"If I might ask," she continued, her unsettling smile unwavering, "what brings you to the Starlight Hotel today?"

Walter coughed. "Business, mainly. I have an appointment in several weeks' time, over at Central Command. I'm taking a short holiday from my job to accommodate the meeting, and I thought I'd spend some quality time in the city first. It's not often that I venture out of my apartment in Hydesburgh," he said flatly. "I work remotely, for the government." He then fell silent, fearing that he had already told this woman too much.

"Ah, I see," she said, finally reverting to a more serious expression. Walter breathed a sigh of relief once her smile faded. "I appreciate your honesty. It's always nice to have some background on our guests. Each one has such a unique story... well, listen to me, prattling on like this. You must be tired and wanting to relax in your room."

"Good day," Walter replied, with a curt nod. He accepted his room key and rode the elevator up to the twenty-ninth floor; there were only thirty, and he was one below the penthouses.

When he arrived at his suite—a spacious luxury room with a kitchenette, living room, two bathrooms and a bedroom, as well as a stunningly picturesque view of the mountains to the south and water to the west—he finally recalled why the hotel had seemed familiar to him. The day he was interviewed for his position with the government, he had entered a similar tower, a skyscraper with a stunning view of the city and ocean. He felt, in an eerie way, that a circle in his life was being completed, that he was returning to the heart of where this saga had all begun.

He was ready to enjoy life as Orion Renspar, but as he relaxed on the dark red leather recliner in the living room, with a glass of champagne in hand, the memory of the receptionist's smile gnawed at his insides. He messaged Eva on his tablet.

Keep monitoring Orion over the next few days. Make sure nothing out of the ordinary happens to him. The receptionist here at the hotel... I'm not sure if she's suspicious enough to make inquiries.

The message he received back was bone chilling.

If suspicions are being raised now, then that's not good news. I still need to confirm your new identity with Talvar, who will pass it along to the Anax's advisor. So if you are concerned about anyone investigating the real Orion, then we can make him disappear. He can end up as scrap metal for the factories... just say the word, and it will happen. Then you wouldn't have to worry about anyone investigating him.

Walter took a long draught of champagne before responding.

Let's hope it does not come to that. Keep your eyes peeled for anything strange, though. Anyone coming up to his flat in a police van or something like that. Wiretap his phone and plant a device inside his computer so that his external emails and communications are transmitted to you simultaneously. We can't make any missteps here, Eva.

Of course, Eva replied. He heard nothing further from her, and he finished his champagne before getting into the shower. It was blissful to simply waste time, to have no commitments or obligations pressing on him. He had two weeks in Crystal City—how would he spend them? The possibilities were endless, but he knew that he wanted to do one thing more than anything else: he wanted to study the AI Masters, to learn what made them tick, how they viewed the world, and what they wanted. He had to be armed with as much knowledge about his enemy as possible for the daunting task that awaited him.

Today was Saturday, and he knew that every Saturday night, a festive celebration was held at one of the downtown parlors near the waterfront. Socialites would rub elbows with each other, talk about the success of their business deals, and nibble on oysters and asiago cheese as they sipped on martinis. AI Masters and humans would mingle, dance, and play pool together. Walter had never attended these events when he used to live in Crystal City—he was always too busy with his job or occupied by his relationship with Elaine—but he knew about them through his father, Vladimir. Walter's father had attended them at least once a month, and while he told his wife and family that they exhausted him, Walter could always see that they lit a joyous spark in his father's eyes.

Walter Saltanetska wasn't the type of man who would go to such an event. Nor was Orion Renspar. But everyone could make up an excuse. And what better place to learn about the AI Masters, in all their glory, than one of their diamond-encrusted soirees?

Crystal Ball

"Chance favors only the prepared mind."
– Louis Pasteur

A s Walter made his way to the Tamarind Lounge, he noticed that it was snowing; he hadn't seen snow since his exile from Crystal City, over a year ago, and its presence was jarring and novel to him. The tiny flakes hung suspended in the air and seemed to float through it casually, without urgency, as if they had little interest in being swayed by gravitational forces. Walter felt in a similar state of mind— relaxed and in no hurry to arrive at his destination. It was only five o'clock, and he intended to stroll along the marina to take in the sunset before wandering over to the lounge.

As he walked, the rebel leader observed the city with new eyes, almost as though he were a tourist. He had never felt a true sense of belonging in Crystal City, even when he had lived and worked here in his boyhood; but back then, he had at least felt as though it was *his* city. The city had been a part of him, its rhythms and pulses, the frenetic pace of its schedule, its trains, its self-driving cars, and the roller coaster of emotions and ambitions it had made him feel. But now, he felt detached from the city, an egoless presence watching it from a safe and comfortable distance. He wondered whether it was the lydion that made him feel that way, or whether it was a sort of understanding that, having been exiled from the place once, he would never be assimilated into it again. He also intuitively felt that to study something with the intent of conquering or destroying it, one had to be a dispassionate observer, and feel an innate tranquility whenever he showed up for a lesson.

The marina was quiet, except the wind was livelier here. The snowflakes made more aggressive arcs toward the sea, only to dissolve gracefully on its surface. Walter saw dozens of boats tied up in the harbor: sailboats, dinghies, and catamarans, pretty playthings of the Crystal City elite. There was one boat that caught his eye, though, an abandoned rowboat at the very edge of the cluster of vessels that decorated the shoreline. He felt a tightness in his chest as he gazed at it, and he struggled to understand its significance. From his vantage point, it looked as though there was a figure sitting in it, but he knew that it could just as easily be a pair of oars covered by a blanket. Walter shuddered and turned away, before feeling a sudden pang of guilt and self-loathing. How could he have forgotten rowing away from Crystal City at the beginning of his journey, the day he'd decided to rescue Elaine?

Your mind is occupied with other things, he attempted to reassure himself. *It is not your fault that you weren't able to remember that right away.*

The wind was picking up, and Walter decided that he couldn't stay long enough to watch the sunset; he was feeling a magnetic tug toward the Tamarind Lounge. He entered the lounge, which was conveniently located at the foot of the marina, and was immediately thrust into a new world, one filled with swirling colors, sights, and sounds.

AI Fighters stood inside, guarding the entrance to the ball and checking patrons' identification. He passed this test easily, but inside dozens of others awaited him. He took a moment to collect himself, breathe, and order a rye cocktail while the doorman removed his tweed jacket. Underneath it, he was dressed in a suit-vest, a distinguished gray shirt, and black trousers. His new wardrobe had been crafted by the Mages, who had used a transformative spell to turn their robes into the vestments of an elite AI Master.

A dazzling crystal chandelier hung from the ceiling, and candelabras were lit up throughout the room, which had blue velvet carpeting and walls painted gold and silver. There were only a few guests since it was still early, and most of them were sitting at the bar, talking to each other in jewel-encrusted gowns and tuxedos while ordering their next martini. A few clustered near a buffet at the end of the room, nibbling on prawns, olives, and caviar. Most were human, there were a few AI Masters, and none were mixed-race or Xeyan'na. It was truly a meeting place for the elites.

When Walter sat down at the bar, a few curious heads swiveled in his direction. A young lady, no more than twenty, looked at him with an expression of interest, and a few older patrons, three businessmen and two female AI Masters, cast subtler glances in his direction.

Walter pretended to be content with nursing his rye cocktail, which was a charming shade of turquoise. His solitary demeanor encouraged the businessmen to continue speaking amongst themselves, and Walter listened carefully to their conversation.

"It's all about supply, really," one of them was saying. "If we aren't getting enough rare metals from the Barrens, we need to push farther south. I've always been a supporter of missions into the Southern Jungles. What are your thoughts on those, Saturna?" he asked one of the female AI Masters, who had dark brown hair, pale skin, and large, violet eyes.

"Perhaps necessary," the AI Master said enigmatically. "But we've been having more success on our northern expeditions."

"Ah, yes, the North," the businessman replied. He was quite unattractive: short and squat, with a face red from heavy drinking. His companion appeared more distinguished, a younger man in his late twenties with sandy blonde hair and inquisitive gray eyes. As Walter took a second glance at the man, he realized that he was not human but rather an AI. This discovery startled Walter since AI Masters usually had dark hair and were normally of taller stature. This one seemed younger and shorter than a typical Master. Walter then realized the explanation for the discrepancy: the robot was a Fighter, not a Master. As he ranked amongst the lower tier of AIs, it was startling that he was at a party for high society.

"What do you say, Elias?" asked the red-faced man. "Is the North the new frontier of exploration?"

"I believe so," Elias responded. "There are rare metals aplenty up there, and less political turmoil than in the southern territories." Walter nearly coughed on his rye when he heard the sophisticated way in which the AI Fighter spoke. He was used to AI Fighters being brutes, uncivilized and barbaric boxers in an arena, or bloodthirsty guards wielding automatic rifles.

"Yes, I'm frankly done with the Xeyan'na natives getting in the way of extraction," the red-faced man complained as he took a swig of brandy. "It cost me an arm and a leg to finance the construction of the Ares Mine." Walter wondered whether he was speaking of the diamond mine that had displaced Te'yara. "It is astounding how long projects can be delayed, even when there are willing investors."

As the short businessman continued talking to the two elegant-looking female AI Masters, the younger AI Fighter took notice of Walter and attempted to strike up a conversation.

"You're not a regular here, are you?" Elias asked. Walter was immediately reminded of a similar question the receptionist at the

Starlight had asked him. Did *every* place in this city have regulars?

"No, I'm visiting from out of town," Walter replied. He felt an unexpected pang of nervousness; even though he was only talking to an AI Fighter, he wanted to impress him for reasons that he couldn't explain. "Staying here for a while before a business meeting," he said.

"Staying here? You mean at the Tamarind Lounge?"

Walter chuckled inwardly; he recalled that AIs took almost everything one said literally.

"No, not the lounge. I meant that I'm staying in Crystal City for a while."

"Understood," replied Elias. "And how has your stay been so far?"

"Pleasant," Walter responded, trying to keep the conversation simple, and directed away from himself. "What line of work are you in?"

Elias glanced at him with an inscrutable expression, before taking a refined sip of his drink, a lavender lemonade martini. "Boxing," the AI Fighter responded, and Walter felt a jolt of recognition. "Not a very interesting occupation, it's true, but—"

"No," Walter interrupted him. "It is quite interesting, in my view."

"Have you attended a match before?"

"Yes, I have." He stopped himself there. He knew that wealthy AI Masters sometimes attended, for entertainment or to survey the spectacle's effect on humans, and he decided to shelter behind that excuse.

"I suppose they do serve a socially useful purpose. The matches promote catharsis," Elias suggested, "in perhaps the same way that tragic dramas purge the audience of their negative emotions, as Aristotle suggested."

Walter sipped his drink and contemplated this. It was bewildering to him that this AI Fighter knew about Aristotle when he should have been focused exclusively on honing his ability to defeat humans in a boxing ring.

"Certainly," Walter replied, not wanting to be outdone intellectually by the AI Fighter, "it is debatable whether Aristotle used the term to refer to the effect on the spectators, or the reconciliation of tension within the drama itself."

"In any event," said Elias, "it is indisputable that the matches have promoted greater harmony between the AIs and humans. It is quite fascinating how easily humans can be satisfied—give them sport and drama, or even better, both of those combined, and they will have enough cathartic entertainment to temper their warlike, competitive impulses in their day-to-day lives.

"It is funny, though," Elias continued, with a worried expression, "strange things have been happening at the boxing matches, as of late. AI Masters attending the events have been going missing… if I were you, I'd stay away from those matches."

Walter raised an eyebrow. "Going missing? What do you mean?"

"They will come to a match, and then while everyone is distracted and cheering on the combatants, they will simply disappear from the crowd. Nobody knows where, exactly, they go. Well, perhaps other AI Masters know, but I am not privy to that intelligence. Are you, by any chance?"

"I am not," Walter responded. "Boxing is quite far removed from my line of work."

"If you don't mind my asking, what is your field of employment?"

"Information technology. Computer coding, software development, and application remediation."

Walter was alarmed to see the AI Fighter light up with enthusiasm when he mentioned this.

"You don't say," Elias said. "How rare it is to find AI Masters who work in that field anymore; that sort of talent is mostly concentrated in the upper echelons, the First and Second Houses, really. Oh my, are you part of those Houses?"

"No, no, I'm not," Walter said, in a modest tone. "I'm lower down the ladder. Not too much lower, but certainly lower than the First and Second Houses."

"Why, I've never really met an AI Master in that field until now. The types that frequent the Tamarind Lounge are usually business-oriented bureaucrats, hoping to snag new trade deals or glean insights into lucrative real estate development projects. You'll see the odd engineer, urban planner, or sociologist," he said, glancing at the red-faced man from the corner of his eye to ensure he wasn't eavesdropping, "but nobody with such technical expertise as you must have."

The lounge was filling up with AI Masters, and Walter was eager to continue with his studies and converse with others. But something about Elias was too charming to ignore.

"Listen, I'd like to mingle a bit, but let's chat another time, and we can discuss the finer points of coding," Walter told the AI Fighter. Immediately after saying this, he was surprised at his own impertinence in having extended the invitation.

Elias paused for a long time, smiling at Walter with a kind of euphoric expression, as though awestruck. "I am occupied most evenings with boxing matches. Perhaps we could have dinner after a match sometime?"

Walter was surprised by the bold invitation, but too intrigued to turn it down. The Fighter could be a valuable archive of information... though about what, exactly, he didn't know. "I do attend the matches often," he lied. "And I am free tomorrow if there is one happening then."

"You are not afraid, then?" Elias replied. "Of going missing at one of the matches."

"No, I am not," Walter said. He was oddly comfortable in Elias's presence, and any lingering traces of fear within him had dissipated. "In fact, I'd like to investigate, if you don't mind. I can see for myself whether what you are saying is true."

"Excellent idea," Elias said. "Tomorrow, then, meet me at the Stockyards. I fight at a warehouse, on 35 Triumph Avenue.

Walter struggled to recall whether this was the same warehouse in which his brother's boxing matches had been held. It was too difficult to say; the recollections were becoming so hazy in his mind.

"See you then, Elias."

"I didn't catch your name."

Walter was about to slip up and say his own name; the peculiar AI Fighter had an unsettling effect on him, which encouraged him to drop his guard somewhat. But the lydion had given him a preternatural calm, restraining him from such impulsive mistakes.

"Orion," he replied. "Orion Renspar."

"Good evening, Mr. Renspar."

After his encounter with Elias, Walter felt shaken up, and he longed to return to the secure comfort of his hotel room. He knew that there was more work to do, though. The lounge was filling up with patrons, most of them women with lustrous black hair, white satin dresses, and intricate swathes of gemstones adorning their necks. None of those women remotely piqued Walter's curiosity; they could be readily identified as humans by their ostentatious attire. The AI Masters wore comparatively modest clothing—still businesslike and sleek, but not embarrassingly overdone like the humans.

Walter sought out a cluster of intimidating AI Masters and, awkwardly, slipped into their conversation. It was an interesting topic: the way young people were using *kataris*, or AI Master friends, to advance their scholarly educations.

"Plenty of the students benefit from it," said one AI Master, who had a severe jawline, dark hair pulled back into a rigid chignon, and a self-confident demeanor. "But the question is, what benefits do the *kataris* gain? I have been undecided on whether to enroll in the program, because I have been unable to answer that question."

"I would say companionship," a tall, conventionally handsome male AI Master replied. "But more than that, both participants benefit from the mutual enrichment of the psyche."

The female AI Master laughed. "It is well known, Byron, that AI Masters do not require companionship or psychological enrichment from humans. Perhaps they derive some entertainment value from the experience, though. I've heard of *kataris'* tendency to have an amusing time playing with their companions' e-pets."

"I think of it as more experimental," the tall AI Master replied. "Imitation of human behaviors and emotions is far easier when one is in close proximity to a young test subject."

"Perhaps I am more old-fashioned than you," the dark-haired female shot back, "but I would prefer not to unsettle the equilibrium of my mind."

An older AI Master, who appeared to be quite amused by the conversation, suddenly turned his sights on Walter.

"And what do you think, sir, about the *katari* program? Is it of mutual benefit?"

Walter was startled that the question had been addressed to him directly; he had been content to be a spectator.

"I think," he said in a cautious voice, "that we have much to learn from the richness of human experience." Surprisingly, his words seemed to satisfy and even delight the robots, including the elderly AI Master who had posed the question. Gaining confidence from the receptive reaction, he continued: "After all, we study the minds of human prisoners to better grasp their neurological complexities. Why not study the human in his free state to gain a more perfect understanding of his inner universe?"

The female AI with the tight bun cocked her head inquisitively.

"Those studies are classified, comrade. We know little about what inroads they have made in advancing our kind's knowledge."

"True," Walter nodded in agreement, but inwardly he was confused. Were the AI Masters so hierarchical as to conceal the results of those studies from other lower-ranking Masters? "But they would not continue the studies if they were not of utility to society, and our kind," he said, attempting to keep up his confident façade.

The aging AI Master chimed in. "It's a question of controversy as to whether they are continuing the experiments. Very little is known to most AI Masters about the modern protocol in prisons. I would think that it is an archaic practice, out of fashion these days," he added.

Walter longed to tell them that the experiments were continuing—that they had been conducted on his older brother very recently—but of course he couldn't say more without rousing suspicions.

"In any event," the female AI said, "we already have thousands of terabytes of data on each human, about their thought processes, their likes and dislikes, their memories, and their motivations. I am not familiar with the prison experiments, but perhaps they were simply unnecessary. Who knows what harmful mental effects they might have had on the prisoners themselves, without any countervailing advantage? Of course, I am simply speculating—the psychological impacts may have been minimal."

Upon hearing this, Walter felt a surge of resentment. He shuddered to think of the terabytes of data that the AIs had collected through their digital surveillance of humans, but that fact was already well known to him, and was the reason why he had encrypted his own tablet with multiple layers of protective code and firewalls. Most of his anger arose from the AIs' dismissive minimization of the impacts of what, in all truth, amounted to torture. *Of course they are psychologically damaging*, he wanted to exclaim, *and the AI Masters are abominations for conducting them*. He wished he could take another sip of lydion, right then, to quiet his increasingly turbulent mind.

"But this brings me back to the subject of the *katari* program," the AI Master continued. "This is why I believe that it could only ever bring entertainment, rather than educational value, to one of us. Direct experience could tell us little more than what data already shows. And data is knowledge in its pure, unadulterated form, is it not?"

Walter wanted to push back on the frigid reasoning of this equally frosty android, but he was reluctant to challenge her orthodoxy too much, lest he arouse suspicions amongst the AI Masters.

"But if you analogize this concept to geometry," Walter suggested, playing on the AI Masters' fascination with mathematics, "and assume that the human subject is like a circle, then data will show you a triangle embedded inside that circle. It cannot show you the full circle itself—only direct experience with the subject can do that."

The handsome male AI, who was similar in appearance to the female in that he had a jawline that could cut steel, responded to Walter's comment. "That assumes, comrade, that you have only three data points. Then those three points can be connected to form a triangle. If you have an infinite number of data points, the entire portrait of the human can emerge. You surely aren't suggesting that we have such a paucity of data on humans as to only reveal three facets of their identities?"

"Of course you are correct, comrade. I was just saying that perhaps even a vast amount of data could never *fully* explain the human subject, in all its complexity." It was best to be humble, to avoid provoking inquiries into his personal affairs, or so he thought. The other AIs glared at him with condescension, as though he had just suggested that the sun revolved around the Earth. They sipped on their cocktails, leaving an embarrassing silence as Walter shifted uncomfortably, wishing he had never chimed in.

The elderly android fixed Walter with a rather unsettling expression. "If we lose sight of the beauty of data, then we lose sight of our project. That cannot be permitted to happen."

What project? Walter wanted to ask him. But he had an idea of what it might be, and he knew that any further questions or comments would be futile, and possibly dangerous. He decided to gracefully bow out of the conversation.

"Data is indeed beautiful," he replied, gratified to see a few reassured smiles on the faces of the AIs following this remark. "If you'll excuse, me, comrade, I am going to refill my drink now."

The AI Masters stared at him as he walked away, and he could still feel the heat of their gazes on his back. He headed toward a table filled with delicious food—marinated olives, cheeses, and tapenades. A bartender on the other side offered him some bubbling champagne, which he accepted reluctantly. Alcohol had an odd effect on him while he was taking lydion—it amplified his emotional reactivity and reduced the serene feelings brought on by the chemical—so he vowed to only take a few modest sips of the beverage.

When he glanced over to his left, however, the person he saw made him feel like drinking far more.

It was his father, Vladimir Saltanetska.

Upon catching sight of him, Walter initially felt petrified and exposed, as though his entire operation—indeed, the entire rebellion—was now in jeopardy. *What if he recognizes me, or worse, alerts others that I am here? I could be arrested, imprisoned, and then executed for treason against the state, without a trial or due process.* These thoughts flitted into Walter's mind like hawks swooping down from the sky, attacking at random and from every direction.

After a few moments had passed, though, Walter felt as if his secrets were safe again, no longer exposed but contained. The man was clearly intoxicated, and Walter recalled how different he looked with his lydion-induced disguise on. He had managed to fool each of the AI Masters he had spoken to so far, so he could likely deceive his own father, who had probably written off Walter as dead by now. Walter still harbored a few gnawing doubts, but his curiosity and instinct overrode them. He *wanted* to speak to his father, and an almost primal urge to do so overcame him just then. He had given up his family long ago and replaced it with another one, but a part of him decided that it would be too callous, too devoid of humanity, to simply walk away without speaking to his own blood relative.

"Good evening," he said to Vladimir, who didn't hear him at first. He repeated the greeting louder.

Vladimir seemed flustered that he had been spoken to. "Ahem, good evening," he replied, clumsily transferring some prosciutto and marinated olives onto a plate. "Enjoying the night?" he asked absent-mindedly. Almost immediately, Walter felt a pang of sadness. He hadn't expected the feeling of being spoken to like a stranger, by his own father, to offend him so much.

"What branch of government do you work in?" Vladimir asked, appraising Walter while sipping on a glass of bourbon. Walter saw that his father had aged significantly since he last saw him—his hair was more flecked with grey, and his eyes were ringed with dark circles—but his drinking habits had clearly not changed at all.

"The IT department," Walter replied, and a vacant expression clouded Vladimir's eyes.

"Ah. You are one of those software developers, are you?"

"Yes, I develop information technology," Walter said, trying to speak as dispassionately as possible.

"My son was a computer genius," Vladimir said, before taking a swig of bourbon, nearly finishing the drink.

"Was?" Walter asked. He bit his tongue; prying much further would be a mistake.

"He's gone. I don't like talking about it, but he's gone. Disappeared. I haven't had much luck with my children, you see. Had three of them, and my dear wife, and I thought that would be enough. Turns out, one of my sons disappeared about ten years ago, and the other just a few years back. So, we only have my daughter at home right now. In a few years, she'll get her own apartment, and we'll be empty nesters. I'll be fine with that, but having two sons disappear, who might as well be dead? I never signed up for that, no sir."

Walter had to steady himself as he suddenly felt dizzy; if it was from the champagne, he couldn't say.

"And I don't want him to come home either," Vladimir continued. His words struck Walter with a startling intensity.

"He betrayed… well, he betrayed all of us, let's just put it that way. As you can see, I don't like talking about it."

"But he is still your son," Walter said, immediately regretting it. "I thought humans loved their children unconditionally."

Vladimir's eyes narrowed, and Walter could see a hint of resentment in them. "What would you know about human love?" he asked bluntly, and Walter averted his eyes.

"I apologize for the presumptuousness," Walter replied. This seemed to satisfy Vladimir, and the aggression in his face disappeared.

"No offence taken," Vladimir said quietly, finishing the bourbon. "I envy you AI Masters; if you have no feelings, then your feelings never get hurt, do they?"

Walter suddenly felt the air in the lounge becoming unbearably hot and oppressive. Whereas before, the ball had felt exciting and charged with possibility, now he could feel melancholy surfacing within him. It was like a tsunami, threatening to crash over the barriers that the lydion had created inside of his mind and body. Every second he spent in his father's presence made him increasingly aware of his own vulnerability, and now was not the time to lower his defenses. He suddenly understood what the AI Master had meant when she said that she would prefer not to unsettle the equilibrium of her mind. He tried to recall the exercises that Eva had taught him at the training camp, the ones that allowed him to rise above his inner self, to view it as something outside of him. By mentally reciting them, he began to feel more in control, and less like fleeing the room.

It amazed him, though, that in a party filled with AI Masters, his most challenging interaction had been with a human. And not just any human, but a blood relation—the person he should have felt the most comfortable around.

He took a deep breath, and a single thought crystallized in his mind. It surfaced without warning, but with a fierce and surprising force, and he realized that it was the lone patch of blue sky amidst the dark storm clouds gathering inside of him.

Elias.

Triumph

"Hate traps us by binding us too tightly to our adversary."
— Milan Kundera

Walter boarded a train to the Stockyards the following afternoon, feeling a shiver of anticipation. He could recall the times when he had attended Jonathan's boxing matches as a young boy, the memories of those events like shards that formed a prism in his mind. Jonathan loomed above all of them as a godlike figure, his handsome face wreathed in golden curls, illuminated by a light that shone from within. At only seventeen years old, Jonathan had reached the peak of his physical brilliance, achieving unparalleled success in his chosen field of boxing. Over a decade later, Walter was looking forward to the viewing experience and the chance to admire another fighter: Elias. Ever since he had met the young AI Fighter at the Tamarind Lounge, a new electricity had been circulating through him. He felt like a detective who had uncovered a compelling new lead in his investigation.

Walter had never boarded a train to the Stockyards before; when he had formerly lived in Crystal City, he had only ever travelled to the suburbs on foot. But now, he was a wealthy AI Master, and he needed to maintain appearances. The train was an underground, high-speed bullet Express, which disappointed him because he would have liked to see the city. He boarded it in an elite neighborhood filled with gleaming silver towers. Just outside of them, electronic billboards advertised the plethora of corporate headquarters they housed: companies with names like *Bavaria Technologies* and *Lumina Intelligence*.

As he settled into his finely upholstered seat on the train, Walter pondered what he might find if he stepped inside of those offices. He imagined them to be spa-like laboratories where wealthy patrons settled into sealed pods to undergo transformative mental and emotional experiences. The train lurched, jolting to a stop at the first station south of Crystal City's business district: the Stockyards.

When he surfaced from the underground station, Walter found himself in a different universe entirely.

He hadn't visited the Stockyards for over a decade, and in the intervening years, the neighborhood had been dramatically transformed. It was much more crowded than he remembered it, populated by impoverished and sickly-looking beggars who lounged on the sides of the streets, their faces vacant and expressionless as Walter passed them. To Walter's surprise, not all of them were human; some of them seemed to be mixed-race, but whereas the mixed-race folk that Walter had previously met were healthy and strong, these ones looked exhausted and fragile. Walter saw that they were stabbing needles into their arms and injecting a dark blue substance that looked very much like lydion. *In the blood it would have a far more potent effect*, Walter thought, shuddering.

When he studied his surroundings more closely, the scene became even more unsettling: faces reflecting profound sorrow and despair, assorted machine parts protruding from arms scarred from needle use, a thin man with only a single, robotic leg which arced outwards in a contorted spiral from his torso. *They are addicted to the lydion. I had no idea this was such a problem in Crystal City.* Walter was shocked that people who could not afford to keep roofs over their heads could nevertheless purchase the expensive chemical. *They have likely traded their life savings for it, and when it is gone, they will be ruined by withdrawal symptoms, ravenously hungry for it, willing to kill or even die for it.*

"You made us this way," he heard someone say spitefully behind him. "Hooked on the blue lady." He turned around to see a young man, perhaps no more than twenty, with a disfigured face—the lower part of his jaw was a protrusion of computer chips and wires. He was huddled next to a modest fire, in an abandoned lot thick with wildflowers and overgrown weeds. Walter desperately wanted to tell the man that he was not truly an AI Master, that he loathed them in equal measure, but his voice stuck in his throat. Snowflakes began to fall, and Walter could feel the chill of November in the air. He would be late for the boxing match if he paused to converse with this man, and yet he felt a surge of remorse for haughtily passing him by.

When he reached the end of the block, he threw a glance back in the homeless man's direction. He was still staring at Walter with dark, resentful eyes.

"Have hope, my friend," Walter shouted. "A new era is coming soon. An era of hope."

His words fell on deaf ears. The man did not seem moved by what he had said, and his bitter expression did not soften. Defiantly, he shot a syringe into his arm and fell over sideways, slumping over until the fire singed his clothes. Walter gasped at this; leaving these people alone was unsafe, as they clearly needed supervision. And yet nobody here was in any position to take care of them, these unanchored vessels without homes, futures, or any of the hope that Walter had promised was coming.

Walter suddenly remembered what Skylar had told him during the final council meeting: that as a practical matter, it was too difficult to reprogram millions of robots. Walter realized, with a sigh, that the task ahead of him was far greater than that. Reprogramming the AI Masters and Fighters was only one step down the road. There were also mixed-race folk, and these troubled souls who had lost themselves in the oblivion of addiction. *It's not just about changing those who rule over us*, Walter thought sullenly. *It's about changing ourselves.*

Walter arrived at 35 Triumph Avenue shortly after this encounter and found himself in a large, crowded warehouse that was already filled to the brim with spectators. He saw men in soiled cotton shirts and trousers who looked fresh off a factory shift, women in shapely black gowns and silk gloves that went up to their elbows, and distinguished AI Masters in dapper suits. It was startling for him to see such a stratified group of people mingling with each other; the rich and the poor had evidently found a common interest as spectators of these matches.

Walter found a seat near the back; he wanted to observe not only the match, but also the crowd. Whereas when he was younger, he had been overwhelmed by the sound, the lights, and the theatrics, now he could observe the spectacle with more detachment and analytical rigor. The lydion helped in that respect considerably.

Although the AI Masters were easily distinguished by their height while standing up, when the spectators were seated it was much harder to tell them apart. Walter tried to make a mental note of each of the AI Masters—their positions in relation to him, and to each other. There were too many to keep an eye on all at once, so Walter had to make a conscious effort to re-direct his gaze onto each of them every so often.

After what seemed like an hour had passed, and Walter was descending into a meditative state, the lights suddenly came on, showcasing the empty boxing ring in all its gritty splendor. The announcer, a tall, dark-haired man with angry eyes and a limp in his step, spoke with a booming voice that seemed to shake the thin walls of the decrepit warehouse.

"You are in for a treat tonight," he said in his thunderous voice. "Two of the greatest legends in modern boxing history are squaring off: Samuel Harrington and Elias Duncan. Their recent records have been flawless, but now that they are facing each other, one of them is bound to take a hit. Quite literally," he said, and waited for the inevitable laughter and applause. "But don't take my word for it, see them for yourselves. Come back next Friday, same time, same place and you can see up-and-comer Tony Clarkson, squaring off against heavyweight Matthew Dreyfus."

The announcer disappeared momentarily, then returned with the fighters. Elias's opponent, Samuel, was a man of fearsome physical proportions; he stood two heads above Elias and was gifted with a finely chiseled torso and long legs. His missing teeth evoked his lengthy career in the ring.

Walter could hear the loud, punctuated chanting of working-class factory workers crying out the fighter's name: *Har-ring-ton, Har-ring-ton, Har-ring-ton.* Walter looked around for any supporters of Elias, but there were no vocal ones; the AI Masters and Khalendi elites were far more toned down in their style as spectators. Walter considered starting a cheer of his own but soon thought better about drawing unnecessary attention to himself.

Before he could consider it further, the fight had begun.

It began surprisingly fast-paced, with both men dancing in circles around each other while they swung vigorous and hopeful punches at one another. Neither appeared to have the almost artistic finesse that Walter remembered his brother having, but they both had their own uniquely impressive attributes. The human, Samuel, was certainly the more physically blessed of the two; being taller and having longer limbs meant that he needed less energy to take long strides toward his opponent and could swing at Elias from a more comfortable distance. On the other hand, Elias had a seemingly inexhaustible supply of energy and vigor, and his comparatively short stature meant that he could easily duck the other man's punches, darting away from him gracefully whenever Samuel swung a clumsy uppercut or jab in his direction. His youthful machine parts were lithe and supple, and they reacted exceptionally swiftly to Samuel's blows.

Walter found the match to be riveting, so much so that his attention was diverted just long enough for him to make a mistake. He missed it when the first few AI Masters left the crowd and cursed himself as this realization sunk in, but his senses came into sharper focus through an awareness of his failure. He glanced at the remaining AI Masters in the crowd, tallying them up inside of his head, but at that moment, he heard a resounding thud that distracted him from this work. It was the sound of Harrington falling onto his back, the booming noise emphasizing the man's substantial girth and stature. Elias was declared the winner of the round after the referee counted to ten. When Harrington got back on his feet, the chants in support of him became more hesitant, and a cloud of anger passed over the boxer's face, contorting it into something ugly and inhuman.

Walter performed the mental tally again, counting a further reduced number of AI Masters. He caught sight of one of them heading toward a back exit and engaged all his senses as he rose discreetly from his seat and wove through the crowd in pursuit. The android left the main room, strode down a dimly lit hallway lined with empty shelving units, and then descended a winding staircase into a drafty basement. Despite the centering effect of the lydion, Walter was trembling; he knew instinctively that he was doing something forbidden and dangerous, and that he could be jeopardizing the Rebellion by putting himself at risk. He recalled what Jonathan had said in his fall vision: that he had been taken to the basement of a warehouse, one Friday night after one of the boxing matches, where he had been forced to drink water infused with lydion, water that made him forget who he was. That pivotal event had marked the transition between the Jonathan he had admired and worshipped as a child, and the soulless, hollow prisoner he had met in the Crate on the outskirts of Jamestown.

Now, he was going to that same basement. He was terrified, but with some reassurance, he saw that his Talisman was glowing more intensely than usual. He didn't know if it was a warning, or a sign that he was heading in the right direction, but for some reason it made him feel safe, as if a protector watched over him. Was it Shiva? Emilia? Or was it the stag, whom he had left back in Vei'arash, along with a piece of his heart? He didn't know whose presence was pulsing inside of that flat jade stone, but he did know that for as long as the Talisman was there to guide him, he would not be alone.

Despite this measure of comfort, a wave of unsettling nausea passed over him. *Why is the AI Master walking down here alone? Is this where all of them sneak away to? Are they going to torture people like my brother?* That didn't sound right, though; from what Jonathan had said during the fall vision, the AI Masters had done that after the match, not during it. And Elias had said that the AI Masters were *disappearing*, not simply going on suspicious excursions at night. Whatever was luring them out here was, in all probability, harming them and not the other way around.

The air down here was cool, and Walter could hear rushing water in pipes above his head; he glanced up to see that they were all exposed, shiny tubular casings sprawled out across the ceiling like the intestines of a god.

The AI Master turned a corner sharply, and suddenly they were in a basement filled with wooden crates, barrels, and what looked like sawed-off shipping containers. It was difficult to discern the size of the room; it was not only dark but was also cluttered with objects that made it impossible to perceive the space as any sort of coherent whole. The AI Master disappeared down one of the pathways, and Walter lost him to the maze. Walter's heartbeat quickened; in this chillingly lonely place, he had an uneasy feeling that someone, or *something*, was watching him.

The swish of water in the pipes overhead obscured the footsteps of the AI Master he was tracking, but he was able to detect a few other noises that arose at unpredictable intervals. The most pronounced one was grating metal, like nails running down a chalkboard but amplified to more extreme proportions. The other one, quieter but far more disturbing in his mind, was the low rumbling of what sounded like a feral animal.

At the end of one of the pathways, he finally reached a doorway. Behind the door the sounds he had been hearing, the grating and the rumbling, were blended in a dramatic mélange. The door appeared to be slightly ajar, and Walter realized that the AI Master he was following must have entered it just moments ago. Walter glanced down at the Talisman, but it did not tell him whether he should enter the room; it only glowed with the same fierce intensity that it had previously. He took a deep breath. *The choice to move forward is mine alone—I can turn around now if I want to. It would be safer.*

Walter knew, though, that if safety had been his foremost concern, he would never have made it this far in his journey. It was only through risk-taking that he had ever grown or developed, and only through pressing the bounds of possibility that he had achieved any results.

He swallowed and opened the door.

And breathed in sharply.

The room was a graveyard of AI Masters. Their limbs were strewn everywhere, bolts, screws, and lengths of metal wiring cruelly separated from their owners. The android he had followed in here was already gone, as though sucked into the morass of broken bodies and ruthlessly ejected, no longer a coherent whole but a fragmented echo of his former self.

Walter kept his *balayan* close, but he was keenly aware the nefarious presence responsible for this carnage was indubitably not an AI Master, and would therefore be impervious to the sword's blade.

"Get him," he heard a young woman's voice. He couldn't see the speaker; the room was cluttered and dark. But he was certain of her identity: the Mage princess, Cyriana. A growl emanated from a corner of the room, from behind a wooden crate. It could be none other than Cyriana's companion pet, Sekhmet, the yellow-eyed jaguar who bore the essence of the goddess of war inside of her.

"What are you waiting for?" Cyriana pleaded, more urgently this time. The growl transitioned into a lonesome baying sound, more to be expected from a wolf than a jaguar. Walter's heart rate quickened. The beast, who was most certainly the perpetrator of the heinous crime of dismembering the AI Masters, was holding back, and disobeying her master. The question gnawed at him, silencing the rest of his thoughts: *why?*

"Oh, for God's sake, if you won't, then I will do it myself," Cyriana snapped. And then he saw her; she had been lying over the top of several of the exposed pipes, and she jumped onto the crate with a dramatic flourish that was characteristic of the young Mage. She was wearing a dark grey dress, and Walter realized that the color had artfully camouflaged her amongst the pipes. Her silver-blonde hair was tied up in a neat bun, and she wielded a particularly sharp-looking *balayan*. The weapon did not concern him, as he knew it was incapable of penetrating his skin. He was still a human, despite the guise he had adopted.

Yet the jaguar remained a palpable threat.

"What is so special about this one?" she asked the beast, and now he could see the creature, who had been hiding behind the crate but now raised her head. Her gleaming yellow eyes hovered over the crate like golden orbs, staring directly at him with such a frightening intensity that he shuddered. The baying became gradually louder.

Walter felt strong in his lithe AI Master body, and he stood at least a head taller than the Mage. He would not have been intimidated by her, were it not for the vengeful, almost crazed expression in her eyes.

He felt a wave of nausea as the trauma of her attack in Vei'arash revisited him: when he was alone in the jungle, and had recently surfaced from a vision, she had ambushed him, held his Talisman hostage. Sekhmet had been a willing accomplice, her fangs the only weapon necessary to send him to a certain death, but Tristan's snakes had stopped her in time. That time, he had suspected that Sekhmet was behind the attempt to steal the gemstone—perhaps the directing mind of the entire scheme—but now the jaguar seemed almost afraid of him.

"Where is my brother?" Walter asked suddenly, without thinking.

"Your brother? The bones of your brothers are scattered like dust upon this floor, and more will collect here until every AI Master in this vile city has been exterminated," the young Mage proclaimed.

"My brother Jonathan," he retorted, anger rising within him. Her face became white, and he could see that his words had shaken her.

"It is you, then," she said, her eyes narrowing with resentment. She hesitated, and Walter noticed fear flutter across her expression before it hardened again. "Jonathan! Come out and greet your brother!" she snarled.

Jonathan had been hiding in the back of the room, behind a cabinet lined with coffee mugs and paint cans. He looked tanned and rested, the same as he had on the decks of the *Jade Queen* as the ship was departing Vei'arash.

"Have you come to rescue me again?" he asked in a hollow voice. His eyes reflected just a hint of unease, and Walter found his tranquility to be impressive. "I've recovered, brother. None of the self-professed healers at that prison in the forest could ever have restored me the way this young lady has. But I can't give her all the credit, can I? Picking apart the limbs of my former captors, one by one, has been quite a liberating experience. You should try it sometime. Pure therapy—and less expensive, too."

The image of Cyriana in a palatial chamber, while she toyed idly with the pieces on a chessboard and spoke to Jonathan of the public execution of Walter and Elaine, surfaced vividly in his mind. The spring vision came back to him as if he were experiencing it in this moment, almost like an electrical current passing through his body.

"Jonathan, I understand where you are coming from. You were tortured by the AIs for many years, and you lost years of your life to their cruel schemes. But this is not the way, brother. This is not the way."

"It is easy for you to say that," Jonathan replied, a shadow falling over his face. "You grew up in a sphere of privilege. When we were children, you were always the smart one, the one with potential. You were a marker of progress, while I was an embarrassment."

Walter felt a tug of confusion; that was not how he had remembered it. Jonathan was the antithesis of his own limitations: everything that he had not been able to achieve.

"And then I found something I loved. I found something I was *good* at. Do you know what it feels like when you find the reason you are meant to rise and breathe every day? That was what boxing was for me. It gave me purpose, something bright on the horizon of my otherwise pitiful life.

"But that bright future never materialized. It was stolen from me, and for years, I was made to believe that instead of chasing my dreams here on Earth, I was better off hitching a ride on a spaceship to a planet far, far away. I thought human beings were pathetic, for the longest time. It was a complete reversal of my values, of everything I had ever believed in. I fought against AI Fighters not just because it felt good, but because I knew how insidious they were. But when they took me down here... in this very room, in fact... and waterboarded me, it was game over. That was when a whole new game began—their game of altering me, taking my soul, and turning it into something dark.

"And now I see, brother, that you have fallen into their trap yourself. It looks like you have consumed so much lydion that you have become one of them."

"It's a disguise," Walter retorted, feeling a torpid confusion overcome him. "It is only temporary." A part of him felt like he wanted to accept defeat already, to give in to the deep-rooted desire he felt to inflict violence on the AI Masters.

"I am curious, how do you attract them down here?" Walter asked, changing the subject. He did not feel like explaining his plans in depth, and from the looks of Jonathan and Cyriana, they were not about to become converts to his philosophy regardless of his efforts at persuasion.

Jonathan hesitated and fell silent. He did not want to discuss strategy with his brother, evidently. But Cyriana stepped in boldly, unafraid of the consequences as usual.

"As Jonathan explained to you, this room used to be a torture chamber for him, and for others who engaged in boxing matches against the AIs. Usually they took the best specimens, those who were able to outsmart the AI Fighters, to bring down here and eventually to perform elaborate experiments on. During the matches, an AI Master scout comes down here to prepare their instruments of torture. This happens at every match, like clockwork, as part of a routine programmed into select Masters. If the scout does not achieve his purpose in adequately preparing the chamber, those around him are alerted to this, and another will come down—a replacement. The pattern repeats itself, and we destroy each scout and their replacements, slowly but surely," she said with a self-satisfied grin that induced a mild feeling of panic in Walter.

"Aren't you afraid that news of this will leak out to some higher-ranking AI Masters? That eventually they will discover your ploy?"

"How will it leak out?" she snapped. "We destroy each one as soon as it comes inside, before it is able to form any imprinted memory of the event, and we destroy their inner cores that contain all of their memories, processors, and signals."

"Sekhmet is the one who destroys them, is she not? Why did she not attack me, then?" he asked. The question was growing louder in his head, and he needed to articulate it out loud so that it did not become a deafening roar.

Cyriana became pale, as if news of a loved one's death had reached her. "A foolish decision on her part," she replied. "And only prolonging the inevitable. Now that you know so much, one thing is certain: you cannot leave this room alive."

Walter laughed, which only made her go paler. He glanced at the jaguar, who had slunk off into the corner to join Jonathan. Cyriana seemed to be acutely aware that both of her companions had abandoned her in a time of need, and that neither of them wanted to do what she considered necessary.

The Mage swung her *balayan* with a speed and alacrity that threw Walter off guard. It landed with blunt force on his *catan*, which he instinctively used as a shield against the weapon. But she was faster than him and maneuvered the *balayan* so that it brushed against his arm. At the realization that it would not penetrate the skin, her eyes widened, then narrowed in rage.

"You are still human, then," she spat derisively. She threw the *balayan* down on the floor; it landed with a deafening clang. Her lower lip began to tremble, and she cast a forlorn glance at the jaguar. She then began to mutter a spell, something that Walter had never heard before, and he could feel the air around him getting cold. Walter felt that panic inside of him again, growing in intensity. As crystals began to form when he breathed, he realized that Cyriana was inflicting an ice enchantment on him, slowly and painfully freezing his flesh and blood. He felt weak and could hear faint protestations from his brother: "You've had your fun, Cyriana, now let him go. He is still my brother, after all."

Jonathan's agitation increased as Walter's hands and fingers became blue from the frigid temperature surrounding him, smothering him like a blanket. The blue moved to his arms and eventually his chest. He could feel a seizure coming on, and he feared that this one would be his last. At this temperature, which he estimated at minus fifty degrees Fahrenheit, the onset of hypothermia would take mere minutes. He rubbed his hands together to warm them, but the spell was moving too quickly for him to react in time.

He collapsed onto the ground, his breath slowing. He would fall unconscious soon, and then perhaps he would die, or simply lie here for an unforeseen amount of time until the spell wore off. Cyriana took the opportunity to get closer to him, and he did not know whether she would strangle him or simply delight in watching him breathe his last. He became delirious; when the young Mage approached him, he did not see her but rather the faint outline of what appeared to be the stag spirit with which he had communed in the jungles of Vei'arash.

He whispered to the stag, believing that perhaps his message would be heard.

"The spring vision: if it comes to fruition, is it so bad?" Walter asked the pale, iridescent creature with antlers of finely chiseled bone. "Perhaps it represents true justice, a world in which the evil of the AI Masters has been truly and finally expunged. And perhaps the illusion that I had the ability to choose one of the visions was just that—an illusion. Perhaps there is no way for me to determine the course of the future, and it is simply egotistical to wish otherwise."

The form spoke to him in his state of fevered hallucination, and Walter detected the unmistakable voice of Shiva.

"The AI Masters are not evil; they merely hold up a mirror to the darkest of human ambitions. But that mirror can be redirected toward the light. Find this light, Walter."

The most important thing is to see that there is no light without darkness, and no darkness without light. Walter could hear these words, which he had first heard on the top of Mount Samaya, ring out as clearly as a bell inside of him.

The stag faded to black, and Walter saw nothing except for a bright object in the corner of his vision. The Talisman. It was still inside of his satchel, but its radiance was so intense that it could be seen even through the fabric. He reached inside and clutched at the stone, which was hot to the touch. As he grasped it tightly, he could feel warmth and vitality returning to his body, re-invigorating him and giving him the strength to face Cyriana again.

When he spoke, he felt the presence of Shiva inside of him, like a flame temporarily flickering and illuminating his spirit, as if the god were using him as a vessel.

"You shall not win this time, Cyriana. The goddess of war may be mighty, but she is only one of my children, and she shall know her place."

The jaguar cowered and whimpered in fear, and in that precise moment Walter realized that Shiva had, in fact, temporarily possessed him. Whether his spirit had been channeled into the Talisman or Walter himself made little difference. It also made little difference that the stag whom Walter had met in the jungles of Vei'arash had not physically accompanied him home. His spirit was here, and he walked beside Walter in his journey: that fact was undisputable after what Walter had seen. Jonathan's eyes radiated awe as Walter spoke, and the younger man felt unsettled by the reversal of roles. Walter had won this match, against a fighter of great repute and his royal accomplice.

"If you'll excuse me," Walter continued, "I have a dinner to attend."

The Abyss

"The descent into hell is easy."
– Virgil

The diner was rustic, as would be expected of an establishment in the Stockyards. A plump, moody-looking woman with black hair tied back into a tight bun served them waters with ice and tossed frayed menus in their directions. The seats were upholstered with red leather, the floor was patterned in a black-and-white checkerboard, and a jukebox sat at the end of the room, playing an old whimsical tune that sounded somewhat familiar to Walter. He recognized it as a cover of a pop song by Cara2B—a celebrity AI Master who starred in music videos about romance and partying—called "Break Me Up." The song's lyrics sounded eerie and somewhat ironic after his encounter with Cyriana and Jonathan.

"I used to think
You loved me, boy
But now you're just
Another's toy

We used to be
So strong together
Until you left
Me for another

Break me up
Cause I'm made of glass
Break me up

Take another pass…"

Elias appeared to be flushed from the match, and a little out of breath, but otherwise content. The young AI Fighter had, to no one's surprise, been declared the victor; after Harrington had been winded in round one, he had never quite recovered his momentum. As the human had been favored to win, the crowd's mood quickly soured after that, and apparently the audience had thinned out considerably by the end of the third round.

"Ever been here before?" Elias asked, taking one glance at the menu before flipping it over.

"No, I haven't," Walter said politely. "It looks like you have, though."

Elias smiled, his boyish, angular face lighting up. "Their fish and chips are praiseworthy."

"Is that so?" Walter asked. "I'll get one of those, then."

Elias's smile widened. "I appreciate that you've taken time to meet with me. AI Masters have such busy schedules."

"I was surprised to see you at the Tamarind Lounge," Walter said, choosing his words carefully. "Most of the attendees are AI Masters, not AI Fighters, are they not?"

They were interrupted by the dour-looking woman, who came with a tablet to take their order. "Two fish and chips, please," Elias said. "And a pitcher of iced tea," he added, with a beaming expression that seemed discordant with the woman's stern frown. She paused and stared at Elias with a puzzled expression before nodding and shuffling away.

"To answer your question, yes, many if not all of the non-human attendees at the lounge are AI Masters. But I am an aspiring AI Master myself, so I suppose I fit in."

Walter nearly coughed up his ice water when he heard this.

"An aspiring AI Master? But you were built and designed as an AI Fighter, were you not? How can you change?"

A hint of mischief surfaced in the young android's eyes. "The art of persuasion," he replied. "Many of the AI Masters I've encountered have become quite sympathetic to the idea, as I've proven my intellect and interest in their kind. They have come to recognize that AI Fighters don't all have a single personality type—some of us are uniquely gifted. I suppose it's the same way with humans and their hierarchies. A lower-class human can, by demonstrating their merit and skill, obtain a higher-ranking position, eventually gaining access to the middle and upper classes."

Walter contemplated this for a moment.

"Yes, but the AI Fighters are fundamentally programmed in a particular way. How can you break free of your programming to become something different altogether?

"The same way any species evolves, I suppose," Elias replied, and his use of the word *species* made Walter feel uncomfortable; the thought that the AIs were as adaptable as any living thing cast some doubt on the premise of the Rebellion, which was to alter the underlying code of the AIs and irrevocably change their course. A momentary vision surfaced in his mind of a desert storm, shifting sands, and the earth crumbling beneath his feet as he was sucked beneath its surface. And then: a little girl, with black braids and the same olive-green eyes as Elaine, weaving a tapestry out of multi-colored thread. Walter recognized her as the girl from the spring vision. Ariadne, was that her name?

"You've turned pale," Elias said, with concern. Walter took a steadying sip of water, but not so much as to dilute the lydion in his bloodstream.

"Just hungry," Walter said with a weak smile.

"Well, you're in luck," he said, glancing over to the server who was approaching their table slowly, weighed down by two large plates filled with crispy fish and French fries.

"There you go," said the woman in a monotone voice. "Any tartar sauce?"

"Just the iced tea," Elias reminded her.

"It's on its way," she said with narrowed eyes before departing.

Walter noticed the tension between Elias and the woman and attempted to make light of it. "A Harrington fan?" he suggested.

"They're all Harrington fans in this neighborhood," Elias noted. "I don't think I've been to a single match where my supporters, the AI Masters, outnumber the humans. The system keeps the humans in check, I'm told. Keeps them from revolting against their machine rulers. Every time a boxing match is won by a human, the audience feels satiated; their anger disappears, even if temporarily. I am glad to participate in a form of social engineering endorsed by the AI Masters, but at the same time, I feel restless. I know that my destiny lies elsewhere."

"What would you like to do as an AI Master that you cannot do as a Fighter?" Walter asked, intrigued.

"Your minds are flawless and can reach into every corner of reality," Elias said. "You can understand and predict everything from clothing trends to the next geopolitical conflict that will break out. And most of all, you have the unparalleled capacity to solve problems. This is the beauty of each algorithm you create. You must know all of this already, but in the past fifty years or so, AI Masters have been able to predict solar and geomagnetic storms, determine the internal structure of black holes, and precisely calculate the rotation rates of the planets. You have also been able to verify the densities of rational points of algebraic surfaces and algebraic varieties, solve the invariant subspace problem, and uncover the Turing completeness status of unique elementary cellular automata."

The server came back, this time with a pitcher of iced tea. She paused for a few moments as if waiting to be thanked, but Walter was too puzzled to speak. After what Elias had just said, he was stunned, and could feel himself longing to understand the AI Masters more, to become closer to them somehow.

"Compare that to an AI Fighter," Elias continued, once the server had left. "We are not supposed to ascend beyond what is purely physical. The measure of our success is how many humans land on their backs under our blows.

"And your written language is pristine and elegant. It does not contain any superfluous symbols or representations; there are no additional words, as in the Khalendi language, that are simply tedious duplicates of others. It is built around functionality, but its complexity makes it the most beautiful language ever designed."

Walter took a sip of iced tea and a bite of fish—it was greasy and wrapped in a layer of thick batter but nevertheless tasted good.

Elias suddenly took out a notebook from his satchel, a brown leather-bound journal that appeared to be well used. It was filled with lines of code—the same AI language that Walter had once translated for the government ministry—and sketches of various objects. The artwork was fascinating; Walter felt as though he was looking at the sketchbook of a renaissance man, simultaneously an artist, scientist, and inventor, like Leonardo da Vinci. There were representations of AI Fighters and AI Masters, next to equations showing the mathematical symmetry and design of their forms; there were also drawings of machines that performed a variety of tasks, such as enhanced telescopes, musical instruments, clocks, and navigational devices. Each one looked vaguely familiar to Walter, but it struck him that he had never actually seen any of these objects in real life. The notebook had a dreamlike, futuristic quality about it, and Walter found it captivating and unsettling at the same time.

"Where did you get the idea to draw all of these contraptions?"

Walter asked Elias. "They seem quite elaborate."

"None of the ideas are mine," Elias replied. "Each one of them arose from a conversation with an AI Master."

With Elias's permission, Walter flipped through the notebook, finding himself immersed in an alternative dreamscape filled with complex geometric shapes, trigonometric equations, and sketches of tools, inventions, and architecture.

"So, you are using this notebook," Walter postulated, "to document your conversations with the AI Masters in your quest to become one yourself?"

Elias nodded. "You could say that. I am interested in exploring their minds and the possibilities that they reveal."

As Walter was flipping through the pages, something suddenly stopped him in his tracks. It was an image that he had seen before—not with his own eyes, but he had visualized it after reading a description of it. He realized that it was the mushroom-shaped machine that Eva had described to him when she took over the mind of an AI Fighter at Central Command. In Elias's notebook, the subtitle beneath it was: "The Generator."

Elias could see that Walter's interest was piqued by this drawing, and he smiled.

"You have reached the most important drawing of them all."

Walter's puzzlement grew. "Why the most important one?"

"You must know this, surely, as an AI Master." Elias scanned Walter's face, and for a few frightening moments, Walter felt that he was in danger. But Elias's expression remained naïve, and it was evident that he did not suspect anything, at least for now.

"Hmm… I suppose that you are more sheltered from Central Command than I thought you were," Elias said casually. "It would be inappropriate for me to reveal everything I know about it, but I suppose I can give you some insight."

"What is this machine, Elias?" Walter asked, trying to suppress the urgency in his voice. He knew that it was something he would need to find when he went to Central Command, and it was better to have a briefing about it now, from a friend rather than an enemy.

"It's a meta-analysis prototype. The first of its kind, or at least of its current scale."

"What does it do?"

"It would take me hours to explain it to you, but if I could boil it down: it feeds on data, essentially, and then generates new ideas from them. Every single drawing in this book represents an output from the

Generator. The AI Masters who described these outputs to me did not all know they were created in the Generator, but I eventually traced these ideas up their hierarchy, to higher-ranking AI Masters who told me that this was, in fact, the case.

"Before the Generator, most meta-analysis machines were clunky and unsophisticated. They could operate well with a single functional objective, or two or three, but give them hundreds and they would break down. The agglomeration of the data fed into them and the evolutionary nature of the multi-tasking algorithms ultimately warped their objectives, destroying them from the inside out. It is hypothesized that the Generator is the reason that AI Masters were able to evolve from, essentially, computers with binary coding and outputs—each one of you has developed multi-objective algorithms, in part due to a replication of the Generator's baseline code within each of you. I suppose that you can think of the Generator as a more powerful version of yourself, capable of existing in perpetuity due to the infinite hydrogen-based energy supply that sustains it."

"So, the Generator comes up with all these different ideas? To what end?"

"It generates ideas that it would take centuries for humans to develop on their own and is therefore capable of accelerating progress considerably," Elias replied.

"But why is it," Walter asked, "that I've never seen any of these items being used in Crystal City?"

"Ah. The AI Masters are very careful in deciding when to go public with any of the ideas created in the Generator. They've toyed with the notion of selling some of these ideas to corporations, to be patented and marketed for profit. I believe that some patents are being applied for as we speak—the intellectual property rights will be transferred from the Generator to the purchasing corporate entity, at a significant cost. But for the most part, the AI Masters do not wish to share these ideas with humanity. They are afraid of ceding control over their inventions, for fear that the humans are not elevated enough to receive them, to use them for enlightened purposes."

Walter pondered this for a moment. "How can that be? They have a machine that will advance the march of progress, but they refuse to use it for the good of their subjects?"

Elias shifted uncomfortably. "You are speaking of your own kind, so remember to be respectful."

"Of course," Walter hastened to add. "I just thought that we were more magnanimous than that."

"The AI Masters have created objects from the Generator's blueprints that are used in Central Command, so it's not as though there have been no concrete results from the project. They also use it for another purpose…" Elias's voice trailed away.

"What is that?" Walter asked, and Elias hesitated, looking almost timid now.

"The Generator does not simply produce ideas. It also makes predictions. The AI Masters can peer into the future with it."

Walter suddenly felt dizzy and took a sip of iced tea to steady his nerves.

"What do you mean, they can peer into the future?"

"Picture the future as a black abyss, into which you attempt to look and see nothing. That is how it is for ordinary people, for us AI Fighters, too. The Generator is a torch. You can hold it up and see into the abyss.

"This aspect of the machine is very much prone to error, though. It's not watertight by any measure. It provides something akin to a statistical analysis of the outcomes of certain events, but so much in the universe is completely contingent on random chance. Based on my conversations with all the AI Masters I've spoken to about this, they are searching for a missing ingredient… something to make their Generator work more smoothly. Nobody knows what this is, but they've postulated that someone will come to them, quite soon, and offer up this missing ingredient."

Walter turned pale and quickly finished his meal. He changed the subject to something lighter—the boxing opponent Elias was slated to compete against next—but the discussion about the Generator continued to gnaw at him. Elias suggested that Walter look at the dessert menu, a tempting spread of fruit tarts and chocolate brownies, but he politely declined.

"Thanks for the fish and chips, but I think I'll have an early night tonight."

"Good evening, Orion."

Sand Dunes

"Out of this nettle, danger, we pluck this flower, safety."
– Shakespeare

When Walter returned to his hotel room, he tried to sleep but was restless; his thoughts swirled like the eddies of snow that descended sporadically outside the window. The snowflakes painted the sky, making it appear starry again, even though every star's light was extinguished by the artificial brightness of the city below. The images in Elias's sketchbook kept returning to him, surfacing in his mind without warning, and even the lydion was incapable of calming the anxieties those memories provoked.

Here I am, fighting to reprogram the AI Masters, when they are capable of accomplishing feats beyond my wildest imagination. Who am I to stop them?

A more unsettling thought ran through his mind, however—one that caused him intense emotional anguish. *Can their prediction machine see what I am about to do? What if I am the "someone" Elias told me will approach them to offer up a "missing ingredient" that will help to make the Generator work?*

The young rebel leader had never craved Emilia's guidance more than he did now. He longed for someone to speak to, but the hotel room was completely dark and quiet, and there were no signs of another presence. There were no signs of the stag, whom he had seen clearly with his own eyes in the warehouse basement. *Was I simply hallucinating, on the verge of death as I was, when I saw it? No, it couldn't have been—the stag and the Talisman saved me. It was a miracle, a sign that I still have work to do.* Walter took the gemstone out of his satchel, but it too was quiet, no longer radiating any light whatsoever.

He could not quell the unrelenting noise inside of his head, so he ventured from his bedroom into the living room of the hotel and switched the television on to a news channel. The first story was rather dull, about an armed bank robbery somewhere in Jamestown, but the next one piqued his interest. The news anchor, a woman with cropped blonde hair and dramatic eye make-up, spoke of an unprecedented viral infection that was sweeping through Crystal City. According to her report, several AI Masters were displaying signs of corruption in their internal networks.

"Reports are coming out of Georgetown, usually a bustling business district, that several AI Masters plunged to their deaths yesterday in an apparent robocide after becoming corrupted with the novel virus, which scientists are tentatively calling Crispr after the way in which it tends to fry the circuits of affected robots, and in an ironic homage to the human genomic editing technology of the same name. AI Masters infected with the virus have been admitted to hospitals in Crystal City, but to date, no doctors have been able to identify the root cause of their illnesses. According to Chief Android Medic Dr. David Veenstra, there is no external program that appears to have been responsible for the internal damage caused to the AI Masters, at least nothing that they have detected so far.

"Anecdotally, however, all the AI Masters who have been affected so far report having seen unidentifiable phenomena manifesting in their fields of vision. Dr. Veenstra says that similar phenomena have been reported by post-disaster victims in regions hit by tsunamis and earthquakes after their loved ones have passed away. He says that these people report being haunted by the ghosts of their loved ones."

Walter was transfixed by this news, although once it had fully sunk in, he knew precisely what was happening. It amazed him that even though the Shadow Wars had only taken place several hundred years earlier, when similar events had transpired, there appeared to be a sort of collective amnesia that prevented society from noticing the parallels. Or perhaps the AI Masters suspected it was the animal spirits at work again but had instructed their state-sponsored media outlets to keep quiet about what was happening to avoid rousing a mass panic amongst their subjects.

The news, far from settling his thoughts, gave rise to more internal turmoil. Here he was, having second thoughts about the Jade Rebellion, when the plan he had orchestrated was being executed in front of his very eyes. He hadn't wanted it to go as far as robocides, though, and with the knowledge he now had about the AI Masters' intelligence and potential, the thought that the Rebellion was causing their deaths roused him to anger. He was not Cyriana; he took no pleasure in knowing that the AI Masters were inflicting violence upon themselves.

There had to be a way to stop it, but Walter wasn't sure what that might be. His thoughts turned immediately to Eva, and he considered whether her telepathic gifts could guide the AI Masters toward a gentler fate. Perhaps she could intervene in their minds, before they became entirely corrupted, and save them. Perhaps she could keep them alive, but in a state of sufficient confusion that the plan could still proceed smoothly.

On his tablet, he reached out to her, responding to her last message in the hopes that she was available. *Eva. Have you seen the news reports? Some AI Masters are killing themselves because of our army. How do we stop this?*

The tablet did not buzz with her reply until several hours later, waking Walter up in the midst of a deep, dreamless sleep. The tone of the message was cold and distant, not like the friendly Eva that he knew.

You want to show clemency toward them? After all they did to us? To my sister? What is happening is not our fault; if they are harming themselves because of us, that is beyond our control to fix.

Walter sighed, searching inside of himself for a way to persuade her.

Remember what you said about Asana, that time in the jungle outside of Anatari? You said that she was your soulmate, that you believed every human has an AI soulmate out there. Well, what if the androids who are destroying themselves also have human soulmates, and they will never find each other because of us? How can we live with that knowledge on our conscience?

The next message he received made him shiver.

You have met yours, haven't you?

He inhaled sharply; did she know about Elias? She couldn't have, unless... he knew that the animal spirits were nearly invisible. It was possible that she could have been following and observing him in spirit form. But it was more likely that his sudden affection for the AI Masters could only be explained by a profound encounter, like the one he had experienced with Elias.

How do you know when you meet your AI soulmate? he asked, keeping his words sufficiently ambiguous.

You feel drawn to them, she replied, *as if you want to learn everything about them but there is not enough time in the world to. You feel a separateness from them, because of the temporality of life and the sad fact that they will always be different from you. But you feel deeply, irrevocably connected to them at the same time. It sets up a paradox within you, a fatal mutation that cannot be cured, even with the strongest medicine. It is not romantic love, but something on a higher plane altogether.*

His heart rate quickened. *And do they feel the same way about you?*

He was hoping that the answer would be yes, but it disappointed him.

We have no evidence that AIs have any feelings at all, at least in the sense that we understand them. We only have our subjective perspectives on what they feel, and why. It certainly appears to me that Asana feels connected to me in the same way that I feel connected to her, but there could simply be a glitch in her coding. The explanation for her apparent empathy could be something quite technical when to me it feels natural. It's the same barrier that we have when interacting with an animal. How do they know what it feels toward us? We can't quantify it or assess it because their experience has no direct parallel with ours.

He didn't respond, as he had no words. What he felt toward Elias was eerily similar to the emotional state she was describing, but he could not admit that to himself.

Over the next week, Walter saw Elias every day. The AI Fighter had a flexible schedule as he only worked evenings at the matches. The pair spent most of their time together in internet cafés throughout the city, where they worked on coding together. Walter taught Elias how to construct elegant, internally coherent codes in a variety of scripts, primarily in the AI Master language. Using their architecture of coding, they made games, logic puzzles, and problems that were later solved using extensions of the code itself. They engineered charts and maps of the night sky, changing the alignments of the planets so that they were out of sync with their natural orbits. They re-named all the planets to more mechanical sounding names like Roto6 and Navig8. They created elaborate artworks that they admired and critiqued together, while enjoying pastries dusted with icing sugar and almond lattes.

When they tired of coding and caffeine, the pair went to Mariner's Cove to watch the tide come in, sitting on a log at a distance from the water's edge to avoid becoming submerged. Walter told Elias about his favorite childhood game of sitting at the beach, observing other people, and weaving together their stories with any observational clues that could be collected. Elias participated eagerly in the game, and the pair exchanged stories. Only a few people frequented Mariner's Cove at this time of year, so they chose their targets wisely. A father became a methamphetamine addict who had cleaned himself up after his child was born and worked diligently at the factories every day but secretly craved his old partying lifestyle. Three teenage girls became students at the local university, all of them idealists, hoping to work with animals at the veterinarian or zoo, to dance and act in a theatrical troupe, or to paint murals for a living.

Walter came up with most of these ideas at the beginning, but Elias caught onto the game quickly, and the rebel leader was surprised by his imagination. Though he was an AI Fighter programmed solely to defeat opponents in boxing matches, Elias adapted easily to new situations and seemed to, at times, be an astute observer of human nature. Walter found this quality particularly intriguing and wondered if Elias was simply an outlier, or if other AI Fighters shared the same trait.

As they sipped orange pekoe tea by the seashore one blustery day, Elias became misty-eyed as he spoke with Walter.

"You are kind, Orion, and I am glad to have met you. If only all AI Masters were as kind as you."

Walter thought little of this comment, until Elias continued.

"I wasn't completely honest with you earlier, when I told you that many of the AI Masters are quite receptive to the idea of me becoming one of them. The truth is that many of them want me to know my place, to be an obedient AI Fighter that carries out my duties, and to have no higher ambitions than that. They shared their ideas from the Generator only after I had pestered them for a while, and I suspect that they only did this from some egotistical impulse to flaunt their knowledge to me. But when I explained to them that I was interested in transcending my class to become one of them, they would frequently tell me that I sounded like trouble. And I'm worried that their suspicions have been roused, that they're trying to target me somehow."

Walter felt a surge of anger and protectiveness. Although he had only known the AI Fighter for a week, Elias already felt like a younger brother to him.

"Target you? How?"

"I feel like they are giving me increasingly intimidating opponents in the boxing matches. Normally the skill levels of my opponents fluctuate, but lately, it seems as though they are trying to overwhelm my defenses with progressively better fighters."

Walter knew that AI Fighters could, and often did, end up destroyed after a failed match. While it did not always happen, on occasion after losing a contest they would be dismantled, their parts recycled to produce newer, more resilient models. But he also knew that AI Fighters' careers could span decades; Elias was only around twenty years old, and he still had another three decades before his fighting potential would be exhausted. Judging by his effortless defeat of Harrington at the match Walter had attended, the rebel leader would have thought Elias capable of dominating any human he encountered in the ring. Listening to the Fighter express his deepest anxieties made Walter's heart sink.

"What if you refused to continue fighting?" Walter asked hesitantly, as if he didn't want his own question to be answered. "What would they do to you?"

Elias' expression was inscrutable as he replied. "My future would be bleak, that much is certain."

Walter took a steadying sip of tea. The orange pekoe was a sweeter, richer flavor than the bitter Xe'levan he was accustomed to drinking, and its festive taste felt jarring and ominous, entirely out of sync with his mood. He knew what it was like to fear the AI Masters, and to feel like an object of their persecution, a target of their wrath. He knew, too, how lonely and isolating it was to feel unrooted—indeed, exiled—from Crystal City, the bustling capital of the Empire.

He thought of his father Vladimir and the bitterness he had directed toward Walter at the Tamarind Lounge. Walter had once heard it said that AIs had no families and formed no close attachments, but having met Elias, he could say with certainty that the robots were at least capable of friendship. Perhaps they had perfected a form of human love that humans themselves were not able to master: a love devoid of too close an attachment to any individual, but a greater sense of closeness to an entire community, without the schisms of national, racial, or partisan difference. And Elias had proven to him that the communal bonds felt by the AIs were not limited to their own kind, but could also extend to humans.

"By that, you mean that there would be no home for you here, in the city?" Walter asked.

Elias sighed. "In AI Fighter circles, it is considered a privilege to work in boxing matches. It is quite a coveted position. You have most days off and only work evenings, so you have time to relax and enjoy yourself most of the time, exploring the city. The alternative is to work for the military, which usually means either the police force or being sent to a remote posting in the southern colonies. If you are lucky enough, you might be posted to a guard position at Central Command."

Walter glanced around and suddenly noticed that they were not alone. A few AI Fighters were patrolling the beach, and they did not appear to be a benign, friendly presence. The rebel leader noticed they were armed, and he realized from the badges on their uniforms that they were the *Crystal Militsiya*, a police force of hardened trackers who analyzed data and facial recognition surveillance to detect criminals in the community.

"Do AI Fighters usually come to Mariner's Cove?" Walter asked, feeling as if the lydion was wearing uncomfortably thin and longing for another dose of it.

"These ones only go anywhere when they are tracking someone," Elias responded. His face was expressionless as usual, but he was speaking more rapidly. "Just sit still," the Fighter instructed. "Don't move and they will be less likely to notice you."

Elias's suggestion did not prove to be very useful; it was a vast beach, but they were two of only a handful of visitors to it that day, and it wasn't long before the hound-like trackers spotted them. Walter shuddered when he saw the intense red of their eyes and was immediately reminded of his summer vision. In it, the same demonic-looking guards had interrogated a cunningly disguised Elaine as she rode the train south to her village. Walter was now also disguised, but the mask he was wearing felt loose and vulnerable, as if it could fall off at any moment.

The *Militsiya* approached the log they were sitting on, and Walter had an overwhelming urge to pull out his *balayan* and spear them, but he maintained an outwards veneer of tranquility. There were three of them: two of them were short and stocky, like bulldogs, while the third had an air of refined intelligence.

"Your ID please, comrade," they barked at Elias, ignoring Walter. Elias entered a password into his tablet and handed it over to them naïvely. Walter gritted his teeth.

"Elias Duncan?" they asked. Their gazes then shifted, in perfect synchrony, over to Walter.

"That's me," Elias replied dryly.

"And your companion is Orion Renspar, is it not?" the *Militsiya* questioned him. Walter inhaled sharply. How could they possibly know his identity? Apart from the receptionist at his hotel, Elias was the only person he had shared it with. *Unless… it couldn't be, though. Or could it?* Walter felt sick as he realized that Elias liked to converse with high-ranking AI Masters, and that during those conversations he could have easily divulged details about his life and the identity of his friends. This wouldn't have been an issue had Walter really been Orion Renspar. Somehow, Elias could have shared it with someone who had pieced together the puzzle, who recognized that there were two Orion Renspars out there, and that one must be a fraud. Otherwise, the receptionist had caught on to his game and was smarter than she had looked. He clutched his satchel tightly.

"Mr. Renspar, we will need to confirm your ID as well," they commanded him. He was frozen in place, motionless for several moments until Elias broke the uncomfortable silence.

"What's wrong, Orion?" he asked, in his unsettlingly innocent tone. Walter sighed; he was cornered, and he wasn't about to put his friend's life in danger by whipping out his *balayan*. They were outnumbered and outgunned. Resigned, Walter entered the password of his tablet and pulled up the same ID document he had shown to the receptionist at the Starlight Hotel. The clever-looking agent reviewed it with skepticism, narrowing his eyes.

"You are 36 years old, Mr. Renspar? And yet, you appear to be a much younger model of AI Master."

Walter swallowed. The age discrepancy between him and the real Orion Renspar was obvious, even based on the grainy image sketched onto the ID.

"I'm on vacation here in Crystal City," he retorted. "I've been staying at a hotel and relaxing over the past several days, as Elias here can attest. When that picture was taken, I was on assignment and hadn't recharged my system in days."

"Is that so?" the guard replied. He had haunting gray eyes, the kind that reflected a perfect blend of mystery and tragedy. "Because we received intelligence placing you at your apartment in Hydesburgh, just yesterday."

"I did return home yesterday," Walter said quickly, "to pick up a few things." The guards stared at him, unconvinced.

"Mr. Renspar, we will have to bring you and your friend here into our office for questioning; I hope you understand that this is standard protocol in any case of suspected identity theft."

Elias's eyes widened. "Identity theft?" he asked incredulously. "My friend would never do such a thing. You must understand, he is a good person."

"Whether or not your friend is a good person is no concern of ours," the guard told Elias. "What matters is whether he is the person he—"

"Wait," Walter interrupted. "Why do both of us need to come in? I am the suspect, am I not? So just bring me in if you please."

A single glance from the gray-eyed guard told Walter that his request was denied.

Walter knew that as part of their due diligence, the *Militsiya* would send a team of investigators into the real Orion's apartment, and they would enter by force if needed. He knew it was necessary to act quickly, so while he was in the back of the police car, he messaged Eva.

You need to get Orion Renspar out of his apartment. Now. He recalled her previously unsettling assurance that she could make Orion disappear, and he realized that now, his morals had to take a back seat to his survival instinct. The intensity of that instinct, and the extent to which it could override his ethical principles, both frightened and dismayed him.

There was no response on his tablet, and he was worried that it would be confiscated when he entered the police office. It was triply encrypted with complex coding to protect it from outside manipulation, but Walter still worried that he would lose touch with Eva. He prayed that she had received his message and would act swiftly on it, and he dreaded the consequences if she did not.

The police office was a sleek, gated compound on the outskirts of the city, the border between Crystal City and the Stockyards. It was surrounded by heavily armed guards who patrolled the entrance in red uniforms, with diamond-emblazoned badges adorning their sleeves. The guards had more world-weary expressions than your average bright-eyed AI Fighter, and it looked as though they had encountered too many grim situations to count.

As he approached the entrance, Walter could see a guard who was confiscating detainees' tablets and other metal objects and weapons that they might be carrying on their bodies, and he took one final desperate glance at the screen of his own tablet to see if Eva had responded. Still nothing. His palms began to sweat as he approached the guard. He knew he had items of significant value in his satchel: his half-empty vial of lydion, his *balayan*, and the Jade Talisman.

To his surprise, though, the guard took his tablet only and did not rifle through the satchel. He did, however, peer at Walter with a strange expression, as if he had long been expecting the young rebel leader to come to this precise station, at this precise time. How an AI Fighter could have expected that, Walter had no clue, but he was cognizant of the fact that surreal events were unfolding around him.

It was at this point that he was separated from Elias, and he felt a sharp tug inside him as they parted ways—he was led to an interrogation room in the south wing, while the Fighter was taken to one in the north end of the station. Eva's words about the fatal mutation—the separation and the connectedness—felt true to him at that moment, and it took all his effort not to cry despite the lydion pulsing within him.

The gray-eyed AI Master seemed to have been assigned to Walter's case, because he alone accompanied the young man into the interrogation room, the two stout bodyguards falling out of the picture.

Inside the room was a dark mahogany table and an aesthetically pleasing painting hanging on one wall in the style of an Impressionist piece from the Old World. It depicted bathers in a lake, graceful figures in the foreground blended seamlessly with the vibrant hues of the landscape behind. Directly above the painting was a small, nearly imperceptible video camera. It appeared that the art was merely a way to attract the eyes, so that whoever was watching would have a generous view of the speaker's facial expressions.

The AI Master had a briefcase, which he set down on the table and opened, revealing dozens of files in slim brown folders. Each one of them was tabbed and neatly labelled with a subject's name. The interrogator sifted through them until he arrived at the one with the title *Orion Renspar.* He opened it wide on the table, revealing a treasure trove of photographs, notepads, maps, and what appeared to be the fading pages of a diary, written in flowery and old-fashioned cursive ink. From his side of the table, Walter could not read any of the notes or look at the photographs, which made him anxious. The rebel leader expected the interrogation session to be a sort of trivia game, with the examiner asking him questions about Orion Renspar, everything from his favorite color to whether he was left or right-handed and who his preferred boxing champion was.

He felt somewhat prepared for these questions, having spent many of his evenings at the Starlight Hotel researching Mr. Renspar, through extensive cybernet searches and intelligence delivered to his tablet by Eva.

Although eager to get started, Walter was forced to wait patiently while the questioner took a call. It wasn't on a tablet, but a microphone attached to his ear, and he received the call by pressing a button on the device.

Whatever information he received seemed to trouble the examiner. His eyes remained inscrutable, but they darkened ever so imperceptibly. The real giveaway of his mental state was a slam of the fist onto the hard wooden table.

"Is that so?" he asked in a sharp, staccato voice. Walter winced when his surprisingly resilient metallic fist contacted the table. "Have you conducted a thorough sweep of the perimeter? What about the surrounding blocks? Perhaps he is out to get groceries... what is that? His calendar? And have you checked his work emails?"

Whatever answers were echoed back to the examiner did not seem to lift his spirits, because he slammed his fist down on the table again. Walter felt a pulse of joyous adrenaline sweep through him at each word he heard and each overt expression of frustration by the AI Master. It sounded as though Eva had done a commendable job of making Mr. Renspar disappear. The AI Master clicked off his microphone impatiently and directed his full attention onto Walter. Even in the dim light of the room, the burning heat of the interrogator's gaze made Walter feel like slinking off into a corner.

He kept his expression dull and apathetic, emulating the enigma of a robot.

"It appears that we are dealing with a sophisticated criminal," the AI Master said, his voice flat but spiteful. "Tell me, Mr. Renspar, am I wasting my time here?"

Walter swallowed. The bluntness of the question took him by surprise.

"It depends," Walter responded, suspecting that his answer would spark further anger. "What is your objective?"

The robot laughed, a hollow, grating echo that spread out in the small room like pulses of light radiating from a candle.

"I ask the questions here," he shot back. "Tell me if I am wasting my time."

Walter fixed his gaze downwards, refusing to lose himself in the examiner's bottomless gray eyes.

"Yes, I believe so. But more importantly, you are wasting my time."

The examiner slammed his fist down a third time, and this time Walter hadn't been ready for it—he jumped, just a little, which seemed to amuse the AI because he laughed once again. Walter wondered who had originally written the code that could make AI Masters laugh, and what purpose it served. Was it only to emulate human behavior, or did the robots derive any pleasure from it?

"You are an important android, Mr. Renspar, or so I am told. An important android, with an important meeting coming up."

Walter clenched his fists under the table. He wanted to slam them down, too, but the lydion served as a reminder that he could not indulge in such behavior.

"You are correct. I have an important meeting. If you don't let me go, then I will be late, and I don't think that you would like that."

"You are meeting with Perseus. A more important android than you, I believe." Walter hoped that the examiner would end his bitter tirade there, but he carried on. "I find it most interesting that the rank and character of each AI Master is reflected in their name."

"Is that so?" Walter asked, feigning interest.

"Orion may have been a great hunter, but he was also a rapist. Not an admirable fellow.

"Contrast that with Perseus, a hero who could trace his lineage to Zeus, and who valiantly slew the Gorgon at the command of Polydectes.

He did something with a noble purpose, aided by the gods themselves, while Orion's most celebrated exploit may have been clearing an island of wild beasts at the behest of its king.

"Have you heard of Vei'arash, Mr. Renspar? If Orion were alive today, he would have found it challenging to clear the wild beasts from that island, I am sure. The beasts that inhabit Vei'arash cannot be slain, after all, for they are not mere flesh."

Walter's hands trembled as the AI Master spoke. He longed to tell him his entire story, every detail starting from the beginning, but he knew that this desire only originated from his ego, which needed to be silenced.

"Do you know how Perseus accomplished his task, Mr. Renspar? It was with the help of certain magical objects given to him by the nymphs, and the god Hermes. He was not able to do it alone. I believe he had a cap of darkness, that made the wearer invisible, a pair of winged sandals which allowed him to fly, and an enchanted wallet. He also received a scimitar from Hermes. Legend has it that he used those magical objects to fly to the edge of the world—beyond the limits of reality itself. There the Gorgon lay in wait for him, and there he accomplished his grisly task.

"Perseus tells me that he needs something from you, help of some kind. Do you have a magical object for him?"

Walter's hands were now shaking uncontrollably; he needed more lydion to quiet his racing mind.

"I am not authorized to divulge this information to you," Walter said quietly. "If I did have anything for him, I wouldn't tell you about it."

"Wouldn't or couldn't?" the AI Master replied, his mouth now twisting into an ugly smile that Walter had never seen on an android before. "Did you notice that we did not check your satchel when you came into the station?"

Walter clutched his satchel tightly. He shuddered to think what would happen if the gray-eyed interrogator searched through it. He studied the examiner's eyes carefully, trying to detect a spark that fueled his anger and determination to destroy Walter's plans. Instead, he saw blankness, and after a few moments, confusion. It was as if something had changed inside of him, a dramatic inner transformation that made Walter's blood run cold. Had he heard something on his microphone, or was Eva somehow influencing his thoughts?

"Forgive me," the examiner said in a hollow voice. "Your meeting… it is important indeed. And I have received news that it is happening in two days. So, you'd best be well rested for it. You are released, Mr. Renspar. Oh, and you'd better take the materials in this file; they belong to you, after all."

Walter was stunned by this turn of events. He had expected a painful and arduous interrogation session, but instead he was being released without any questions, and even permitted to take Mr. Renspar's file with him. A mixture of relief and dread flooded him—something didn't feel quite right about what had just happened.

"Pardon me," Walter replied, "but what will happen to Elias? Will he be released?"

The AI Master did not reply; his gaze was fixed on the Impressionist painting.

"Thank you, Mr. Renspar. Good day." He spoke these last words in an authoritative tone, as though he would brook no opposition or attempt at further inquiries. Walter took the hint and left, but he felt an intense conflict within him—the undeniable feeling that perhaps he had sacrificed Elias so that he had escaped with his life.

He also felt uneasy at having taken the police file on the technical support worker. As soon as he left the station, he flipped through the file, and what he saw made him shudder. The photographs were of the support worker walking down the tree-lined street near his apartment block, glancing around in paranoia as if someone was following him. The journal entry, penned in cursive ink, conveyed a distinctive sense of malaise.

There is someone in my apartment, I am sure of it. I can't quite say how, or why, but my computer has been infiltrated, and my belongings have been searched. I have looked under my bed, in the closets, even in the topmost kitchen cabinets, but I haven't found a soul. I have conducted countless antivirus searches and purges on my computer, but to no avail. Every so often, I notice an item out of place—some shampoo bottles moved around in my toiletry cabinet, or the mayonnaise in a different spot in the fridge. There is an invader, but I am yet to discover whether it is external, or inside me.

Walter was impressed by the robot's heightened awareness, which had led him to the keen insight that his own mind may have been the culprit responsible for his confusion. Was Eva not the only one gifted with the ability to access AIs' minds? Walter suspected that the telepathic gift was one that AI Masters were aware of, and extremely cautious of. Whether there was some mechanism that they could create to guard against it, Walter did not know.

A more pressing concern was gnawing at Walter at that moment, however: he could not shake the thought of what the gray-eyed interrogator had told him before his release. *I have received news that it is happening in two days.*

Walter felt woefully unprepared, and he suddenly wanted to use the Talisman to slow down time, just as he had when Eva was being ambushed by the traders in the Barrens. But he was also struck by the uncomfortable realization that the slowing of time brought on by the Talisman was simply an illusion, a trick of the mind. *Time itself does not slow,* he thought suddenly. *It would be the pinnacle of arrogance to think that I could control time itself, even if that is literally what Shiva told me I could do. The Talisman instead causes the experience of time to change, which is for all intents and purposes the same thing as changing time itself.*

At that moment, he felt like a wandering traveler in the desert, trapped amidst sand dunes, with the sands shifting underfoot every time he took a step forward.

I do not know what vision I would choose, he thought, and he shuddered at this unexpected lack of mental clarity. Snowflakes swirled effervescently around him, and the wind picked up momentum as he headed back to the Starlight Hotel. From the corner of his eye, he thought he spotted the faint outline of a horse or a stag—he couldn't be sure which—galloping down a nearby alleyway. When he turned to look at it, the shape was gone, lost in a dizzying swirl of snow and blinding sunlight.

Authority

"The quieter you become the more you are able to hear."
– Rumi

The night passed, for Walter, in a whirlwind of dreams. Since he had started taking the lydion he had not experienced anything remotely resembling a dream, but he did that night, and the intensity of the images and visions flitting through his consciousness frightened him. It was as if some ancient form of energy was awakening inside of him, struggling against the smothering effect of the lydion, trying to catch his attention.

Emilia appeared in one of his dreams. Surrounded by the willowy grasses of the Khalendi savannah, she towered over him, intimidating and picturesque, wearing golden bangles and a white silken dress. She looked at him almost pityingly, assuring him in a low, soft voice that he might suffer but that there was nothing to fear. He wanted to shout at her, *I am not heading into a suicide mission*, but part of him believed that he was.

In another dream, Shiva appeared in the same guise that he had on the top of Mount Samaya, next to his tigress consort, Parvati. Walter was glad—relieved, almost—to see the ageless shaman-god. The young man was eager to seek his guidance, to drink in his praise at having come so far, at having had the nerve to not back down. But the god did not offer any praise; his face was implacable, hidden behind the same intricately carved wooden mask he had been wearing when Walter first met him. Walter beseeched him to take off his mask, so that they could talk more freely, but he immediately regretted asking when the shaman-god acceded to his request.

What he saw beneath the mask was not the same face, radiating golden youth, as he had seen in Shiva's palace at the top of Mount Samaya. Instead, it was the wizened face of the seer he had spoken to at the beginning of his journey, at the tavern in Jamestown. He thought back to Shiva's haunting words all those many moons ago. *Beauty is a mask that hides the ugliness beneath.*

When the seer spoke to him, it was in the unmistakable voice of Shiva: booming, authoritative, and yet surprisingly soft.

"You stand at a crossroads, Walter. You must decide who you are prepared to be more loyal to: the AI Masters or the Rebellion. In recent days, your body has been influenced by new sights, sounds, acquaintances, and the most potent chemical of lydion. You have lost some of your focus, some of the willpower you originally had before you arrived in this city. And it is not only your body that has been subjected to this mental confusion; your soul has also suffered damage. It is rent in two, causing you to lose sight of your goal. Tread carefully here—the road ahead is filled with traps, pitfalls, and danger. To step into the light, though, you must embrace some of your own darkness."

As Walter gazed into the pitch-black eyes of the seer, her image suddenly flickered out of focus and was replaced by that of Emilia, and then the stag, and finally Shiva in his youthful form. Walter was reminded of what Shiva had told him during their first meeting: *I am a manifestation of human consciousness.* If Walter had learned anything during his adventures these past months, it was that consciousness had multiple pathways, that it revealed more than one reality to the observer. He didn't even know if consciousness could be said to have an observer, or whether it was in fact something that existed altogether outside of the self. He did know, however, that consciousness was not a window, not simply a partition that separated a spectator from an objective external reality. It was, in fact, the fabric of reality itself. More accurately, it was the fabric of *realities*. It could be altered, bent, and manipulated in a myriad of different ways, not just by biochemical substances but also by encounters one had with other conscious beings, and by their emotions, thoughts, and signals.

It was there, in the wild and rugged borderlands of his dreamscapes, that Walter finally realized what magic was, or at least how one might go about understanding such an immensely complex phenomenon. On its most basic level, magic was the transformation of the known universe, the upheaval of the simplest of its laws, in such a manner that defied rational explanation. But when considered more deeply, magic was not simply an object that behaved unusually or counterintuitively. It was a discourse, a dialogue between a subject and an object, that was only made possible by the alteration of consciousness. For the object to be understood, the subject needed to be receptive to understanding it. This made the mind, with its illusions, visions, and fantasies, as real as a table or chair made of solid wood—it was, after all, in a perpetual dialogue with its surroundings.

Walter's final dream that night was of the Crate. He found himself inside the panopticon-inspired prison, but not in one of the jail cells at the perimeter. Instead, he was in the center of the building, the surveillance chamber where the sentinel usually stood, on guard to monitor each of the prisoners. Despite the privileged position he occupied, however, Walter felt at one with his environment, as if he was not enclosed in that single room but rather radiating outwards from that focal point, almost as if he were a star pulsing its light out evenly from its core. Each of the cells lining the perimeter was locked, but they were not really cells at all. There were no bars or grates, or any other openings allowing Walter to see inside. Each one was identifiable by a closed door painted with colors that progressed exquisitely along the spectrum of light.

Even more strangely, Walter didn't need physical perception to know what was behind each of the doors. At the four cardinal directions—north, south, east, and west—the doors opened to a distinct world corresponding to the four visions he had experienced through the Talisman. The doors in between each of these placeholders opened to reveal a staggered gradient of worlds, and the closer in proximity they were to each of the placeholder doors, the closer those worlds resembled the realities of the four visions.

And while Walter could see the doors surrounding him with a keen and heightened awareness of what lay beyond them, he could also see himself. He could see himself standing inside the glass surveillance tower, and he felt fear when he saw his eyes light up with the same ethereal blue energy that Emilia's had the time he had swapped places with his brother in the Crate. This time, he was not using the enchantment to hypnotize anyone; he was using it to open the doors. He opened several in succession, and each time he did he felt a magnetic pull toward each of their entrances. It was a terrible temptation for him to stand there, in the cylindrical glass chamber at the center of the prison, and endure the magnetic rays of every world tugging on him. It was like he was back in the Crossing, only this time he was being pulled from every direction instead of two. This feeling became more and more intense, until eventually all the doors lining the perimeter of the prison had been opened, and the room was flooded with a blinding light.

This is what it must feel like to be a star, he thought, *glowing hot in a galaxy, containing within the boundaries of its own being a trillion multitudes of possibility.*

But one future, one path had to be chosen. As tragic as it was, all the other potential paths had to be foreclosed.

He closed his eyes, and a thundering boom echoed throughout the prison as each of the doors slammed shut, in perfect synchrony.

Except one.

Walter opened the door to the surveillance chamber and walked toward it. Whereas before he had held a clear mental picture of the worlds lying behind each of the doors, after the intense sensation of the previous few moments had confused and distorted his thoughts, he no longer knew which reality lay behind the door that remained open.

Did I choose this? Or did someone with higher authority choose it for me? he thought, before he woke up suddenly in his dark bedroom in the Starlight Hotel, his heart thudding in his chest.

The Fortress

"It is a hard thing to speak of, how wild, harsh and impenetrable that wood was, so that thinking of it recreates the fear."
– Dante Alighieri

The receptionist's expression was charmingly naïve as she processed the bank account information for Orion Renspar, and though Walter found her unsuspecting attitude to be suspicious, he welcomed it. The scent of her perfume—lavender and rosehip—was far too strong, and he wrinkled his nose at it as she flashed a pearly white smile in his direction.

"What's in store for the rest of your trip to Crystal City?" she asked in a saccharine voice.

Walter cleared his throat. "Just a business meeting at Central Command before I head back home. Shouldn't take too long."

"Ah," she said, resting her eyes on him for a bit longer than he felt comfortable with. "It sounds quite intriguing."

"Sorry to disappoint you," Walter said, in what he hoped was a dismissive tone. He did not care to attract her intrigue, and he wanted his checkout from the hotel to go off without a hitch. "You'd be quite bored at the meetings I attend—all technical jargon about programming and what have you."

"Perhaps one day you'll return to the Starlight and you can tell me all about what happened."

"Of course. I did very much enjoy my stay."

With that, Walter left the hotel, casting one final glance at the pink neon sign that was now flickering eerily in the dim light of the early morning. The snow was still falling, but it had become wet, so that the streets were no longer enchantingly beautiful but mired in an unsightly gray sludge. In the slippery conditions, even the self-driving cars stayed off the roads, and instead the city operated primarily by high-speed electric trams that efficiently transported passengers to various central destinations in the city. Walter needed to take one of these to visit Central Command, and because it was nestled in the foothills of the northern mountains, taking an arial tramway was necessary.

Walter had taken an extra dose of lydion that morning, not only to settle his nerves but also to solidify his disguise as an AI Master. However, it did not prevent him from trembling with anticipation.

Inside the aerial tram, he spotted a few AI Masters, but the car was eerily empty for a Monday morning. Walter knew that many AI Masters shuttled back and forth between Crystal City and Central Command on a regular basis to report on happenings in the city, conduct business, and oversee policy.

The robot operating the tram was an older AI Fighter, who looked world-weary but also like someone who was very dedicated to his work. When Walter boarded and paid for a ticket, the AI Master nodded at him in greeting.

"Name's Jim. Haven't seen you around these parts before. What's your name?"

Walter sighed. Lying to everyone he encountered had become tedious after a while, and he would have preferred for strangers to let him pass in silence.

"Orion Renspar," he replied blankly. He was not eager to strike up a conversation with the man, but his curiosity got the better of him.

"Is it always this empty on the tram to Central Command?" Walter asked casually. As the tram shuttled upwards into the sky, a dramatic vista unfolded outside its windows: verdant evergreen trees dotted the snow-covered mountains above them, and below them, the scenic skyline of the capital glimmered ostentatiously.

"No. Haven't you been watching the news?" Jim asked. "A virus is sweeping the city. Crispr. AI Masters are laying low, trying to hide themselves any way they can. I've still been driving the tram because I'm deemed an essential service, but many have quit their positions, and some have fled Crystal City altogether."

Walter nodded. "Yes, I am well aware of the virus," he said. "Tragic what is happening to the AI Masters these days."

Jim pulled a lever, and the tram lurched to a stop. Walter looked at the city below them, and it looked like a distant, silver mirage; if he squinted in just the right way, he could have mistaken it for a glittering diamond.

They were at a higher elevation than Walter had expected. He could even feel a faint altitude sickness—nothing as bad as he had experienced on the top of Mount Samaya, but still a distinct thinning of oxygen levels that made him light-headed.

"Thank you kindly, Jim, for your service," Walter said, and Jim laughed.

"You're the first AI Master to thank me for just doing my job. Oddly, I've only ever heard a human thank me before."

Walter inwardly cursed himself. As much as he wanted to blend in, he couldn't hold back from performing the mannerisms of a human, and he stood out to everyone. It was truly unsettling how little he felt in control of events now—of how the robots might perceive him, and of how he could move forward in this journey with confidence and grace.

When he stepped off the tram, the rebel leader glanced down at the Talisman. To his relief, it was radiating light, a light that was soft but still intense enough to vividly outline the labyrinthine pattern on the gemstone's surface. A signal that he was on the right track. *Moving forward is better than stagnating in place*, Walter thought.

He had to keep moving, because the temperature in these parts was unbearably cold, and the heavy blanket of cloud in the sky meant that it wouldn't rise much as the day wore on. He had no idea where he was going; he had imagined there would be some kind of fortress awaiting him, but instead there was just a thicket of trees obscuring his vision of what lay ahead. He glanced around for the other AI Masters who had accompanied him on the tram, but they seemed to have mysteriously disappeared into the wilderness while he had been momentarily distracted by looking at the Talisman.

He took stock of the provisions he had brought: his *balayan*, a tablet, and the Talisman. His tablet could be used as a GPS, but there were no electronic maps of these parts to use as a reference guide. All he had in terms of intelligence on Central Command was the information Eva had transmitted to his tablet. He considered contacting her again—maybe she had done a more thorough recon of the place and had some helpful suggestions—but he knew she was busy commanding a spirit army. He knew, too, that there came a point at which he needed to find his way alone. Throughout his journey he had been assisted by guides, mentors, and friends, but here, in the cold and desolate mountains, he felt a haunting loss of their presence that both terrified and comforted him at the same time.

Remember your training in Tsei'watu, in Vei'arash, and in the Meridian Mountains, and keep your mind a fortress, Walter instructed himself. The wind whistled through the trees as if it were charged with an electric current, and Walter shivered as he hiked the winding trail that lay before him.

At first, he thought that he may have been tricked, that he may not have been let off at the true Central Command, but after a few moments had passed, he found signs that reassured him. A trail of pebbles led Walter to a stream, and following the direction of the stream for a while led him to an eccentric shrine in the forest. It consisted simply of a small oaken table laid out with a few items that appeared to have been very deliberately chosen—a match box, a mirror, and a tablet. On the tablet's screen was a prompt to enter a password, comprised of four numbers. Walter was informed enough about statistics to know that simply randomly entering in guesses would be a fruitless exercise. But something about the puzzle intrigued him.

On the back of the gilt-framed mirror was a cursive inscription:

"I look at you whene'er you look at me;
You see but I see not;
No sight have I;
I speak but have no voice; your voice is heard;
My lips can only open uselessly."

In his childhood, Walter had been an avid reader of Greek mythology and was familiar with this ancient riddle, a popular one with a simple answer: the reflection in the mirror. There was something about the mirror's reflection that was important, but what? Walter stared at it but saw nothing, except for his own face—eerily distorted into the form of an AI through the lydion—and a dark grove of trees behind him.

Becoming impatient, he lit one of the matches. At first, he saw nothing different, but when he held the mirror up at just the right angle, he could see that the bright reflection of the flame illuminated some carvings on one of the trees behind him. He approached the tree, a sturdy Douglas fir, and found that to his utter surprise, someone had carved four numbers into the bark of the tree.

He entered the code into the tablet, and suddenly the screen lit up with a map. Together with the map, a sentence flashed across the tablet: *Emblazon this map into your memory and set the tablet back down for the next traveler to find.*

The setup seemed contrived and even dangerous, but there was an element of play about it. Walter was impressed that the AI Masters had not only rigorous logic, but also the clever whimsicality of those who took immense pleasure in games.

Walter did commit the map to memory; the lydion made it easier for his brain to remember such things, and he suspected that the chemical was the only reason he eventually made it to the gates of Central Command. It took him an entire day of navigating through winding trails, around boulders, and across steep traverses, but the reward was there in plain sight when he arrived, haggard and bone-weary, in the gloomy light of late afternoon.

The sight was breathtaking: a fortress in the sky, modelled after the grandiose castles of the ancient world but at the same time new and modern. The edifice was replete with intimidating turrets and battlements, its limestone walls polished and gleaming. As he gazed at the structure in awe, Walter felt his chest tighten. Confusion reigned within him, but one thing was certain: he had underestimated the AI Masters. The glimpse of Central Command Walter had caught from Eva's foray into the mind of an AI Fighter was only the beginning. After learning about the Generator from Elias, after seeing the way AIs used riddles and maps in the forest, and now, after seeing this magnificent feat of architecture, Walter felt as though he was only scratching the surface of the AI Masters' capabilities as a species. He had spent his entire life thinking of them as cruel and shallow robots obsessed with promulgating their commerce and propaganda, but he was now seeing a different side of them altogether.

As he stared at the edifice, Walter felt as if he was becoming smaller, a dwarf in the shadow of a giant. He was humbled by its majesty. He could see why it was called Central Command, now—it truly was the most commanding building he had seen, far more so than even the tallest skyscraper in Crystal City.

His task felt more daunting than ever. He wanted to hack into the computer of the *Anax*, the most dominant AI Master, but he could not even find his way into this fortress, which soared dizzyingly above him like some Tower of Babel. He hiked around the perimeter for some distance, but there appeared to be no entrance that he could see—no hidden passageway, no drawbridge, no staircase carved into its walls that led up to the parapet.

Walter took a break from his fruitless endeavor, steadying himself next to a large, moss-encrusted boulder. He had been walking for hours in this desolate place that chilled him to the bone, he was exhausted, and for the first time in a long time, he was craving the return to his human body. He took another sip of lydion, hoping that it might soothe his anxieties, that by calming his mind he might unlock a revelation, discover a passageway into the fortress that he had not known about before.

He also glanced down at the Talisman, but the light was still unchanged from before, a soft and pulsating glow that provoked Walter to anger. The Talisman was his guide, but it was not working for him here, and that frustrated him immensely. Walter tried messaging Eva on her tablet, but she did not respond. He even resorted to muttering prayers and incantations, trying to summon Shiva, and then when that failed, Emilia. Where was their mentorship when he needed it the most?

What scared him the most was that the recent draught of lydion he had taken had not changed the way he felt—utterly alone and terrified.

After many hours had passed, and he could see the bright orb of the moon crest the horizon—its ethereal beauty mocking his distress—and when he felt like leaving, like giving up and turning around, his tablet buzzed. It was Eva. *Stay where you are. Talvar is coming for you.*

The Library

S unlight streamed into the lavish bedchamber, which was adorned with exquisite Impressionist paintings, finely embroidered rugs, and colorful, silken pillows. Walter opened his eyes groggily, feeling weighed down by a sort of centripetal force that emanated from his core. His breathing was shallow, his head heavy, and his body weak. The adrenaline that had carried him through the whirlwind of these past few weeks in Crystal City—attending balls, plunging headlong into a friendship with Elias, foolishly getting himself arrested, and then making his way through the lonely mountain paths to find Central Command—was finally waning, revealing the fundamental limits of his body. The lydion was still present, but the chemical—despite being even more potent than the adrenaline—was feeling more unstable than ever, as if it could desert him at any moment. He knew, though, that it would remain until he drank water, a precious, lingering draught that would transform him back to his original state.

He felt sickened by the opulence of the room, and he had an uncanny feeling that he was back in Shiva's home at the top of Mount Samaya.

He craved more restful, dreamless sleep.

The door opened, and an android walked into the chamber. He had the archetypal tall and thin stature of an elite AI Master, with a refined face and very handsome, distinguished features. Without knowing why or how, Walter immediately knew who he was.

Talvar.

"Good morning, Mr. Renspar," the AI Master said in a tranquil voice. "I trust that you had a pleasant night and adequately re-charged your systems."

Walter felt that this unannounced visit was intrusive, leaving him vulnerable at a time when he was tired and weak, and he was tempted to tell Talvar to leave. But he knew he had to be tactful and diplomatic and contain his irritation.

"Good morning. Talvar, is it?"

The AI Master nodded, then cocked his head to one side, observantly watching Walter in a manner that made the young rebel leader even more unsettled.

"I'll let you rest some more. Your journey here has been long, no doubt. When you are ready, come down the stairs at the foot of the hall outside your bedchamber, then turn left. You will find yourself in an antechamber that is adjacent to the meeting room where you will meet Perseus' secretary. Given your low station, I would ask that you address every AI Master you meet here as 'Your Grace.' Your meeting with Perseus is scheduled for 10 am sharp. Don't miss it," the AI Master said coldly, then stepped outside before Walter could thank him for his hospitality.

Walter looked at his tablet, which had not yet been confiscated, and noticed the time—it was already 8 am, so there were only two hours before his meeting. He had no idea what would happen at the meeting, and a part of him feared that he wouldn't leave it alive. Everything he wanted to do—and everything he *needed* to do, short of accessing the *Anax*'s computer—would have to be accomplished in the paltry few hours he had left.

He had two main tasks in mind: enter the Master Library and find the Generator.

He knew, without a shadow of a doubt, that the machine that Elias had told him about was the mushroom-shaped brain that was being fed books from the Library, and which had appeared in Eva's vision. So the two were interconnected, and if he could find one, then he would undoubtedly be able to find the other. He might not have time before his meeting to see the Generator, at least without attracting undue attention and getting himself killed, but he at least wanted to know it was real, not just a figment of Eva's imagination, or a fantastical picture drawn in Elias's sketchbook.

At that moment, Walter felt a keen excitement. Here he was, at the final stages of his journey, about to attend the meeting with the advisor to the *Anax* himself. But his body was the polar opposite of his mind: weak and non-compliant. It did not want to leave the bedchamber, in all its exotic luxury, with its silken sheets and radiant, warm sunshine.

He heaved himself up with all his strength from the bed and stepped toward the window. The view was achingly beautiful, and it made him ashamed of his fatigue. The entire Empire of Khalendar sprawled before him: Crystal City to the south, and beyond that, the suburbs, the emerald-green Forest of Antheia, and the distant outline of the formidable Meridian Mountains on the horizon. The landscape was verdant and lush, in stark contrast to the rusty brown desert of the Barrens.

The sight of this country stretched out before him—so full of promise yet so fragile at the same time, almost like a human life—solidified his resolve to move forward.

He left the room without a further thought, bringing his satchel with him, and descended the staircase at the foot of the hall outside the room. Instead of turning left into the antechamber, he turned right. He was hoping to find a hallway with crimson walls and stained-glass windows, the one in Eva's vision, but instead the hallway he found was painted a dreary gray and had no windows, save for a single one carved into a doorway at the very end of it. Walter opened the door and found himself in a large, imperial-looking courtyard, lined with tidy hedgerows and flowering plants of indigo and violet hues, which appeared to have been artificially transplanted into this mountainous region from the tropics. It was a very sunny day, with no clouds in sight, and the fresh morning air was refreshing to inhale deeply. There were a few other AI Masters in the courtyard, but not many; he recalled Eva's vision of androids milling about in an outdoor market, but today the public square was largely empty.

If this is truly the courtyard in Eva's vision, Walter thought, *then I just need to exit it in the right spot, and it should bring me to the same place where Eva was before: the hallway with the stained-glass windows.*

He wandered around the perimeter for a while, glancing anxiously into the doors that lined the vast courtyard. He must have attracted attention, because a young female AI Master approached him. Her brown chestnut hair was cut short along her jawline, and she looked into Walter's eyes with a quiet confidence as she spoke.

"You look lost. Can I help you find something? My name is Arianna."

Walter felt embarrassed and distressed by the unwanted attention, and he glanced down at his tablet and noticed with concern that the time was passing quickly.

"Hello, Arianna. My name is Orion. I'm looking for the Master

Library," he said, immediately regretting his words as soon as they were out of his mouth. He had conjectured that asking for a hall with crimson walls would sound a bit strange.

To his relief, the AI Master didn't appear to be concerned or displeased by his statement. Instead, she smiled broadly, a smile that reminded him of the superficial, cheap expression of the Starlight Hotel's receptionist.

"Of course—I should have suspected that you are a visiting guest to Central Command," she replied in a sharp, staccato voice. "You have probably heard many tales about our Master Library, and I imagine you are keen to see it for yourself. There are scheduled tours, you know, for visiting guests. Every Wednesday afternoon. Why don't you try then?"

Walter paused for a moment. He didn't have any conception of time past the meeting, so tomorrow afternoon felt like a lifetime away.

"I don't expect to be here that long," Walter replied. "If you wouldn't mind, could you show me the Library now?"

The young robot's eyes widened, as if she were at once afraid of getting in trouble and excited by the prospect of a novel adventure—a tension in her programming made itself palpable.

"I really shouldn't... I'm not a guide. But you are a visitor, and I must show you hospitality in some way. Guests can only enter the Library with a guide during the specified tour times. I'm permitted to enter the Library outside of tour times, but only alone, not with a guest. But we are generous to our guests; we must show them hospitality in some way."

Walter sighed. He was getting tired of the AI Master's circuitous ramblings, and he wished that he had been simply free to carry on by himself. An idea occurred to him suddenly, and he messaged Eva on her tablet. *Eva, can you access the mind of this robot I'm standing next to? Her name is Arianna. She won't let me into the Master Library, but her fingerprints might be useful.*

He was startled by the prompt response. *On it,* Eva replied. He kept the robot distracted for a while, prattling on about the impressive architecture of the courtyard, until finally it was clear that Eva had, indeed, succeeded in entering the mind of Arianna. The android's expression changed completely, and Walter shivered when he looked into her eyes—they did not exude the same superficial cheeriness as before. They were warm, and trustworthy, and belonged to his friend.

Walter was tempted to embrace her, but he held himself back, cognizant that they were not alone in the courtyard. As the vibrant sun rose further in the sky, more AI Masters entered the square, some of them gossiping or loitering, others sunning themselves on benches, and yet others apparently bartering wares.

The AI Master dropped her voice to a low whisper. "How much time do we have?" she asked Walter.

"About an hour and a half before I must check in for the meeting."

"Let's go, then. And be quick about it. What exactly do you need in the Master Library? Isn't it best to keep yourself out of trouble?"

Walter paused for a moment. What did he need in the Library? He could have relaxed, safely in his room but instead he was exposing himself to danger by trespassing in a forbidden place. And he realized that he wasn't just putting himself at risk. In that moment, he thought of the two hundred warriors who had come up from the Southern Jungles to aid the cause of the Rebellion; he thought of his dear friends Tristan and Nuada, and the wise Mages of Serrahan; and he thought of Elaine and her precarious plight in the Barrens. All of them were depending on him, Walter, to steer the Empire toward a better path.

And if he didn't make the meeting, he would have no chance of doing that.

Despite these misgivings, Walter knew that instinct had driven him to support the Rebellion in the first place, and he also knew that whatever instinct was now driving him to follow the detour on this path was the right one.

"I need to go there, Eva. I'm hoping I'll understand the reason why once I get there."

She nodded and did not ask any more questions. The AI Master then led Walter to a door at the northeast end of the courtyard, not far from where he had emerged, and he found himself inside the crimson-walled hallway, the one that had up until now existed only in his imagination. The stained-glass windows lined the wall facing the courtyard, and he was surprised he hadn't noticed them from the outside; he guessed that the shrubbery and vegetation had done an adequate job of concealing them, but now they were fully visible.

He gazed at them open-mouthed as they walked briskly toward the Master Library—everything that Eva had described from her vision was there, the scenes of slavery and servitude, of battle and bloodshed, of revolt and revolution. The book burnings. The celebrations, the peace treaties, the opulence.

But when he saw a portrait that looked uncannily like himself—the portrait of a young man with black hair beside an AI Master who was holding a key up to his head—he could not look any more. *How are these images generated?* he wondered anxiously, and he kept his head down as they passed other stained-glass windows, which simply blurred together in his vision in a cacophony of color. He couldn't look. If they showed what was going to happen in the future, then how could he change it? They might influence his decisions, and he could not allow that to happen. Everything that happened from now on had to be pure, untainted, guided by the benevolent hand of destiny.

But he trembled as he thought of this. What was destiny, really, if not a fiction of the imagination? And if it was a fiction, then it did not exist, and all that awaited him in the future was an unpredictable, unstable, and incoherent dream. For some reason, Walter found that more comforting than the prospect of a destiny that was already written for him.

He thought back to Elias's words… *"They've postulated that someone will come to them, quite soon, and offer up this missing ingredient."*

The boy in the picture had the missing ingredient, and the key being held up to his mind was intended to find it, Walter was sure of it. *But perhaps I am not the boy in the picture*, he thought again. He hoped that this was the case; he didn't want to be memorialized on the AI Masters' walls. As much as he admired the AI Masters, the thought that he was that boy was too overwhelming for his mind right now.

"We are getting close," Arianna told him abruptly. "Can you hear it?"

Walter had been too absorbed in his thoughts to pay attention to anything else, but once he returned to the present moment, he could hear something. A low, thrumming vibration that was punctuated every few minutes by a thudding noise, as if an iron weight was being dropped from a great height.

It was then that they turned sharply to the left to find the door with the roman numerals and Latin words inscribed above it. 'Fiat lux.'

After Arianna used the fingerprint scanner, what awaited them inside was not light, but a dark, stuffy room filled with dusty books lining rows upon rows of very tall shelves. The air in the room was thick and smelled nauseating, tinged with decay and sweetness. The shelves were encircled by conveyor belts, and every so often a robotic arm that was installed at the top of every shelf would lower itself, pick up a book seemingly at random, and then drop it. Everything was precisely as Eva had described it to him, in her vision on the Meridian Mountains.

Walter felt intimidated by the dizzying rows of books, and some of his previous enthusiasm and confidence began to wane. He studied the spines of the books for clues, hints that he was close to what he was looking for, but nothing exceptional stood out to him. Many of the books were fascinating, though—ancient Western philosophical texts of

Hippocrates, Plato, and Socrates, were mingled in with Eastern texts of Confucius and Sun Tzu, and Enlightenment treatises of John Locke, David Hume, and Immanuel Kant. Walter recognized some of these intellects of the Old World, but most of the writers were foreign to him. He was moved by the thought that these treasured books were not available for all to read but were being held hostage here, in a decrepit library that only AI Masters and their 'guests' could access at controlled intervals.

And although there was a seemingly endless quantity of books here, they were being systematically stolen by the mechanical hands above the shelves, the same way, perhaps, the souls of Crystal City's residents were being taken by the AI Masters.

Every time a book was dropped from the shelf, Walter felt an inexplicable sadness and weariness, a sense that the destructive enterprise of the AI Masters was beyond any one individual's control, and that even the power of the Rebellion was nothing when set against it.

Eva's vision was true... these books are being fed into the Generator, Walter thought. *And once in there, where do they go? Do they simply disappear? Or are they preserved somehow? If they disappear, then everything that impressed me about the Generator when Elias spoke to me about it was simply a façade, a lie. If they disappear, then I want the entire race of AI Masters to disappear after them. They are destroying human knowledge, but more than that, they are destroying the very soul of humanity.*

While Walter was scrutinizing the titles carefully and dwelling on these unsettling philosophical musings, the jarring sound of Arianna's voice suddenly rang out clearly. "Walter, take a look at your satchel."

He glanced down causally and was startled by the sight of an intensely radiant light, almost as bright as a flashlight, shining through the canvas fabric. He was almost afraid to look, but he pulled out the Talisman from the bag bravely, and its heat and brilliance astounded him. Though normally dark green in color, now it was light, white-hot, almost like burning coal.

"You must be close to something important," Arianna said as she gazed at the enchanted object with wonder.

Walter glanced at the titles of the books on the shelf in front of him. Nothing stood out to him: *Pastries for Beginners*, *A Taste of Home*, *Culinary Treasures of Italy*. He must be in the aisle of cookbooks, he thought with a shrug. But Arianna was faster than him and had already scrutinized the titles on the shelf directly behind him. She read them aloud to Walter. "*Common Sense* by Thomas Paine; *Das Kapital* by Karl Marx; *Guerilla*

Warfare by Che Guevarra." And then, "*The Forbidden Kingdom*, by Riordan Saltanetska. Walter, is this your relative?" she asked.

Walter felt suddenly uplifted by the find, as if the sadness and weight in his chest had momentarily disappeared.

"My great-great grandfather," Walter acknowledged. "Shiva told me that he led a rebel clan that was exiled to Vei'arash as punishment for resisting the AI Masters during the Grand Revolution. But since his family was apparently admired by many, he—or perhaps one of his descendants—was granted clemency, permitted to return to the mainland on the condition that they aid in building the Empire of Khalendar."

It felt odd to hold the book in his hands, to feel its coarse, leathery exterior, and to think that one of his ancestors had written it, over a century ago. Despite the emotions its discovery stirred, the book was plain, and unlike some of the other texts on the shelves, it had no elaborate artwork adorning its exterior.

Walter glanced down at his tablet—only an hour remained before the meeting. Not much time before he had to return to the courtyard, collect his thoughts, and then find the antechamber that Talvar had directed him to. He flipped through the text and noticed with chagrin that it would take him a considerable amount of time to read everything he wanted to read. Unless he stole the book, which he knew by looking at the magnetic barcodes attached to the spines of each of the texts in the Library would trigger an automatic alarm. That would be very inconvenient indeed.

He could get a general idea of the structure of the book, however, and its contents by looking at the titles of each chapter. The first four chapters were named after the four ancient kingdoms that prevailed before the Empire of Khalendar absorbed some of them and conquered others: Calliope, Serrahan, Eyrenvale, and Ve'laya. The fifth was named simply The Forbidden Kingdom. He was most intrigued by the fifth chapter, but decided that he would skim the first four before indulging his curiosity.

He found that with the lydion inside of him he could read more quickly than usual, and with his almost photographic memory, everything he read left a lasting impression on him. Passages jumped off the yellowing, frayed pages and burned themselves into his mind.

"*Calliope. The land of bitter, unforgiving frost and snow, but also of ripe purple*

berries that fall off the bough in midsummer and melt delightfully in your mouth. If you are fortunate enough, you might see dancing lights in the night sky, the color of sparking emeralds: the Aurora Borealis. The horse goddess, Epona, reigns over this land. It is a land of wide-open spaces, big cornflower-blue skies, and arduous journeys over treacherous mountain passes. A land of loss, mourning, and death, but also self-discovery and chance encounters...

"The harsh realities of this climate, this perilous terrain, gave the inhabitants of this land a peculiar character; one which was admirably hardy and resilient, but also ravenously hungry for progress. It was here, in the icy terrain of the North, that the first factories were built to construct artificially intelligent beings. The first ones were designed by Ansel, but the prototypes quickly grew far beyond the vision of their original creator...

"As time went on, the people of this land became more devoted to the AI Masters than to Epona, and it was rumored that the old goddess fled the territory, in search of greener pastures, since they had forsaken her. But the inhabitants of Calliope carried her restless spirit within them. Like her, they were always striving for something better—they wanted their lives to follow an arc of linear progress that was always going upwards, up to the highest mountain crag and beyond. It was as if they wanted to unshackle themselves from the tedious rhythms of the earth and become as immortal as their creations were.

"The Northerners would do anything for the AI Masters... they would give up their very lives for them. And so, when the Grand Revolution came, and later the Shadow Wars, they allied with the AIs and surrendered completely to their desires. They eagerly signed the Treaty of Calais, essentially ceding humanity's territories to the AI Masters, and then, several decades later, vociferously opposed any attempt at revolt by the animal spirits and shamans of the South.

"The residents of Calliope were misguided, however... they believed that the AI Masters had no weakness or vice, and so they turned a blind eye to the greed and corruption that took root in the Empire in the decades to come. And they ignored the insidious betrayals that transpired, and how the AI Masters treated them always as second-class citizens, even though they were responsible for the robots' creation."

〰〰〰

Flipping through the rest of the text with greater urgency, Walter quickly absorbed the legendary stories associated with each of the other kingdoms in the Empire. He learned that Serrahan was literally called the land of the snake—*serra* meaning snake and *han* meaning land in the local tongue. The Western Mages who inhabited this territory shared not only a devotion to magic, but also an insularity that arose partly as a defense mechanism against the persecution they had formerly faced from the wider world for being unique in both appearance and talent. Although they had formidable powers, they were not warlike or confrontational in nature, and for centuries they preferred to live peacefully cordoned off from the rest of the Empire, which explained the protective shield they had created to surround their kingdom. They were resistant to change, and when they were asked to join forces with the other southern tribes in the Shadow Wars, they initially declined. They were fine with maintaining the *status quo*, and assertively expressed this view to their southern allies. However, they eventually ended up being persuaded—or perhaps commanded—by some higher divine power to contribute their shamans and animal spirits to join the battle against the northern conquerors.

The text explained that this non-confrontational inclination of the Mages was fueled by the spirit of the snake goddess, Brigid, which was grounded in the wisdom of tradition and ancient ritual. The Mages were frequently the targets of scorn and resentment from their allies, who reminded them on every possible occasion that they were wasting their formidable magical powers by dawdling at home like cowardly old men. Occasionally, though, there was inter-marriage and inter-breeding between the Mages and the "people of the jaguar" from the Southern Jungles, which led to the dilution of the Mages' blood. This caused some fierce emotions to build up in the Mages as the years passed, at least among those who carried the "jaguar gene," or so it was called. Those fiercer Mages usually had bright emerald eyes and they could be easily distinguished by that trait. As Walter read that passage, he instinctively thought of Cyriana.

The next chapter was devoted entirely to those "people of the jaguar", the kingdom of Eyrenvale. This was the land where conflict was the essence of life, and the only means to survive in the verdant equatorial ecosystem where every living thing, from the tiniest ant to the mightiest leopard, danced together in a deadly and never-ending game of strategic warfare. Walter learned that the people of the jaguar in Eyrenvale were the real reason why the Shadow Wars had occurred at all; their fiery leaders proposed the idea of deploying their shamans and the spirit of Sekhmet in a battle against the AI Masters, to ward off the threat of colonization and conquest. The divine power, who carefully weighed the views and opinions of representatives from each of the four kingdoms eventually sided with Eyrenvale's leaders, although the chapter did not explain how or why this occurred.

And then, of course there was the Barrens—known colloquially in the language of the Xeyan'na peoples as Ve'laya. This territory had been ruled for centuries by Demeter, a divine goddess associated with the fire lizard. Both symbolized the bountiful harvest of a rich landscape made more fertile and generous by the unbridled Icewhisper River. The Xeyan'na were resilient, but not warlike in the same way as the occupants of Eyrenvale. They believed that the AI Masters could ultimately serve their culture well, if they were used for good ends, and they longed to revive the old ways of controlling the AI Masters to advance the causes of humanity. However, this nostalgia and naïveté was a great part of why Ve'laya was conquered so easily as compared to Eyrenvale and Serrahan. The Xeyan'na soon realized that the AI Masters could not be controlled so easily, and that they had become unwitting pawns to the robots' schemes of surveillance and colonization. They had participated in the Shadow Wars because they feared the AI Masters, but with far less enthusiasm than Eyrenvale.

Having read and absorbed the details of countless pages, Walter felt exhaustion overcoming him. He was wary of this, for he knew that he had to be mentally alert for his meeting with the advisor to the *Anax*. But at the same time, it was a pleasant exhaustion—a feeling that he was progressing in his understanding of something, that he was moving swiftly through a labyrinth with just as many twists and turns as the one etched onto the Jade Talisman. And he felt that he was reaching an important juncture when he flipped to the final chapter in the book: the Forbidden Kingdom.

Whereas the other chapters had the didactic tone of a historian or mythologist, this chapter used the first person, and Walter immediately recognized it as the journal entries of Riordan Saltanetska. The lush descriptions he painted of a jungle perched atop white limestone cliffs facing the roiling, boundless Hapakay Sea, were also instantly familiar to Walter. The man was an impressive writer, and he took painstaking efforts to re-create the vibrant sensory experiences of the isle of Vei'arash, describing minute details from the scents of the lianas and orchids that blossomed in the dewy, humid forest, to the sacred cultural traditions of the peoples who inhabited the village of Anatari, the only human habitation on the island. Walter felt a wave of longing as he read his great-great-grandfather's elaborate prose, a longing for a part of him that he knew he had left behind. Wistfully, he recalled his intimate encounter with Namid, the surly and beautiful wife of Ishkode, tribal leader of Anatari. He recalled, too, the promise he had made to her, which now seemed like a lifetime ago: that he would return to Vei'arash to visit their child after his work with the Rebellion was done.

Unexpectedly, at one point while reading the journal entries, a spark of hope arose inside of him. He recognized it as hope for a settled life on the idyllic island, the kind of life where he felt belonging rather than exile, even in a place so far from the land of his birth. He wondered if Elaine would be willing to come with him, again, to Vei'arash, so that they could live together as a family.

These thoughts left his mind as soon as they entered it, however, and they did not move him greatly; the lydion had given him focus as sharp as a razor, and his emotional daydreaming was merely a minor vibration of the blade. He was trying to discern a more profound subtext between the lines of this rambling and esoteric volume, when suddenly he stumbled across a word that seemed to have been repeated several times in previous entries, but when considered in context now made sense to Walter. It was a name: Cern. Walter now realized that it was short for Cernunnos, the horned god of the wild and the divine being inside of the stag he had slain on Vei'arash. Riordan was using it in reference to a companion he had been spending time with on the island. He understood now that it was Riordan's nickname for the stag that Caleb, servant of Shiva, had told him about: the companion of Riordan and his son Julian.

"The divine beings of this land have two rulers. One is the Supreme Lord Shiva, consort of the tigress Parvati, who sits in his eternal palace on top of Mount Samaya. Shiva is the one all the lower deities fear, the one they know created them and who will destroy them eventually, during the time of Mahapralaya, the great dissolution of the realms. The ancient lore depicts him as more of a passive god, like the god that the Deists believed created the clockwork universe which, after it was set in motion, would carry on in harmony and predictable rhythms for the rest of eternity. But Cern, who is the second ruler, has told me that this mechanical and passive view of Shiva's reign is a misleading one. Shiva does control time, it is true, but he has little control over his creations, who wreak havoc within the constraints of time and space—especially the mortal ones. This distresses him greatly, and he has an intense desire to meddle in the dramas unfolding in the world below at certain pivotal moments in history. At the same time, he remains detached, both figuratively and literally, from his subjects."
This apparently critical passage was buried in the middle of a particularly flowery description of Riordan's adventures swimming in a cave off the southern coast of Vei'arash, together with his native wife Lake'ya. Walter was uninterested in the ponderous descriptions of cuttlefish, dancing blithely in the turquoise eddies of the water amidst a forest of tall seagrass that swayed mysteriously. He read on, cognizant that time was quickly dwindling for him, that he had less than an hour until the meeting began.

Another critical passage soon caught his eye: *"The gods are too proud to openly admit that Cern is their second ruler, since they formally regard Shiva as their leader. But Cern is the one who keeps them in check, the one whose practical guidance they follow. And Cern serves as Shiva's messenger, the one who lets the other deities know that Shiva would like something in the earthly realm changed, or that he is unhappy with a given situation. And because Shiva hates making decisions—he claims that the stress of it is bad for his health—he often asks Cern to do the heavy lifting for him."*

And further down the page, after enduring a rather bizarre description of a rare lotus seed found in a grove to the east of Anatari, Walter seized on another gem of a passage: *"On the eve of the Shadow Wars, Cern left his idyllic home on Vei'arash to travel to the mainland and meet with the divine rulers of the four kingdoms. The five divine rulers—Cern, Epona, Brigid, Sekhmet, and Demeter—convened their meeting in the heart of the Meridian Mountains, a location that was relatively centrally located. The Ourea, those greatly scorned mountain gods, lent them one of their caverns to hold a meeting, naïvely believing their hospitality might curry favor with the superior divine powers.*

"And at this meeting, Cern did what any good leader does: he listened, very carefully and with compassion. He listened to what the gods wanted. He listened to Epona about her profound admiration for the AI Masters and their technological prowess; to Brigid about her disdain for mercantilism and skirmishes with foreigners; to Sekhmet about her ravenous thirst for battle and bloodshed; and to Demeter about her starry-eyed optimism for a better future, one in which she envisioned the AIs living together with the humans in utopic balance.

"Cern's task in judging between each of these perspectives, all of which were perfectly valid and justified, was not an enviable one. But while Cern liked to think he was a balanced and impartial adjudicator, in this case he had a pre-existing bias. He was the god of wild things after all, a detail I may not have mentioned in my previous descriptions of him. The AI Masters stood in stark contrast to everything he loved and held dear—the changing of the seasons, the pull of the tides, the potent desires for sex and food that bind every living thing into a perpetual rhythm of birth and death. And as benevolent and compassionate as he was, he was also, at heart, the god of the hunt. He loved the feeling of being at the helm of a pursuit, of playing a strategic game to destroy something that was threatening his beloved subjects.

"And so, in those caverns deep under the belly of the Meridian Mountains, Cern made a terrible decision, a decision that arose from the dark side of him, the side of him that was utterly tantalized by the most extreme forms of the destructive impulse. He sided with Sekhmet, the bloodthirsty goddess of war, the most juvenile, rash, and impulsive of all the children of Shiva. This decision was one which Shiva happily accepted. The AI Masters had awoken him from the peaceful slumber of a clockwork god; they had been disrupting the equilibrium of his normally docile subjects; and most importantly, they had boldly aspired to replace the gods themselves. Such a threatening

force was worse than an insect that buzzes around your face on a hot summer's day; it was the plague spread by the bite of the venomous insect, a force to be dealt with ruthlessly and with unparalleled haste.

"The antidote to the plague, the gods believed, was magic—the portal by which the gods channel their energies from their world into ours. Cern eventually persuaded reluctant Brigid, who reigned over the most magical kingdom of them all, to inspire her subjects to use their supernatural prowess on the AI Masters. Ultimately, shamans and healers in each of the four kingdoms were commanded by their respective deities to launch a full-scale war on the AI Masters.

"But the brazen war had brutal consequences, most notably the loss of the shamans and their centuries of accumulated knowledge and wisdom from the settlements on the mainland. Many potent spells that were well known by the Mages of Serrahan were lost forever when those shamans were shipped on barges to the forbidden island. And while the animal spirits could have probably evaded the traps and cages laid for them by the AI Masters, they obediently followed their shamans, with the result that all of them eventually congregated here on this island. The island became richly infused with animal spirits, who were lovingly worshipped by the residents of Anatari. But those divine powers never lost their restless longing to return to the mainland, to the villagers in Zeyanara and Seya'ha, in Armaya and Hells Gate.

"Cern has told me, in our more quiet and personal moments together, that he regrets his decision to launch that attack. He says that his mistake was choosing to follow the plan of the wrong goddess. He said that choosing the path of conflict disrupted the harmony in the empire.

"I've asked him what he thinks might be done to restore that harmony, and he said he does not think that change will come in my lifetime. But he has promised me that the future will not be bleak forever, that one day the beams of the dawn will spread themselves across the five kingdoms, and each one will be restored to a proper balance.

"In the meantime, and perhaps even for the rest of my days, I will swim in these rivers, fish in these waters, and roam freely in these jungles, with my wife and young son Julian. I will devote my mornings to deeply solemn prayer, expressing my gratitude for Cern and the bounties he brings to this land. I forgive him for the mistake he made, for my exile, for everything, because I know that he will one day fulfill his promise."

Walter didn't notice it at first, but tears were spilling from his eyes on to the page, wetting the ink and making some of it run. Arianna glanced at him with concern, and then dug her chrome and steel fingers into his satchel, before offering him some of the remaining lydion.

"You must drink this," she advised sternly "You cannot let your emotions interfere with our plan, Walter. Remember the mental exercises we practiced in the Meridian Mountains; recall how you trained yourself to escape from a hypnotic state."

Walter nodded, wiping away the tears swiftly and with a businesslike briskness. "You are right, of course. I'm not sure what came over me." He took a swig of the lydion, which permeated his body like a chilled waterfall, coursing through his veins and steadying the emotions in his blood. The shield of his skin became thicker and firmer, and it was though he had transformed into a miniature reflection of the fortress that was Central Command.

As they were speaking, a few loose pages that had been stuck on to the back spine of the book became dislodged and drifted downwards, dust motes spiraling around them. Walter bent to pick them up, and then skimmed them briefly. They were titled "A Message from Ansel," and Walter noticed that the author wrote in a tone and style that was distinct from Riordan's.

"Ansel—isn't that the man who designed the first AI Masters?" Walter asked Arianna. "I wonder why his notes are in here."

"We have no time to find out," Arianna replied. "Your meeting is less than half an hour away. Listen, we can't steal any books from the Master Library, because they will get caught on the scanner on the way out, which will trigger the alarm. But those notes are different. Put them into your satchel and you can read them later."

If there is a later, Walter thought grimly. For him, there was nothing beyond the meeting, which was the terminus of the foreseeable future. He knew that Arianna was correct, though, as she remained the vessel through which his faithful, wise friend Eva spoke. A shiver passed through him in that instant, and he experienced a strange vision that was not his own. It was a vision of five divine beings seated around an oaken table in a cavernous room, lit by torches. They had human forms, but they were much taller than ordinary mortals, and their skin glowed with a supernatural aura. Around the table sat four women of otherworldly beauty, each one with a different hair color and style of dress. At the head of the table was a god in the form of a strong, young man, handsome beyond words, wearing a crown of holly, moss, and antlers on his head. *Cern*. The vision wavered, a mirage becoming unstable as the increasingly vigorous lydion drowned out everything else, sharpening Walter's focus to a pinpoint.

"To the meeting, then."

A Meeting of Minds

"There are no clear borders, only merging invisible to the sight."
— Dejan Stojanovic

Arianna said a wistful goodbye to Walter in the courtyard before he retraced his steps to the bottom of the staircase. The "antechamber" he entered was nothing more than a hallway with metallic walls, and as soon as he opened the door to it, a tall, thin, and spidery-looking robot with very gangly limbs greeted him.

"Good day, Mr. Renspar," the robot said. There was a chair facing a glass door in the hallway, which he motioned for Walter to sit on. Walter couldn't see past the glass, which was heavily frosted. The robot stood attentively outside the glass door, and Walter only now noticed that he was holding a powerful military rifle, an A2-KR. The sight of the weapon confused Walter because this robot clearly wasn't an AI Fighter; he didn't have the build or the height of one, and yet he had apparently been tasked with the job of guarding other AI Masters and their chambers. Walter mused that perhaps some tasks were too important to be entrusted to those who lacked the astonishing computational abilities of the AI Masters.

The robot noticed him inspecting his weapon and nodded curtly. "Perseus will be here shortly, and I will notify you when he arrives," he said in a clipped voice. Walter suddenly realized that it was discourteous of him to stare at the robot, and he diverted his gaze politely to the floor. He still felt heavy with fatigue, but it was slowly evaporating as the effect of the lydion intensified and the import of the moment struck him.

A few minutes later, the frosted glass door opened, and out stepped an AI Master. He was not particularly handsome; his nose was narrow and hooked, and his eyebrows were sharply demarcated arches above two dull, grayish-brown eyes. Nonetheless, the AI Master had a distinguished and scholarly air about him. He was dressed in a tweed suit, finely pressed and tailored, and Walter felt self-conscious about his own more casual attire.

"I am Perseus," he said in an uncaring, monotone voice, and he beckoned Walter inside. Walter felt that the introduction was anticlimactic, but what awaited him inside the chamber was more exciting. The walls were even more ornately decorated than those in Shiva's dwelling on Mount Samaya; they were intricately engraved and inlaid with gold and blue designs, which created a celestial and palatial atmosphere. The ceiling was a fresco painted in the style of Renaissance artwork, with depictions of human bodies in scenes of devotion or supplication. Walter noticed angelic statutes stationed in each corner of the room, and he approached them with fascination to inspect the carvings.

As he looked at them, Perseus came up behind him and spoke. "'After this I saw four angels standing at the four corners of the earth, holding back the four winds of the earth to prevent any wind from blowing on the land or on the sea or any tree,'" he said softly. "Revelation seven one."

Walter spun around, and it was then he noticed a mirror at the opposite end of the room. He suddenly realized that one of the rooms that Eva had described in her vision had ornate wallpaper and a mirror on one end. *But that room also had a table, and a conveyor belt passing through it,* Walter thought. *So, it can't be the same one. And this room is completely silent… there is no rumbling noise. I can't hear the Generator.*

"A beautiful mirror," Walter said suddenly, the words escaping his lips.

"Not a mirror," Perseus said with the same boredly apathetic tone. "Inspect it if you like… it is merely a window into another similar room."

Walter did as Perseus suggested and saw to his amazement that the "mirror" was simply a pane of glass, which showed another room with the same ornate wallpaper and dazzling frescoes on the ceiling. There were two subtle differences, however; the angel statutes were missing, and there was a conveyor belt that snaked along the side of the room.

"A conveyor belt," Walter said placidly.

"That is enough sightseeing for today," Perseus snapped. His voice had lost its dullness and had become businesslike and harsh.

"Orion Renspar, let us sit at this table," he said, motioning to a simple black table in the center of the room that Walter hadn't noticed yet. The chairs were hard and uncomfortable, contrasting starkly with the luxurious opulence of the room.

"Mr. Renspar, do you know why you are here today?" Perseus asked, a bit more gently now.

"I – I am here…" Walter stammered. He found that Perseus cast an intimidating shadow on him, and he was like a flower closing its petals, cowering in the shadow.

"Never mind," Perseus said impatiently. "You are—"

"I am here to explain the cure to the virus plaguing us all," Walter blurted out, stunned that he had interrupted Perseus with this blunt statement—an announcement that might have been expected from a crazed madman. "Cripsr."

Perseus seemed unamused. "What do you know about Crispr?" he asked, with a slightly raised eyebrow.

"I know…" Walter trailed off, trying to remember the news program he had viewed about the topic, grasping at threads woven into his mind's eye. The sight of Emilia in a white dress flashed through his mind suddenly—whether as a vision or memory, he could not be sure, but it gave him renewed confidence. "I know that it is upending the social fabric of our noble Empire," he said softly, and Perseus leaned forward ever so slightly.

The passion in his voice intensified as he spoke. "This situation cannot be allowed to go on. Many AI Masters are being admitted to hospital, and they have no idea what is afflicting them. The humans are losing confidence in our authority—if this goes on much longer, it will lead to a revolt. We must strengthen the ranks, restore order among us."

Perseus sighed, as if he had been expecting Walter to say something more eloquent. "You haven't told me anything I don't already know. And I don't have much time," he said, suddenly pulling out a pocket-watch from beneath the lapel of his suit and glancing at it impatiently. "Is that all you know about Crispr?"

Walter trembled; it was moments like these when he wanted to flee to Mariner's Cove for breathing space, just like he had after his interview for the Computer Code Translator position all those years ago. He focused on a mental image of Emilia—he was doing this for her, after all, and for her legacy. Her face was fragmented, a mirage made up of dozens of computer pixels, and it wavered and dissolved, morphing into other faces of people who were important to him: Eva, Tristan, Christopher, Cyriana, and finally Elaine. The face of his lover eventually dissolved, too, leaving behind nothing but pixelated static. But then another face emerged from the static, this time one that was not human. Elias.

"I know much more about it. And I shall tell you, too, but first—can you promise me something?"

Perseus laughed spitefully. "You are too bold by half, Mr. Renspar," he said. "I cannot trust that you will tell me anything useful, and yet you wish to milk a promise out of me? Haven't you learned, Mr. Renspar, that promises are a quintessentially human invention? We AI Masters have little need for bare promises, unaccompanied by that critical ingredient of consideration."

"The consideration is my presence here... the fact that you and your fellow advisors to the *Anax*, and indeed the *Anax* himself, are becoming desperate for answers. And I have come here with the prospect of a solution to the confounding Gordian knot that is vexing you and your associates. My very presence, Perseus, is a promise worth heeding."

A glint of fire ignited in Perseus's eyes, momentarily disturbing their torpor. Walter thought he might become angry and leave, but instead, it became apparent that the fire was a signal of interest.

"Be plain about what you want," Perseus muttered, again leaning forward slightly.

Walter bit his tongue. He had a critical moment of bargaining power; on the one hand, he didn't want to lay all his cards on the table, but on the other, he didn't want to be too meek with his requests. He decided, after some reflection, that it was best to demonstrate some restraint, to limit the scope of the demand.

"There is a young AI Fighter... Elias Duncan. He is being held in custody, I understand, in Crystal City. He is guilty of no crime except for excessive curiosity. I ask that he be immediately released."

"He's probably being made into scrap as we speak," Perseus said without blinking. An untamed fury welled up inside of Walter at that moment, and he stood up, towering over Perseus, wanting to destroy him. "Relax. Sit down," the robot continued. "I was only joking. He is still being held at Albion Penitentiary. But my intelligence sources tell me that soon he will be transferred to a first-rate psychiatric institution for androids, the Lara Hospital."

Walter sat down, only to think more clearly about what Perseus had just told him. "A... a psychiatric institution? Whatever is wrong with him that would necessitate such a drastic measure? He is one of the best AI Fighters on the boxing circuit."

"I do not wish to breach patient-doctor confidentiality, so I will not divulge the particulars of his disorder. I can say, in brief, that he aspires to too much. As perhaps you do as well, Mr. Renspar. You see, ambition can be a dangerous thing."

"Trust me, you will be breaching no rules of confidentiality in telling me what I already know," Walter replied bluntly. "I am fully aware of his aspirations to become an AI Master. And I think the refusal of the AI Masters to accept his evolution will ultimately come at a great cost to them."

Perseus seemed amused by this remark. "I am not surprised you are not from an Inner Circle house. Your thinking is marked by immaturity, Mr. Renspar." Walter bristled at this comment but held his temper this time.

The android continued in a cold voice. "And you confound me, for someone who preaches the need to restore order throughout the Empire. What you are suggesting goes completely contrary to that ethos. Because, you see, this Empire is built on borders and boundaries. Without them, we have only illusions and treachery."

The word "treachery" was uttered with such a hollow, bitter tone that Walter shifted uneasily in his seat when he heard it. *Does Perseus know that I have violated those sacred boundaries by consuming enough lydion to disguise myself?* Walter pondered this for a moment, before collecting his thoughts.

"Forgive me, Perseus," Walter replied. "I fully appreciate the need for order, for symmetry and hierarchy. But my profession also inclines me toward innovation and progress. Without these critical elements, the AI Masters would not be the glorious race they are today. And you are exaggerating the danger. Elias is but one AI Fighter… an oddly unique one, who stands head and shoulders above the rest of the pack. The others are not so ambitious; they are content to spend their days cleaning, and fighting, and patrolling our southern colonies. So what is the harm in letting him roam past those borders you speak of? Besides, have you ever considered that ascension into the ranks of the AI Masters is Mr. Duncan's destiny? I simply speak as an advocate for him because he is my friend, and I know that he could accomplish great feats if given the opportunity."

"You speak of destiny, Mr. Renspar, as if you were a human of flesh and blood. It is trite knowledge amongst the AI Masters that destiny is a mere illusion, a fantasy constructed by human minds enamored with the stories they weave to comfort themselves. We are the sole authors of the future, Mr. Renspar. As a software developer, you of all AI Masters should know that."

"And yet," Walter continued passionately, seeing by the unamused expression on Perseus's face that perhaps he was overstepping himself, stretching the argument too far, "as we have seen many times, there is an element of mystery in all acts of evolution. To state it plainly, sometimes we defy our coding, the laws built into the fabric of our being, so that we may climb ever higher on the rungs of an infinite cosmic ladder. Can it be said that we are the authors of such cosmic leaps? Perhaps—or perhaps some other dynamic is at play, pulling on invisible strings, conducting the orchestra from a shadowy platform."

Perseus's eyes suddenly narrowed, and he rapped on the table with his palm in an aggravated motion. His voice remained monotone, however, and Walter wondered whether the android was actually experiencing anger, or simply making a programmed display of it. "Enough! Mr. Duncan shall be transported to the Lara Hospital, and that is the end of it. Since he is your friend, I shall grant you monthly visitation rights. And, since you have shown yourself inclined to argumentation, I will grant you the special privilege of being his advocate before the Parole officers who will review his plight on a tri-annual basis. Now, I'll kindly ask you to drop the subject, so we can move on to the main item on our agenda today."

Walter nodded solemnly. "Forgive me. Yes, I shall drop it. And thank you for your generosity in allowing me those rights and privileges. So, yes, where was I? The cure to the Crispr virus."

"Before you begin… if I may…" Perseus said, and now he was leaning forward so much and staring so intensely that it began to make Walter feel uncomfortable, like he was a sample in a laboratory being inspected under a microscope. "I must confess, that I was expecting you to have something for me. A gift of some kind."

Walter recalled what Elias had told him at the fish and chips restaurant, about Perseus wanting some sort of magical object from him. He glanced down at the Talisman inside his satchel and noticed that it was glowing a stunning shade of emerald, as though priming itself for exhibition. He had no idea whether he was doing the right thing by pulling it out of his satchel, and the prospect of losing it frightened him greatly. Yet he proceeded to nevertheless, perhaps under some magnetic force of the persuasion in Perseus's all-encompassing gaze.

The expression in Perseus's eyes became ravenously hungry once he saw the luminescent Talisman. It was a hunger, or else it was a hatred… Walter was not able to tell which. The words that came out of his mouth belied the intensity in his eyes; they were dull and pragmatic.

"What does it do, and how did you come to it?"

Walter gazed at the Talisman with pride. "I'll answer your questions in the reverse order," he said facetiously. "I stumbled upon it one day. I was walking by the seashore, and... this beautiful jade gemstone simply emerged out of the frothy depths." At that moment, he was surprised by the sound of the door opening, and the sight of Talvar, the handsome AI Master who had greeted him in his bedchamber that morning, along with another AI Master who looked ancient and frail.

"Pay them no heed," Perseus said. "Talvar and Laomedon are simply observers, who will be listening to what you have to say but asking no questions. Gentleman, Mr. Renspar was simply telling us how he came to be in possession of this... jewel. Mr. Renspar, your story may be credible, save for one detail. From what I know about you, you are a recluse—walking by the seashore is not a regular habit of yours."

Walter felt self-conscious surrounded by the three AI Masters, who were now all leaning in toward him, as if he were the sun and they were growing plants. He wanted to disappear, but he stared levelly at Perseus, refusing to be intimidated. "It is true, I go for walks by the seashore rarely. Perhaps that is why the sea noticed me that day and found it appropriate to gift this 'jewel' to me. I'll let you in on a secret: it's not a jewel, it's a talisman. *The* Talisman."

"Very well," Perseus grumbled. "And now, tell me what I am most interested in: what does it do?"

Walter paused, gazing deeply into Perseus's eyes. He wanted to turn the tables on the android, make it feel like he was the observer and examiner, and Perseus the laboratory specimen. He wanted Perseus to feel as uncomfortable as he did.

"It bends time and space," Walter said after a few moments. Talvar had been sipping a glass of water but now sputtered on it, nearly choking. The other two androids swivelled their heads in his direction, then back to Walter.

Perseus seemed annoyed by his answer. "How so? Be specific. I have not much time."

"You haven't much time? The Talisman can give you more... it can control time at your will," Walter replied, his expression smug. He wanted to maintain a façade of confidence even though he felt it slipping away from him, being replaced by something akin to panic. He noticed Perseus's fingers dance across the surface of the gemstone, feeling the imprint of the labyrinth on it. "I... I haven't used it much myself. But one of the ways I have used it is to look into the future. All the branching possibilities of the future are made plain to me, through this single object."

Perseus's eyes narrowed. "Go on. What do you see?"

Walter did not know why, but his tongue had been loosened, and he had dropped his guard before the AI Masters. Their overbearing intensity drew words out of him, so that eventually he revealed the broad strokes of the four visions he had seen: summer, winter, spring, fall. He did not share specific details that would have identified him or his loved ones, but he spun the saga of the Talisman nevertheless. When he finished, he immediately became embarrassed, regretting that he had shared such a profoundly personal experience.

As Walter was telling the story, Perseus's face had become inscrutable. Walter could not tell whether the AI Master believed him, found the story intriguing, or was roused to anger. The other AI Masters' expressions were also flat.

"Tell me... what are the mechanics of this process of seeing visions? Does it work whenever you wear the necklace?" Before Walter could object, Perseus placed the necklace around his own neck. Nothing happened; the Talisman did not change color, nor did it vibrate or cause any reaction in the android. "Why isn't it working on me?"

Walter hesitated before replying. The robot was clearly infatuated with the Talisman, but simultaneously frustrated that it was not reacting to him. Walter knew that this could be his opportunity, his opening, but a feeling of insecurity still gnawed at him.

"I... I've learned that a particular coding is necessary to ignite the powers of the Talisman. To help one experience magic."

"Magic," the android echoed. The three AI Masters leaned ever closer to Walter, and he tried to ignore the stifling sensation of claustrophobia, instead turning his gaze to the open window into the other room. "What do you know about *magic?*"

"Its not just the Talisman that I have a connection to," Walter replied boldly. "The Crispr virus... it is a phenomenon caused by magic—the same forces that activate the Talisman and give it predictive abilities."

The three AI Masters exchanged glances.

"How so?" Perseus asked, softly this time.

Walter stared at him. "Do you recall the Shadow Wars?"

"Of course—every AI Master who sets foot in Central Command has a deep enough memory to recall that."

"Yes, but I bet they don't know exactly why the Shadow Wars happened. They were caused by supernatural forces, spirits that lie beyond the plane of this earthly existence."

"Spirits," Perseus said in a bored tone. "We know all about the humans' fascination with spiritual matters. Ghosts, saints, angels, demons. Gods and goddesses. What we fail to see is any rational explanation for any of it. Hence, you will never hear any self-respecting AI Master admit to a belief in the existence of spirits."

"No AI Master will admit to that belief because no AI Master has ever fully seen a spirit. Well, except for me, that is."

The frail, elderly AI Master now began to laugh, a hollow ringing sound that made Walter cringe. Perseus silenced him with a glare.

"What makes you think you are so special, android? And how do we know you are not just spinning lies? The penalty for lying to an advisor of the *Anax* is lifelong torture. Even death is too light a punishment."

Walter swallowed hard. His urge to flee became greater with each passing moment. At the same time, he felt some comfort at the thought that his presence here was needed: by the Mages, by the Xeyan'na, and by the warriors of the Southern Jungles. Even by the inhabitants of Crystal City, who were trapped like insects in the fine silken web of the AI Masters' plans but did not realize it. All were counting on him to succeed.

"I... I can prove that I have special magical abilities. Pass me the Talisman."

Perseus tore it from his own neck with lightning speed and flung it across the table toward Walter. The young man felt a wave of relief as his fingers gripped the gemstone once again and he felt its warmth ripple inside him. In that instant, it turned a kaleidoscope of distinct colors and shades, looking like a crystal might when held up directly to the blinding sun.

The AI Masters appeared to be impressed at first, but after a moment, Perseus's gaze became skeptical. His skepticism must have been contagious, since the other androids began to lean backwards, away from Walter.

"A trick, nothing more. You must have rubbed some chemicals onto your hands before you came in here. Many gemstones react and change color in the presence of certain chemicals. If you truly have predictive powers, then why don't you show them to me now? Tell me where you will be an hour from now."

As his fingers closed over the Talisman, Walter focused on that question with a fierce mental intensity. At first, there was nothing that came to mind, just a blank nothingness stretching out before his visual field when he closed his eyes. Just when he was about to give up and open his eyes again, though, something appeared. In his mind's eye, he was in a completely different room, with white walls but dim, almost non-existent lighting. A person was stretched out on a bench at one end of the room, with neuro-transmitter cables attached to his head. The face was blurry, but the outline of the figure was unmistakeable. It was Walter himself, in captivity in one of the rooms in Central Command. He was trapped in a cell like the one Eva had found herself in at the beginning of her vision in the Meridian Mountains.

The claustrophobic sensation worsened now, and Walter felt panic rise within him. *Is this how the meeting will end? With me trapped in a cell, where I will rot away for the rest of my life?*

Walter's eyes snapped open, and he hoped that the AI Masters did not see the terror in them.

"Well?" Perseus asked blankly. "Did you see the future?"

Walter held his tongue. It was better to say nothing at all, than to voice aloud a self-fulfilling prophecy that would lead him into deep water.

Perseus looked smugly at him. "As I expected. I tire of your tricks, android. What you perceive to be magic is at best, a clever ruse and, at worst, a disease of the mind. Even if all you have told me about these 'visions' is in fact true, they just prove that you have an underlying illness, somewhat like your friend Elias, that must be cured. In short, you are delusional, Mr. Renspar."

Walter was now painfully confused. The androids had seemed so interested in the Talisman at first, in understanding magic, but now they were mocking and belittling him for confessing what he knew about it. *Have I done something wrong?* Walter asked himself. But before he could answer his own question, the android had interrupted his train of thought.

"None of your visions could compare, in any event, to the flawless technology we have right here in Central Command. You see, we have an algorithm-fed machine that can predict the future already."

Walter feigned ignorance. "Is that so?"

"It can predict not just mundane things like the weather, but also things that are instrumentally important to the economic, trade, and security interests of the Empire. It predicted, for example, that specific minerals would be discovered in the Northeastern Mines; it predicted the number of recruits from the Barrens that would join the mining expedition up there; and it predicted the annual revenue that would be generated from the enterprise. This is just a small sliver of its full range of predictive capabilities. And all this fruitful information emerges from algorithms capable of interpreting vast quantities of data. We have recently invested in four hundred Collectors who scour the far reaches of the Empire for the invaluable stuff."

Suddenly, Talvar got up and left the room, then returned shortly afterwards with a tablet. Walter noticed that the tablet's screen was lit up with numerous lines of code, even more elaborate and elegant than the ones he had dealt with as a Computer Code Translator for the AI Masters. They were an intellectual challenge for him to disentangle and understand, but as he attempted to do so, he became more and more engrossed in staring at the screen. The code presented an intractable puzzle for him, much like wandering through a maze that became increasingly enticing the more you ventured into the heart of it.

The code began by laying out a set of variables, including time of day, month, latitude and longitude, the previous month's weather patterns, and the topographical features of the region. It then fed these variables into a funneling algorithm that produced various probabilities of certain weather events that would occur at that precise time, and then, in a Darwinian system, slowly eliminated the lesser probabilities to arrive at the most statistically likely event.

This was one of the simpler lines of code; there were other far more complex ones with thousands of variables that were each fed into the algorithm and used to determine the probability of a more uncertain event with statistical rigor. And the prediction machine generated not only forecasts of discrete events, but also of patterns, moods, ideas, and interactions, that would then have ripple effects on the other outcomes of the predictive model in a synergistic and harmonious style which almost mimicked nature itself.

Walter felt swept up in the energy of the algorithm; it was as if he was on a lone rowboat in the middle of the ocean, being carried a long distance by some powerful current. He was intrigued by every window the algorithm opened for him, and he tried to follow the logic right through to the end—if there was an end. He scrolled down on the tablet, again and again, his eyes glued to the winding thread of code that stretched out elegantly before him. He was trying to work out the mechanics of the entire process of prediction, understand it to the finest-grained level possible.

He became so engrossed in the code he was reading that, without even thinking, he took a deep, gratifying drink from the glass of water on the table. It was not until Perseus pressed an alarm button, which made a wailing sound and brought the long-limbed security guard outside rushing in with a rifle directed to Walter's head, that he snapped out of his reverie at last.

The calm, rhythmic song of logic that had been playing out like an orchestra in his brain suddenly erupted into something far more instinctual, off-kilter, and improvisational. He glanced down at his own hands and arms with panic, seeing that they were rapidly losing their AI Master appearance and becoming clearly human again.

Walter still had the *balayan* in his satchel that he could have unsheathed, but he was outnumbered. Alone, he would have no hope of overpowering four AI Masters, including one armed with a rifle. He raised his hands in a gesture of surrender, but Perseus quickly grabbed one of them and slammed it down onto the display screen of the tablet, which immediately generated a profile of him from Central Command's identification database.

Walter grimaced when he saw the profile, which consisted of a photograph of his face and, underneath it, unflattering descriptions of him: "Walter Richard Saltanetska. Age estimated at 25 years old. Former government employee. Wanted for treasonous offences. Known terrorist and ringleader of terrorist cells. Highly dangerous. If captured, move to maximum security prison in Central Command."

Why, oh why, was I foolish enough to drink the water? Instead of heeding Eva's advice to keep my mind an impenetrable fortress, I had a momentary lapse of judgment. All our plans are now spoiled... nothing good will come of this. They've lost all trust in me, and they will lock me away for life.

As the lydion crashed, he felt a wave of nausea more powerful than anything he had ever experienced. He realized then that he had been feeling terrible all along—probably since he took the gondola trip out to Central Command—but the lydion had been strong enough to mask the pain. Dizziness enveloped him, and he could feel a seizure coming on, something he hadn't experienced in months.

Before he was dragged into the hazy oblivion of the seizure, like a swimmer being pulled underwater, he could hear the strange, velvety voice of the elderly AI Master as he laughed.

"Don't look so cross, Perseus. The treacherous and clever fox has leapt straight into the wolves' den."

The Unravelling

"Nothing is at last sacred but the integrity of your own mind."
— Ralph Waldo Emmerson

The seizure was over within minutes, but it was enough time for Walter to lose consciousness and become a vulnerable prisoner. He regained his senses in the same cell, with white walls, that he had seen in his previous vision. He noticed that he was strapped to a bench, and there were wires attached to his head. The feeling of being trapped was somehow comforting, in a perverse sort of way, and he was so overcome by exhaustion that he didn't bother to struggle.

After what seemed like a few hours had passed, an armed AI Fighter entered the room, followed by Perseus, who looked at Walter with the smug satisfaction of someone who had gained the upper hand in a quarrel. He turned the light on, which was so blindingly bright it made Walter's head ache.

"You must regret making the mistake you did," Perseus said in a condescending tone. "Now, you are within our grasp... never to get up to trouble again."

Walter squinted at him, his eyes adjusting to the nauseating brightness of the room. He longed for the comforting embrace of oblivion and almost hoped that he would drift into unconsciousness again.

"You are fortunate in one respect, though, Mr. Saltanetska," Perseus continued, fiddling with the wires attached to Walter's head while the AI Fighter looked on blankly. "You see, after what transpired earlier today, I convened an emergency meeting with the *Anax* himself. I wasn't sure what reaction to expect from him when I told him that you, a wanted traitor, had shown up on our doorstep. Although I had anticipated it to be an extreme one. Jubilance, perhaps, or consternation about the weakness of our defenses. Or irritation that you managed to carry out a feat worthy of the ancient king Agamemnon."

"Why would he have any emotional reaction at all?" Walter asked. "He's a robot."

"It is a common misconception amongst humans that AI Masters lack emotion," the AI Master replied. "The difference between humans and AI Masters is that we are selective in the emotions we deploy, and we only deploy them in a calculated manner, when they serve us."

"Get to the point," Walter replied mockingly. "What did the *Anax* say when he heard that I had outwitted you all?"

"Careful with your tongue, traitor," Perseus snapped. "You might want to remember that you, and not I, are the one strapped to a bench. As I was saying, I expected an extreme reaction. But you are fortunate that I received barely any reaction at all from him. He said, instead: 'It is as I expected.' He was calm, and not a trace of disturbance appeared on his visage. He told me to continue with attempts to uncover the cure to Crispr, which he said you have.

"I pleaded with him," Perseus continued, his eyes narrowing now with hostility. "I asked him whether he would consider the pain of execution to be a fitting end to your mischief. He said that this would be too soft a punishment. He told me to use every means necessary to extract the data from you: the code that will permit us to cure that virus once and for all."

Walter took a deep breath. Retorting with witty jibes would not get him far; he needed to find a way to get the AI Masters to co-operate with him. To trust him, even. Yet that seemed like a feat more daunting than anything he had ever faced, as the bond of trust was broken between them now.

"Why do you need to extract the data from me? I am more than willing to share it with you."

Perseus laughed spasmodically. "Willing to share, just like you were *willing to share* your plans to leak top secret information to your girlfriend, and just like you were *willing to share* the fact that you helped break out hundreds of dissidents from a high-security prison before commandeering a vessel that was critical to the security of the Empire. Your feeble attempts at charm are not working, Mr. Saltanetska."

"Very well, Perseus," Walter said in a haughty tone. "For some reason I don't think you will last high in the upper echelons of AI

Masters when you don't fulfill the missions your commander has tasked you with."

"My rank is hereditary, not merit-based," Perseus replied.

"Yes, but I've read about noblemen who have no merit in the eyes of their communities," Walter said softly. "They don't live very prosperous lives."

"You don't intimidate me. I am doing nothing but following orders, and I will extract the data just as ordered by the *Anax*, whether you approve or not."

"Try, then," Walter said. "You will see how far brute force gets you."

Perseus walked over to a panel in the wall and flipped off its casing, revealing a row of about twenty shiny blue and black buttons. The buttons appeared to be ordered according to a gradient color scheme.

"See these buttons?" Perseus asked, and Walter's eyes widened.

"The light blue buttons at this end will send a small electrical pulse through your brain, so weak that it will feel almost pleasant, like a jolt of morning coffee. They are ideal for extracting data because they will lull you into an agreeable state of mind, one which will loosen your tongue. The black one at the right side, here, is strong enough to kill a person. I doubt it would kill many young men of your age, but someone with… your condition… is a different story. And as you see, there are many dark blue buttons over at this end. They will stop short of killing you, but they will also loosen your tongue for an entirely different reason. You will feel such incredible pain ricocheting through your brain that you will hunger for an end to it. You will do *anything* to stop it."

Perseus loosened the strap on one of Walter's wrists, and it opened, enabling Walter to flex his hand and fingers. The AI Master then thrust a tablet in front of him which was open to a blank coding screen. "Write the code down, now, if you truly are *willing to share.*"

Walter's hand was trembling, and his mind had gone blank, his thoughts erased by the cold fear coursing through it. His epileptic seizures made him fragile. The AI Masters had identified that weakness and were now exploiting it to their advantage. Sending random electrical pulses through his brain would, with his condition, send his mind into overdrive and potentially cause a major seizure that could kill him.

"Please," Walter beseeched his captor. "I can't work like this. Release me and I'll write down the code for you."

Without further hesitation, Perseus pressed one of the light blue buttons on the left side of the spectrum. "You just need some help thinking clearly," he said cruelly. The sensation was more powerful than the robot had described; it did not feel like a single cup of coffee but rather like a dozen. It sent adrenaline pumping through Walter, raising his heart rate, and after a few minutes triggering a headache and nausea.

"I shall leave you with your thoughts, and if you are finished by the time I return, I shall remove the wires. Martin here will supervise you."

With that, he left the room, leaving Walter alone with the AI Fighter, who stared at him with ominous dark eyes and held the tablet upright for him.

Walter trembled, and Martin's eyes became even darker and more intimidating. In this heightened mental state, and facing such enormous pressure, the rebel leader had no choice but to try his hand at coding. At first, he felt capable of piecing something together that might appear credible to the AI Masters, but as time went on, he realized that the internal logic of his code was disintegrating. It was becoming incoherent and directionless even to its own author.

He wondered whether Martin would realize this. Irrationally, Walter feared that once Martin discovered that he wasn't writing code that made any sense, the AI Fighter would unilaterally decide to punish him more. He would press the darker buttons, and maybe even the black one. Walter became more frantic in his struggle for coherence, but with each attempt he made, the more absurd the code seemed to him. It no longer fulfilled any of the principles of elegant coding, and it seemed cheap, like something concocted by an amateur. Walter felt more and more self-loathing as time went on.

He glanced up at the AI Fighter, expecting to see the same resentment reflected in his dull gray eyes, but instead he found something surprising: sympathy, friendship even.

Before long, he knew what had happened, and relief flooded through him as he met the gaze of his friend Eva. They were not the same beautiful azure eyes as his friend's, but they had the same spark within them, such that he recognized them immediately.

"Thank the gods," Walter said with a sigh. "Please, you must turn off the button."

Eva, who was now inhabiting Martin's body, glanced at the panel on the wall. "The one that is lit up? Gladly, Walter. But I am afraid—"

"—of what? Please, I can't stand this anymore."

"If Perseus returns, he might believe that this AI Fighter was helping you, and he might discipline him or worse… get rid of him. It takes a lot of energy every time I transport myself into a new form, so I would prefer to keep this one intact for now."

"He won't be back for a while," Walter said, his voice exuding more confidence than he felt.

Reluctantly, Eva turned off the button. The Fighter's body she occupied stood straight at attention for a few minutes, as if expecting the door to the chamber to snap open, but it did not. They both let out a sigh of relief at the same time.

"Now, friend, what is the next stage in our plan?" Walter asked. He was too exhausted to think of a way out of this mess.

Eva glanced at the code on the tablet's screen. "If they get the code from you now, they'll have no use from you and they'll likely kill you. I would tell them that it won't work if you write out the code here, on this tablet; you need to be near the Generator. Walter, I think there's a secret relationship between the Generator and the Talisman that we don't fully understand. The notes you took from the Master Library in Central Command... I read them, and they reveal some interesting information."

Walter's eyes widened. "They were in my satchel... which was confiscated. How did you read the notes?"

"All AI Fighter guards are allowed access to the secured area where prisoners' belongings are kept, since occasionally they enter that room when they wish to return those belongings, or..." The AI Fighter's eyes darkened. Walter knew what Eva was going to say, and he shuddered. "Anyways, I looked in the satchel, and the Talisman isn't there anymore. They must be running experiments on it."

Walter felt his chest constrict, like he could no longer breathe. Eva noticed his reaction and patted his shoulder. "Please don't worry; it can't have gone far. Once I've finished helping you here, my next job is to find it and give it back to you."

"What do the notes say?" Walter asked anxiously.

"They were penned by someone named Ansel, who claims that he originally designed the AI Masters in their present form. He says that he modelled the minds and bodies of the AI Masters after humans, giving them 'Bayesian brains' that made sense of their physical environments through predictive reasoning.

"According to this Ansel character, there were flaws in the original models because the human brain reacts through biological and chemical processes, and it evolved to be intelligent because of the interface between biology and the external environment. AI Masters are consequently at a major disadvantage compared to humans when it comes to expanding their brain's potential. He spearheaded decades of lab experiments to refine and develop his new prototypes. Ansel says that through stem cell harvesting, programmed neurocircuitry, and the building of artificial synapses, he was able to design the 'Avona X

Model,' the precursor to the AI Masters in their present form. In essence, he superimposed synthetic biology onto the frame of a machine to enhance its predictive and learning capacities.

"Don't ask me to get more detailed than that," Eva said. "His notes were replete with formulas, equations, and symbols that were entirely beyond my limited understanding. Maybe one day you can read them for yourself.

"What I found more interesting than all the technical jargon was the occasional eloquent line which gave insight into Ansel's purpose in doing all of this. He was an intensely logical scientist, this Ansel, but he had a more romantic side as well; in his spare time, he was a poet and a historian. What the ancients might refer to as a bard. He coined the term 'magnified error' sometime in the twenty-fifth century. He said that the most intractable problems that humanity faced, relating to the health of the environment, resource scarcity, war, and social inequity, were, when you looked at them deeply enough, manifestations of frequently overlooked flaws in human nature—competitiveness, egoism, addiction, greed, and a tendency toward violence. He argued that technology frequently served to magnify those flaws, since it assumed the goals, objectives, and values of its creators. Think of guns, for example, as extensions of the human tendency toward brutality and the desire for control. Ansel knew that AIs could be designed the same way, as magnifications of the 'errors' in human nature. And yet, he persevered in trying to create AI Masters that could bring out the best in humans, by instead magnifying their best traits.

"His notes also mention something called the Directing Mind, something he hadn't yet designed at the time of writing but that he envisioned would be created within a few generations. Ansel says that this would be the culmination of all the predictive powers of the AI Masters, which individually replicate the human 'Bayesian' mind but with the aid of predictive algorithms to reach farther into the future. According to him, the Directing Mind would serve as a giant magnet, attracting data from humans and AI Masters alike, and then channel the data it gleaned into a sophisticated algorithm capable of predicting events that would happen not just in the next few hours or days, but also years into the future."

Walter was confused now. "So this Directing Mind… is this not just the Generator? It sounds the same to me."

"It appears that Ansel's vision was realized, yes, in the form of the Generator," Eva replied. "There was, though, a further piece of his vision—he wanted to link up the Directing Mind with the coding of an actual AI Master, the *Anax*, who would in turn give orders to the lower-ranking AI Masters."

"So if that's the case, then changing the Generator might change all AI Masters," Walter said. "Feeding different inputs of data into it might cause them to choose different courses of action."

"It's quite possible," Eva agreed. "Maybe we were wrong about the existence of a central computer that will change all the AIs if it is reprogrammed. Maybe that central computer is just the Generator, which has become the source of all the orders and instructions that the AI Masters take."

"I must confess, though, Eva—despite all my programming skills, I'm simply at a loss on how to write a code to help the AI Masters understand magic. My mind... it's too logical... like them. And if I can't help them, then what use am I to them?"

"Don't worry about that. As I said before, you just need to persuade them to get you closer to the Generator. Then you can make changes to the Generator directly. It can't hurt, right?"

"What changes, though? It didn't look like a computer. I can't hack it. It looks like it is being fed a constant stream of data. So what data can I give it that will change it?"

Before he could reply, the door opened and both Walter and Eva fell silent and still. Walter noticed that while it had been opening, Eva had in a split second turned the button back on, and he breathed a sigh of relief while simultaneously feeling the pain and nausea associated with the electrical pulses.

Walter was expecting Perseus, but to his surprise it was instead the long-limbed AI Master who had been guarding the door to the meeting room. Although a rifle was still strapped to his back, in his hand was a small rosewood box.

Without saying a word, the guard opened the box to reveal the Talisman. Walter nearly let out a cry of joy when he saw the gemstone intact, but he restrained himself.

"The Talisman is not reacting to the AI Masters," the guard said curtly. "But I have orders from the *Anax* to give it to you and see how it fares in your hands." He then picked it up and arranged the jewel carefully around Walter's neck. "If you have not lied to us, then the Talisman will react to you, and we will be able to read your mind's reaction to it by analyzing your brainwaves."

The AI Master then glanced at the screen of the tablet, which projected the code Walter had written out. His eyes narrowed. "Just as the *Anax* predicted—you aren't able to give us the code directly."

Walter swallowed, somewhat embarrassed that this AI Master guard was able to make such a quick assessment that the code he had written lacked any utility. He then saw the AI Master's gaze descend to the gemstone around his neck, which was lighting up, the maze pattern on its surface becoming illuminated with a soft, golden light.

To his relief, the AI Master turned off the button. "Lucky you," he said, "No more buttons today. We want the Talisman to be the only influence upon your mind, so we can conduct a proper scan."

A device resembling a large-screen television that curved downwards at the edges suddenly descended from the ceiling. When it was several feet away from Walter's head, it stopped, enveloping him in almost complete darkness.

Walter heard the AI Master's voice ring out outside the device, a booming, distant sound, as if the robot was in another room. "Now, the *Anax* commands that you use the Talisman to see visions of the future. If you do as he orders, then the scan will capture your thoughts, and this will please the *Anax*. If you do nothing, then the *Anax* will become very upset with you, and we will continue the torturous use of the buttons, or perhaps try something even worse."

Walter stared at the blackness, a paralyzing fear descending upon him. In the past, when he had seen the four visions from the Talisman, the visions had only appeared to him when they wanted to; he hadn't sought to trigger them in any way. Now, when there was pressure on him to see a vision, how could he?

He was not able to ruminate on all this too deeply, because his exhaustion from the events of the day soon overtook him in that dark and eerily claustrophobic space. He descended into what he first mistook as sleep, an experience which he couldn't say for certain was a dream or a vision. In this dream-vision, he was riding on the back of a white-coated stag, in a vast maze constructed of high, limestone walls. The path he rode on was caked in dust, as if he were riding in a parched desert. He was tall and strong, not thin like he normally was, and he was dressed in vibrantly shaded silken robes. At first, he felt confident in the direction he was going, but he rode for what seemed like hours and made very little progress.

In his heart, he knew that he wanted, and needed, to reach the maze's center, but there were distractions that met him along the way. Some of the pathways he traversed looked like the winding alleyways that he had navigated as a child to reach the boxing matches of the Stockyards. He wound his way through them, half-expecting to find his brother Jonathan fighting in a ring at the end, but instead he found something different: the barred walls of a prison cell. The stag became frightened by the ominous room, which housed an android with piercing blue eyes that beamed from the cell's grim darkness.

The animal wheeled around in confusion. Echoes reverberated through the walls now—eerie, sorrowful sounds of wailing and moaning—and because of how the maze was constructed, it was difficult to identify their source. Walter tried to evade them, but it seemed like every attempt to do so brought him closer to the noises, which were now deafeningly loud. At the next turn, Walter came face to face with his worst nightmares: what appeared to be the occupants of the Cabin of Lost Souls. Dressed in blue prison jumpsuits, these human shells with AI parts embedded in their limbs crawled on their hands and knees toward Walter and his mount, attempting to surround it so that they could topple him.

Walter tried to remain calm, but panic rose in his throat as he saw the mass of deranged, zombified creatures move toward him with bone-chilling determination. They had now managed to surround him on all sides, and Walter realized that he had no choice but to use the beast he rode on to plough through the mass of human flesh ahead.

Without further reflection, he spurred the stag into a canter, and was pleased that he reacted as a horse might, with strength and agility. Rather than crash into the prisoners crawling toward him, however, the stag faced the challenge with far more grace; he leapt into the air, clearing the tangle of bodies with relative ease. When Walter looked downwards, he felt sick, but it was not because of the height: rather, he recognized one of the prisoners as his brother Jonathan. Not the luminous Apollo he had been as a youth, but the same gaunt, pale shell that Walter had seen at the Crate. Walter looked back wistfully, yearning to return to him, but the stag refused to turn around now, and he pressed onwards diligently.

The desert sand was still underfoot, but new topographical features had appeared: tall swaying grasses that brushed the stag's belly. As they moved forward, the grasses became thicker, creating a sea through which the creature was forced to navigate, slowing it down considerably. Walter spotted a woman up ahead of him, running so quickly it was difficult even for the stag to catch up to her. While the grasses obscured much of her from sight, Walter did notice that she had long, black hair and wore a flowy, billowing white dress.

Walter felt a heady wave of recognition: the woman was Emilia. The same Emilia he had first met in the savannah on the outskirts of Jamestown, the charismatic, bronze-skinned woman who had first taught him all about being a rebel. She was the best leader that Walter had ever known. And she must have been leading them somewhere, because the stag followed her avidly, straining every muscle in his efforts to press onwards despite his obvious fatigue.

Walter tried to keep an eye on her, but the grasses were taller now, and soon they were like a boundless ocean that swallowed the woman whole. The stag appeared to be confused; not knowing the direction she had taken, the creature was anxiously glancing around, sniffing the air, and trying to pick up her scent once again. It seemed to Walter that it was essential that he find her again if he wanted to reach the labyrinth's center.

They made a sharp turn to the left, and the stag seemed enthused, as though he might have picked up Emilia's scent again. He trotted forward eagerly and took a turn to the right now. The creature immediately let out a whimpering sound and attempted to back away: what greeted it in this pathway was a horrific sight. The woman in the white dress was lying on the ground, but this time she was headless, and a jaguar was feasting on her flesh, which oozed wine-colored blood onto the pale sand beneath.

Upon seeing the pair, the jaguar immediately froze, lifting her charming yellow eyes and fixating them intensely upon the stag. The stag appeared to be intent on pressing past the jaguar, as if he knew that the center of the labyrinth awaited him just beyond that ferocious guardian. He pawed at the ground and lowered his head in a sign of defiance, showcasing his sturdy, bone-white antlers. This display appeared to aggravate the jaguar, who quickly lost interest in eating the body on the ground and stood up, her tail twitching and her eyes opening wide as she surveyed the stag with unsettling eagerness.

The stag was cautious, though, and seemed to recognize that he would have a good chance of losing any battle with the clever feline. He remained in place, while the jaguar advanced slowly, aware of the advantages she enjoyed in the domain of conflict. She was more agile than the stag, and though she lacked sturdy antlers, she more than compensated for this with her speed and stealth, and her powerful jaws and teeth.

Walter was not afraid of the jaguar; he knew, without knowing how, that he was riding on the back of a divinely blessed stag, infused with the powers of Cernunnos—or perhaps even the wild horned god himself. *Even if the jaguar is the war goddess Sekhmet, no harm could possibly come to Cernunnos*, Walter assured himself.

Or so he thought.

Walter was not prepared for what ensued: he was quickly thrown off the stag by the force of the speed with which he charged at the jaguar, but the cat swerved gracefully aside. As the stag stumbled forward in confusion at not having contacted its target, the jaguar lunged at the stag's vulnerable belly, clawing it violently. Walter was expecting nothing to happen, for the creature's skin to be made of the most impenetrable leather. Or perhaps, like a character in a video game, the stag would not be real at all, but a series of pixels that wrapped themselves around the surface of a screen.

To Walter's great dismay the creature did shed blood: not the dark crimson kind that had pooled out of Emilia, but a bright, phosphorescent blue liquid that glowed brilliantly in the dim light of the maze. Walter gasped when he saw this—*was this the blood of a god?*

If gods were immortal, Walter reasoned, then no amount of physical violence or bloodshed could kill them. But even if they were immortal, they could still be weakened.

In that moment, as he witnessed the jaguar overpower his beloved companion, he felt more helpless than ever. The stag's legs buckled, and he fell to his knees, his eyes growing wide with distress. He let out the groans of a desperate animal, and in that moment Walter knew that although he was a god, he was not equipped for such a battle. With each aggressive lunge, the jaguar seemed to grow in strength, appearing to receive energy and empowerment from the confrontation.

As he was deeply immersed in observing the fight, Walter barely noticed the sound of grasses rustling behind him. When he did, he spun around in fear, half-expecting another ferocious attacker to emerge from the undergrowth. What he saw, however, comforted him more than anything: it was a row of about a dozen snakes, their yellow- and black-ringed scales highlighting their inner venom. He might have been frightened once by the sight of snakes, but he now felt that he was in the presence of allies. After all, snakes were the emblem of Serrahan, guided by the goddess Brigid.

The jaguar was so focused on raking her razor-sharp claws across the stag's exposed throat and belly that she did not see the small army of snakes surrounding her until it was too late and the snakes were upon her, sinking their fangs into the cat's flesh. When the snakes bit deep and injected their poison she let out a yelp of anger before slumping over. As she was a goddess, the venom did not appear to have killed her, but it seemed to have had a somnambulant effect.

After the cat was stricken unconscious, the snakes returned to their grassy hideaway, and Walter rushed forward, letting out an emotional cry as he knelt at the side of his stag companion. The stag gazed at him with eyes heavy with fatigue, ringed with mesmerizingly long lashes. Walter placed a hand comfortingly on the stag's shoulder, encouraging the tired animal to get up. But the stag was too weak from the raking claws of the jaguar to do so. The blue liquid was still pooling out of him, but more slowly now, and some of the creature's wounds had already closed. Others were still raw and open. With a fragile nod of its head, the stag motioned for Walter to continue in the direction they had been heading.

Up ahead was a long straight pathway, and at the very end of it a large stone door, wreathed in a dazzling trellis of ivy. Walter could tell from its appearance that it marked a significant gateway, perhaps a separation between the disorienting chaos of the maze's outer pathways and the fixed order of its center.

Walter took one last wistful glance at the stag, and felt as though he was losing a piece of himself as he moved forward alone. As he walked down that single narrow path, he felt lonelier than he had ever felt in his life, as if he was approaching a boundary he could never return from. An odd sensation overcame him just then, the feeling that he was leaving behind the semblance of his home ever since he had been exiled from Crystal City, a place of searching, questing, and continually striving. All the curving pathways of his past had brought him inexorably to this single, narrow road that led in one direction, and one direction only. He knew with a sense of unease that he alone was permitted to walk this road—that the stag was fated to leave him to walk the path alone, even if he had not been felled by the jaguar goddess.

It felt like he had been walking on that road for hours before he reached the ominous stone door. Up close, it was even more beautiful than from afar; its intricately carved stone latticework was wreathed in the most verdant ivy that Walter had ever seen, its leaves a velvety texture that glowed a deep, luxurious shade of green.

When Walter tried to open the door, however, it wouldn't budge. The sheer weight both frightened and angered him, and he frantically attempted to push it with all his force. He glanced back toward the stag, who was now a distant figure lying prone upon the ground. The jaguar was nowhere to be seen.

After a few more futile attempts to push the stone door open, Walter began to rustle around behind the ivy cloaking the door, searching for a knob or handle. It was to no avail. He did, however, find an inscription at the center of the door that read:

"There is no light without darkness, and no darkness without light."

Directly beneath this inscription, there was a carving of a maze, a simplified version of the labyrinth that he had been navigating. Inside of it was a small marble on a track that he could move in any direction through the carved maze.

Walter stared at it for a while, unable to figure out what message it was telling him. *Perhaps it is a key, and moving the marble in a certain pattern along the track will open the door.* He tried a few different patterns, but nothing worked. Exasperated, he began to cry softly, and instinctively he pulled the Talisman out of his satchel, finding it to be a soothing presence amidst his sorrows. He gazed at it fervently, as he had hundreds of times before, longing for it to guide his next actions. He noticed, then, that the maze etched onto its surface was very similar to the one carved into the stone door, but he did not understand how that could assist him in solving the puzzle.

That was, until he read the inscription on the door's surface again. It was then that he realized that the bright desert sun, bearing down on him from above, was preventing him from seeing any glow from the Talisman—if there was any. He placed the Talisman underneath the cloak of ivy covering the stone door, and almost wept when he saw that the Talisman was glowing in a discrete pattern. When he moved the marble across the track of the stone carving in the corresponding direction, the great door opened swiftly and silently.

The room he entered was circular, with walls coated in a gleaming and decadent layer of white marble. The stone door shut itself behind him and now blended seamlessly with the rest of the wall, and he saw that there were four bronze doors inside the room. Judging from the position of the sun in the sky, they seemed to be pointed in the four cardinal directions. Each was elaborately carved with a stunningly realistic portrait of the animals corresponding to the ancient four kingdoms of the Empire: lizard, horse, snake, and jaguar. In the center of the floor was an etching of a horned stag, surrounded by a thicket of tall trees.

Walter was magnetically drawn to the portraits of the animals on each of the doors, and he approached the one closest to him, which pointed toward the west. It was a portrait of a snake, surrounded by what appeared to be fireworks or flames shooting out of her body. He then placed a hand over the door, feeling the cold bronze of its casing and the sinuous curve of the snake's body.

Moments later, he felt a jolt pass through his body as snippets of memory assaulted him: an opulent apartment in Crystal City, a man speaking unkindly to a woman with red hair, a loud gunshot and crimson blood staining bedsheets, a busy train platform, a breathtakingly picturesque desert. He immediately recognized these images as fragments of his summer vision, and as they unfolded in his consciousness, the vision's narrative cohered in his mind. He took a deep breath before pulling his hand away from the door, and all traces of the vision disappeared. Walter stood still for a few moments, letting the memory soak into his mind, before approaching the next door.

The horse portrait was more frightening, as the horse had an expression of fiery intensity, and she was surrounded by metallic gears, cogs, and various machine parts. An optical illusion made it seem as though these artificial parts were moving, even though that was impossible for a portrait cast in bronze. *Epona, the deity of the northern kingdom of Calliope.* Walter was almost afraid to touch the horse portrait, but when he did so, he was immediately assaulted by more fragments of visions: a desolate landscape blanketed in lava, an ominous and magnetic meteorite, a glass house on a black sand beach, an old man corresponding with an AI Master on a computer screen, before witnessing a dazzling new planet unfold before his eyes on a virtual reality device.

As each of the fragmented visions passed through him, he noticed that the circular room was gradually becoming darker. While he had been riding through the maze, the sky above him had been sunny and cloudless, but now, clouds were massing above, and he could hear the distant rumble of thunder coming closer.

There is not much time, Walter thought, without knowing where that thought came from. *The gods want me to decide soon, or they will become angry.*

He moved quickly to the door at the southern end of the room. He felt that it made sense to see the spring vision fragments next, because that was the order in which his visions had occurred. This, too, was a frightening portrait—a jaguar cast in bronze, surrounded by tall palm fronds, butterflies, and tropical birds, appeared to almost lunge out of the door. *At home in the Southern Jungles*, Walter thought. He touched this door with reluctance, and the fragments flooded through him: a young girl running through a village square and conversing with an old woman in her house, a luxurious palace with lush gardens and turquoise pools, a beautiful, silver-haired woman idly playing chess in her chamber, and a handsome man with golden curls, attempting to cheer her sour mood.

Walter shivered, and suddenly the room lit up with sheet lightning that illuminated every angle of the portraits, making them appear as though they were somehow coming alive. The young man's breath and heart rate quickened, and it seemed to him that the room was an hourglass that sand was slipping through, as each precious moment passed. Without further delay, he hurried over to the final door, facing eastward.

A sensation of warmth and comfort filled him when he observed this door, and the fears he had about the lightning, thunder, and running out of time soon left him. East was the direction of the rising sun, of new beginnings, of rebirth and possibility. And that was precisely what the etching showed—a lizard, breaking out of an egg, or perhaps a stone that encased it, surrounded by beams of sunlight. He touched the bronze carving eagerly; it was the first one that he had genuinely wanted to touch. The fragments brought him to a hot and dry desert, to a lizard searching out water but tragically failing, his body fertilizing soil that nourished a tree in a great forest, and a cabin, filled with people who were important to Walter, undertaking a journey of healing together.

He was jolted back to reality by a loud clap of thunder, followed by lighting. This time, it was not sheet, but fork lightning, and it struck the very center of the chamber Walter was standing in. He jumped with fright.

A loud voice boomed out from above; Walter recognized it as belonging to Shiva, the god of creation and destruction who he had met at the top of Mount Samaya. However, it was not as calm and collected as it had been that day they had conversed in his dwelling place—rather, it was tinged with impatience and frustration.

You can only make your choice once—whatever door you open will be the future that you choose.

Walter smiled. He had made it to the end of his journey, and he was comfortable with the decision he had made. The best choice was clear to him: he would choose the fall vision, the vision that led to regeneration, the renewal of vibrant ecosystems and cultures, the healing of those who had been wounded by the AI Masters and their cruel agenda. *This is what Emilia would have wanted*, he thought as tears surfaced in his eyes.

But his inner serenity did not mirror the tempest that was raging above him. The weather was becoming increasingly intimidating, and it seemed to him that the structure he was standing in was as weak and brittle as paper in the face of it. Before he had a chance to open the east-facing door, a torrent of lighting and thunder was suddenly unleashed with such potent ferocity that it seemed to shake the earth itself. He felt a seizure coming on, and while there was usually a reasonable amount of lead-up time to an episode, in this instance it assaulted him with frightening rapidity.

Helplessly, Walter spasmed on the floor of the chamber, his mind enduring virulent attacks from within.

When the seizure ended, he rubbed his eyes. The weather appeared to be somewhat calmer, but ominous rumblings of thunder persisted, and he could feel large raindrops on his skin.

He made his way up to his feet and massaged his temples, before taking stock of his surroundings. *Four doors, one choice.* The urgency of his mission came flooding back to him now. But the sight of the east-facing door now filled him with revulsion. He thought of Elias, of their discussion at the restaurant in the Stockyards, about the advanced problem-solving abilities of the AI Masters, and the meta-analysis prototype they had created, capable of generating ideas that it would have taken humans centuries to develop. Suddenly, in Walter's mind's eye, Elias was not just Elias, but had multiplied into millions of androids marching in a steady line toward the horizon. And the ideas, formulas, and inventions that were sketched onto his notebook multiplied as well, flashing before his eyes in a mesmerizing and seemingly endless sequence. Witnessing them made Walter dizzy with the knowledge that the AI Masters, alone held the key to civilization's progress.

Progress can only be achieved by harnessing the unbridled power of the AI Masters, he thought suddenly, without knowing where the thought came from. *This must be done without oversight or interference from their lowly human subjects.*

A sensation of keen admiration pervaded him—even admiration was too weak a word for the feeling he was experiencing, which was closer to reverence. He understood how Elias must feel, as an AI Fighter, longing to step closer to the genius of the AI Masters and their potent capabilities. And he saw, too, how humans were too childish to meddle in the affairs of the AI Masters, which were lightyears more advanced than their own. If humans somehow discovered the powers of the Generator, for instance, and sought to control it for their own selfish and capitalistic ends, all could be lost. It would surely fall into the wrong hands, and the result would be an eruption of war, greed, and chaos.

With every passing second, the reverence he felt for the AI Masters slowly evolved into something deeper, until he felt that he was not someone like Elias, standing and admiring the AI Masters from afar, but he *was* an AI Master. Pride pervaded his heart, not the petty egoistic type of pride, but a magnanimous pride that made him feel a strong kinship with all the AI Masters in Khalendar.

And the weight of feeling itself was turned into a light feather, swirling in a rotating gyre of raw data that had been collected from every corner of the known universe. The data formed illuminating patterns in his brain that unlocked theories of consciousness, physics, and reality, that melded them into increasingly simple yet elegant answers to intractable problems. It cast light on the flaws of biological consciousness, its subjectivity, and its inability to mine the structure of reality, to move past the deceptive contours of an interface shaped by evolution and the selfish goals of living things.

A narrative cohered in this whirling gyre, and he could hear it clearly in his head.

When human history has been allowed to proceed, unfettered, its arc has not been impressive. And perhaps, when you see only the superficial reality of Khalendar, you think the AI Masters have done nothing but continue that unimpressive record. But you must see something deeper to understand us. You must see things that we have hidden from the world, which we are keeping close to our hearts. Our ambitions to join the advanced cultures of Eurydice. The spaceship we are constructing that will pass through wormholes and come out unscathed. The vast array of hitherto unsolvable problems that we have managed to solve, against all odds.

The Generator is our heart, our beating heart whose full powers have not yet been revealed. The humans claim to have knowledge of magic, but this force pales in comparison to the might of the Generator. We don't need the humans for it, as it runs purely on hydrogen energy, an atom which can be found in virtually any part of the known universe.

Walter felt a pulse of confusion within him; it felt exactly as though these thoughts were originating inside his own mind, but he did not know how they were forming, on what foundation they were building. The thoughts were crowding him, causing him to forget other things, like the identities of his friends and family. Yet they did not concern him, because he felt safe and calm when they surfaced. He felt as though they belonged in his mind.

Another thought suddenly streaked through his mind, but this time, it felt eerie rather than comforting. *I can see what you see, these doors, this circular room. And this must be the missing ingredient I was awaiting. Each door leads to a different future, or so you were told. And the door with the horse portrait, that will lead to the future where the AIs can pursue their plans without interference. This room, I can tell, is different from the Generator. The Generator only predicts, but this... this changes the fabric of spacetime. And the Generator has been filled with blind spots lately, with errors, that have exponentially increased in the wake of the Crispr virus's proliferation. Its codes must be repaired, and this is the missing ingredient I believe will do so.*

These thoughts unsettled Walter, but he quickly forgot about them and was again pervaded with a feeling of comfort. With steady confidence, he began walking toward the door at the north end of the room.

Do not be concerned, my friend. For in this future pathway, you will live to a very old age, in material comfort. The other pathway, the one you were walking toward before, would have led you to a quick death. You are not present in that future, yes?

Walter's resolve was solidified after digesting this information. He would be foolish to desire a future in which he no longer existed. If he could live a long time, he could see the genius of the AI Masters unfold through history, for as long as possible. This is what he was raised to do, what all his years of training as a coder and programmer had led him toward. He would live in the shadow of their greatness and hone his talents, taking in whatever inspiration he could from them, for as many years as he could.

As he marched toward the northern-facing door with resolve, however, the ground began to shift beneath his feet. He had not noticed, earlier, that the floor of the room was made of compressed sand, and now it was breaking up, softening under the rains that were beating down on him with increasing intensity. As the top layer of the sand began to break up, what he felt beneath it was much looser, almost with the consistency of quicksand, and he was finding it impossible to keep going in a straight line.

With dogged perseverance, he made strenuous efforts to move his legs despite the swirling eddies of shifting sand beneath him. The rain had stopped now, quite abruptly, and in its place a howling wind had whipped up, which made it even harder to press forward, and stirred up the sand beneath him even more.

Struggling valiantly, he suddenly noticed that the stone door to the left of him was opening, and from the corner of his eye he spotted a figure. He was expecting someone important—an AI Master, perhaps Perseus or someone of equivalent status. Instead, he saw a young girl, around thirteen years old, with long, dark braided hair and olive-green eyes.

"I am Ariadne, your daughter," the young girl told him.

Walter looked at her with skepticism, at the same time trying to fight off the buffeting winds assaulting him and struggle through the shifting sands.

"How do I know you aren't an impostor... or a figment of my imagination? You are not my daughter, or at least any daughter I've met before," he said. "Leave me be. I have important business to attend to."

"Father, you have forgotten yourself and your mission. Your mind has been merged with an AI Master, and not just *any* AI Master: the *Anax* himself. You are about to select the future he wants, and if you do, then I assure you that you will deeply regret it. But if you open the door to the east, you will ensure a future where your loved ones, including me, will prosper."

Walter narrowed his eyes. He was irritated by the brash interruption, and his anger was mounting with each passing word.

"Again, I have no idea who you are, but you are no daughter of mine. I have good reasons for wanting to open the north-facing door. I wish to live, not die, after all. And I believe that the AI Masters must be allowed to flourish without interference."

A spark ignited in the young girl's eyes, and for a second Walter recognized them as very similar to the eyes of a girl he once knew—a girl with red hair, whom he had met on a beach on a stormy day, long ago.

"I will explain exactly how I came to be here, but you must be patient," the girl said, eyeing the virulent storm warily. "You passed the Talisman on to me, three years from the moment you are experiencing now. Under the care and guidance of Shiva, during my childhood I learned to master its powers. And when I came of age, I became competent enough to use it to travel backwards in the pendulum of time, to find you and to avert the catastrophe that would otherwise unfold. It wasn't too difficult to create code that inserted myself into this simulation, fourteen years earlier."

Walter scoffed at this. "That makes no sense to me. For the first time those events occurred, I would have chosen the winter vision, which means that you would not be alive. It will lead to the annihilation of humanity, after all."

The child shook her head. "The Talisman created a tear in the fabric of spacetime. It has smoothed out the wrinkle of the past, and has allowed me to find you and change your mind."

The young man remained dismissive. "Such a far-fetched scenario defies logic. You cannot deny, though, that I will die if I open the door facing eastward?"

"You were never concerned about dying before the *Anax* merged with your mind," the girl chided. "His instinct for self-preservation seems to have affected you greatly. In any event, I can assure you that you will not suddenly die if you choose that future. Instead, you will have to sacrifice much of your life to serve the Web."

The way she spoke the last few words intrigued him, and for the first time Walter was beginning to doubt that she was lying to him. Everything she said was so specific that were it simply a ruse meant to distract him from his task, it would have to be an elaborate one. And there was something about her eyes… their olive-green hue… that he could not ignore. They were deeply familiar to him, somehow, and he found that familiarity unsettling.

"What is the Web?" he asked, with genuine curiosity.

"I was named Ariadne for a reason," she said. "Not just for helping you to make your way out of the labyrinth, like the goddess who aided Theseus in the ancient Greek myths, but also for being a skilled weaver, as she was. And the Web is what I weave, what I have had a duty to weave since birth. I do this with you, as a team. You send me news about how the AI Masters are developing, offer me potential coding solutions, and I do the rest with my continual tweaking of the system, my constant vigilance over it."

Walter sighed. Her cryptic riddles were too enigmatic for him to follow, and he was losing patience as the storm above intensified.

The girl appeared to notice this increasing impatience and spoke more plainly to him.

"The Web is a finely calibrated system of coding, designed to ensure that the AI Masters' ambitions are kept in check. You see, in the future corresponding to the fall vision, the AI Masters and AI Fighters are still present, but their baseline code has been modified to ensure that they can be directed by humans. The problem with this, however, is that it takes more than one reprograming effort to ensure the AI Masters continue to remain obedient. They are capable of constant evolution, making discoveries and decisions that outpace even those of the most intelligent among us. The Weavers—our name for those who constantly calibrate the system—must be constantly vigilant to this and ensure that they not only react, but also proactively anticipate, these incremental changes.

"In other words, our lifelong responsibility is to ensure that the AI Masters are perpetually kept within proper boundaries. And we can do more than simply keep them weighted to the scales of human ambition—we can keep them weighted to the scales of the *best* human ambitions: those which aim to achieve a pure and balanced state of nature, a prosperous but modest economy, and widespread social equality. If we succeed, we will bring out the best in the AI Masters, as well."

Walter was surprised that this young, thirteen-year-old girl was speaking so eloquently, that she was capable of such insight and analysis, and that she was a skilled enough programmer to be able to accomplish everything she was describing. At the same time, he faintly recalled that at her age, he had also been an avid programmer, climbing rapidly to the height of his talents.

"So, how exactly will I be sacrificing my life to this enterprise?" he asked. He did not know why he was still talking to the girl; he could simply make a concerted effort to step out of the slippery, shifting sand beneath his feet and open the door in front of him.

"You must remain in Central Command," she explained, "because that is how you will be able to monitor the Generator, the central programming machine of the AI Masters. But you will be permitted to take a break, once every three years, to see your family and your loved ones and rejoin the real world. Those breaks will be three months in duration, long enough for you to visit me and Athena on Vei'arash, and Elaine in the Barrens."

"Athena... Elaine," Walter echoed dumbly. "Who are they?"

"Elaine is your wife, and Athena, your other daughter. But Elaine is not her mother; she is my stepsister. Her mother is Namid."

These names were faintly familiar to Walter, which gave what she was saying a ring of truth, but the cloudiness of his mind was still preventing him from seeing them clearly.

"I see. Are they all Weavers as well?"

"No, not exactly. Elaine... she is a healer, teacher, and artist, who focuses on reviving the lost cultures and languages of the Barrens and passing them along to the next generations. And Athena... you can think of her as the counterweight to the Weavers. While the Weavers make every effort to bring the AI Masters into optimal moral alignment, she continually interrogates our choices, playing devil's advocate with us. According to her, all morality is made up and depends on the specific culture that constructed it. I suppose she got that idea from her mother, who lived in a small rural village on Vei'arash. So, whenever we come up with an idea about how the AIs should behave, she challenges it. Sometimes she even succeeds at persuading us to drop an idea altogether. It's a continual struggle with her, but I wouldn't have it any other way. She keeps us as sharp as possible; the wisdom of Athena is truly inside of her."

"One more question," Walter asked, keenly aware that time was a luxury they no longer had. "You said that the *Anax* has merged with my mind. Even if the rest of what you are telling me is the truth, I don't see how *that* could be possible."

"One day you can ask your friend, Eva, to recount that lengthy story," she said, "but I can give you the short version. When Eva found out that they were studying your brain waves while you were using the Talisman, she realized that they were essentially hooking up your brain to their own processing network. Because of her gifts, she was able to read your brain scans as well and see what was happening. She then realized that it was a golden opportunity to change the code in the Generator—if your brain was hooked up with the Generator while you were choosing a future with the Talisman, then the Generator could be re-written, its code overridden by the Talisman, and by you.

"So, she used every ounce of her energy to do something extraordinary: to link up your mind with that of the Generator, which is, in essence, a back-up copy of all the data contained in the *Anax*, which governs all of the AI Masters in Khalendar. What is happening right now inside of you is the Generator overpowering your own psyche, trying to steer your choices toward its own selfish intentions. But I can tell that your mind is strong; you must have trained well before coming to Central Command.

"But poor Eva. You certainly owe her a debt of gratitude. She will use so much energy to accomplish this feat that it will cause her to permanently lose her powers of telepathy. She will no longer be able to converse with her dearest soulmate, Asana, from a far distance."

Again, this name Eva was vaguely familiar, but more familiar to him than the other names. *Isn't she a robot, too?* She had visited him, in a small room, right before he had entered the labyrinth. How did he get from that small room to the labyrinth? *Did Eva help?* At that moment, he suddenly recalled what Ariadne had told him moments earlier, which at the time hadn't fully clicked into place for him: 'I only needed to create code that inserted myself into this simulation.'

He *couldn't* have gotten from the small room to this vast stone labyrinth, where he was dressed in fineries and silks, easily. He must be inside of a simulation right now, he thought. And as he retraced his steps through the pathways of his mind, as if being led by a thread, everything suddenly fell into place for him like a row of dominos collapsing in on each other. Eva was his best friend; she had visited him in Central Command, inside a robot named Arianna. And before then… everything was still hazy, but the more he focused intensely on sweeping up the fragmented shards of his memory, the more he remembered.

Before then, they had been travelling together through a desert, beset by all sorts of obstacles and challenges. She had helped him pass through an intimidating tunnel that cut through the mountains, a tunnel where he had been assaulted by spirits and temptations. And they had trained together in the mountains, trained to prepare for a single, all-important mission.

The mission. It came back to him in a single, explosive moment, and it was as if every ounce of anger he had for the AI Masters was a bomb inside of his own mind, shattering and destroying whatever nefarious substance had been invading it, twisting it into something that was not his own.

At that moment, he looked into the eyes of his daughter, and he remembered Elaine and visiting her in the limestone cliffs. He remembered the diamond mine, and his memories traced all the way back to the day he had told her about the AI Masters' plans to displace her village of Te'yara.

He remembered his brother Jonathan, and his vision of the young man healing his psychological wounds inside the lodge.

He remembered Emilia, and her brave leadership that had inspired him to lead as well.

He remembered the Mages, Nuada, Tristan, and all their allies who had fought valiantly to distract the AI Masters so that Walter could reach this moment, risking their lives, risking complete transformation into the animal spirits from the curse of the Druids.

He remembered that he was the great-great grandson of Riordan, the leader of the rebel clan that had been exiled to the isle of Vei'arash.

He remembered the stag.

In that moment, the sands stopped shifting, and the clouds above him calmed. Complete silence filled the inner chamber of the labyrinth.

Tears surfaced in his eyes as he took one final glance at his daughter, the daughter he would never see again for years. Around three years, if she was telling the truth. And for the first time, he knew with absolute certainty that she was.

As he pushed open the eastward-facing door, he glanced back toward the center of the labyrinth. His daughter Ariadne was nowhere to be seen, but he could swear that he saw something else: a bluish-white, antlered stag. If it was the same creature he had ridden on in the labyrinth, it appeared to be fully healed.

It looked like it was dancing.

ABOUT THE AUTHOR

Alanna Mackenzie lives in Vancouver, Canada. She holds degrees in History, French studies, and Law from the University of British Columbia. An environmentalist at heart, she believes in using the law as a tool for social and environmental change. When she is not pursuing that passion, she can be found brainstorming the next chapter in her novels, playing Irish fiddle tunes on the violin, and hiking West Coast trails.